ATACAMA

ATACAMA

Sherry Leonard

ISBN: 1983976393
ISBN 13: 9781983976391

"It is darker than you think...this little light
and then the night"

Tocko, the Clockmaker
The White Deer
James Thurber
1945

HctorVera   Gerrit   Rita) Blain
                              Ian

Bowens   Barrento mine forman Cort Raicher Mine manager
  Alice   Art. mine forman   nellie
  Wes   Clane

  Swenson   Felix Alford   JuanOrtega
   Lief   mike Marshall   Ned Tully
   Greta   Huge Dillon

Zungor   Chet Weir

mollie Prichard - teacher

For the mineros of the Atacama
SL

Alchemist symbol for copper

CHAPTER 1

Slowly winding its way through thick air in the Antofagasta streets, like a tear running down a dirty cheek, the white station wagon began a journey home. Gerritt Wells stared blankly at the passing Chilean slums, seeing instead the loamy soil, wet and fecund, his Uncle Shem waving from the tractor. Perhaps he and Shem were the same person. As his Aunt loved to say on cold January nights in a room made warm by the wood stove and her keeping of the house, Gerritt and Shem were born under the same moon and meant to hate the filling of the world with people. With a genuine distrust of humanity, Shem taught him to move away from civilization. That there might come a time when there was no further escape did not occur to them. There would always be somewhere else to go.

At one time the farm had provided that kind of liberation, a kind of free will sharing between earth and man, and Gerritt liked it there. Raised by these farm folk from age six when his parents died of something sudden he could not now remember, he permanently stored an unexplained loss. As a student he excelled and went to a local Montana mining college on scholarship. If it got too crowded on top, he would simply dig down. In the apocryphal traditions of blue-collar professions, miners are generally a solitary lot, even the educated ones, preferring the company of ore and machinery to each other. Gerritt fit in. And in the sense that he loved the vibratory feel of a drill in his hand as it bit the rock, he had not made a mistake. But it wasn't long before he had enough of Montana. The town, once eight miles from the farm, was now four and filled with grain elevators and a tailings dump that hid the sunset and clouded the air in summer. It was clearly time to leave.

There was quick advancement in the mines of South America owned by American companies and Gerritt didn't like working for other men. Taking this job in northern Chile seemed a way to find isolation and autonomy.

What he needed in the car right now was endurance and the saved up memories of the farm in spring, the creek big with snow melt rushing in his ears and loud enough to cover the insipid voice of Rita Blain, the Mine Superintendent's wife, in the front seat, holding forth on the relative attractions of life on the pampa. Relative because Gerritt had no experience with which to compare life in a foreign mining camp in a desolate desert at 10,000 feet. The Atacama in northern Chile is one of the driest places in the world. In parts of the high pampa no rain ever falls.

Next to him in the back seat was another couple from the States, the Bowens, from their looks probably green as he was. As though Rita's words could infuse them with knowledge of coping with any adversity, Alice Bowen leaned toward Rita and chewed away at a piece of loose skin on her chapped lips.

Alice's face was flushed in a healthy way, but she looked tired after the twenty-hour plane ride, the sinister customs agents and the lunch of duck at the hotel, which Gerritt was convinced, had been seagull. Thank God there was wine and plenty of it. He had tried to leave Rita's voice at the table telling about locos, which were like abalone, but had to be pounded on the concrete and pressure cooked before you ate them. Out the window of the hotel the ocean broke on the basalt beach and the seagulls for tomorrows lunch waited on the rocks for theirs.

Gerritt watched Alice and her husband, Wes, on the plane, and was surprised to find they all had a common destination. He didn't like flying and tried to forget the closeness and how the fuselage narrowed at each end, pushing the passengers together. He'd been told in New York, after taking the required two-week Berlitz course where he learned how to say useful phrases such as "el lapiz es rojo" that another mining engineer would be starting at Cerro Verde at the same time. The man he imagined was not sitting in the car with him. Wes Bowen had curly, red hair, was nearly a foot taller than Gerritt's six feet, and wore a tweed jacket, his shoulders supporting the coat as if it were thrown over a chair by the stove.

In the heat of the afternoon, the slow speed of the car through the crowded and dusty streets made the air heavy with stale, traveled people. Gerritt rolled his window down halfway. Ian Blain, the Mine Superintendent, stringy but not as tall as Bowen, sat in front with his wife, vaguely talking about the desert stretching away from them to the east. The driver, a local Chilean named Hector Vera, maneuvered the car expertly, but distantly, like water running over an oily surface. Vera's neck was thick, widening out from his head on which sat a small, white hat and dark glasses. The head remained motionless, concentrating on the dirt road ahead, fuzzy with the rising heat and smell of fresh garbage. He slowed as a child of sorrow ran into the street for a dirty ball, slowed enough for the boy to look Gerritt in the eye, grab onto the moving window and push his face, its dark skin pulled tight over young bones, into the car.

"Gringo bastard!" The child spit on him, his lip curling stiffly over yellow and black teeth. The decayed breath brought a wave of nausea and Gerritt could taste the duck from lunch in his mouth again.

"Shit", he said, forgetting where he was and for a moment locking on the eyes of the boy and making them his to remember. He wiped the dirty spit on his sleeve, looking at it in disgust; the kid was chewing something green and black. Vera sped up, his wide neck turning red, mortified to have his passenger defiled by a beggar.

"Get the hell out of here!" Ian Blain ordered after Vera had already made the decision, and turned abruptly into a narrow street, the houses carelessly constructed of mud brick and metal calamina.

"Altido, Señor!" Vera inched along, honking at people in the way, who looked at them as though the car intruded on them personally.

"What was the kid chewing, concrete?" Gerritt asked as he wiped the spit off his sleeve with a tissue from Rita.

"Coca leaves and ash," Ian explained. "The ash forms a weak alkaline effect that extracts cocaine from the leaves. It's used here in northern Chile and in Bolivia at high altitude; it dilates blood vessels and gets more oxygen to the brain."

"Great," Gerritt answered sullenly, wondering if it also made you spit on people.

They passed an open market with smells of fish and overripe tomatoes. Up and over a rise ahead, the mountains rose toward a blank, white-blue sky, to which Gerritt looked, longingly. He was already beginning to feel easier with the brown cliffs in sight and wasn't ready for a second abrupt stop. The street ahead was filled with people in black in front of a small church. Vera muttered something that sounded like a curse.

"What's this?" Wes Bowen leaned forward, ducking his head to see out the open window, which made his neck arch like a goose. He breathed in, but Gerritt could see from his puckered face that it didn't smell any better outside, just thick and dirty. He continued to wipe the spit from his face, knowing Alice was watching him with a sick expression.

"Funeral," Vera replied in Spanish, without turning around. Gerritt and Wes looked at each other, realizing simultaneously that Vera understood English.

The station wagon came to a complete stop as the crowd ahead filled the street, mostly women in tired black mourning, lumpy from the years of their lives. If there was a through street in Antofagasta, this was not it. They wouldn't be allowed passage until these people were done helping the deceased complete his journey.

Five or six men in dusty black suits, buttoned around middle-aged bellies, spilled out the doors of the church and down the cracked steps, then turned around to wait. The church was of crude construction, adobe blocks, white-washed in some past year. A metal calamina roof held up a crooked, empty bell tower.

The crowd began to move; the women wiped their eyes with wrinkled white handkerchiefs, which fluttered like lights against black dresses. Music seeped out from the church, muffled at first, and then a small band emerged on the steps playing a funeral dirge woefully out of tune. The coffin followed, carried by six younger men. It was narrow and constructed of unfinished wood. In the end was a glass window against which heavy brown hair pressed when the box was tilted going down the steps. Gerritt pressed his own thick black hair against the frame of the car window as he watched. The box was loaded into an old blue panel truck as the women began to moan and sing to the dirge. The band climbed into a dented pickup never missing a sour note and the whole scene slowly sank down the hill past them.

The mourners looked into the white car with the same angry eyes of the boy who spit on Gerritt and he defensively rolled up his window. This was not Montana. A dust devil blew down the hill after the funeral, sweeping the gravel after it. The tiny rocks whispered against the side of the car as Vera started the engine.

"Why do they have a glass end in the coffin," Alice shivered next to Gerritt as the car grew silent. "I've never been to a funeral". Gerritt turned to look at her, realizing that he had never been to a funeral either and wondered what it would be like to understand this common custom, particularly when it was personal.

"A lot of people here bury their dead that way. The pampa desiccates everything, just dries it up and those people will be able to go look at their dead relative until they get put in a coffin themselves. Don't let it worry you." Rita frowned at Alice's disgust for the ritual.

"I find the custom quite acceptable. Your makeup would last a long time, maybe forever."

Rita lit a cigarette, the smoke rising up and around her pale fingers past a large diamond that reflected light on the dashboard. Her other hand fingered the ring, carefully turning it around as though it was unfamiliar. Gerritt found her out of place. She was soft, a city girl who did not fit the pampa. He leaned against the car window, noticed the grimy fingerprints left by the boy in town and tried to imagine what the kid was doing now and whether the act of spitting at a Gringo had been satisfying. The glass felt cool. He pushed his hair back trying to see the top of the mountains into which the car was moving.

Vera started up a narrow paved road that led into switchbacks, leaving the tangled labyrinth of Antofagasta in a smoky haze below. Then the mountains swallowed them. On a road so narrow two cars could barely pass, that had been blasted from the sides of the brown peaks rising from the sea and protected nowhere by guardrails, the light grew dim from taking so long to reach them. It was dark and close as they neared the summit. Gerritt felt as though this must be what being born felt like. Finally the light grew brighter and the road widened some and he knew the Bowens had also experienced something, as they breathed in deeply and looked at each other a long while. Vera slowed the car, opened his window and tipped his hat toward what looked to Gerritt like a small dog-house, painted white and covered with bleached paper wreathes and flowers that flapped in the wind.

'What in hell was that all about?' he thought, watching Vera carefully, but there was no sign, only the stiff head pointed again to the business of driving. Ian Blain sensed their curiosity and turned his head to the back, wrinkling the leathery skin on his long neck.

"Hector Vera's brother was killed here four years ago, went right off the edge in a truck loaded with marble from one of the quarries up north. The little house is supposed to be a home for his spirit. They're all over, another one up the road. Hector knows they would do as much for him." It seemed to give Ian pleasure to talk about the local customs, in the way you are fed by those things you love without reservation.

"I was born here," Ian went on. My father was the Mine Manager. Went to a military academy in Miami and then to Mines in Colorado. But I had to come back to the pampa, to Cerro Verde." Ian smiled, looking at Rita. "She was a young schoolteacher. Has wanted to move back to the States for years, but I know I couldn't be happy without this place. It's just part of me." Ian seemed so content as he put his arm around Rita's shoulder. Gerritt wondered how one reaches a place where you are completed in that way.

The road straightened as they approached the altiplano, becoming a narrow ribbon disappearing into brownish haze far ahead. There was nothing green to break the bland surface and it looked devoid of life. The road surface was barely wide enough for the car and soon decomposed into strips of pavement, one for each wheel, and even these were cracked and heaved up in spots. Vera did not slow down and they flew across the pampa, a flood of brown in every direction.

Mine ruins floated by, a few walls still standing in testimony to a past time of mineral prosperity. Rita droned on to Alice about the Feria, an open market in New Camp and the smuggler who came down from Bolivia occasionally with peanut butter and corn flakes. Gerritt wanted to sleep, but Ian occasionally said something about the mine and he thought he better listen.

"..Mine is a mile-and-a-half long, big S.O.B., and you'll know it when you try to drive a pick-up around, roads don't make any sense. Doesn't rain so the cables are on the surface. Been 15 years here and want to retire in the south." Gerritt watched Rita's response to Ian's last comment and figured she would make the decision when the time came.

Day vanished, gold tones brushed the hills with an almost artificial illumination, as though someone had turned a light on somewhere as you do at dusk, not because you can't see but it makes the room seem warm. Gerritt noticed the bus first, a black speck ahead in the distance with some dust around it haloed by the setting sun. And Vera in front of him stiffened noticeably, his neck becoming thicker and red under the white hat. Beyond the bus were the lights of a town and smoke from the mine plants trailed faintly off to the south.

No one else anticipated the conclusion of a duel, Vera swerving out of the way at the last possible moment. The bus drew closer, reflecting the low sun off its windshields as if it were winking at them. It was nothing like Gerritt had ever seen, a clown of a vehicle stuck together by hand, of wood, metal and leather straps, painted a flat, blank blue. Stuffed and trussed, the baggage tied on with rope, it came rolling unsteadily at them faster than Vera was going and Gerritt had assumed at first that the thing would slow and give way to them, leave the spotless whiteness of the station wagon to the sparse pavement strips and pass slowly on the gravel shoulder. But the bus did not acknowledge their claim to the road and came on even faster as Gerritt realized with a shock that it would not give way and he must have raised off his seat not knowing the words to say, just pointing and hitting Bowen on the shoulder, who saw in an instant what would happen.

"My God! They aren't moving over!" he yelled.

"What?" Rita screamed, turning from Alice who had gone as whitely sterile as the car.

The blood in Vera's thick neck rose in the pulsating vessels under his ears, his chubby hands on the wheel were ashen.

"Turn!" yelled Blain, as Vera had, again, already made the decision himself and then they were passing the bus on the left, the car fish-tailing in the soft gravel, then skidding to get back on the gripping surface of the concrete ribbons that couldn't really be seen for all the dust. Hector Vera never took his foot off the accelerator as he regained the roadbed and Gerritt watched the redness in his neck slowly deflate as he spat out the curses.

"Chuchah! Putah!" the words squeezed between clenched teeth.

"What was that?" Alice asked faintly from the seat where she had crouched, afraid to sit up.

"One of the Goddamned homemade buses that run on a can of alcohol and a piece of rope, and probably no brakes at all!" Ian was furious.

"What nerve!" Rita seethed. "They know where this car is from. They always pull over."

"Never seen anything like that!" Wes breathed heavily.

Gerritt sensed from Vera's reactions that the bus did, indeed, know them and that was why it would not pull over. Vera had given way and what did that mean? A sense of unrest and not belonging permeated the car like a fog as the moment passed and conversation returned to their arrival. It was nearly dark, the lights of the town pushed at them from above, like lanterns signaling from a hill.

CHAPTER 2

The inhospitable blue bus faded with the light, to be filed with the things you don't understand. Colors faded to shapes and shadows. They passed through New Camp, the town downhill from Cerro Verde, the mine. New Camp was small; the tiny stores bore unfamiliar names in Spanish and were tightly shut against the coming night by heavy metal gratings and doors. The town said closed, not saying for what or to whom, just closed. There was an up street and a down street, a surprise for the town's size, but Ian explained it allowed the huge mine trucks to pass without destroying the houses. Nothing had changed here in a long time.

Rita pointed out the Feria, an open market, barely glimpsed through the dark buildings. A Union Hall was white in the early night, making it appear large and isolated. A Catholic church sat on the edge of a square with its rooms for the faithful.

Then a long incline past the houses of the empleados, the section chiefs in the mine, and they were stopping in front of a low, brown building. Gerrit could tell by the finality of Vera's movement forward and slamming the car into park that they had arrived.

"You're not going to think much of these apartments," Rita's deep voice whined apologetically. "Try to remember that we all start here."

The air was dry and chill and smelled faintly of sulfur, drawing Gerritt's nostrils together. Vera opened the back of the station wagon and began to take out their luggage, but made no move to carry it anywhere.

Both apartments were in the same long building of brown adobe blocks, which looked to Gerritt very much like Shem's chicken house. In deference to

Alice, he helped take Bowen's bags inside, stepping over a pile of dirt blown through a crack under the door, which spread out as their feet pushed inside. Ian switched on an overhead light providing harsh illumination. They saw what were some three or four rooms, sparsely furnished with leather-seated, wood benches and chairs. It could not in any way be called home. If anything, it resembled the train station in Rosalia, near the farm, where people were always waiting to go somewhere else. The bright light bounced off the curtainless windows and bare walls. Gerritt was glad he had not brought a woman here; you would always have to say you were sorry.

"I'm sure you would like to get settled," Rita's eyes rolled upward. "We'll look for you around eight." Rita and Ian were having them to dinner to meet some of the mine personnel. Gerritt looked at his watch. It said seven but time seemed meaningless here. His place was a smaller version of the train station, the wood chairs chipped and with one seat torn. At least it was warm after the chill of the pampa air. A small electric stove had been turned on in each room and the shower was hot. Garrett put on a clean blue shirt.

Vera was back in the white car within the hour to deliver them to Blain's. Alice had changed into a brown polka-dot dress, but Wes still wore the limp, tweed coat. The houses grew larger with gardens indiscernible and colorless in the yellow street light as they went up the hill. Gerritt thought about the trip from Antofagasta, the car still smelled close and stale, like a room with too many people. They stopped in front of a large frame house, where cars were parked on the street in front in no particular order.

"Aqui estamos," Vera announced. Lights blazed from every window and music with a slow, rocking beat came from inside.

"Wes, was there a garden at all down there where they put us?" Alice asked hopefully.

"Doubtful," he frowned. "Wonder how many years you have to put in to have a place like this?"

A young Chilean boy in a starched white coat and black tie opened the heavy brass-trimmed door. He carried a small silver tray. Warm smells of furniture polish and food greeted them. Gerritt looked at his image in the beveled mirror over the foyer table, saw that his mouth was open and shut it.

"Here they are," Rita floated across a room carpeted in green and gold, four times as large as their train station. She had changed into a dress that matched the room and waved like a flag as she moved. Behind her the men rose from their seats and the women looked at them expectantly.

Rita took Alice's hand warmly and led them inside. "Welcome to the pampa! I need you to meet the rest of the mine management."

"Your home is lovely, Rita," Alice said in amazement as she looked through glass French doors into a large dining room where two maids in grey were arranging the table and beyond to a glass garden full of climbing plants and flowers. As Rita patted her hand and laughed, a diamond bracelet reflected the light. Her other hand held a heavy crystal glass of scotch.

"Of course. Miners can work miracles, darling! In a few years, you will have a place like this, too." The contents of her glass could not remain inside as the glass tipped and bobbed, and dripped on the floor, but Rita didn't seem to notice as she began introductions to the dozen or so people at the party. Gerritt wanted to turn around, away from the waiting faces.

"This is our Mine Foreman, Art Barnett, and his wife Elaine. He's the man you will be working directly under, and he's a tough one, let me tell you!" Rita laughed loudly. Her red hair was puffed and sprayed so it didn't move when she did and Gerritt didn't like her perfume.

Art shook hands, firmly, his hand warm and rough, letting go sooner than you should, as though the gesture was something he had to do rather than wanted to do. Barnett was a stocky chunk of a man, not much older than Gerritt, with a hairline receding too early and a soggy, chewed cigar in his hand.

"Well, you better be used to hard work—we don't screw around here. This hole in the ground is not forgiving!" Barnett growled, his voice deep and gravelly. He was standing very close, close enough for cigar breath to wrap sourly around each word. Dark brown eyes looked closely at Gerritt as if trying to see inside him.

'Who the fuck does he think we are.' Gerritt thought, taking an instant dislike for the man. He glared at Barnett; whatever this was, it was not a good beginning.

Wes laughed nervously. He had an easily recognizable, deep laugh that always put people at ease. Gerritt thought it sounded this way because it came from so far down in his lungs up through that throat and out his tall frame. It reminded him of voice echoes off canyon walls.

Elaine Barnett sat down on the couch and made room for Alice. Introductions were made quickly to the rest, too fast to catch all the names. Curt Reicher, the Mine Manager and a Swenson. Few of the people were from the States and Gerritt was glad. He was on a foreign contract and he wanted it to be that. It was part of the escape from the encroaching town at home and there were already too many people. He looked carefully at Elaine Barnett. She was tanned, with hair the same color as her skin, and in a white dress that framed her in a nice way. He wondered why she would be with Barnett, but his thoughts were interrupted as Art followed him and continued talking.

"I'll be around to pick you up tomorrow morning at 10A. You get a *re*prieve tomorrow," he emphasized the first syllable and chuckled. Gerritt could see he was enjoying their naivety, just beginning to find their way in this foreign place he knew so well.

"Thereafter you better show up for your shift an hour early. That means 6 AM where I come from!" He bit down hard on the cigar, the end bouncing in his teeth as he talked.

"I've been looking forward to this," Wes said tentatively. He didn't seem to know how to begin and his height forced him to look down on Barnett and tip his head to the side to make eye contact. He looked over at Alice, sitting on the couch with Elaine Barnett.

"This is my first real mining job, except for a summer in Colorado. I hated to uproot Alice from a job she liked and her family to bring her to this isolated place. She was thinking about graduate school, and, well, here we are," he said anxiously. "Tell me what exactly it is that you do in the mine?" Wes smiled at Barnett. There was silence as Art looked up at him carefully.

"I'm the Mine Foreman, damn it!" Art sputtered loudly around the cigar. "In charge of all three shifts and that means you! When you get your own shift, at the end of your eight hours you'll turn in your ore and waste tonnages, feet of track laid and a few other things to me. There's a lot going on and it's a big hole. How's your Spanish?" The smile disappeared from Wes's face.

Rita leaned in between Gerritt and Wes, her diamond bracelet flashing, handing them each a drink. The glasses were large and heavy-bottomed, filled with ice and scotch. A mozo behind her, the kid at the door, smiled and offered a small silver pitcher. He diluted the liquor with what seemed like a teaspoon of water. They had not eaten since Antofagasta and the scotch felt warm going down.

"We learned some from that week at Berlitz in New York, but nothing useful for a mine—just how to ask where the head is," Wes laughed.

Barnett smiled. If one would make it, it would be Wes Bowen, he decided.

"How about you, Wells? Know any Spanish?"

"Not much. I'll learn," he said, fixing his eyes on Art. Gerritt moved off to talk to Blain who was familiar from the drive up and drinking with Curt Reicher by the fireplace. It wasn't new, this gravitating to heat, it was the same with the stove in the general store at home in Montana. And Gerritt had enough of Barnett.

Curt Reicher, the Mine Manager was short in stature. Gerritt noticed he wore elevated shoes and puffed his chest out like a grouse in mating season to make himself seem taller. He'd heard Reicher was Swiss but born in Chile, in the south. Reicher was head man in the mine and Gerritt wanted to impress him.

"Settled, Wells?" Blain asked, raising his glass in welcome.

"Reicher, isn't it? Curt Reicher?" He wanted to get the name right before Ian reminded him.

"Yes," Reicher turned and offered his hand, which was small and dry. "We're happy to have you both here and need the help."

"I've read about the mine—pretty impressive," Gerritt said confidently. He had planned this carefully and was pleased with the look it drew.

"Yes?" Reicher's eyebrows rose. They were heavy, outweighing the man. "Cerro Verde is definitely a rich hole; it's hard not to make money. The native Chilenos have mined turquoise here for a thousand years." Gerritt knew it was the richest body of ore in the world. The tailings dumps contained more copper than many mines in the US.

"Well, I'm looking forward to getting into it," Gerritt said enthusiastically. Reicher nodded, looking up at him thoughtfully as he tipped back on his heels.

"You won't be able to get into it literally, Wells," Blain cautioned. "Doing Obreros' work isn't allowed here, not so much by us as by the Union and the men themselves. They don't like to see their Jefes get their hands dirty."

"Who isn't going to get his hands dirty?" Gerritt turned and looked down on Leif Swenson's short, thin crew cut through which you could see a shiny head. The Chief Geologist, sitting on a nearby couch, was stocky and healthy looking. His wife Greta was his twin, except for her large breasts, which leaned heavily into the front of a low cut flowered dress.

"I only meant that I'm anxious to start the job," Gerritt said quickly, squatting down to their level. Next to Greta was Nellie Reicher, a diminutive woman, precise in speech and dress. Greta was relaxed and friendly.

"Welcome, Gerritt! How nice to have two handsome young men in camp." She pinched his cheek.

"Greta," Nellie Reicher admonished. "You will embarrass him. Gerritt, we will have you over for dinner soon."

"And that will be a treat!" Greta laughed. "Nellie is from Switzerland and a marvelous hostess. She carries civilization with her, packs it with the china and moves it to the next mine."

The faces began to look the same through the scotch, healthy and white; there were no Chilenos. There were obvious questions about how they liked the mine and pampa, neither of which they had seen. It was like taking an exam when you haven't read the book. Gerritt decided it was affirmation everyone wanted from them, that it was all right to be here 8000 miles from anywhere, and that Cerro Verde was special in some way he had not yet discovered.

Was it OK? Gerritt felt flushed and uncomfortable. He was accustomed to a casual arrangement of few people, the old men in Shem's kitchen discussing the coming of rain, where it smelled of old wallpaper and day old bacon. Rita swept in from the dining room, opening up the wide glass doors to announce dinner. If anything, Gerritt was grateful. Another scotch would have been deadly. There was a glow from candles in sconces on the walls and the sound of water from the garden room, visible over the table. Gerritt could smell grass and earth and coolness, the way the brook next to the house at home smelled.

"You must sit next to me. I haven't had a chance to talk to you, Gerritt." It was Elaine Barnett. He had glanced at her when he could. Her tanned skin was shiny, as though oiled. She took his arm and pulled it to her; he could feel her breasts. She was soft and smelled good. As his eyes moved down to hers, he caught a peripheral glimpse of Art, staring at him.

Rita took Wes's arm and they were seated. She rang a silver bell and maids, dressed in grey and white, immediately surrounded the table. They were served locos and then what Rita explained was pastel de choclo, a dish with meat, chicken and fresh corn, flavored with albahaca and garlic. You shook powdered sugar on it, which was strange to Gerritt but good. The wine was a heavy Chilean red, Sangre de Toro.

"You will have to see some of the pampa around here, Gerritt," Elaine said. Her eyes were direct and personal, or was this how she was, he wondered. "My father is a doctor here and has a clinica in one of the pueblos. We go out often." If this was an invitation, he wanted to accept, but Alice spoke.

"I've been reading some history about Chile. Did the Incas get down as far as Cerro Verde? Are there ruins?'

"Yes, and from even earlier," Leif Swenson replied. "The road they built survives, but the Incas went back to Peru. Most of what is left here is pre-Incan."

"This is great, Rita," Wes raised his wine glass and Gerritt followed. Rita smiled. She liked to cook and she liked men who liked to eat. These two would do well in her eyes.

"You must eat every bite," Greta, sitting on his left, gestured to the few bits of salad left on his plate. I was a little girl during the war in Europe and we had very little to eat. Not one morsel was wasted." Her Swedish accent sounded motherly, or what he thought a mother might sound like and he cleaned his plate. It seemed easy to satisfy these people. But there was Barnett; perhaps not him.

More drinks came after dinner, menta and more scotch. A mozo fed the fire and Gerritt felt warm and content. Vera was waiting outside. The wind blew chill and dry as they got in the car. When Gerritt and Wes said good-night, they shook hands. There was no moon, only the stark light from open bulbs on the porches and Gerritt could not see Wes's face well. There was a connection anyway, not friends yet, but people a long way from home doing the same thing. The apartment seemed even starker after the warmth of Blain's party, but Gerritt was too tired to think about it. He fell into a bed where the sheets smelled faintly of sulfur and listened to the wind whistling against the outside walls before he fell asleep.

CHAPTER 3

Gerritt opened his eyes, slowly remembering where he was. Light coming in through the window formed a halo around a dark green shade, making the edges fuzzy and white. He looked at his watch.

'Already nine! Crap,' he thought as he jerked himself awake. He rolled over to pull back the shade. The window was scratched and dusty, spraying the brightness of the day, watering his eyes and making his head hurt. He thought about the scotch at Blains. Ian had told him to watch the alcohol as the altitude made you feel it quicker and he guessed that was about right.

What he saw out the window was not encouraging; a bleak, and roughly paved street ran past the metal fences that kept in a small dirt patch with a few sorry weeds. Gerritt wondered if this was supposed to be the garden and thought briefly of Alice. If it was indeed her garden, she wasn't going to be pleased. The wind was swirling fine, brown dust, moving it from one place to another. Across the way stood a building, made of metal calamina and painted a flat green, holding a sign declaring it to be El Club Condor in plain black letters. A mozo in a white coat, a waiter in the club, moved debris and more dust around on the steps with slow and deliberate sweeps of an ineffective broom. Gerritt let the shade clatter back into place and lay back down, staring at the high ceiling and thinking of how the mornings were at home with the sun warming the earth and the ground absorbing the sounds in the air like an upholstered room. This place was empty, as though the people and buildings stood there on a surface with nothing underneath. Then he thought about the mine and smiled. Nothing underneath, that is, except money. Copper ore was money and that was his business and he liked it.

He felt cold and got up to dress quickly in the khaki work pants and shirt he had brought with him. They were stiff with newness. The rest of his clothes he put away in drawers without taking the tags off; it didn't take long. There would be other things coming, boxes with his life, books, stereo, more clothes, an old horseshoe from his room at Shem's that would arrive by ship sometime. He didn't need much.

Gerritt's footsteps clattered in the kitchen and echoed off white walls and metal cabinets that smelled of fresh paint and antiseptic. There was coffee and bread. Instant coffee. He made a cup from the hot tap water. It tasted burned and bitter, but he drank it anyway and took it outside. He was ready. At the end of the street, mine tailings rose against a milky sky and the muted rumble of a working mine sang to him. God, it was good to hear. The mechanical aspect, the expectancy of smooth machined parts working, well oiled, back and forth in complete order pleased him. The cables were pulled up, the shovel bucket went up; cables let down, the bucket went down, picking up, dumping, over and over. He smiled again, pleased at the reliable prospect and then his mind moved back to the evening before, all the endless faces and personalities to work on. The machinery was so simple and beautiful, each action predictable. People were another matter.

"Gerritt?" It was Wes's red head hollering from the door of his apartment. "Bring your cup, I'll get you a refill". He waved his arm for Gerritt to come on over. He hesitated, wanting to be alone on this first morning, but in a way Wes seemed like him, not yet a part of this place. There was that, some sort of understanding in the handshake of the night before. The empty cup needed a refill. There was no lock on the door, but he shut it and walked over.

"Hey," Gerritt greeted Alice and looked around at their apartment. "This stuff doesn't look any better in the daylight, does it? My place is the same."

Alice was in a bathrobe. Her dark hair was combed smoothly back and she looked clean and alive as she frowned, shrugged her shoulders, and refilled his cup.

"I know it's awful and after being at Blains, it seems worse. I hope we don't have to stay here too long. At least we have some things in the kitchen that the Welfare left for us."

"Welfare!" Gerritt exclaimed. Shem didn't believe in social support, felt everyone could earn his way and more of that ethic had rubbed off on Gerritt than he might have liked.

"Not what you think," Alice smiled. Her touch on his shoulder was somehow comforting. "Rita said it's the department here that handles all the furniture allocations and has dishes to rent and things like that. She's going over there with me today and we'll get some things for you, too."

A truck screeched to a stop outside, the dust coming in through the open door. Their coffee cups hung in the air for an instant and then dropped on the table as they heard the door slam shut and Barnett appeared in the door. It was a different person than the one they had met the night before; a boiling came from inside him and he seemed larger.

"Get your butts in this truck now!" he screamed. The veins in his temples bulged from the effort of yelling with a cigar clenched between his teeth, the sound going around it and out, making his voice have a slightly muffled sound.

"When you sons of bitches get your own trucks you can fuck around all you want, but when you ride with me, you be out here waiting. This isn't a date!" He seemed unaware of Alice's presence, but then turned to her and softened. He took the cigar out of his mouth briefly.

"Morning, Ma'am", he said pleasantly to Alice, then replaced the cigar, put his head down and walked out.

Gerritt and Wes jumped in the truck, putting on yellow hard hats that were thrown at them, their shoulders pushed together by the massive Barnett, who elbowed Wes in the side every time he wanted to emphasize something. Wes waved goodbye to his wife who stood, mouth open in the doorway.

"Now, I run a tight shift, and I expect things to be done the way I want 'em done. Our job here is to get ore out of that mother's ass-hole up there that's farting all that dust and get it anyway we can, understand?"

They bumped over brown dirt roads, dust rising in clouds around the truck when Barnett skidded around corners, enjoying their inexperience.

"Roads are oiled; the fucking dust explodes if we don't." The lesson continued as they went up a slight grade.

"Towers in the mine are for communication with the railroad and second-arily to provide info to the pickups and shifters. That's you, and you better damn well remember that! The Jefe Patio doesn't have any frigging time to spend helping you find your ass, so don't bother him. Just listen to him and you'll know what's happening."

Barnett then calmly veered, turning the wheel with ease and no explanation to the left side of the road in front of an enormous fully loaded truck and waved to the driver. If there was ever a time in his adult life when Gerritt came close to pissing in his pants, this was it. Recalling the near collision on the road from Antofagasta the previous night, here it was happening again. He could feel the huge truck's momentum like a heat wave off the summer street at home, pushing him back and away, but coming all the same. It would roll right over them and never notice. Didn't the bastard Barnett see it, for Christ's sake? He could feel the cold sweat rise on his skin as Barnett raced past the Dart on the left side, never taking his foot off the gas, and he was laughing, the cigar clenched tightly in his teeth, laughing at them, slapping the wheel in a personal ecstasy at their fright. Gerritt instantly cooled, realizing this was a perverse stunt Barnett pulled on new men in the mine.

"Road changes right-of-way at that point, didn't you see the sign?" Barnett's voice surrounded the cigar, preachy and condescending. "Oh yes, it's in Spanish, guess you wouldn't have caught it. The cabs of the Darts are on the right sides, so if they drive on the left side, it improves their visibility and be-lieve me you want those fuckers to see where they're pushing those mothers." Art continued to laugh, but there wasn't time to reply as he pulled abruptly into a parking place in front of some low buildings that looked to Gerritt like huge cardboard trailers without wheels.

"Mine offices," Barnett growled. "Temps. We'll have to move them again when we need this bench." The dust floated up off the pickup when he slammed the door and stomped inside.

"Nice guy," Wes shrugged and they followed. The door was heavy and on some sort of vacuum hinge which nearly slammed shut on them as they entered. Gerritt looked around the large main room and surrounding offices. Barnett was nowhere to be seen, but a few men sat around the tables, staring at them. Wes was about to introduce himself when Barnett burst back through one of the office doors. He'd discarded his hard hat and his baldhead reflected the fluorescent light.

"Here's the new help," Art waved some papers at them unenthusiastically. "About pissed in their pants at the right of way change." There was sweat rolling down the sides of his forehead as he bit down on the cigar and wondered off absorbed in the paperwork, leaving them standing there like exposed prey.

Bastard, Gerritt thought. Christ, how does this place function. He had a bad taste of uncertainty in his mouth. It felt like he could vomit and looked around for the toilet. One of the men slid off the table and walked over to them. He was slight of build and dressed in starched khakis that looked uncomfortable.

"Well then," he said in a heavy British accent. "Never mind Art, he's a decent chap. I'm Felix Alford, one of the Shift Foremen." When he smiled, you could see the space between his teeth, and his hair was thinning, but his offered hand was warm.

"Art's OK", he said again as if it was necessary to confirm this comment. "You'll get on once you learn the mine. Let me introduce you round." Gerritt wasn't sure. There was a rumbling discontent coming around the cigar that eating new shifters couldn't cure.

"This here's Juan Ortega, another shift foremen," Alford gestured to a dark head bent over a mass of papers. Gerritt and Wes were told in New York of a Chilean shift boss already here for some years. Ortega had a stateside education and two years experience here before he was made a shifter but Wells and Bowen were coming in green as his equals. Ortega's black eyes moved slowly up from the pages in front of him to Gerritt's face and then to Wes's, searching for what it was that gave Gringos the edge. Cerro Verde was an American company. They owned the mine; they didn't own the land. As long as it was their trucks, their shovels, Gerrett knew any white asshole would have precedence here. It was one of the reasons he had come; the Gringo was in charge. In another place Gerritt might have liked Ortega, but not here. Ortega's cold stare validated his thoughts.

"Pleased to meet you," Juan managed, pushing his chair back as he stood up. "I just finished the shift. Got to get these tonnages to Art." His eyes flashed at Gerritt as he passed them without shaking hands and disappeared into Barnett's office. Juan was not going to be much help. "And that," Felix smiled, pointing at a man slouching over a cup of coffee," is Mike Marshall, the Track Foreman.

"God, you look terrible! Looks like you had quite a night of it, Michael."

"Shut your bloody mouth, Alford," Marshall snapped. Ignoring Wes and Gerritt, he retreated into the contemplation of his coffee cup. Marshall was slight and pale looking, his thinning, sandy hair was uncombed and fell down over his forehead as if to shade his eyes from the morning.

"Is Mike British, too?" Wes asked Felix, since Marshall appeared to be no source of information at present, even about himself.

"No. Mike is from New Zealand and I'm actually South African. We've quite a cosmopolitan group here, but not so many Americans." Felix took in the new men. Bowen was enormous and gangly. Gerritt, however, moved from one foot to the other, anxious for something undefined, not saying what it was.

"I've been working in South America a good many years, mostly up in Bolivia around Potosí, and there were some bad times. One gets on best, I think, by waiting things out. Change requires patience." Felix explained calmly. Gerritt could feel Alford looking through him and he wanted to get on with it. The door banged shut again, this time on Hugh Dillon.

"Good morning, been expecting you!" he said cheerfully. A skeletal man with bad teeth and a warm core, his presence in addition to Alford removed the chill of Barnett and Juan Ortega. Gerritt relaxed a little.

"They seen the engineering offices yet?" Hugh looked at Felix.

"I was just introducing them round. Julio isn't here yet-he's the other shifter, or rather acting shifter until you two come on. Go on with Hugh, I've got my shift to ready."

"Geology is on the other end," Hugh pointed with his hard hat to the rooms as they followed him through the wide hall.

"Reicher's office, then Barnett's." They looked in on Barnett absorbed in paperwork and the first of many cups of black coffee.

"The last office is Ned Tully's. He's the blasting foreman and checks out the new drill holes on his way in each morning. He'll be in after awhile. Desks out here you can use, his hand indicating a few dented and dirty metal desks behind them. Coffee's in here in the engineering room." They followed him through the door into a large room lit by fluorescent lights and furnished with three large drafting tables on which were maps of the mine.

"In there," he said, pointing to a sort of closet off the main room. "It used to be a dark room until Zuñiga complained about people spilling coffee on the files and he moved the pot in there near the sink."

In the corner next to a drafting table, his head bent down, a slight and older Chilean was busy straightening the maps and papers that cluttered the big design tables in the center of the room. The collar of the dirty white shirt he wore was wrinkled and rolled out, and the shirt wasn't tucked in completely which gave him a look of being pulled down toward the floor. He sighed in seeming frustration at his task.

"Zuñiga, these are the two new men I told you about, Wells and Bowen. Can you get them some coffee, please?"

"Buenas dias, Señores. Cafe altido," he looked at them apprehensively and then quickly headed for the coffee. Either he didn't watch where he was going, or maybe he was near-sighted, as he walked right into a wastebasket filled with maps, spilling them and depositing himself flat on the floor in the middle of them.

"Lo siento, Señor," he looked at Dillon. "Lo siento, siento, mucho." He turned very red in the face, embarrassed by his awkwardness in front of the new men, as they all bent to help him retrieve his maps. Hugh didn't act surprised, as though this was a common occurrence, something Zuñiga did to start the day. Instead in a patient, if somewhat tired voice, Hugh began to explain his work, briefing them on the support his engineering department offered the mine. Zuñiga shuffled around in the background, finally bringing them some steaming mugs of coffee, real coffee, not instant.

"We try to maintain a five-year plan and stick to it as best we can. I fight with Operations all the time! They just want to get ore out of the pit; they don't give a damn about all the waste that has to be moved. So my job is to keep it all making some sense." It was obvious to Wes and Gerritt that Hugh enjoyed his work.

Wes ran his fingers over the drafting table. Drafting was his favorite class at Colorado School of Mines. He felt in Hugh a stable presence, as though they were settling in and this man would help them arrange their tools.

Gerritt was only mildly interested and looked out the window at the dust rising from the pit. Engineering had its place, but he also knew you moved a lot more ore if you thought about the ore first and the waste later. Hugh flipped the light on underneath the table so they could look at the plans for current operation.

"Numbers are the shovels, so we know where they're mucking," Hugh explained. "The highest benches were dug back in the 1890's; we're a half mile down now. Semi-permanent track is the hatched lines. Most of the track gets moved as the shovels move. Roads aren't on here, they change all the time. It won't take you long to learn your way around."

"Could I see the mine plan for this year?" Wes asked, thinking it would give them a better idea of the layout and also he was anxious to see what kind of engineering work was done.

"Hell with that, Wes," Gerritt stood up and put his hard hat on.

"Let's go on back out and see what they're doing with the shift. We can look at this shit later on." Hugh and Wes looked at him in disbelief of his casual dismissal of the mine plans.

Wes shrugged. "Well, later then?" he asked Hugh.

"Sure, anytime." There was a loud muffled hollering from the other room.

"There you are!" Barnett stuck his head in the door.

"Get your God-damned asses in my truck, I haven't got all day!"

He stormed out of the engineering office and on out the front door, which nearly slammed shut on him before he got his mass through it and it did knock his hat off. Art opened the door and came back in red-faced and furious.

"Somebody get this fucking door fixed, nearly cut my ass off!" he spit out around his cigar. There were suppressed smiles, even from Gerritt who had already seen enough of Barnett to find a door talking back to him amusing.

Art ripped the pick-up out of the parking lot and drove around the mine offices and out onto one of the mine roads. The huge pit opened up canyon-like underneath them. The benches from antiquity stepped down to the bottom where what looked like a toy shovel raised small puffs of smoke. Barnett turned on the radio in the truck. A garbled voice, speaking in Spanish and static came over the speaker.

"That's the main dispatch tower, the Jefe Patio," Art explained. "There are other patios around the mine, but this one is the Jefe, the head dispatch, he knows what's going on all over the mine. You better listen to him, you'll learn a lot. He'll be way ahead of you most of the time and can save your ass."

He had driven them around the south side of the mine and pulled up on the Visitor's Bench. You could see the whole mine from here and smell it on the wind. They got out and walked over to the edge where heavy posts had been sunk. The chain that connected them was a gesture only, a setting of limits. If you wanted to go over the edge, it was there and only the bottom would stop you.

"Shit," Barnett said looking at one of the posts, "Somebody must have hit this, it's leaning out. Remind me to tell Marshall to reset it." It didn't lean much, was just pulling on the chain connecting it to the next post. It wasn't the focus of their day.

What Gerritt noticed first was that there was no noise. The enormous air space more than two miles long and a mile and a half wide swallowed the mechanical sounds and it seemed as though the mine existed in a vacuum, and they were somehow outside it. Occasionally, the wind would bring the faint sound of a train.

"See that shovel working in the bottom," Art pointed his chewed cigar down to the machine loading rock into a line of railroad cars. Gerritt thought of the train he had played with as a child, the coal cars, the caboose, and felt control running coldly in his veins.

"That mother is the biggest one we have. It could crawl right over two pick-ups parked side by side and never touch them!" Art looked to see if they were impressed and bit down on his cigar. There were thirty shovels and they drove down to several of the sites where Art gave directions or asked questions.

"The 121 is loading oxide today," he indicated. They watched as the green ore was loaded into 65 ton metaleros, the huge railroad cars that went to the oxide plant where the ore was dumped, crushed, dissolved and electrolytically converted into copper bars. Another shovel loaded sulfide into a train that would wind around the mine to the smelter.

"Waste is mostly trucked or hauled in side-dump cars to dumps around the mine. Every shovel, truck, tower and bench has a number and you have to know where things are and how to get to them fast, understand? Not all the benches in this fucking hole have interconnecting roads so learn your way around. Shifts are expected to move 80,000 tons of rock in 8 hours and it takes 10 minutes just to drive from one side of the mine to the other. That's if you know the way!"

"Descarrille D-2," spat out the Jefe Patio over the radio.

"Derail! Fuck, better get our butts down there," Art said, wheeling the pick-up around on the dirt road and heading in the opposite direction. The mid-morning sun illuminated the light brown dust and reflected off the 80-foot high benches of the mine, making Gerritt squint. As they wound down into the deep pit toward the derail, he felt the place weighing, leaning on him. Though the top was open to pale, dusty sky, it got darker as you went down and the wind didn't whip around like it did on the upper benches. He longed to get out of the stale truck and look at the machinery more closely, to smell the familiar oil and grease.

The descarrille was near the big shovel at the bottom of the pit. It lay quietly now, the bucket resting on the bench above like a giant spent prick, its cab puffing ineffectively. They got out and walked over to where a group of men were trying to get the wheel of a rail car back on the track.

"Shit! They'll need a crane," Barnett spat onto the dry dirt, got back into the truck and picked up the radio. "Patio Siete?" he growled into the mike.

"Si, Señor Barnett," crackled the voice on the end, obviously knowing who was calling.

"Mandale una grua a D-dos, y altido!" His voice sounded tired, as though he had made this request many times before. They didn't stay long; the crane would be coming. He ordered Gerritt and Wes back in the truck. Three of the great metal cars were off the track, the front one contorted at the connection to the locomotive.

"Bastards steal the copper brake tubing off the bottom of the cars until they don't hold anymore. You get enough cars without brakes and you get a descarrille or worse yet a chokey. You'll see it all the time. Look at the faces on these guys, they don't give a damn whether the ore gets out of the mine or not, they still get paid.

Gerritt frowned. "How do you work them then, to get the tonnage you want? Are they all paid the same?" he asked Barnett.

"Well, no, the shovel operators get more and then they get a bonus according to how much ore they load. You have some control there. Train engineers make more and of course the Patios. Bonuses go to the chofers, too, for the number of trips they make."

Both Gerritt and Wes nodded, taking careful note of how Art handled the men. He was forceful, but didn't lose his temper. There seemed to be an unstated understanding between Barnett and the men. They all knew why the descarrille occurred, but that didn't seem to matter. Nothing would be done about the cause. The cars would be put back on the track. The event was just part of the day and a different day than they had seen in the mines on summer jobs. But every place has rules, pacts of acceptance that make progression and productivity possible. They knew they had just watched such an accommodation. But Gerritt was already thinking about how to take advantage of such a situation. He knew he had to get ahead here; he didn't want to go home. It was too crowded and you had to wait years to get a promotion.

They were glad to see the end of the shift. Julio Romero, the afternoon shift boss was in the office when they returned. A plump, happy man, he seemed genuinely glad to meet them. They forgot to remind Art about the leaning post on the Visitor's Bench, but he remembered anyway. Mike Marshall had mumbled something in response about it not being the first time.

When Barnett was finally done with them, he assigned pick-ups at the garage. Gerritt was sure they got the oldest ones in the mine. His had a hole in the floor around a gas pedal, which was only a thick, metal rod extending up through the open floorboard like an erect penis. It sputtered and whined, but ran and he drove back to his apartment, being careful to cross back over to the right-hand side of the road when he left the mine.

Barnett told them about the bar in the Club across from their apartments, and Gerritt had been thinking about that first beer for hours. Wes went on home to see what kind of a day Alice had, and Gerritt went over alone. The Club was cool inside and smelled of wax and something cooking somewhere. The entrance opened onto a large room where Gerritt's dusty boots left footprints on the polished floor. More rooms lined the sides, and he could hear the clink of glasses and voices from a hall. The steps down to the bar were worn in the center and it was dark, coming in from the light of day, the glare of the mine. At first he couldn't see who was there.

"Over here, Wells." It was Hugh Dillon seated at the counter with Felix Alford and another man.

"Chet Weir," he said, offering his hand. He was short and squatty with a ruddy face and a small reddish goatee under his smile.

"You weren't at the mine today, were you?" Gerritt asked.

"God, no!" Weir laughed. "I don't go out to that dirt hole unless I have to. You bastards can have it!"

"Chet, here, is the Oxide Plant Super," Felix explained. "They think we're dirty muckers up in the mine."

"Pleased to meet you, Weir," Gerritt returned his firm handshake. "You been here long?"

"Four years now, not long, but I'm second generation. So's Hugh. Our Dads retired here. How'd you like your first day?"

"Big place," he replied. "How do you get a beer around here?" Gerritt didn't want to talk about the mine. There were too many things to sort out and this Weir had no connection to all that. Maybe he'd talk to him sometime, but not now.

"Cuatro cervesas, por favor," Hugh waved to a mozo in a white coat. Gerritt wondered if it was the same one he saw ineffectually sweeping the steps earlier in the day.

The Cervesa Escudo was good. Cool and heavy, it melted the day away. Wes came later and they were able to laugh about the door slamming shut on Barnett and their dilapidated trucks. Hugh told them there was a picnic planned for the weekend out near Chieu-Chieu on the Rio Loa.

Gerritt ate dinner alone in the Club mess hall for the solteros and drove back out to the top of the mine. The dark was just coming on and lights from the shovels and other operating machinery twinkled faintly, not yet being of much use. He parked his truck and turned on the radio that responded with static and the barely perceptible voice of the Jefe Patio. Gerritt took out a small pad and began to write the words down he did not know, looking them up in a small dictionary.

CHAPTER 4

Learning a mine operation was easy for Gerritt, but sorting out how to get his way with the people around him was always difficult. After two days the labyrinthine roads finally made sense and evenings with his Spanish dictionary at the top of the mine made the radio comprehensible. Wes was slower, more methodical about the mine plan, the questions he asked. Gerritt liked him, but there were differences in their views of the operation. Wes examined; Gerritt watched. And Gerritt liked working on his own, he was just fine on his own. Most of the staff was tolerable, except for Barnett. If Barnett had a purpose, Gerritt was quite sure it was up his ass. The guy never stopped yelling. It was his normal way of talking and like the train that rumbled by at the edge of the farm, you slowly stopped hearing it.

On Tuesday after shift he drove up to the visitors' bench again where he would listen to the radio before going down for a beer and supper. The altitude of better than 10,000 feet made the nights cold, the sun intense and the wind a force. But the air was still for a change; he opened the pick-up door and slid out. There were shadows already down inside the pit, obscuring the lines of the benches. Standing in the sun on top, Gerritt felt warm, a growing sense of knowing his place here. He didn't see the person sitting against the chain post until he heard rocks being thrown over the edge, skidding and clicking going down. When the figure got up and walked toward him, he saw it was a girl, small and athletic-looking, in worn jeans and a grey sweatshirt that said Property of the University of Iowa.

"You're a long way from home," he managed to say. Gerritt was neither good nor bad with women; he liked them but didn't want one around all the time. It felt nice to be near a woman, but they interfered with getting on with things. He found it was always easier to define what he didn't want than what he did. The latter always implied that something could be fixed. So he had stopped trying to explain; when he was ready, he just moved on.

"I know. Molly Pritchard, I teach school here," she laughed and extended her hand. It was warm and she was standing close enough that he could smell her hair, dark brown curls and tangles fell to her shoulders and there were small freckles across her nose.

"How'd you get up here?" Gerritt took a step back away from her, which Molly noticed and moved away from him toward the edge of the bench.

"I come up here all the time, walk up from down there," she pointed toward the camp. "I like the mine, the machines. I like the sound the shovel makes when it bites the dirt. Look at that!"

Gerritt walked over and looked down to where a shovel was working three benches down, gouging the earth, taking a mouthful and spitting it into a truck. He was standing close to her again. She wasn't beautiful, just clean and strong, wound up in her own ideas about what she saw.

"I know what you mean," he said, looking down at her.

"Do you?" she turned and examined his face carefully, then turned back to the gaping pit.

"I suppose you do, all men do--think they know about machinery, I mean. But I see it a different way, probably."

"What way is that?" Gerritt was amused.

"Its movements, the movements of the different parts, like the boom on that shovel down there, so regular, so predictable, up, down, up down. It reminds me very much of sex." She said it so carefully, never taking her eyes off the shovel to look at him.

They stood there a moment, both looking at the shovel move back and forth. Molly shivered; the wind was coming up, blowing from the east off the Andes where snow still lay.

"Yes, I think I know why you would see it that way," Gerritt turned to her. "I identify with it, though, with the machine itself. It's more an extension of my body, letting me to do things I can't alone, like a tool," Then he chuckled, realizing that's exactly how she saw it.

Molly looked at him again as closely as she could in the fading light, but couldn't read anything that made any sense.

"I better get back."

"I'll drive you down."

"No, you came up here for some reason. It's OK, I walk all the time."

Gerritt had the urge to extend his hand, as he would to a man, and ended up doing so; he felt awkward. She took it briefly.

"You must be Gerritt Wells, one of the new shifters. Rita said Wes Bowen is seven feet tall and that definitely isn't you. Bye." And she was gone before Gerritt could think of something to say, whatever that might have been.

He noticed that the cables connecting the posts along the edge of the bench were stretched tight, the posts were leaning out toward the pit. Gerritt made a mental note to mention this to Barnett. He got back in his truck, smiled, thinking about Molly, then turned on the radio and the Jefe Patio.

The next afternoon Barnett sent Gerritt down to B-4 near the bottom of the pit to pick up a gang of men who had been laying track. He told Barnett about the posts and cable, but Barnett blew it off. And Gerritt was tired; after Molly left he stayed in the mine listening to the radio, but only hearing it peripherally. His mind was on Molly and the shovel, trying to sort out what she said and why to him.

Near where he was to pick up the men, he saw a huge dozer sitting partially on the road. It was orange, oil dripping from its sides and the seat empty. Gerritt slowed his pick-up, looking hungrily at it, wondering what it was doing idle. He looked around for the track gang, didn't see them and stopped to look at the dozer more closely. It was quiet there, near the bottom, the noise from the other machinery stilled by distance and the end-of-shift crew changes.

'I'll just sit in it,' Gerritt thought, smiling to himself at how the girl would like doing this, as he climbed up the six feet to the oily leather seat.

'God, the gearshift felt good, smooth and cold in his hand.' He shut his eyes so hard they watered and could feel the coolness on his cheeks. In his mind he was remembering the dusty summers on the farm, plowing Shem's fields until he was covered with good rich earth, remembering the showers and muddy water going down the drain. And then he was really there and it seemed the most natural thing to him to reach down for the key, which was there, and to turn it and to feel the vibration in his fingers as the engine turned over and over and finally caught, and the familiar black oily smoke belched out of the pipe above him.

He saw the men from the track gang waving their arms at him as he backed the thing out onto the road. He waved at them, scraped the side of his pick-up as he went past, not really seeing it. It all felt so good, so very good.

Gerritt didn't see Wes Bowen jump onto the dozer and turn off the key, didn't see anything except things behind his eyes, hearing the sound of the engine. When the motor stopped, he was back in Cerro Verde and he looked incredulously at Wes, who had hopped down from the machine and stood furiously contemplating him from the ground.

"What the shit do you think you're doing?" Wes's eyes were bulging out of his head. With his height, he was an awesome sight, even on the ground. But Gerritt didn't see him, as though he wasn't in the present situation at all, but somewhere else.

"If Barnett saw you doing this he'd have your ass. You've scraped the side of your truck!" Wes looked at the track gang Gerritt had been sent to pick up. They stood around staring at the two Jefes arguing. One of them was the dozer operator, a machinista, and he knew the dozer had been left there for the next shift's use. If this was an example, it was not good and Wes turned back to Gerritt to pull him off the machine. He seemed to be coming back from wherever he was and smiled at Wes and the others.

"Jees," he said, the words coming loosely. He felt exhilarated, free. "I haven't been on one of these in years."

"Well, you can't do it here either. Don't you remember what Blain said about doing the Obreros work? It's not done! It doesn't go in this place. Come on, let's get out of here."

"Jesus, Wes, it's no fucking big deal." Gerritt wasn't quite sure what had just happened. He was sweating freely, totally relaxed and wanted to let what he was feeling continue. But the look on Wes's face told him to put whatever he felt back in the closet for another time, only he knew it would be gone and he couldn't get it back.

He climbed down, smelling his oily hands and smiling. They piled the men into the backs of the two pick-ups and headed for the mine offices. Gerritt whistled softly to himself. Barnett glared at them walking in late for the end-of-shift meeting, but Wes didn't mention the dozer again until the weekend when they were sitting by the Rio Loa drinking beer.

CHAPTER 5

He thought about the dozer, going over what made him start it and how he got lost for those few moments. He could remember the pleasure it gave him, but not the impetus for doing it. Wes hadn't said anything to Barnett; for that he owed him. Gerritt was already painted with the yesterdays that formed him and he carried those colors. In Montana enough people pushed him into a ready-made, custom designed trough to make him leave and come here. Now, new fences were going up. He really didn't want to go on this picnic with a lot of people who would ask questions, but there wasn't anything else to do on a Sunday in this place.

And the weather was good. Later he learned that the weather was always good; it never rained. There was, instead, an absence of weather in the Atacama. It was hot in the day and cold at night; the altitude simply engendered extremes. The pocket encompassing the desert was a vacuum, sucked dry from two directions; the Humboldt Current on the west and the Andes to the east. Weather was rarely a topic of conversation, only as a comment that it wasn't there or on the one or two occasions when it rained, as a disaster. The electrical cables in the mine were laid above ground and cracked in the dryness. While the children in camp went around pointing at rare raindrops falling on the ground, the cables shorted and the mine shut down for the few hours it took them to dry.

Having no reason to stay in camp, Gerritt went. Cerro Verde was an island and he decided that living here for a while probably gave people something like cabin fever. And the Atacama mothered past secrets, different from what he knew, swallowed in high flat brown land a thousand miles long.

He rode out with the Alfords, his pick-up was in the shop having the fender repaired where the dozer had scraped it. Felix's wife, Thea, was a thin, delicate woman with pale blond hair. Molly Pritchard came with Wes and Alice. The Dillons drove the geology Land Rover with their five children and all the food. They turned east after leaving camp, the dirt road passing in back of the oxide plant and tailing dumps ribboned out ahead of them, pink in the early morning sun. There wasn't much wind and the trucks stayed well behind each other to avoid the dust. Gerritt breathed in the dry air and felt himself floating out into the vastness of the pampa. It went on as far as he could see. Empty was a good word. Empty fit the desolation of where they were and Gerritt liked it.

"The surface of these roads is somewhere between cement and sand," Felix Alford said loudly over the engine noise and the rush of wind through open windows. "They've been scraped out of the desert with a road grader. Up higher they get pretty rough from the llareta trucks. Llareta's about the only fuel source up here since there's no wood. But it's going fast; only grows on the north side of the mountains and slowly."

"Where were you up in Bolivia?" Gerritt asked. He had wanted to ask Felix about his time there from their first day. Bolivian mines were also isolated in desert.

"Up near Potosí in the tin mines. God awful climate, high and cold. Indians are partially paid in coca leaves to keep their blood vessels dilated and to keep them from leaving. I was up there a while ago when it wasn't a good place to be. We got chased out of one small mine, by a bunch of Bolivianas hopped up on chicha and coca. Left our passports, everything. They strung one poor bloke up and picked his eyes out with those big hatpins they wear in their hats.

"Felix, I don't relish that story." Thea said softly. Her Leicester accent was brittle and the fine, white hair blew around her face. She seemed too fragile for the pampa and was half Felix's age. He put his hand on her knee.

"I know. Things are different now," he said to Gerritt, "It's pretty civilized. I wouldn't mind going up there again."

"No thank you," Thea looked at him, frowning. Felix told Gerritt they were married when he was on holiday in England the previous year. Thea barely knew him. Felix had lived a whole lifetime before her and Gerritt figured he probably had other adventures, things he would rather she didn't know.

The day began to warm up and the pampa and dust strung out golden in the light. Gerritt sighed with pleasure at the immensity and space.

"Not much wind today," Felix pointed at the rooster tails, which obscured the trucks ahead. "Sometimes you can follow behind twenty feet back and never get dusty. Today's a rotter; we'll be filthy by the end of the day."

That didn't bother Gerritt, but he supposed the women wouldn't like it much and looked at Thea. Her small hands were white and thin.

"You didn't meet Ned Tully, yet, did you?" Felix asked.

"No, he was always out in the mine or down at the pulverine with the explosives trucks when I was in the office. Barnett wants us on the road."

Felix smiled and shook his head, knowing Art Barnett well. "Ned was up in Bolivia for a time, too, back in the old days. He's quite a chap, knows everything about drilling and blasting. Never been to college, but knows powder by the feel and smell."

"Yeah?" Gerritt answered. He was distrustful of old-timers. They reminded him too much of the old men who sat around Shem's stove, talking about how they could do a better job of most everything, particularly the government.

"Well, you wait until you see his work. He can lay a million ton an inch from your foot!"

Felix put his foot on the brake; the other trucks were stopped up ahead. They could see Hugh waving a beer.

"We're near the quebrada, a small canyon, where we can get down to the river."

Felix pulled up in back and Hugh and Wes threw them beers. Gerritt's mouth felt like cotton, though they had been traveling less than an hour. The beer tasted as though someone was pouring a bucket of cool water over him. Molly tied her hair back and wore a red and white checked shirt, buttoned low in the front. He moved over to talk to her when Hugh called to them.

"Walk up here." Hugh headed out in front of his truck. Hugh had already lit a cigarette and talked with it in the edge of his mouth. Ahead the road curved slightly and there was what looked like a large crack in the earth. When you made the turn, the crack became a small canyon dropping from the pampa to the river and invisible from even a hundred feet away. Down inside the quebrada, far below, Gerritt could see green things growing and a narrow brown stream of water. He looked up. San Pedro and San Pablo, two extinct volcanoes always iced with snow rose in the distance. Below them lay the brown-yellow pampa and then the mouth of the quebrada opening to its bottom of soil and growth, watered by the river. It was a continuum of opposites, ice and moving water, bareness and growth.

"That's Lasana," Hugh pointed at a few wood and calamina buildings in the valley. "About a dozen people still live down there by the river where it's protected and warm. This place has been inhabited a long time. The Rio Loa's the only river in Chile that makes it all the way from the Andes to the ocean. The rest dry up on the way."

Driving about half way down into the quebrada, they stopped again. The ruins of the Pukara de Lasana, a pre-Inca fort, ascended a small hill next to the canyon wall and were intact enough to see where rooms had been. Gerritt climbed up the narrow stone path behind Molly, feeling the walls, thinking that other hands, long dead now had touched these blocks, put them in place and crawled inside away from the cold. Shelter was an ancient need. The form had changed, but the motivation for building in a place near water like this was common.

"God, I couldn't have lived here," Molly shivered even though it was hot in the canyon. "Imagine how hard it must have been, their lives I mean." Gerritt looked at her; it hadn't occurred to him to compare amenities. He was simply feeling a rapport with the builders of this place in their choice of site, considering the alternative of the dry, harsh pampa above them.

"What if you had to, what if it was all you knew?"

"Then I'd want to run, only I wouldn't know where." Molly could see there was something in Gerritt she didn't understand, some empathy and satisfaction with the land itself and only the land. Gerritt bent over to pick up a stone and rubbed at it with his shirt. His dark hair fell down into his face as he spit on the stone and kept cleaning it.

"Look," his pale eyes lit up as he handed her the stone. "It's an arrowhead, finely made, too." He hadn't heard what she said. The object definitely was an arrowhead, small and black with a finely chipped point and a notch for tying it to a stick. Gerritt went running back down to show the others his find, a connection to this place.

They picnicked by the river. Hugh told them there was a place south of the mine where you could find a lot of arrowheads, something like a primitive factory. Dillons were the only ones with children and Hugh found a small stone corral with a decrepit old horse for them to ride. It was owned by an equally decrepit and toothless old man who furtively skirted the fringes of their picnic, disappearing quickly behind a stone wall when anyone looked his way and then popping up somewhere else entirely.

"Who's the spy?" Gerritt asked Rene Dillon as she handed him a piece of fried chicken. Rene was a farm girl, also from Montana, with healthy freckled skin and warm eyes. She had married at eighteen forever and after five children still wanted more. Gerritt liked her, she was the kind of woman he imagined his mother might have been, when he was able to imagine her at all. The youngest Dillon was only three months old. He started to fuss and Rene turned to pick him up.

"We're not sure where the old guy lives, but he's always here when we come and it's his horse," she said as she patted her now quiet baby on the back. "He won't ever come over to eat, but we leave food for him when we go back."

The food was good and the beer made them sleepy. Felix stretched out under a tree, his head in Thea's lap. Gerritt wondered off toward the river. Here, the ground sloped gradually down through the thin, grey pampa grass to the water where he bent down to wash grease from the chicken off his hands. The river was narrow, hardly what he would have called a creek at home, and was clear, cold, and slightly salty when he licked the wetness from his fingers.

"Hugh said it's salty," Wes had followed him down. As tall as Wes was, it was difficult for him to squat down to the water.

"A little, but the people down here seem to use it for crops, so it can't be too brackish."

"Apparently, there is another river running into this one down about ten miles, the Rio Salado, that has salt deposits all along the edges."

Gerritt nodded without answering and turned back to the river. He didn't feel like talking, wanted instead to watch the running water, hear its motion across the rocks and around the grass.

But Bowen wanted to talk about the dozer.

"Just wondering if you'd thought about why you started up the dozer when we aren't supposed to do anything mechanical in the mine?" Gerritt picked up a rock and threw it in the stream. How could he answer when he hadn't figured it out himself. Wes stood back up and Gerritt looked up at him for a long time.

"It felt good, so I did it," was all he could say. And that was the end of it. Gerritt turned and looked down the river. It was clear to Wes that either Gerritt didn't know why he had started the dozer, or if he did, it was a private thing, something he didn't want to share. Wes hoped it was the latter. He liked Gerritt and wanted to know him, but the guy was closed like an exclusive game preserve. Wes walked back up to the others thinking that he'd keep trying, that maybe at some point Gerritt would open up.

Gerritt felt heavy from the beer and the exchange with Wes and lay back in the grass. When he opened his eyes, it was with an awakening sense of the smell of someone near him. Molly had come looking for him.

"There you are. We're about ready to go on to Chiu Chiu, it's getting late." She knelt down beside him. She untied her hair and it was nice, heavy and falling on her shoulders.

"It's pretty here," she said quietly. "Like a secret place. Did you ever have a secret place when you were a kid? I bet you did." He didn't answer, but he reached over and touched her arm where her shirt was rolled up. The softness of the light hair was like fur and reminded Gerritt of a small and vulnerable animal.

"Well, you must have," she watched his hand, but didn't move. "Or you wouldn't look for a place like this. Come on, we have to get back." He was the first to draw away and stand up. He didn't want to leave; it was cool and shady.

The trucks were hot inside until they headed out on the road to Chiu Chiu. Gerritt rode with Bowens and, thankfully, Wes seemed to have finally forgotten the dozer. Alice was ebullient, thrilled with being in a place so different from the States.

"Well, Gerritt," Alice said, "What do you think of Molly?"

"She's OK, nice looking." He hoped he sounded non-committal; it was really none of Alice's business.

"She certainly seems to prefer the company of men," Alice raised her eyebrows. "She hardly talked to me at all." Gerritt wasn't surprised. Alice wouldn't have interested Molly in the slightest. He ended the conversation by turning around to look out the back window of the truck to where the quebrada had been swallowed in the flatness of the brown pampa. No break in the landscape told you where its edge began.

After ten minutes, Wes turned off the road, following the other trucks. Up ahead a few miles was a village, larger than Lasana, with trees and adobe houses. The dust came up through the floor of Wes's old truck when they stopped on the top of a rift, from which the ground fell away sharply beneath them. It was windy when they got out and walked over to the edge. Alice gasped and grabbed onto Wes's arm and Gerritt felt his lunch rise in his throat. Spread out over the floor of the small valley below them were what was left of 300 or so people, mummified by time and the desert.

"This graveyard is more than a 1000 years old, actually older than the Incas," Hugh explained seriously. "We were out here a few months ago, but looks like somebody's been in here with some large equipment. Let's go down." They walked and slid down a steep embankment, the dry rock and sand rolling down in front of them.

The mummies sat cross-legged on the ground looking up or at each other as though they were caught in the middle of a conversation. The condition of some verified the reality; not all were whole. Some had unattached feet and hands, the joints still bent and fingernails intact. In one place five heads were lined up, one with a hole in the skull. The graveyard was dug up disrespectfully and cruelly, the dead left where they fell. If a peaceful eternity was what they had in mind, it was not here. Their gold was gone. Baskets with seeds to feed them and a few tattered blankets to keep out the cold survived, blown around by the winds of the pampa. Otherwise, there was nothing left.

"How long has this been here, been opened?" Gerritt asked.

"It's been going on for years, and it isn't the only place. Grave robbers take the gold and leave the rest. Eventually, the natives take some of the mummies up in the hills to rebury them, but for the most part nobody cares." Hugh kicked at a stone that went nowhere, just deeper into the sand.

"What about Padre Simon, he cares!" Rene said emphatically.

"I'm not so sure he does, Rene," Hugh said sadly and turned to explain. "Simon Gherts is a Flemish priest, old now, been out here since before my father came down here to work. He's got a museum of sorts in Santa Bárbara de Atacama with enough gold and beads, mummies, all kinds of things, to fill this whole quebrada. I doubt he did the digging, but I'll bet he was out here shortly after."

They walked around among the people and pieces of people. Molly picked up a few turquoise beads, rubbing them over and over in her hand to give them life.

"If the mummies are being reburied in a different place, how will archae-ologists in the future be able to make sense of the new site?" Wes asked Hugh, who had no answer.

Near the side of the canyon, Gerritt bent down, pushing the sand away from a bone. It was greyish, a femur, he decided, somebody's femur that had once walked around where he was standing right now. He squeezed the bone and it came away easily from its burial place. There was yellowed skin and dried blood, thousand-year old blood, on one end and a small piece of torn cloth stuck to the other. It was part of this place, and Gerritt wanted it.

"You aren't going to take that, are you?" Molly stood with her mouth open staring at him.

"Yeah, I think I will." As he said it, he was making the decision. The bone was light; it hardly weighed anything.

"Put it back! Can't you leave them alone! I wish they would bury all these people again, at least leave their bodies intact. It's too personal, what you're doing." She turned away from him and ran back to the pick-ups, her hair flying around her face.

He took it with him anyway, because he wanted it to be personal, to be with these people. To Gerritt it was saying he cared about what was done to them, and he didn't want or need anyone's approval. He rolled the femur in a rag Wes gave him and laid it in the bed of the pickup. Wes did not comment or ask him what it was. The dozer conversation was strange enough.

They went back to camp by another road, the sunset painted the high snows red and brown dust bloomed pink behind them. Gerritt looked on all sides of the road where time and wheel marks of previous trucks lay. Nothing ever seemed to leave the pampa. If it came here, it stayed. He would put the thighbone on his mantle.

CHAPTER 6

Julio Romero described himself as a weed. Gerritt was put on Julio's shift with the understanding that when he learned enough, it would be his to run. Julio was filler, a bright engineer who happened to be Chileno. He would work for the other Jefes and maybe, if he stayed as long as Juan Ortega, he would have his own shift.

"So you see, Sr. Gerritt, they need something to cover the ground until the grass grows." Julio seemed resigned to the situation; it wasn't the first time it happened. His job was to teach the new Gringo shifters and to that he had acquiesced. He liked to evaluate them quickly when they first arrived and then to see how they developed, who made it and who ended up getting shipped back home. If these kids wanted an easy job, Cerro Verde was the wrong place to come. The shift changes came every two weeks; just when you got used to sleeping nights, you had to sleep days. The rock was acid and ate your clothes eventually. Your pockets usually disintegrated first, then the cuffs of your pants. There was Barnett, always pushing for higher tonnages. Julio found him sadistic. Art seemed to look for ways to twist situations around that would enable him to embarrass you. He didn't bother Julio, Juan Ortega or any of the other Chilean shifters, but he seemed to have no respect for his own. And the heaviest thing about Cerro Verde was the isolation. It carried a lot of men away who couldn't deal with it. You worked and played with the same people, engendering an intimacy not found in most places. There were no secrets here. If you couldn't cut it, everyone knew.

Julio liked Gerritt and was impressed with his quick command of the language and the radio. They worked day shift together that first week, a lot of the time spent with Mike Marshall, the track foreman laying track to the new cuts and with Ned Tully, the blasting foreman.

Ned was a large, heavy man, nearing retirement and from a day in mining when you learned with your hands. He loved the taste and smell of explosives and had a feel and respect for their power that he demanded of everyone who worked for him. Ned combed his grey hair, which he allowed to grow long on one side, over the top of his bald head, a habit his wife found aggravating and which always became detached in the wind of the pit causing him to trip over things because he couldn't see. And he was never without a wad of tobacco in his cheek, spitting the brown rank juice in whatever wastebasket was handy and wiping his mouth on the back of his sleeve.

One morning at shift meeting, Tully told Gerritt to have a shovel moved before the shot that afternoon. Gerritt had already made plans for the crew that would have to move the shovel and he said so.

"Can't do it today, Ned." He felt confident of his position. He had looked at the shot plan and with loading thirteen holes, he didn't think the fallout would come close to the shovel.

"The crew working down there will be busy moving track today."

Tully stared at him, stopped chewing his wad. Barnett suppressed a smile. This would be interesting. The others at the meeting, Dillon, Romero, Reicher and Marshall didn't move.

A mouthful of spittle twanged loudly into the empty metal wastebasket near Reicher's desk. Tully's face flushed and swelled, his neck pushed fatly against his collar.

"God-damn it, Wells! You better move that fucking shovel or I'll cover it with the shot!" he roared.

Gerritt looked at him without emotion. If the crew laid track down there, they'd be loading ore from the shot the next day, increasing the daily tonnage. And anyway, he was sure the old man was wrong.

"I don't think it will fall that far," he answered, never taking his eyes from Tully's. "Why don't we recheck the calculations?" And then Tully was on his feet over him, brown spray coming out of his mouth with every word.

"Just you move it, you son-of-a-bitch, and don't you ever try to tell me where a shot will fall! You stand where that shovel is this afternoon and you'll get your fucking ass covered!" Ned stomped out, the office door slammed behind him and he ground the gears in his truck as he peeled out to load the shot. Nothing more was said; the shovel would be moved.

Gerritt had the sour taste of crow in his mouth all day. Tully hadn't scared him exactly, but Gerritt didn't want any part of an argument with him again, at least not in front of Reicher. It was too important that Reicher thought well of him. If he had a problem with Tully, he'd see Tully alone, welcome the chance to prove the old man's blasting techniques wrong. There was a reason he went to school and it wasn't to take shit from an old grunt.

At the end of his shift, Gerritt went down to G-2, where the shovel was sitting that morning. He would wait there when the shot went, just to see where Tully would lay it down. He put on his brakes as he passed the shovel in its new location. Sitting against it was the track gang who had moved it, waiting for the end of shift. Stopped, he leaned out of his truck, now repaired, only to choke on the dust blowing up from his tires.

"No se van trabajar mas oy dia?" he asked, spitting dust out onto the ground.

"No creo, Señor." One of the men stood up and walked over to the truck; the others only looked blankly at him.

"Y porque?" Gerritt asked why.

"No hay mucho tiempo, diez minutes no mas." The obrero pointed at his watch.

Gerritt looked at his watch and then at the men. There were fifteen minutes until the end of shift, not ten. What the hell, he'd just let them go early, they weren't going to get anything else done anyway.

"Bueno," he said. "Vayase pocito temprano."

"Ah, gracias!" the man smiled as he waved at the other men to leave. Then they were all smiling and thanking him. It took them only a few seconds to jump into their truck and then they were gone; they had been packed and ready. Gerritt stood there watching the dust of their truck disappear at the end of the mine.

'That was too easy,' he thought, rubbing his chin and realizing he'd been duped. Next time he wouldn't be so generous. Maybe they'd remember they owed him, but not likely.

He must have stood there until 3:30 PM, because the explosion took him by surprise. It was close, the ground at his feet shook before the sound reached him. He turned in time to see clouds of dust erupting from deep holes in spurts of energy from a bench higher up. As if geysers were going off in domino order, the brown water of earth moved up to the sky and then the casings, the long narrow tubes shot up like cannon and began falling, breaking apart with the rock itself. The bench, what had been a bench, cracked and crazed and fell into the pit below in large and small boulders and dust, dust so thick and muddy, Gerritt had to get back into his pickup to breath. As small pebbles and sand-like earth whished and pinged on the truck roof, he felt alone, sweating, knowing that Tully had been right. The dust began to clear with the wind, rising up and out of the mine. He strained his eyes to see ahead of him. Not more than 50 feet from his truck lay the rock from the shot. If he was closer to where the shovel had been, not exactly there because that spot was completely covered now, but only the 50 feet closer, he would have bought it good, just like Tully said.

'Shit on the old man, he knows his stuff,' Gerritt thought. His neck felt cold and he wanted to get out of the bottom of the pit. The truck started easily and moments later he was roaring up the mine roads toward the offices. Barnett met him about halfway, drove in front of him, stopped and jumped down from his truck.

"Where the hell were you?" he screamed at Gerritt. "No, don't tell me, fellah, I know! I talked to the track gang you let go early. What the shit do you think you're doing? You're supposed to be out of the mine before 3:30. Didn't you hear the whistle? Maybe Tully was right, maybe you ought to get your ass blown off." Barnett was red in the face, the cigar end blooming brightly as he waved his hands around.

"OK, OK, I hear you! Jesus!" Gerritt wasn't going to take anymore. He wanted only to get away from Barnett, away from everything right now. Barnett seemed to cool off, sensing Gerritt's reaction. He'd had his say. Art didn't bring up the argument at the post-shift meeting, but it was there between them.

The shift had gone well, Gerritt and Julio had more tonnage than any of the other shifts for the last three days and Barnett liked that, as a dragon might who gets enough to eat.

Supper didn't sit well and he went to find Molly's place. It took him a few minutes to find it in the dark. She lived in a long, drab building with four apartments much like his, but she had put red and white curtains at the windows and pillows on the railroad furniture.

Molly was pleased, but was not expecting him and had a craft project spread out on the floor. Even that was nice.

"You look like you need a drink," she offered. Gerritt had a strained look on his face and was tired.

"Yeah, scotch, if you have it." She turned away from him and he followed her into the small kitchen, watching her tight rear end move in her jeans.

They sat at the kitchen table with their drinks, bending over towards each other and talking softly. The scotch felt warm and good on his throat. He told her about the run-in with Barnett, the explosion, the gang he allowed to go home early. She listened, watching his eyes.

"Barnett wants a firm, black line between us and the men and I have a hard time doing that. Christ, they're people, with sense. They get tired, they feel. I don't like a lot of people around me, but I can't move them around like chess pawns either." He stopped and looked at her. She was listening, listening carefully, not only to what he said but what was behind the words.

"I see what you mean, but it's different down here," she said slowly, then looked away.

"I mean, we don't have these class differences. At home, being rich doesn't make you better or different, it only means you have more money. Here in Chile, the laboring class is a separate society, not worthy of close association."

Her lips tensed as she talked and Gerritt could see this bothered her, too. She ran her hand through her hair.

"All the dollar-row people here, not just the Chileans making dollars, but the Europeans and Americans, none of them would think of interacting socially with the empleados and obreros. Why do you think the American camp was built up here on the hill away from the laborers' houses and all the stores? Rita Blain is a good example of your fine Gringo lady; she looks down her nose at anyone who lives further down the hill than she does! And you ought to hear children at school talk about their maids and gardeners, as though they were another variety of being than themselves." Molly was quite red in the face and her brown hair tossed as her voice became louder.

"Well, shit, I just can't understand it," Gerritt shook his head. "Julio Romero is a friend. I don't care if he's Chileno or what he is. It's not going to change what I think of him."

Molly was quiet. It was a useless argument and anyway they agreed. Most of all there was absolutely nothing to be done about it. She reached across the small distance between them and touched his arm.

"I know. I'm sure Julio Romero is a good guy, but you're not going to get far in Cerro Verde if you see him out of the mine. This is not home; this is a country with centuries of conditioning. You aren't going to change anything."

Gerritt laid his hand over hers on his arm. She was such a mix. The macho female who liked heavy equipment and still had a warmth and sense of fairness. He felt her shiver.

"Are you cold?" Gerritt stood up and pulled her close to him. She fit under his chin where he could smell her hair, it was warm and clean. Molly fixed him another drink and took him into her bedroom where they talked for awhile longer before he kissed her. The wind whistled at them through cracks around the window, the gusts rattling the shade.

Gerritt would have liked sex with her to be different, though he couldn't think exactly how. Molly was forceful in bed, strong, nearly taking him. He lay there afterwards, with her sleeping quietly, her breaths sometimes drawn in restless gasps. The sounds from the mine were audible on the wind and Gerritt wished he were there, on a Cat, or pulling a convoy up the ramp with a loco-motive. He smiled, it wouldn't be unlike being in bed with Molly.

Wes was on night shift. Gerritt wondered how he was doing, thought about what Wes would have done about the gang, decided that, yes, Wes would probably have made them finish the shift.

CHAPTER 7

It was dark, no moon and the shadows had long since raced their way down to the sea a hundred miles west. The only light came from his truck as Wes sped along the top edge of the mine. In a few places lights from the locomotives and shovels blinked in the void beneath. Things were going well and he liked working with Juan Ortega, the Chilean Shift Boss. Wes was meeting him on the visitor's bench for lunch. Juan was hard to get to know, but his instruction and assistance were extraordinary. Juan knew mining as though reading the backs of his eyelids, from a sentient knowledge of what was needed in any situation. But Wes knew Gerritt was suspicious of Juan's reservation.

"I can't trust a man whose soil I'm on," Gerritt said, "He'll be waiting around to get it back."

There was a point to that; an American company taking ore from Chilean soil. But Barnett told them Condor Copper, the owner of Cerro Verde, paid the government plenty for the privilege of mining here.

'Anyway,' Wes thought, 'I'm being paid to run the mine not argue property rights, and this is a great chance for experience.' He was feeling comfortable with the operation now, learning the radio, the roads, and the shifters. Alice was happier. Henri Duvillárd, the French Jefe of the Welfare warehouse had brought more furniture and replaced some. Nellie Reicher had introduced her to some of the other women in camp who played bridge every week, a game Alice loved.

Wes arrived at the spot early, parked and unfolded his long form, leaving his radio on in case they were needed somewhere. You couldn't sense the depth of the pit in the darkness. It was black with a few lights where shovels worked and he could see the headlights of trains shooting ahead on their way to the oxide and sulfide plants, illuminating the rock a few feet on either side. It was still, the wind dying down as it did every night after midnight. Wes was glad he came here. He heard about Cerro Verde from one of the old miners in Leadville, where he worked one summer.

"Richest pot of copper in the world", the old guy said. "Tailings dumps have more copper than Bingham Canyon!" That was hard to believe as the Utah mine was one of the biggest and most successful in the States. It made Cerro Verde an exciting place for a young engineer.

Wes turned as Juan pulled his new GMC up beside him and leaned out the window.

"Hola, como te vas?" Juan asked.

"Ah, mas o menos," Wes answered, laughing. That's how it was, not bad, not good. He pulled the lunch Alice made him out of his truck and climbed into the GMC.

"We don't have much time to eat tonight, I want to be sure that tread gets changed on the D-2 dozer." Juan reached over to turn down the radio. There was silence as they opened their lunches, making Wes uncomfortable.

"How long have you worked here, Juan?" Wes began, wanting to know something, anything about the person he was welded to for the indeterminate duration of his training.

"Too long," Juan stopped chewing. In the only light, coming from the dashboard lights, it was hard to read his eyes. Juan pushed his heavy black hair away from his face.

"Nearly ten years now, why?"

"Oh, just wondered," Wes turned to look in his lunch sack for dessert. "Barnett hasn't been here that long has he?"

Juan didn't answer right away. He was peeling an orange and Wes watched him as he threw the peelings out the window with some force.

"No, he was passed over me. So was Hugh Dillon. They're good men." Wes was thinking they weren't better than Juan. He started to say something, but Juan got out of the truck and walked over to the edge of the pit. Wes got out and followed him.

"I know how this company works."

"What do you mean?" Wes asked. Juan jerked his head up from the orange he was peeling.

"Oh come on, Bowen! Gringos love Gringos! They look after their own. The dollar-row Chileans have been getting screwed since the Americans took over this place. You get tax help and free transportation back to the States for vacation. Shit, I could go on and on, but don't get me started on this subject. I don't want to talk about it."

"But why do you have to take it? You went to the same school in the States that I did?"

"Yes, but yo soy Chileno"! It makes a big difference. If I want to leave here and make the same kind of money, I'd have to go to another fucking Gringo company with the same problems. And I like it here; our families are all here. It's home." Juan threw the rest of the orange down into the dark of the empty pit.

"And mostly because I don't think about it much anymore."

Juan opened the door of his pickup and turned up the radio. The conversation was over. Wes got back into his own truck, staring out into the blackness. He felt guilty, as though he were taking something away. Their roles could be reversed, and yet he would still need Juan's help. That was a miserable realization. However, Juan seemed resigned and not ready to take back what should rightfully be his, theirs, his and all the other Chileno's.

"We better move, Wes." Juan started his own truck and hollered through his open windows. "Before you come back down to the dozer, see if you can find Arias. I heard he's been moonlighting again and he's probably parked someplace sleeping."

Wes welcomed the time to himself; he wanted to sort out what Juan just said. There was the guilt, sure, but he wanted the job, to be Shift Boss, not Juan's assistant. If guilt over working someone else's land went with the territory, it went with the territory. And maybe like Juan, he wouldn't spend a lot of time thinking about it. He couldn't think about it now, anyway, he needed to look for Arias.

Guillermo Arias was one of the "chofers", the drivers of the huge trucks in the mine that carried ore and waste. He worked another job during the day and invariably tried to sleep on night shift. Wes couldn't blame him. Juan said Arias had nine children and his parents to feed. As with many of the men, family ties were strong and frequently several generations lived in one or two rooms. Arias would drive his big Dart up to one of the benches no longer being used, cut his engine and sleep there in the darkness. He'd been caught, but there wasn't anything to be done except wake him up; Arias had more than 25 years with the company. The Union would never let him be fired and he knew it.

The night air was chilling and the heater in the truck felt good. Wes found Arias and his 80-ton truck parked up on F-2, a bench unused at the moment but where the mine offices would be moved eventually. There was no sound from the truck. It loomed, a giant yellow-orange shape in the night, the cab six feet up and black as the pit. Wes pulled up behind him and honked several times, but there was no response, no sound, no lights.

'Shit, the guy must be deaf,' Wes thought, ramming his truck into park and jumping out. He looked up at the seemingly empty cab of the Dart, then seeing a piece of old rail on the ground reflecting his truck lights, he picked it up and banged heavily on the cab door.

The Dart exploded with sound and light, the engines whined as they started up, the exhaust belched out, huge lights came on. The gears ground and with a sick feeling Wes remembered his pickup was in back of the Dart. Arias backed right over the quarter-ton truck, never even noticing it, probably thinking he had backed over a small boulder so common on the benches. He simply put the Dart in forward gear and roared away, not waiting to see who had waked him again or what they wanted, if anything.

Wes grimly surveyed the damage in the dust from Arias's hurried departure and it was not encouraging. His truck was completely crushed, the cab lying flatly on the front seat, the tires splayed out as though they were knock-kneed. Impotent headlights still beamed, but pointed at nothing and the heater still belched its warmth. The radio crackled on, directing the mine. The Jefe Patio was calling him.

"Señor Bowen, donde esta? Donde esta, Señor Bowen?"

He tried the mike, but the transmitter didn't work. He turned the key off and dejectedly began to walk the mile back to the main road leaving a dead truck behind asking him where he was.

Juan was hot about it, partially at Arias, but also at Wes for parking behind the big machine.

"Madre de Dios," he screamed when Wes took him back up to the bench, "it's totaled!" Then there had been a small silence when Juan looked at Wes, remembering their talk at lunch.

"I'm glad you weren't in it, amigo."

When Wes went into the office at the end of shift, Gerritt had just arrived.

"What's the matter with you?" Gerritt asked. "You look sick." Wes was sick. Not only was he worried about Barnett, he was coldly realizing that he could have been, as Juan had said, the filling for a steel sandwich.

"I wrecked my pickup."

"Is that all? Well, you can have my place in the shop." Gerritt said lightly.

Wes sat down heavily, shaking his head. His clothes were sticky with perspiration, clinging to his back and itching under his belt.

"The shop's not going to be able to glue mine together; Arias ran over it with a Dart. There's not much left, it's flat!"

"Christ, Wes," Gerritt sat down, grimacing and finally serious. He was surprised; Wes was a careful person. Barnett was going to have his ass.

"I know, I know." he drove his fist uselessly into his big hand. "Juan's going to tell Art. I just as soon not be around. I'll see him this afternoon after I get some sleep."

Wes went home in a sweaty chill. Alice was, thankfully, still asleep. He wouldn't tell her about this, couldn't tell her; she worried too much about the mine machinery and injuries. He'd say the truck had broken down, yes, that would be good, it was in the shop. And then it would stay in the shop, be replaced eventually. He tossed back a jigger of scotch and went to bed.

Gerritt took time that morning to go up to F-2. At first he couldn't see the truck, thought the shop had already come for it, and then he was on it, nearly running over it himself. As he stood over the flat and tangled mass, crushed into the gravel, he wished he wasn't seeing the truck. The wind was beginning to whirl small gravel into the wreck and Gerritt wanted to help cover it, bury it. He was suddenly angry with Wes; his sweat chilled him in the wind, seeing a working piece of machinery come to this. He took off his hard hat and wiped his forehead with his sleeve, remembering the scratches he had put in his own truck.

'Well, hell,' he thought, 'At least Barnett would have a bigger bitch with Wes than him now, at least he would leave him alone.'

The shift was good that day, no choques and he and Julio Romero loaded more ore than the other shifts; he wanted to celebrate.

"Hey, Julio, let me buy you a beer?" Gerritt simply felt good. He was going to have a few beers, eat and then there was Molly. Absorbed in his small and private euphoria, and finishing up the paperwork from the shift, he didn't see Julio's face tighten and turn a pale grey. When there was no answer, he looked up.

"How about it? A day like this deserves a drink, como no, Julio?"

All the old things, the traditions of the pampa were going through Julio's head, the acceptance of his station in the mine. There was some peace and contentment in knowing one's distance, one's place on the shelf. His job was teacher, not Jefe and his space in the mine hierarchy was small and located on a lower floor. Somewhere, though, somewhere inside rested thoughts that responded to Gerritt's invitation, as though it were only a matter of one man asking another to simply go, have the drink, talk about the shared shift, the shift he now ran, the mine, laugh a little and then go home. But Julio had too many years of saying "yes, Jefe, no Jefe". Conditioned by his culture, he could not go to the Gringo club, have a drink with Gerritt there or anywhere.

"Lo siento, Señor Gerritt, pero no puedo," he said with some sadness.

"Oh, for Christ's sake, why not?" Gerritt knew exactly why not and it made him want to retch.

"You're with me, Julio. Who the hell is going to care whether you're an empleado or a Jefe or a cow pie for that matter!" And he literally dragged Julio into his truck, and Julio did not resist. They arrived at the Club together and went in the side door and down the worn steps into the darkness of the bar.

Felix Alford and Wes Bowen were sitting in a booth and Hugh Dillon was at the bar getting a beer. They all looked up, staring and not saying anything. The mozo behind the bar, the young one, froze, knowing what he would have to do, incredulous that Julio would test rules which were not posted, but which did not need to be posted because they were understood to a depth that no one could make such a mistake, at least until this moment.

"Hollah," Gerritt waved, ignoring the silence and knowing what he would do, must do.

"Dos Escudos, por favor." The mozo didn't move at first but his eyes rolled over to Julio and then he looked down and began to wipe the counter slowly with a towel.

"Dos cervesas para mi!" Gerritt was bent over the bar, snarling, screaming in the boy's face which flooded with fear and drew back.

"Si, Señor," the mozo said weakly, unable to confront Gerritt further, and produced the beers. Gerritt threw some money on the bar, handed Julio a beer and they sat down with Felix and Wes. It was over, but not over. Julio was not accepted, but it was the mozo's choice to avoid conflict, since he couldn't think of a way to answer Gerritt, the Jefe, who purchased the beers. The air relaxed some and the men began to move around, but an electric charge floated in the room; what Gerritt did was to put a foot on the scale of propriety and all felt the imbalance.

"Did Barnett hear about your truck?" Gerritt asked Wes, shoving the confrontation back into his mind.

"Yeah, Juan called me at home. Barnett threw his hard hat on the floor and broke it--those are great hard hats!"

"Yeah, hecho in Chile! Just don't get under a falling rock," Hugh laughed from the bar. "We're supposed to get some better ones, but they never arrive."

"I went up to the mine this afternoon after Barnett cooled down some," Wes said, wiping the frost off the side of the beer. "You know, he was almost reasonable, and I sure wouldn't have blamed him for kicking my ass. Anyway, I'm going to be without a pickup for a while, for sure. There are some new ones due in next month, so Juan says; maybe I'll get one of the old ones, then.

Barnett said I could walk until the Incas came back for all he cares. I was grateful to Juan Ortega for softening him up."

Julio smiled, knowing how Juan handled Barnett, then took a swallow of beer.

"Yeah, Juan's a good man," Hugh agreed, lighting a cigarette.

Gerritt didn't say anything. He didn't owe Juan and didn't want to. The guy thought something was owed him, that a stateside education and a dollar-row salary made him a Gringo. It was better to work with Julio, he was paid in escudos and he had no pretensions.

There was an awkward silence. Julio drained his beer and stood up quickly.

"I must go. Thank you Señor Gerritt. Thank you Señores. Hasta luego." He nodded to the mozo, wanting to thank him, too, thank him for letting this moment pass. It would not happen again. He retreated backwards toward the door as if he was afraid to expose his back, then turned and ran up the stairs, the air outside was at least for everyone.

"What the hell did you ask him in here for, Wells?" Hugh asked when Julio was gone, coming to the booth where the mozo would not overhear their conversation.

"We had a good day. Why shouldn't I buy him a beer?"

"That's OK in Montana, but doesn't go here, you can't buy empleados a drink in the Club bar, old bean," Felix explained as patiently as he could. The local class system was like home in South Africa for Felix and he had no real patience for Gerritt's misuse of it.

"Well, I just did buy him a drink!" Gerritt was adamant and he had indeed done just that. He wasn't good at following rules when they made no sense and remembered a licking as a child from his Uncle Shem when he let the cows out of the pasture. Pleased with himself, the beer tasted especially good today, sinking coolly down his throat and he went to Molly. It was better this time, his energy nearly matching hers.

CHAPTER 8

The Gerencia sat alone, a white jewel, at the top of Camp Hill from where one could see a hundred miles across the brown pampa to Lincancabur, a dormant volcano that had not yet reached its angle of repose. The party was an annual affair for the mine and plant Jefes, required by the New York office. As the traditional home of the current Mine Executive Director for over fifty years, the Gerencia's green shutters and pillared porch were kept in constant and careful repair, providing a solidarity and permanence to the small community of Cerro Verde. Gerritt heard often about the current residents, Joe and Anna Driscoll and the daughter, supposedly retarded. As with most people who are seldom seen, they were much discussed. Anna Driscoll stayed at home; her maids did the shopping. Though household help freed her from the routine of constant care required by a disadvantaged child, Anna seemed not able to return to the social world and they did not participate in the rounds of bridge and parties in the camp. Gerritt met Joe Driscoll at the mine. A heavy, surly man, his face was pitted early by acne and he was quick with opinions and orders.

Gerritt rode to the party with the Bowens, in their recently purchased car, a silver 1938 Chevy. Because there was no car insurance in Cerro Verde, people tended to drive cars forever, reselling them over and over.

"I like your car, Alice," Gerritt said warmly. "Where did you find it?"

"Henrí Duvillard's father was getting a new one and wanted to sell it. I love it! The curved horns on the side remind me of an Elliott Ness car and it has an on and off switch!" She laughed, her laugh pleasant and warm.

"The engine is aluminum," Wes explained. " It was recently rebuilt in the mine shop. I had to do something. With my truck wrecked, we had no transportation and Alice wanted her own car, anyway. Isn't it great?"

"A real find," Gerritt replied. He loved old cars and this one was a classic.

They parked in the lot in back of the mansion. Gerritt was feeling more at home, liking the endlessness of the pampa, the working machinery. Having finally written to his uncle about the camp and mine, the farm was now behind and he didn't miss it. Gerritt failed to mention the trouble with Barnett or Julio Romero's beer, but only because Shem didn't know such people. Work at the mine progressed well and Gerritt was comfortable with the Spanish, had settled into the routine of the shifts, not forgetting the farm, just filing it away.

He smiled as he climbed the steps of the Gerencia for the first time with Wes and Alice; their shoes scratched the grey marble, making sounds of a knife on a wheel sharpener.

Light flooded out from every window and there was music playing somewhere; a mozo in a starched white jacket, which pushed his neck stiffly upward, held the heavy, carved wooden doors. Inside was a central hall, more marble, the roof supported by columns covered with flowering bougainvillea vines; light in the day came through stained glass skylights overhead like a prism, making plays of color on the walls and floor. Rooms opening onto the atrium were filled with Spanish antiques, purchased in Santiago over the years by the succession of occupants. The Gerencia was a museum of time, a representation of successful stability within a constantly changing and transient population.

But mostly it was the daughter, Eve, about whom people talked. She was Driscoll's only child, was meant for them as if ordained, a promised gift. Eve was not their own daughter, she had been found.

"Found her in a cage in Antofagasta," Julio told Gerritt one night on shift.

"Her mother died in childbirth and her father left her alone while he worked." Felix said when Gerritt asked about her.

Hugh told him Eve's father built the cage himself and used it during the day until she was two, when the Driscoll's were contacted by a priest and came to take her away.

"Never had a bath."

"Psychological impairment. Lovely girl now, but not really all there."

Gerritt pieced the story together; everyone knew something. Eve would be about twenty, he thought. She had apparently been away at school in Santiago for a time, but could progress no further and was returned to the safety of her parent's house and the small mining community. He decided that she couldn't be empty; instead she would be filled with different thoughts and experiences than most, something Gerritt understood. There were times when, unable to communicate a meaning or feeling, he found himself retreating into his mind, taking himself completely away from the conversation. When jolted back by the other person, he sometimes felt disoriented, preferring his own thoughts. Maybe Eve lived inside herself in that way.

Gerritt saw the reception line, the Blains and the Driscolls smiling to greet them. He sensed his hand being crushed by the man Driscoll who smelled heavily of alcohol, his smile moving in and out of the pocked scars on his face. And then the mother, her grey hair pulled tightly back, her small dry hand turning him toward Eve. He was unprepared for her, he realized quickly; he had expected a girl with the northern Chollo flatness of face. Instead, she was pale and tall with the fine facial features of the southern Auracanians. Her thin arms hung from a black dress with no sleeves and a long strand of ivory pearls fell from her neck, matched her skin but looked too heavy for her, as though she might have to bend over under their weight. Long black hair was woven around her face, the dark eyes offering nothing but inviting him to enquire about the secrets inside. Gerritt thought of a place he used to go in the woods to think and imagine. Eve's hand was limp, but warm and faintly damp like the earth on a summer night. She stared at him and pulling him toward her she reached her white hand up to his neck and grasped the ends of the western bolo tie he wore. Gerritt pulled back slightly, embarrassed at her attention and not knowing at first what she wanted. It was the only kind of tie he owned, the only kind Shem ever had in the house.

"Look at this tie, Daddy," Eve exclaimed, her black eyes delighted at her find. "Isn't it too pretty. I've never seen one like this." Her voice was soft, but had a hoarse quality like a young boy's voice when it changes. She looked closely at him, as Gerritt imagined she might look at a magazine.

Joe Driscoll rolled his eyes back, taking her enthusiasm lightly and turned to the next guests arriving. But Eve continued to hold onto the tie and Gerritt began to wonder how he could extricate himself from her grasp without seeming awkward. Anna Driscoll flushed hotly.

"Well, why don't you have it then," Gerritt said, watching Anna's face instantly cool in relief. "It will look much better on you." And now everyone was watching them, Driscoll arrested in mid-handshake with a guest. Gerritt took off his tie and put it around her neck, having difficulty getting it over her ample hair and getting close enough to smell the soap and perfume on her skin. Rita Blain walked over and laughed too loudly as she admired Eve's new necklace, but the harshness in her voice broke the moment and the line began to move again.

"Oh, Gerritt, now you don't have a tie," Alice exclaimed worriedly as they accepted glasses of champagne from a mozo.

"Well, she wanted it, and I didn't think she was going to let it go. I can't say as I miss it." He loosened the collar of his shirt, looking back at the reception line where Eve was straining her long neck to see him, her mother pulling her back to the guests. Gerritt smiled at her simplicity and directness. Eve's life must be easy with no gray areas; if you wanted something, you took it. She was obviously spoiled, but without guile, a fragile child in a glass house. She is so lucky, he thought, to be with the Driscolls. The eyes and dirty teeth of the boy in Antofagasta flooded back and he tried to picture him clean and whole in this place, but could not.

He walked with Bowens into the living room where thick, red carpets, furnishings and wood-paneled walls hushed the conversation of what looked like a hundred people. Gerritt recognized only a few faces; there were many employees in the oxide plant and smelter, and offices whom he hadn't met. They waved a greeting to the Tullys, Reicherts and Barnetts, but neither Gerritt nor Wes cared to sit with Barnett and they were pleased to find Felix and his wife Thea sitting with Rene and Hugh Dillon in a book-lined alcove. They switched to scotch; the mozos kept their glasses filled and Gerritt felt an intensity of well being, rich and secure.

"This is an amazing place when you consider where we are," Gerritt said, thinking of the spartan simplicity of his home with Shem.

"I wish we could see it more often," Rene said longingly. "There are so many beautiful things, I forget what's here. Oh, here comes Henrí."

The tall, dark and neatly dressed man joined them. His black hair was combed back as though with glue, making it look thick and shiny and his narrow mustache was blessed with the same compound.

"You haven't met Henrí, have you?" Hugh asked Gerritt and Wes. "This is Henrí Duvillárd, our resident Frenchman. He's the Bodega Superintendent, the man you call if you need furniture or repairs made on your house."

"Ah, you're just the man I wanted to see," began Wes, smiling and glad to have made such a valuable and pertinent an acquaintance. "Thanks for the help with the furniture. You made my wife very happy!"

"Yes," Alice said enthusiastically moving toward him. "It was wonderful getting some padded chairs and a sofa? I got splinters in my legs from those wood railroad things." Duvillárd chuckled, admiring her legs.

"Of course, Madame, glad to be of service." He bowed slightly and graciously.

"One thing," Felix Alford said, teasingly. "Hugh forgot to mention that whatever you want, Henrí is out of at the moment. He even had a stamp made up that says 'No hay in La Bodega'!" Felix danced around waving his drink in the air.

Henrí only shrugged his shoulders and laughed. He was used to the Jefes' humor and took it as it was intended, easily and cheerfully. It was harder than they knew to run a bodega and still keep everyone happy. You had to give a little more attention to the bigger Jefes, but he liked to be sure the new people stayed around, too.

Gerritt leaned on a mahogany sofa table, setting his drink down to light a cigarette. He didn't smoke often, but liked it. A box caught his eye, slightly smaller and narrower than a cigar box, inlaid with colored woods. He let the lighted cigarette dangle from his lips, picked up the box and opened it, more to see how it was constructed than what was inside.

"My God, what's this?" he gasped, the lighted cigarette falling on his arm. He caught it quickly and stubbed it out in the ashtray. "It's a voodoo doll, or something!" The others peered with surprise and curiosity at the contents.

Inside, stuffed tightly, so tightly it barely fit was a small doll made of colored cloth with finely painted facial features and black hair that looked human. She was dressed like a Boliviana in a tiny black bowler hat and a shawl around her shoulders. Piercing her stomach and legs were pins, sharp, ceramic-headed pins, placed precisely in the joints and to the left of center in the midsection where the stomach might be if the doll were human.

'If the doll were human,' the thought ran through Gerritt's head. 'Who was this supposed to be?'

"How awful," Alice was repelled. Her face contracted and she shuddered. "What is it?"

"Witchcraft is still practiced out on the pampa," explained Hugh as he lit another cigarette from his and handed it to Gerritt. "Some of the festivals remain fairly pagan. They dance in costumes with demon masks and in some of the more remote villages they still make animal sacrifices. But, they go to mass and the Catholic priests have accepted integration of the old ways. It's a strange mix."

'No it isn't,' Gerritt thought. 'It isn't strange at all. People on the pampa are more tied to the earth than you are.' Shem would understand it, as he did, know the meaning and dependence on nature. Like the bone, the femur from Chiu Chiu Gerritt had on his mantle, the doll in the box was a link to the insides of the earth, to things the doll maker understood and accepted.

"Hello, everyone." A tinkling voice behind made them turn and there was Eve, her large eyes moving over them all slowly until she found Gerritt. She walked over to him, barely seeming to touch the carpet, and looked into the box, Gerritt's tie moving against her chest.

"Oh, that's one of Hortensia's dolls," she said. Gerritt marveled that what it represented didn't seem to bother her. "Mum told her not to leave them around, but she still does it."

"Who's Hortensia?" Gerritt asked her.

"She's one of the empleadas and cooks for me. She is from Ayquina and brings the dolls from there. But I don't know why she sticks the pins in them, maybe she's sewing them, do you think?" Gerritt looked at her, incredulous at her failure to see the cult symbol in the doll. She was different, in a way that surprised him. Untouched by evil, she lived in a world that lacked malevolence and would, therefore, be unable to comprehend the abstract idea of the fetish. Gerritt decided to approach her on her terms, as he couldn't think of a simple way to define wickedness, nor why it should have been brought into her house.

"Well, let's have some fun with Hortensia," Gerritt said, with a mischievous look at the others. "We'll rearrange her pins for her. Let's see, we'll put some in the arms and feet and one in the head. There, now someone will have a headache."

"Oh, I don't know if Hortensia will like that," Eve didn't understand what Gerritt was doing, but knew Hortensia didn't like anyone touching her dolls. Eve had been scolded, repeatedly, for playing with them, and it was this she remembered.

The others also felt threatened by the change of the pins. It looked like just a doll, but to Hortensia it was a person and someone to whom she wished ill. The whole thing was too personal for interference.

But there wasn't time to talk about it. Rita Blain swept in on them, a flash of red hair and green dress. Her strong perfume dominated the alcove and as they all turned from their preoccupation with the doll, Gerritt shut the box quietly and put it down.

"Oh there you are Eve, dear," Rita said, her low voice filling the small space completely. "There are more people coming and your mother needs you.

Come now." She disconnected Eve's reluctant hand from Gerritt's arm and they disappeared in the crush of guests. Gerritt felt the loss of her warmth; his coat sleeve was wrinkled and damp where Eve had grasped him.

"Mustn't touch the baby," mocked Rene Dillon, shaking her finger at Gerritt.

"Seems to me like she's still in a cage," Gerritt said sadly. "It just has a different kind of bar."

"No Gerritt, I don't think that's the reason," Felix put his hand on Gerritt's shoulder supportively. "She's too easily hurt and they try to protect her. Cerro Verde is a good place, quiet and isolated."

"I'm not so sure of that," Rene said, looking at Gerritt. She couldn't read his eyes but had seen Eve's and wondered if Eve would leave him alone. "She's pretty self motivated. I remember a few years back seeing Eve at a Christmas creche at the church in New Camp, crying for hours, wailing because she could not take the lamb home with her."

They moved into the dining room to a table heavier with food than Gerritt had ever seen, excessive almost in its volume and variety. Whole lobsters, sides of beef and stuffed turkeys sat beside gelatinous fruit and vegetables he had never tasted. Chefs from the Club, dark faces in white hats, rushed around to refill already full serving dishes. Gerritt returned to fill his plate several times, thinking about the food in the mess hall at the Club. Nothing made sense in this place.

He felt his head get heavier after the meal but had no idea how much alcohol he consumed. You never knew with the damn mozos refilling your glass constantly. Some people were dancing in the marble atrium. He wished Molly were here, but she was on vacation in the States. In any case, it was only a fleeting remembrance that didn't burn through the scotch and the introduction to Eve.

It was late when everyone began to leave, not to see the place for another year. The Gerencia was meant to be tasted not digested. He looked for Eve, but she disappeared after the people stopped arriving and Gerritt pictured her sequestered in an upstairs room, waited on by Hortensia.

The Tullys walked out just ahead of Gerritt and the Bowens. Ned's wife was an older, portly woman with curly blue hair and an old brown fur coat that hung nearly to her ankles. Her arm was linked through Ned's and they were weaving slightly. Behind him on a long string, as though he were walking his dog, was a whole lobster shell, the redness visible in the dim light from the house. Ned was clucking and cajoling it along.

Gerritt looked up across the camp toward the reason they were all there. He could detect a slight sulfur smell to the dry night air and hear the grinding of machinery down the hill in the mine. The light from the Jefe Patio's tower was just visible.

CHAPTER 9

Gerritt was up early on the Wednesday after the Gerencia party, unable to sleep. He jumped off a rail car on shift the night before onto cold feet. A buzzing numbness spread quickly up his legs, like bumping a funny bone, and then his legs gave way and he fell, hitting his hip on the car bed. It wasn't a bad bruise, but his leg stiffened overnight. He sat now in the early morning, licking the edge of a cup of hot coffee and looking out the window at the wind blowing dirt up the steps of the Club. The phone rang, a new phone installed just that week. The shock of hearing it calling him jarred his hip and meant he had to get up. He thought about Tylenol.

"Hullo," he said coarsely into the receiver, expecting it to be Molly and not wanting to see her at this hour. He tried the day before to tell her about Eve and the party at the Gerencia, but she seemed uninterested and babbled on about her new niece, how cute babies were. That was an uncomfortable topic for Gerritt and smelled of attachment. Now he only wanted to be left alone; it was 5:30 in the morning and his leg ached.

"Is this Gerritt?" The voice on the other end was soft, child-like in its lightness. Who was it? It couldn't be Eve. "Hello, is that you, Gerritt?"

"Yes, it's me." It was, it was her. Christ, what was she doing calling him. He saw her in his head, the pale arms, the dark hair.

"I have on the tie you gave me. Can you come up and see it?" Come up? To the Gerencia? No he couldn't possibly. Not only was his leg hurting, but the whole thought of going alone to the Gerencia was an absurdity that bounced around in his head making the pain worse. How did you answer, discuss social rules with an illogical person. Gerritt began to laugh at himself.

"I don't think so, Eve," he said lamely.

"Well, and why forever not?" She sounded pouty. Gerritt could almost see her lower lip stick out and wondered aimlessly if her hair were down and how long it was. This wasn't happening. Maybe if he could just go back to sleep.

"I don't know why not." And not being able to think of a reason that would make any sense to someone like Eve, he began to think 'And why not,' the suggestion a seed, a beginning of an idea. It wasn't in any way complete and Gerritt was not even sure what it was he was thinking or beginning to think. Only that why should anyone say he could not go to the Gerencia. She asked him, the Director's daughter. Why should it matter to him that she might not know what she was doing? No, he decided, it didn't matter at all. She called him.

"Where is your mother?" he asked, wondering if Anna Driscoll knew Eve was talking to him. How could she, it was 5:30 in the morning.

"She's asleep with Daddy."

"Did you ask them if I could come?"

Eve didn't answer right away. 'Oh shit,' Gerritt thought. 'Hang up, hang up, now.' His eyelids squeezed tight, trying to shut out what was happening.

"Look Eve," he said slowly and carefully. "Why don't you ask your parents when they get up and call me later."

"No, no, no! You come up now, right now! You come!" And she hung up, the last being a raspy whisper, as though she had screamed a command at him.

He got the Tylenol and sat back down on the bed with the bottle in his hand, trying to believe that he had imagined the conversation. He had done that before, thought he talked to someone when he only intended to. Sometimes what he did got confused with what he thought he did, or he would think he saw himself phoning, listened to himself calling, talking.

'He wouldn't go, that was it', he decided, took three Tylenol with his coffee and got in the shower. As the hot water flooded him, he forgot the pain. But drying off it reminded him, brought him back to the room. Then, well, hell, he would go. She wanted to see him and he was curious. Where did she spend her time, what had happened to her mind?

He dressed slowly, partly in pain and partly because he was reluctant to do this thing. He looked at the day outside, the usual cloudless sky that gave you no information about the temperature. It was almost always cloudless. If there were clouds, they were never serious. Gerritt longed for a summer thunderstorm and the humid smells that came after.

The altitude made the early morning cold and the wind blew at him as he used his arms to grab the steering wheel and pull himself into the truck. Maybe tomorrow he would be able to put more weight on the leg, but today he had to sit a moment waiting for his muscles to settle into the new position. He realized he was sweating and wiped his forehead on his arm. Through the windshield were San Pedro and San Pablo, the twin mountains with their eyes in snow, which were turning pink with the dawn light. The night shift was still on; the machine noises were faintly audible, arriving in waves as the wind chose to send them. Gerritt didn't have to report until three for afternoon shift. He would see Eve and then have some more Tylenol and a nap.

The street rising to the Gerencia was deserted, but he wondered if anyone looking out the windows of the houses recognized his truck, wondered what he was doing up here. He passed Barnett's and Reicher's homes and they were dark. Gerritt wasn't sure yet whether he cared if he was seen or not. There was certainly no reason for him to be at the Gerencia, especially at this hour and everyone seemed to know everyone else's business in this place. If they weren't looking now, Gerritt supposed they would know anyway, it was too small a place.

A maid let him in the front door. She had obviously been waiting for him because it opened before he could knock. He looked quickly around for the Driscolls, thinking that surely by now they would know he was coming; she would have told them. But there were only the silent bougainvillea vines in the dark foyer. It seemed much larger without people and conversation. Gerritt could hear himself walking.

He was encouraged along impatiently and followed the dark-skinned maid down a few steps to the left of the atrium into a small sitting room where the carpet was the color of the sky and which he did not remember from the night of the party. Eve sat at a small table, a child's table, her knees poking up into a white gown as she sat on the low chair. She looked up at Gerritt and smiled with her whole body. Her black hair was undone as he imagined. It hung in heavy masses down her front, framing the tie around her neck, which rested lightly on a full chest, moving up and down as she breathed.

"Oh Gerritt", she began softly, "I'm so glad you came." She stood up and he took a step back, realizing that she wasn't dressed. The white gown was nightwear and though he couldn't see through it, the shape of her body, the gentle curves and points of nipples under the light, white material were clearly sensed. He was confused. Why would she greet him this way?

"Come sit with me, Hortensia will bring breakfast. I waited and waited for you." The crack in her voice was natural, but sounded as though she was hoarse from a cold. Eve motioned for him to sit down in the chair next to her. He looked at it, below him, but she didn't seem to notice that the chair was small, just patted the seat of it and smiled at him. He shrugged and lowered himself onto it, his leg hurting as he stretched it out to the side. He was awkward and huge in her presence; though he was not a big man, the table and chairs made him seem so.

"That was Hortensia...?" Gerritt jerked his thumb toward the door, trying to recall her face. She was like so many of the women from the pampa he had seen in New Camp, flat faced, braids, the flowered dress. But Hortensia had suddenly become a person who left a definite intension in a box, a person who could hate enough to hex.

"Mmm-hmm," Eve said, her hand over her mouth trying unsuccessfully to stifle a giggle as she watched Gerritt's amazement. It wasn't at all clear to her why he should react this way to Hortensia's doll.

"She looks pretty harmless," he said, trying to laugh at his own discomfort.

"Harm less, what's that?" Eve asked. Her mouth fell open. It was pink and wet inside and she hugged her knees, pulling the shirt down over her toes.

'What you are, Eve,' Gerritt thought. 'My God, she was a child, like Molly said, nothing but a child, in every way except her body. No wonder they kept her shut up.'

"Harmless means you won't hurt anyone," he said softly, bending close to her. "Do you understand that?" Her black eyes were rimmed with long lashes that moved slowly as though weighted.

She seemed to be considering what he said, bit her lip, which was naturally berry-colored. The word was an abstract for her, it wasn't a real thing she could touch or see, and she didn't understand.

"Yes, I think so," she said tentatively, then "Are you harm less?"

Gerritt had to smile at that, but he didn't know the answer.

"I try to be harmless," he said, wondering if it would be true. She was fragile. And he thought of a yellow and white teacup, all that was left of his Aunt's china, sitting now in Shem's pie-safe at home. Gerritt used to take it down, turn it gently over in his hand. You could see through the cup when you held it to the light, all the way to heaven, Shem used to say.

Then Hortensia was back with warm rolls full of nuts and sugar and coffee thick as syrup. Gerritt examined the maid carefully, but she kept her head down and wouldn't look at him. She was a heavy woman with graying hair wound in braids around her head. Her features were sharp and severe, and Gerritt thought she must be from the south as well, not the alteplano. He wondered whom the doll was supposed to be and whether it was still there in the box, whether she knew who moved the pins. Again, he felt with something like a chill that he should not be there.

The rolls were warm and soft. Gerritt realized he was hungry, or perhaps he was nervous. Eve watched him eat, offering more rolls and pouring his coffee with ceremony.

"There, isn't this fun? Now I want you to meet Alfredo." She turned toward the corner of the room where a half-dozen large stuffed animals sat sleepily. "Fredo, this is Gerritt. Isn't he wonderful?"

"Meet who?" Gerritt was startled, looked around but didn't see anyone. Who was she talking to?

"Alfredo, silly, over there! He's the big brown fuzzy one. I love him so." She pointed to the full corner. There was indeed a brown bear, inanimate and cold, but her eyes told him that to her the bear was as alive as he was.

"You mean the bear?" He laughed uncomfortably. "Well, hello Alfredo." Gerritt stood up, partially because his leg was hurting and bowed deeply. Eve began to laugh and clap her hands, rocking back in her chair and then her expression changed abruptly. Gerritt turned to see Joe Driscoll in the doorway, dressed for work.

"Eve, what is this?" Driscoll hadn't moved from the top of the stairs and though he was not a tall man, he seemed as though he were about to fall forward, cover them both.

Gerritt walked quickly over to him and extended his hand, which shook air. "I'm Gerritt Wells. You met me at the party the other night." He smiled weakly, letting his hand withdraw slowly. The man was furious. Driscoll's countenance reddened down through his neck and Gerritt imagined his whole body as being that flushed.

But Driscoll was not looking at Gerritt, he was totally concerned with his daughter and obviously incapable of sustaining anger towards her. His neck faded quickly and he walked down the blue steps, passing Gerritt as if he wasn't there, and knelt down by Eve.

"Baby, what are you doing? You aren't even dressed," his voice now higher, coaxing, loving, his arm around her lifting. "Come now, let's ring for Hortensia."

But Eve pushed him away. "No, Daddy, No! I want to finish my party with Gerritt."

Driscoll wheeled around to face him, as though he had expected Gerritt to be gone, and his face began to redden again.

"Get out!" he growled, his lower lip extending over bared teeth and the pocks on his face seemed to become deeper.

So this was how it would be. He should have stayed home with his hurting leg and let Eve Driscoll go to hell. He turned without looking back at Eve, but then he heard her begin to cry.

"No, wait you!"

"Wells, Sir, Gerritt Wells," Gerritt enunciated carefully, as if the precision of his speech could control his own anger. He hadn't asked for this.

The two men stood, their eyes locked on one another. Driscoll was seeing another insolent kid; they always flocked to Eve. She was too pretty, too rich and much too helpless. He couldn't let them near her, wouldn't. And this one acted as though he belonged here.

Gerritt watched the older man cool perceptibly again and wasn't sure what to do. He started to turn slowly toward the atrium and the bougainvillea.

"Uh, Wells. I know who you are. Wait in the library across the hall, I want to talk to you." And that was all, he turned back to Eve.

"Now lets get you dressed, young lady. Your mother will be down soon."

Gerritt left them, walked across the entrance hall in the direction Joe Driscoll had indicated, his heels scraping on the marble floor. The morning sun coming through the glass roof was warm. In the library, thick oriental carpets and book-lined walls silenced his footsteps. He hadn't seen this room the night of the party and quickly became immersed in the books, many of which were old. An hour passed before Driscoll appeared.

Joe Driscoll meant for it to be a long wait for Gerritt, wanted him to have time to think about where he was, worry about what was coming. Joe attended to Eve and then woke his wife, Anna, who immediately became hysterical.

But the hour went quickly for Gerritt; he found a book on the history of the Atacama and had lost himself in it, forgetting time. There were maps of the pampa, the pueblos as they were in the early century, the silver mines indicated, silver mines that now were dry and deserted holes. He remembered reading such a book about the early days of mining in Montana and it all sounded so familiar and comfortable, as though he were really back at home. When Driscoll came in he simply closed the book and placed it soundlessly on the table as he stood up.

Eve pleaded with her father and mother not to send Gerritt away. Before, she hadn't cared much when they discouraged other young men. Her reaction to Gerritt worried Joe Driscoll, but he usually gave in to her and this would be no exception.

"Ah, yes, so here you are," he said clearing his throat as he came into the room.

"I'm sure sorry to upset you, Mr. Driscoll," Gerritt began. He was cool, now. The book and the library had been a quieting influence where things fell

74

into some perspective in comparison with the vastness of the desert and the distance from home.

"Eve called this morning and I just assumed it was OK and..",

"I know, she does that sometimes. You don't know about her, Wells, and you must not take her seriously. She, she's very naive, particularly about men."

Naive? Maybe, but Gerritt knew now she was also manipulative.

"I think I know enough about her, sir," Gerritt said, deciding to be forward. Her father must know that Eve's origins were common knowledge in camp.

"Do you now?" Driscoll tipped his head slightly, eyeing the other man. "Are you a charitable person, Mr. Wells?"

"I think so. In any case it's pretty hard to say no to Eve. I tried when she called this morning and you see where I am," he gestured hopelessly.

"Yes, I do see." Driscoll turned to the wall to hide a smile of shared understanding. You didn't often say no to Eve, because she never understood the reasons. "She tells me you have asked to take her to the movies on Saturday afternoon."

"What?" This took Gerritt completely by surprise and the other man saw it in his face. There was no discussion about going anywhere together. There was breakfast, the stuffed bear, and then Driscoll found them. He went quickly over all their conversation, knowing that he would never have made a direct invitation, but wondering if something he said could have been misunderstood. And then he decided that no, it was a decision made by Eve, just as she decided to call him that morning without asking anybody. Gerritt flushed with anger. She was spoiled and she was using him.

"Well, what do you have to say? Are you taking her to the movies at the weekend?"

He realized he must have been standing there, unresponsive, or Driscoll wouldn't be leaning toward him asking for an answer. And then he heard himself answering as though it was another person.

"Oh yes, yes, sure...that is if it's OK with you."

"It's fine. Be here at three in the afternoon; she doesn't go out at night." And that was all. Joe Driscoll quickly became footsteps scraping the marble floor in the hall.

Gerritt stood a moment looking after him, not sure what he was expecting, then walked outside into sunlight that made him squint after the cool interior of the Gerencia. He wondered how he managed all this, or mismanaged it really. There was no intention of seeing Eve again, or was there. Now he wasn't sure. Why had he come? Curiosity? Partly, but there was something else, something related to liking the thick carpet, the cool shade. There were things he wanted there, or maybe it was the feeling of having those things he wanted. Then he remembered Molly. How was it he had forgotten they had planned to spend Saturday together. She would drive because his leg was hurting, they would take a picnic to Lasana. He would have to tell her and she was not going to be pleased. No, she would be pissed as hell.

The shift went smoothly except for his leg, which throbbed. After work, all he wanted was to go home for a scotch, but he headed for Molly's.

"What are you trying to do?" she yelled when Gerritt told her about seeing Eve. In his mind there was no conflict, but this was always how it was with women. They wanted a piece of you, a plot of ground to plant and water, where before you knew it you were buried and growing with your roots stuck in one place like spring wheat.

"What are you looking for? What is it you want, Gerritt? This is too incredible! I swear, I just don't understand you. Eve Driscoll doesn't exist, she's not a real person." Molly glared at him in disbelief and he had no answer for her, it was too soon for answers.

"I don't know why, Goddamn it! I don't, and that's it." He touched her arm, but she drew away.

"Just go. I don't feel like having you here tonight."

Gerritt looked at her, trying to think of something that would save this and couldn't think of anything. Maybe there wasn't enough between them to save, a preservation of the few good times seemed suddenly to require an enormous effort. And his leg hurt and all he wanted then was to be alone.

The movie on Saturday, the only movie for three hundred miles on Saturday or any day, because the nearest other theatre was in Antofagasta, was in Cerro Verde's very own Teatro Chile. The films were always old, this one a jungle picture with John Wayne. Teatro Chile was a large quonset structure painted a flat barn red, with two classes of seats, one for the Jefes and one for the Empleados and Obreros, the supervisors and workers in the mine. The Jefes sat in a small reserved section raised above the main floor, furnished with padded seats. Gerritt thought briefly of Julio, knowing he would have to sit down below with the Empleados.

"I'm glad we don't have to sit down there," Eve whispered to him. "Hortensia says she always gets fleas." Eve had on a soft yellow dress and her hair was piled on top of her head and braided together, the dark of it framing her face.

She wouldn't have any notion of Julio's value as a man, or his for that matter, Gerritt thought. Eve had her place and her place was with the Jefes; the others "down there" only represented something that was unacceptable. She would be unable to weigh things, he could see, and he wondered how much of her naivety was due only to lack of experience and how much to incapacity to experience.

They were noticed. Reichers and Blains were there.

"How nice to see you, Eve." Nell Reicher said, her mouth opened so wide she could barely manage to smile.

"Gerritt," acknowledged Ian Blain, frowning.

Rita Blain squeezed his arm too hard as she sat down behind them. Gerritt couldn't read the faces; there was either indifference or disapproval. The movie started quickly. He was so absorbed in Eve's reaction to the film that he soon simply turned off whatever else was happening around them.

The movie was filmed in Africa. Eve was laughing and clapping at the animals. Her enthusiasm bubbled out of her like a spring thaw, tearing at the banks that held it. Gerritt wished for that kind of uncomplicated happiness, empty of any thought but the pleasure itself. There was a scene in a bedroom, rather inhibited, but he watched Eve for her reaction. Her chin went down and she studied the screen carefully, picking at her fingernails. She turned to him when the two actors climbed into bed.

"They're tired, aren't they?" she asked uncertainly. Her large eyes said she didn't understand, but Gerritt couldn't think of how to explain the emotion of what was taking place on the screen, much less relate it to her perceptions.

"I'm sure they are," he whispered slowly and looked away. What could she be thinking? The scene was so obvious.

There was a brief and tense exchange of greetings with Blains and Reichers outside the theatre and then they escaped to his truck. The Driscoll's were waiting anxiously when he returned Eve to the Gerencia. Anna barely acknowledged him, put her arm around Eve and urged her out of the room. Eve swiveled her head around to watch him, as she was lead away, chattering about the film. Anna was small, shorter and lighter than Eve, but obviously the stronger woman.

An uncomfortable silence fell as the two men stood watching. Gerritt turned and realized Driscoll had been looking at him carefully.

"Would you like a drink?" he asked.

"That would be fine." Gerritt replied. He needed something. He was beginning to feel as if the whole afternoon was an experiment in which he was the laboratory animal. It was difficult to talk to Eve, Molly had been right about that. She would listen to you and then she would drift off somewhere and then come back in another place.

"How was the movie?" Joe asked him as they walked into the library.

"Great! Eve liked it, at least I think she did." He tried to read Driscoll's pocked face, but he remained stoic.

"Yes," he said contemplating the drinks he had just poured. "Yes, I'm sure she did. Gerritt, I want to hear about you, why you came to Cerro Verde, what you want from your experience here."

Driscoll handed him the heavy scotch, then looked away, down to the polished toe of his shoe which rubbed the nap on the rug, making the color change. Driscoll seemed anxious rather than angry. Gerritt was trying to understand if there was a difference between what this man wanted to hear and what was the truth, or what he knew to be the truth. He must have taken too long as Driscoll finally looked up straight into his pale eyes with a look that was almost a threat and Gerritt began to talk.

"I grew up on a farm in Montana with my Uncle Shem, my mother's brother." Gerritt explained. "My parents were killed in a car accident when I was six." It came out haltingly, the shyness with people, the preoccupation with the machinery, the realization that he wanted to work the earth in some way came through he thought.

"Yes, I had an early attachment to heavy equipment as well," Driscoll nodded as he spoke, seeming to identify with him. What Gerritt couldn't say was how alone he had felt, how alone he still was. How there was an island inside him that no ship could reach. His description of those days came out making him strong, only he wasn't strong. But maybe saying he was made it a fact. Gerritt felt himself becoming confused, but the other man only smiled in approval. As Gerritt limped out to his truck, he shut his eyes in relief. He must have said the right things. Whether they were true was something else.

CHAPTER 10

The following week, Gerritt was made a Shift Boss. He stood in Art Barnett's office listening to the words uttered in an unenthusiastic monotone and felt himself grow numb. It was what he wanted, but sifting through the events of the past few days, Eve and her father came up again and again behind his eyes and he knew it shouldn't be happening.

"As far as I'm concerned, Bowen is better qualified, but the word came from Reicher, not me. You start with day shift on Monday next, take over from Julio Romero," Barnett growled, considering carefully Gerritt's reaction. "Julio can help, I don't want the mine completely fucked up."

Art Barnett didn't like Gerritt much. He worked hard enough but was spacey and his motives weren't clear. Barnett much preferred an up front person like Wes Bowen; you knew he listened and that there was someone inside that understood what you were saying. With Gerritt, the iced eyes never looked directly at you and whatever you told him you had the sense that he would do as he pleased. If that was in agreement with what you had ordered, fine; if not, that was fine, too. Things moved fast in the mine and Gerritt would just have to suck it up. But a promotion out of order coming from Reicher, aroused Art's suspicion. It was an arrangement, he was sure of it. How had Wells done it? Barnett looked at him, but Gerritt was far away someplace searching, too, for how this happened and Art couldn't reach him.

Yes, Reicher must have gotten the word from Driscoll, or perhaps through Blain, Gerritt thought as he stared at Art. The promotion was premature. Gerritt knew neither he nor Bowen were really ready to take over a shift. But here it was, handed to him by the bastard, Barnett. Gerritt wanted to laugh.

He doubled up his fist in his pocket, feeling the arrowhead he found at the Pukara.

Yeah, yeah, his face revealed nothing, but his fingers turned white with pressure on the stone. Yes, he wanted this. No, it didn't matter how it happened. He needed this to show them what he could do. Gerritt could see the boardroom in New York going over his tonnages approvingly. He was floating. Soon he wouldn't need anybody, particularly Barnett. For some reason he thought of Wes Bowen. It was important that Wes would think this was a good thing. Yes, of course he would and then, Wes could come along with him. He would let Barnett tell Wes about the promotion. They were on different shifts and Gerritt wouldn't have to see Wes until the meeting at the end of the week. By then, Wes would grow into the idea, yes, he would think it was good and they could talk about it over a beer. Gerritt felt suddenly weak and had to get outside. He nodded to Barnett, acknowledging that he heard and left Art sitting there expecting further conversation.

Art Barnett had bigger problems than Gerritt's promotion, though he knew it was forced and untimely. The Union contract, the pliego, remained unsettled and that was trouble. It meant the possibility of a strike in the mine. It was Art's opinion that the obreros were asking a lot of piss-ant things which made little sense, and that the whole thing was a power play by the Union. He thought about Gorges Hidalgo, the Union chief, who had been arrested for embezzlement last year, and then released on his own word. Corruption was a given; you learned to deal with it. It made Art think about retiring to California to sell real estate and lately, he was thinking about that more often. His wife Elaine's father, Jason Stoddard, the doctor in Cerro Verde, talked about California all the time and it was sounding better this morning after Gerritt's promotion. Art rubbed his balding head and lit a cigar. He had to think about a possible strike.

The pliego had gone three rounds and the possibility of some kind of settlement now looked remote. Art looked out the window at an operational mine, knowing that if the negotiations didn't go well, the Union would tell the obreros to strike, but the New York office would still expect the same tonnage delivery. Sometime he'd like to get those bastard suits down here. He'd show them what he had to deal with, the petty thievery of copper tubing from the brake systems, the increasing amount of waste that had to be removed to get at the ore as the pit grew larger, and assholes like Gerritt Wells. Art knew Gerritt was seen at the Teatro Chile with Eve Driscoll and was fairly sure how the promotion had come down. Maybe Wells would end up owning him someday, but it didn't solve the present problems. If the pliego wasn't settled, Art would have to keep the mine running somehow and Gerritt wasn't going to be any help with that.

"Art, got a minute?" It was Mike Marshall the track foreman.

"Yeah, what is it?" He didn't look up.

Marshall didn't come into the office. What he had to say was something he said before and he already knew what Barnett's answer was going to be. Instead, he leaned against the door jam. He'd seen the schedule for the next week on the board in the outer room, listing Wells as a Shift Boss, but that wasn't what he wanted to bring to Barnett's attention. Mike Marshall knew his place and his job.

When he had first come to Cerro Verde, Marshall began as Bowen and Wells. It didn't take Barnett, or Mike himself, for that matter, long to see that he couldn't cope with the pressure of the shift. Rather than send him back to the States, Art found a place for him as Track Foreman. The focused, repetitive tasks suited him well and he thrived. Mike owed Art Barnett, understood the depth of the kindness. He did the job well, track was laid on time and there were fewer derails after Mike took over. There was still a sadness about Marshall, though, which drinking didn't lift away, the feeling of settling for less than you hoped.

Barnett was moving paper around on his desk, trying to locate the previous day's tonnages for his report to New York. There was a silence and he looked up at Marshall.

"So what do you want?"

"It's the posts on the visitor's bench, Art. I know you think I'm nuts, but they're leaning out again. I recemented the suckers in and reset the chains three months ago. Now they look like they did then and six months before that! Something weird is going on!"

Barnett tried to be patient. Posts didn't move themselves.

"Maybe someone hit one of them with a truck, Mike. Fix it, OK." Art didn't look up.

"But, I did!" Mike threw his hands up.

"Fix it!" Barnett yelled. "I don't want to hear any more about it!" And that was it.

"Como no, Jefe," Mike replied deferentially in Spanish, and putting his hard-hat back on he went out the door and let it slam behind him. He'd fix the posts, all right. Again. Barnett knew Mike was a lush. He'd certainly come in more than one day with a hangover so bad that even Zuñiga's coffee didn't help. But Mike was mostly lucid and there was something strange about posts that grew to lean toward the empty, open pit of the mine when they hadn't been touched. Despite Art's indifference, he knew that Mike did his job. One day Barnett would have a look.

As the door slammed on Mike, it knocked his hat out of his hand and the wind blew it across the parking lot. He didn't see Gerritt coming through the door behind him.

"Oh, sorry Gerritt," Mike said as he turned around. "Fucking door! Zuñiga doesn't seem to be able to get anybody to fix it right."

"I know", Gerritt responded, smiling. "Hecho in Chile, no cierto?"

"Si, Señor", Mike acknowledged, laughing. Then he remembered the schedule inside.

"Oh, congratulations, Jefe! Don't know how you did it, but around here mostly the unexpected happens, trust me." He winked at Gerritt and went to pick up his hat before Gerritt could reply.

Julio Romero pulled up next to Gerritt's truck, and saw Gerritt frowning as he stared after Marshall's truck.

"You OK, amigo?" Julio asked Gerritt. Julio knew Gerritt was now his boss. His job as a weed cover was over for now; a new Gringo shift boss had been planted. But he liked Gerritt. Even though the beer at the Club had been a bad idea, Julio recognized Gerritt's good intention and would help him; he would need it. Julio held out his hand.

"Guess you are my Jefe now," Julio said warmly.

" Yeah and glad you will be on my shift, Julio," Gerritt replied, raising his eyebrows. He started to turn away, but Julio had more to say.

"Jefes are talking, Señor Gerritt. Wondering how this happened so quickly. Ten cuidado, entiende?" He looked directly at Gerritt.

"Si, gracias Julio." Julio waved and went inside, the door slamming behind him.

Gerritt broke away from his thoughts, which had been of Eve and how the last few days had changed everything. It was what he wanted, but Mike and Julio's reactions indicated the undercurrent in the mine that was sure to follow the promotion. Gerritt knew Wes would avoid him until he had chewed the matter around awhile. There was plenty of time. Time was something you had a lot of in Cerro Verde. Gerritt could wait.

CHAPTER 11

Alice Bowen was planting flowers she purchased in the feria, the open market in New Camp, when she saw the white car between the slats in the fence. Thanks to meeting Henrí Duvillard at the Gerencia party, Bowens had a new house. Henrí took a look at their furniture on a particularly windy day when dirt had again blown in under the door. He managed to find a small vacant place, one block up the hill. It wasn't much, but it was painted and Henrí had a fence built around the small garden on the south side.

The new house gave her something to do. Alice was bored. She read the half dozen books she brought with her from the States and several from the Cerro Verde Library, an institution stocked with gifts from the residents and lacking any semblance to a library at home. She and Wes brought their textbooks from Mines and she often pulled the biochemistry book out to remind herself that one day there would be a return to academia. Wes had promised.

It was the same white car they arrived in many months earlier and Hector Vera was driving, but it was coming down the hill, not arriving from the coast at all. Alice leaned back on her heels. The planting stiffened her back some and it felt good to stretch and breath in the sulfury smell of the wet, sandy soil.

"Why do you think the dirt here smells so sulfury," she asked Wes.

"Comes from the sulfide plant," Wes said. "Sulfur dioxide is a product of the smelting process and can form an acid with water. Hugh Dillon says if the wind is blowing off the pampa into town, the tops of the grass can turn white!" Alice hadn't seen that yet, but the sulfur certainly flavored the air.

'The geraniums will do well', she thought as she looked at the soft green leaves and red buds. Geraniums were one thing that grew in this place. They could take the dramatic changes in temperature between day and night, the acid soil, the dry air and the wind, always the wind.

She heard the doorbell ring, but didn't connect that with the car until she went to the door, ripping off her muddy gloves as she went.

Hector Vera rang the bell and then opened the car door for an obviously impatient Eve Driscoll who was waving and talking, though Alice couldn't hear her. And then Alice was on the porch and thinking about whether Wes had eaten the last of the chocolate cake. The greeting between the two women was awkward. Eve was all over Alice, hugging her, exclaiming about the flowers, not even noticing how dirty Alice was.

"The flowers are so pretty. Hortensia planted new flowers in our garden in the back. Can we go inside? Where is Gerritt, is he here yet? Where is he, he said he'd be here? Can I have some coffee? Mama never lets me have coffee at home." She turned around to her driver, waving him off.

"Go home, Hector, I don't need you anymore." And she opened the door to Bowens house and let the screen slam shut as she went inside. Alice stood for a moment trying to understand what just happened and then looked at Hector Vera, who was smiling at her with a helpless look. Then she quickly remembered that Eve was in the house and wheeled around to find her. The garden was forgotten.

She found Eve in the kitchen looking through the cupboards and Alice was suddenly angry. Eve was obviously used to having her way and people to wait on her. The sight of her going through things that didn't belong to her was more than annoying. Alice watched her for a moment and then took a deep breath. Unfortunately, this willful girl was the daughter of her husband's boss and that meant Alice couldn't just go in and break her arm, which is definitely what she felt like doing.

"What can I get you Eve?" she asked sweetly. It was like planting the flowers, an attempt to make an ugly situation beautiful. Alice looked at her watch. It was 3:30 PM. Wes would be home soon and he could deal with this.

"Coffee. I asked for coffee. With lots of sugar and milk". She turned and for the first time looked at Alice with some sort of recognition. Her black eyes were framed in large lashes and her heavy hair pulled away from her face and tied in back, where it lay against a simple blue dress.

"Why don't you sit here," Alice offered as she pulled a chair back from the kitchen table. "I'll fix you some coffee. Gerritt doesn't live here, Eve. I'm Alice Bowen. My husband is Wes Bowen. Do you remember us from the party at the Gerencia?"

"I know," Eve answered quickly as she sat down and looked up at Alice, but continued with her fidgeting.

Eve was truly gorgeous, Alice decided, even if she was hopelessly spoiled, naïve, and incorrigible. And she set about making a large pot of coffee.

"Gerritt comes soon?" Eve asked again. She had taken all the fruit out of the basket on the table and was now putting it back in, one piece at a time, as though it was a set of children's blocks.

"Gerritt coming here? No, I don't think so. My husband will be home soon and you can ask him." Alice looked at her and slowly realized what was happening. Eve must have arranged to meet Gerritt here. Why here? She wondered if Wes knew. Wes didn't always tell her everything, but he certainly couldn't have overlooked this.

Alice gave Eve two cups of coffee that were half milk and sugar and a piece of cake before she heard Wes's pickup, but Eve volunteered no further information other than asking about Gerritt.

"Hi, hon, I'm home." The screen in the front door banged shut and Eve was instantly on her feet and ran into the living room, running directly into Wes. She barely came up to his chest.

"Gerritt, where's Gerritt?" Eve yelled at him. "I want to see Gerritt".

Wes grabbed her arms to calm her and looked up at Alice whose look told him she didn't know what this was all about either and also that she was pissed.

"Hold on, little lady! Here sit down here with me." Wes made her sit down on the couch. "O.K., now it's really nice to see you again, Eve. Do I smell coffee?" He looked up questioningly to Alice, but his eyes wanted more than just a cup of coffee. Alice rolled her eyes up in response and turned to the kitchen. Let him try to get something out of her.

Eve calmed down. Wes was able to ask her about the Gerencia and the town and her parents place on the coast. He was just about to get back to why she was there, when he saw Gerritt walk by the window and knock at the door.

"Well, at least he knocks." Alice said, but Eve didn't hear her, because she was up and running to the door and into Gerritt's arms. As he put his arms around her, Gerritt handed Wes the note he just found on his own door.

See you at Wes Bowen's house. I love you.

Eva

"I guess none of us knew about this!" Wes waved the note at him and handed it to an incredulous Alice.

"Right," Gerritt said, embarrassed. Alice softened then, realizing that all of them were being used by a girl who might be slightly dim, but was definitely determined to get what she wanted and what she wanted right now was Gerritt. He probably wasn't going to have any more choice in the matter than they did.

Eve softened and entered a state of complete tranquility, once Gerritt arrived. She did continue to touch him and he found that he liked it, just as it felt good when she had pressed herself to him when he came in the door. This wasn't going to be easy. Maybe if he could see her at Bowen's house, with them there, it would be OK. He would talk to Wes about it.

The conversation was rather disturbing for Gerritt, who discussed the mine, the pliego, Alice's garden and the day. Eve seemed to have no knowledge of life in the camp. She interrupted every once in awhile with a totally irrelevant comment about something in the small circle of her life at the Gerencia.

"I better get her home," Gerritt said after a few minutes. There were awkward goodbyes, and although there was no invitation from Bowens for her to return, they both knew she would.

On the way up the hill, Eve clung to Gerritt's arm. He explained to Joe Driscoll, who met him at the door, what happened. No one at the Gerencia had yet missed her and Driscoll wasn't too upset.

"Just take care of her, Wells." Driscoll demanded from the door, but didn't ask him in. Gerritt wondered what that was going to entail and then smiled, thinking of the feeling when Eve was next to him.

The visit left both Wes and Alice a little numb. Gerritt's new position in the mine came as a surprise to Wes. He had counted on it for himself, worked his butt off. And Barnett hinted that the job was his. But it wasn't his; he was still on with Juan Ortega. Wes knew he had done some stupid things, like getting his truck smashed by the bastard, Arias, but that wasn't the reason. The reason just left his house.

Over the last few months, Gerritt had definitely been irrational at times. In spite of the fact that Wes knew part of the disappointment was jealousy, he wasn't at all sure Gerritt could handle a shift or deal with the men. Gerritt was always more interested in fiddling with the machinery. And the previous week he left a trainload of waste in the bottom of the mine. Wes had to move it out before he could begin to haul any ore on his shift and it brought the total tonnage way down. Ortega was sore as hell. Gerritt said he told the Capitas to move it and the guy forgot, but Wes found the Capitas who quakingly told him that Señor Wells had specifically told him to leave the loaded cars there on the bottom track.

Wes wanted to trust Gerritt. There were the times before Gerritt had his own shift, when they would be working together and look up at each other over a greasy engine with shared understanding of the mine and how it worked. And it wasn't only professional interest, there seemed to be more. They were becoming friends. Now Gerritt was wading into water with an unstable bottom and he knew the friendship wasn't going to be equal. He sensed that Gerritt was going to need him.

Bowens slowly got used to having Eve around. She relaxed some in their presence and they found her unaffected and totally honest, if naive, ways of dealing with life rather refreshing. Somehow, in this isolated place, she belonged. The four spent their Sundays on the pampa. Eve loved the earth and the vastness of the desert. It delighted her to pick up handfuls of dirt from the road and let it blow away from her hand. She didn't remember much of her past and the Driscolls didn't tell her much. Yet, Eve knew what a cage was. She brought Alice little gifts from the Gerencia, flowers and tiny china vases. Hortensia's cat had kittens and one day she brought a little black one.

"Oh, Eve, how perfect she is," Alice exclaimed as she cuddled the little ball of fur. "Let's make her a box to sleep in." Alice found a box and Eve watched as she spread an old towel in the bottom and put the tiny kitten in. As she watched it feel around and mew softly, Eve's face changed from sweetness to fear.

"No, no box," Eve yelled, taking the kitten away and throwing the box against the wall. There were hidden things that none of them could understand about her early life, even Eve.

A few weeks later, the white car again came down the hill to Bowen's house, this time in the morning. Rita Blain arrived with no warning, knocked on the door with one hand. The other held a cigarette.

"May I come in, Alice?" she asked smiling. "I'd like to talk to you." Rita Blain was seldom seen at houses down the hill, unless it was for a baby shower. She wanted something.

"Of course," Alice said, graciously, thinking as she held the door for her how fortunate that she had taken a maid and the house was clean. Rosa was from Santa Bárbara de Atacama, a small village on the pampa and was a sister of Sonia, Dillon's maid. Rosa spoke no English and Alice spent days with a dictionary, trying to communicate with her.

"Can I get you something, some coffee?" she asked as Rita surveyed the house, which was meager compared to her own.

"Yes, thank you," she smiled blankly at Alice. "Some gin and ice would be fine. Maybe with some lime if you have it." Alice blinked. It was ten o'clock in the morning. But she calmly asked Rosa to bring two gins. Rosa frowned, but disappeared into the kitchen to get the drinks. Alice looked at Rita's face. Rita was sitting in a shaft of sunlight, the beams came through her dark red hair like a fire halo. The brittle transparency of her skin made her seem papery and artificial. Alice pushed her own brown, straight hair back and felt healthy.

"You seem to read a great deal," Rita observed, looking at the stack of library books on the table. Her voice was deep and a little hoarse like Eve's.

"All the time," Alice confessed. "Wes thinks that's all I do."

"Well, one has the time here, don't you find?" She crossed her legs, the stockings not hiding the fine freckling of her skin, and settled into the chair after accepting the glass from Rosa. Alice smiled at the warm brown girl.

"Yes, especially with the help. Do you like to read?"

"Too much," she answered as if it were an understatement. "A bookstore in Miami mails books to me. I'll have Hector Vera bring some down for you. The library is pretty grim." There was a silence. Rita took another long draw on her gin and looked Alice in the eye then, making her quite uncomfortable.

"Alice," Rita began carefully. "How much is Gerritt seeing Eve. They come here don't they?" Her chin rose probingly as she watched Alice's reaction, which seemed sad.

Alice realized that Rita was there for information, not to give her books away. She took a big drink of her own gin and didn't look directly at Rita.

"Often. She's a nice girl, spoiled, but happy, I think. They seem to enjoy each other." She sighed, disappointed. What was it Rita really wanted to know?

"They don't go anywhere but here, then?"

"No, I don't think so. Eve probably does pretty much as she pleases, but she seems fairly innocent about men. I doubt she would encourage anything but the "play" relationship they have now." Alice paused, wondering if what she was saying was really true. She and Wes talked about that, but they wanted to think it was, indeed, still innocent. And then she remembered.

"Oh, and Gerritt has Molly." That's right, there was Molly. Only Alice was quite sure Gerritt wasn't seeing her much anymore.

"Molly......?" Rita waited.

"Yes, Molly Pritchard. She's a school teacher."

"Oh, yes, of course." Rita smiled, pleased. She had been a schoolteacher when she came to Cerro Verde. But then she married Ian and began the move up the hill. It seemed a long time ago. The gin and lime was relaxing.

"How nice for him." Rita replied, thinking that at least Gerritt had some other outlet. She knew exactly how frustrating Eve could be. Gerritt wasn't the first stud to chase after Eve. Rita felt a certain responsibility, partly because she liked Anna Driscoll and also because she considered it her position to know everything that was going on in camp. Everything.

They talked about the mine and books for a suitable length of time and then Rita stood up to go. She had the information she needed.

"Thanks for the gin, Alice. Do drop by sometime." The latter was said unconvincingly and she was out the door and into the white car that was waiting by the porch, having been instructed that the visit would be brief.

As she poured her gin down the sink, Alice wondered if Rita heard her answering goodbye. It didn't matter; it wasn't a social call.

Hector Vera brought Alice a stack of new books the next morning and returned every few weeks to exchange them for others. He handed them to her stiffly, as though he too, had no place down the hill. When Alice saw Rita at the Recova, the grocery store, or in New Camp, their visit was never acknowledged. Alice took it for what it was, a business arrangement, the books a payment.

CHAPTER 12

"Padre Simon, you just must visit him," Eve exclaimed one afternoon at Wes's house. "He's El Padre de Los Viejos. I love him!"

"Rene Dillon said he's a Flemish Catholic priest, been at Santa Bárbara de Atacama for three decades," Alice explained. "He's a kind of amateur archeologist who dug up half the desert surrounding the pueblo and put all the artifacts in his own museum."

"Sounds pretty eccentric," Gerritt replied.

"I think that's probably a kind description of him. He loves the pampa and tries to protect what's left of the culture here, that's all." Wes heard that an archeological team from Columbia University had come to the Atacama and, appalled at what Simon Gherts was doing, saw to it that he didn't do any more excavation. But Simon kept his collection. They tried, but couldn't get that away from him.

"Well, I love him and I help at the museum," Eve said proudly. "You have to come see him, Gerritt, you have to!" For Eve, Padre Simon was a tie to something she didn't understand, but to which she felt attached. Her parents often left her with Gherts when they had to travel. Santa Bárbara was safe.

It was an easy Sunday to get away. Curt Reicher and Ian Blain were in Santiago, where the pliego, the labor negotiations, were ongoing. There were rumors that things were not going well and the mine that week seemed to wind down in expectation of a strike, though no definite word filtered up from the South.

Santa Bárbara de Atacama lay on the edge of a huge salar, one of the drying salt lakes of the northern pampa. The salar supported flocks of flamingos on the remaining small patches of brackish water with fresh-water shrimp.

Santa Bárbara was fed by a spring, which provided pasture and watered gardens, one of the rare patches of green that seem like jewels against the desert brown. The way to Santa Bárbara from Cerro Verde wound up and over a hilly range, highly mineralized, and through a canyon of grotesque rock formations that jutted in every direction on the narrow dirt road.

Gerritt felt somewhat apprehensive about meeting this man, wondering what Eve told him. He actually wasn't sure how Eve saw their relationship. She didn't seem to understand the physical part at all and he carefully avoided intimate contact, though she touched him frequently. Simon was man of God and would take such matters seriously. Gerritt experienced only a brief religious education before his Aunt died and he didn't care to resume the persuasion; he didn't believe. And Simon dug up graveyards. That sounded incongruous for a priest and increased Gerritt's unease. Wes, however, didn't see the conflict at all.

"For Christ's sake, Gerritt, even if the guy isn't educated he probably has learned on his own," Wes said. Maybe Wes was right. Other people he talked to considered Padre Simon a harmless amateur. Bowen's maid, Maria, was from Santa Bárbara and according to her Padre Simon was regarded there as somewhat of a saint.

"He keeps the old ones", Maria said lovingly.

The pueblo had a small square similar to Chiu Chiu, rather overrun with dry flowers and other foliage, a small church, and the familiar water conduits for irrigation running down the edges of narrow, unpaved streets. Eve pointed out the museum that stood on one corner of the square, rather obviously opposite the church. The two buildings seemed to tie the pueblo to the earth. Dogs barked at the trucks as they rolled into town and the Padre must have heard them as he came streaming out of the museum, his robe flowing and his arms extended to Eve.

She ran to him and was engulfed in a wad of brown cassock. Padre Simon was a huge man, dark and intense. He came toward them breathing heavily, almost snorting through a grey beard in which small bits of food were lodged.

"Y quien trajes contigo?" the Priest said still holding Eve to him. His voice rumbled deeply as though coming from his stomach, which protruded amply into the heavy robe.

"Son mis amigos, Padre," she answered, kissing his hand.

"Habla Ingles, Padre?" asked Gerritt, extending his hand.

Simon took it but pulled Gerritt closer, leaning over him, almost sniffing at him like a dog. Gerritt felt pushed back by the bulk of the man and an odor of yesterday's dinner. Yes, Simon knew about him, he was sure of it. He was being examined as carefully as an archeological specimen.

"Pocito, Señor," Simon said testily. "I speak little Ingles, you try Castellano, no? Venga."

They followed him to the museum where he pulled a huge key from somewhere in the depths of the dirty cassock to open the door. Inside it was musty and cool, the result of thick adobe walls and few windows. There was an odor of dank things and age and it was silent. Only their breathing made a sound. Padre Simon wheezed and Gerritt thought briefly that perhaps he had asthma and that's why he never left the dryness of the pampa.

A central skylight let in the only day and stood over a model of an ancient grave in the process of excavation.

"Aqui, is how I do," Padre Simon said, pretending he was hoisting a spade with dirt over his shoulder. "Are many tumbas, pero muy lejos." He indicated the far pampa. "Las cosas aqui son de Chiu Chiu, de Toconao, de Lasana, entiende?"

"I think so," Gerritt said, staring into the heavy dark eyes of the Padre. Then he thought of the femur he had taken from the graveyard at Chiu Chiu because it tied him to the earth. He realized he vaguely understood at least one level of this man.

"Ahora, Los Gringos come, stakes y cuerda. Tell me no dig. Quiero ofrecer al pueblo. Es la historia de la pueblo, el dominio de la pueblo!" His size and voice were convincing and he was filled with an overwhelming sadness that seeped from him like sweat.

"You see," he gestured with his hands, being able to explain no further.

It was hard to believe one man had done all this. Display cases ringed the room, but nothing was labeled. There were dozens of everything. One case held buckets of arrowheads, so perfectly made they looked machined. Baskets were stacked inside each other, nearly to the sloped ceiling, each one with a different design woven by a precise and careful hand. It all smelled of death, but not of decay, only a silent and cold smell of earth cover and loss.

In one alcove were the dead themselves, or a good representation of them. Nearly perfect mummies, much better preserved than those now left at Chiu Chiu, sat on or inside glass cases.

Wes and Alice were overcome with the exhibit, having seen displays of South American artifacts in other musems, which couldn't compare to this. Gerritt was quiet. He was trying to pay attention to Simon, but there was a tension between them he could nearly feel on his skin. The Priest watched only him, following him closely to see which cases he noticed, what things caught his eye.

"What are these over here?" Gerritt asked, stopping abruptly near some wood coffins, so abruptly in fact that Simon nearly bumped into him and Eve into Simon. Eve had been babbling constantly about all the things to see, but she stopped as Gerritt spoke. There was a small silence.

"Ah si," the Padre said slowly, surprised that Gerritt was interested in these mummies. "Son de Los Caracóles, silver mine. Not old, 80 years dead. Un bombero, fireman."

Wes and Alice walked over and they all looked at the two crude wood coffins, the lids lying up against the sides. In one lay a man with a red handlebar mustache, his face only slightly sunken. On his head was a tarnished fireman's hat, less well preserved by the dryness than the fireman, himself. The other coffin held a woman laid out in a lace dress, her hair still done up in a bone comb, sleeping quite peacefully except for one foot which was broken off and lay askew still in its black shoe, leaning in an awkward direction, the dried flesh and bone sticking out, a dark brown-red.

Somehow, these later remains were more disturbing, were closer to their time. They had been people, whose lives and habits were more familiar to them, reminding them of their own mortality. Alice turned quickly away and went outside. Wes shrugged and followed her. Gerritt watched Eve twist her head to line it up with the woman in the coffin at whom she looked with amused interest, as though waiting for her to awaken.

"I think we better go, Padre," Gerritt found his voice cracking and hoped the Padre did not notice. Thank you, muy interesante."

"Bueno," he replied. "Eva, vamos a La Hosteria para almuerzo?"

"Si, Padre, tengo hambre," she answered, smiling and rubbing her stomach.

The sunlight caused their eyes to water when they came out from the dark museum, but the air was fresh and warm. Alice and Wes were waiting on the stone steps. This was not like the sterile museums at home. In this one, you felt that you descended into the earth to visit the antiquities in their original location. Both of them looked a little pale, and Gerritt was thinking that the femur maybe didn't belong on his mantle, but here instead. He thought briefly of Molly and the day they first saw Chiu Chiu.

"What did he say, Eve," Alice asked.

"He wants us to eat lunch with him, at the Hosteria." She grabbed hold of Gerritt's arm.

"Quisas, vamos por la Iglesia?" the Padre asked as he turned to them after locking the museum door.

"Oh, yes," Eve said enthusiastically. You want to see the Church don't you?" She was a little disappointed that they didn't spend more time in the museum; she so loved it. Eve's hair was down and the breeze blew it around making her release Gerritt's arm to brush it away from her face.

Seeing the church seemed like a good idea. Gerritt didn't feel like lunch right away and was sure Bowens would welcome the walk around the square.

The church was small, built of adobe and wood from the saguaro cactus, which grew on the pampa at higher elevations. They walked inside and stood in the cool of the spartan sanctuary, their voices echoing off the lumpy white walls.

Eve and the Padre, followed by Alice, went up to the altar railing and knelt on one side before a velvet virgin. There were several other statues in niches and Gerritt examined them carefully as his fingers traced the edge of a rough-hewn wood pew, the architecture of the place more important to him than the meaning.

"Do you ever wonder, Wes, why it is that women and priests do most of the praying?" Gerritt whispered.

Wes bent down to him to keep the others from hearing his comment.

"I don't feel a need to, that's all," Wes whispered.

"Well, why do they?" It was something Gerritt was not able to sort out. His Aunt went to church every Sunday and made him go, when she was alive. His Uncle never went, not even at Christmas. And Simon's God had seen fit to take Gerritt's parents away from him, an unmeasured loss. The supplicants rose and silently filed to the back of the church. Wes and Gerritt followed them out the door.

"No son Católicos?" the Padre asked them both, but was looking directly at Gerritt.

"No," Gerritt answered resolutely. Simon seemed about to say something and then looked down and set off quickly in the direction of the Hosteria.

Lunch was dry bread and cheese, which suited them perfectly, drying up the juices of uneasiness in their stomachs. Gerritt sat next to Simon who asked him about the mine and clapped him on the back a few times. He and Eve seemed to have many private jokes, which they told in Spanish and Gerritt wondered if they were laughing at the Gringos. Eve was obviously happy.

Lunch didn't last long. They needed to get back to camp. Wes was on night shift starting at 11 PM. Gerritt was relieved to get back in his truck, which felt familiar, and to head back across the pampa. Eve was tired and soon the rocking of the truck and the lunch put her to sleep, her head falling into his lap. He caressed her heavy hair, pulling it back off her face. The pampa turned pink and gold as the dust blew quickly away from the back of his truck and he could see Wes following behind. The pickup was pushed sideways by the wind and he kept a firm hand on the wheel. The day with the Padre made him feel pushed personally, blown in a direction over which he had little control.

Padre Simon hung on in Gerritt's night dreams and punctured the fringes of his daytime thoughts. Eve's reliance on this brown cassock was a reminder of her frailty. Priests were men he had no need of, nor desire to explore. To him they were keepers of a tenantless house, supported by an intangible and uncaring force. The only reality for Gerritt was something you could touch, that had substance, like the rock in the mine and the machinery. And maybe Eve.

Eve's world was a simple place where dragons live only in dreams and disappear when you wake. Simon was obviously her protector, a person she clung to and needed. He was of her land, the earth she loved to hold in her hand. The Padre touched her world like no other, took the dead back, collecting, caring for them. Gerritt understood it, but couldn't accept it as his own. His reality was the mine, its urgent needs and schedules comforting and dependable. He walked around Eve's world, pressing on a glass ball from outside, but receiving her kindness and caring, feeling it running down over his shoulders like a warm coat in winter. And then he would see the coat as the brown cassock. He was in two planes, floating in her world and then descending to the solid and real ground, to what he knew to be important.

CHAPTER 13

Eve went to Santiago with her parents early the next week, leaving Gerritt to concentrate on the mine. Joe Driscoll was not confident the pliego could be settled and was headed down to help with the negotiations.

"What's the problem, Joe," Gerritt asked during dinner at the Gerencia the night before? "The mineros have a good deal here, housing, discounts. What more could they want?"

"It's not the mineros who are causing the problem. I talked to Juaquin Arco, the Jefe Patio, and he tells me it is the Union. There is an election soon and Hidalgo wants to look like he's in charge. And not the money; his family has vinyards in the south." Joe dropped a piece of toast in his lap and retrieved it.

"Well, let's hope they don't go out. We need the mine working." What would he do if there was a strike and idleness? The mine was keeping Gerritt from thinking about Eve and Molly and why he was promoted so quickly. Wes heard the Jefes might run the trains and shovels for a while; what a blast that would be! A shiver went down Gerritt's spine at the exciting thought!

Gerritt was struggling with the responsibilities of running a shift and was receiving help from only a few people. He knew Barnett was hoping he would fall on his ass and then could replace him. Juan Ortega ignored him. Gerritt was just another Gringo who was passed over him. Felix Alford and Hugh Dillon were helpful, but it was Julio Romero who picked up the pieces when Gerritt let the shift get out of control. It was Julio who made sure the waste got hauled out as well as the ore, Julio who had the track laid and Julio who wrote the shift report for Barnett, while Gerritt drove around the mine checking on the equipment.

Gerritt was falling into bed each night exhausted, more from the mental effort of organizing that part of the operation in which he had no interest, managing the obreros and equipment efficiently, than from hard work. He was gradually letting Julio take back the shift; it was easier than dealing with the men. Molly let Gerritt come to her place occasionally, but there was something lost now between them.

"Why don't you go to Eve?" she asked him.

"I don't touch her," he answered flatly as they lay in bed. He made love to Molly loosely, promising nothing.

"Not like this." Gerritt kissed Molly's breasts, then moved on top of her as she clasped her legs around him. The time together quickly became a satisfaction of physical need that Gerritt approached with a desperate hunger and which angered Molly. She accused Gerritt of using Eve and he could not answer; he didn't know, so said nothing. Molly stopped asking.

Driscoll, Blain and Reicher were all in Santiago with the pliego negotiations and it was not going any better than Gerritt's shift. Hidalgo and the Union were stubborn and this time the demands were unreasonable. They wanted double the present salaries and no overtime; the latter would force the company to hire more people.

Curt Reicher returned from Santiago after two weeks and called an immediate meeting in the mine. Gerritt didn't want to go. He was on night shift that week and it meant he had to stay after shift, when all he wanted was to go home to bed. While Julio turned in the tonnage and made the report to Barnett, Gerritt pushed a chair back against a wall and quickly fell asleep. He opened his eyes when Wes Bowen shook him.

"Gerritt, wake up. What's this all about?" Wes sat on the desk, his long legs draped over the side were touching the floor. He had arrived for day shift to find Gerritt still there and the rest of operations beginning to assemble in the large meeting room.

Gerritt woke with a start. He was dreaming about lying in a meadow by the creek again, a place, his place, where he felt safe and unencumbered. Wes reminded him where he was. It made his head hurt.

"Christ, I don't know. Maybe the pliego's been settled. I hope Reicher isn't going to be long-winded, I'm beat." He rubbed his unkempt hair and yawned, a sour taste in his mouth.

"Well, since Hidalgo wants to be reelected, I guess anything can happen. God, how can people be that stupid to vote for a Union president that's been caught with his hand in the till." Wes dropped his hard hat on the desk in disgust.

Hugh Dillon walked over to them, a cigarette hanging out of his mouth.

"Did you get that track laid on D-4 last night, Gerritt?" he asked, shuffling the shift report.

"I don't know," Gerritt replied, disinterested. "Ask Julio".

"You're supposed to be the Shift Boss, Wells." Hugh wondered off shaking his head. Gerritt didn't feel like arguing, Hugh would get the information from Julio and forget about it. Felix Alford was walking in from Engineering with a cup of coffee in his hand.

"That looks like what I need," Gerritt said to Wes, heading for the coffee room. Wes frowned. Maybe Gerritt was just tired but Wes was fairly sure from his reaction that the track had not been laid, another job that would have to be done by Wes's shift.

Juan Ortega was stirring some sugar into his cup when Gerritt walked in.

"Morning Gerritt," he said without smiling, pushing his heavy hair off his face. "How was shift?"

"So, so. Everybody seems to be slowing down, waiting like crouched dogs."

"Si, they're waiting alright, and we're caught in the noose."

"Say Juan, this man Hidalgo, what's with him anyway. You're a Chileno, what's he got?" Gerritt cocked his head in a challenging way. But Juan responded explosively.

"That bastard! He's been around awhile and is sort of a folk hero, a known quantity. He likes to fight the Gringo and that means solidarity to the people in a way. He makes them feel like he does it for them, do you see what I mean?"

"You mean nationalism, don't you Ortega? Not fight the Gringo! Fuck the Gringo!" Gerritt felt hot inside and he did not know why. Maybe he was tired.

Juan's expression did not change. He eyed Gerritt carefully, wondering how Gerritt would feel if the Chilenos were digging in American soil. It didn't matter, that wouldn't ever happen and Juan lowered his eyes, the moment over.

"I suppose everyone is nationalistic in his own way." he said quietly and walked with his coffee around Gerritt back to the meeting room.

Gerritt stood there a minute thinking about what had just happened, what was behind the dark look in Juan's eyes. He knew Juan didn't like him. Well fuck him. Gerritt knew there wasn't much Ortega could do to him. They were both Shift Bosses now.

The room was full when Gerritt returned with his coffee, which burned his tongue but felt good in his throat after the long night on shift. Everyone was there, all the shifters, engineering, Ned Tully the blasting foreman, Swenson, the geologist. Too many people for the room and the acid smell of mine dust mixed with sweat made Gerritt sit down at the edge of the group. He didn't want to get any closer to all this than he had to. Curt Reicher was in his office on the phone. When he slammed it down, his face screwed into a wrinkled grimace, and he came out to the meeting.

"Well, what's up, Curt?" Barnett asked, handing him a cigar.

"There is no agreement on any part of the pliego," he said slowly, taking the cigar and then pausing to bite the end off.

"Hidalgo is adamant, wants to start the negotiations at half what they were asking and go up from there. There will definitely be a strike and the Santiago office thinks it could be a long one." Reicher lit the cigar, waiting for this to sink in. No one said a word.

"They go out at midnight tonight. There are threats that some of the mines down south may join in sympathy."

Murmuring and swearing began then among the men. Gerritt felt sick. Working the mine was keeping him from thinking too much about what he was going to do. It was easy in his pick-up driving around the mine, especially at night, to be anywhere but where he was, transport himself back to the farm, the coast, any place he could remember, any place away from Cerro Verde.

"And that's not the worst of it. If you'll just shut up so I can continue here!" Reicher was getting impatient, and Gerritt didn't envy him.

"New York is not pleased! They have ordered us by Telex to continue running the mine at least one shift a day." He said the last slowly, rocking back and forth on his heels and pulling on the cigar.

"Run the mine," Gerritt thought out loud, "We're going to run the mine?" He was incredulous, shocked at such an action, and then began to smile to himself. So it was true, what Wes heard. Why, it was just what he wanted, to run the machinery, feel that surge of engine boil under him. He looked over happily at Wes, but Wes wasn't smiling.

"Christ, Curt, how can I load a shot with just three or four of these idiots, it will take weeks! And it's dangerous!" It was Ned Tully, the blasting foreman speaking up first and spitting brown tobacco juice into the wastebasket.

"Take it easy, Ned," Reicher said. "You won't have even that much help. Just go ahead as fast as you can. I doubt there will be any need to blast anyway. There is plenty to load right now, waste and ore, and with only the one shift a day and all this "experienced" help we've got here, we probably won't need another shot."

"You mean to tell me these guys are going to run the shovels and trains, too?" bellered Art Barnett, slamming his fist on the table. "Half of them can't drive a pick-up!" He looked over at Wes Bowen, who sheepishly recalled his smashed truck. He was now driving the oldest truck in the mine and grateful to have that. Everyone smiled, it took away some of the tension. When the men quieted down again, Reicher continued.

"Yes, they are going to run shovels and trains," Curt replied sternly. "And cranes and trucks and anything else we need driven. Also, we'll need a night watch up here, to see that the office isn't broken into. Set it up, Art. One day shift until further notice. I want to see that schedule this afternoon. Your jobs will be posted then, so everyone's responsible for checking in and being here in the morning. And be careful, I don't want any accidents. The idea here is just to keep the mine running."

The meeting broke up, but the men hung around the room. It was too fresh an idea in their minds and it was as though they had to grasp it collectively.

"Where'd this idea come from anyway, Curt?" Hugh Dillon asked as he stood up and ground out his cigarette. All turned to listen. Hugh was usually quiet, did his job competently, and the men valued his opinion.

"New York doesn't know how hard this is going to be."

Curt Reicher sighed. Hugh was right. Sitting in their plush offices on Broadway, most of the head office had forgotten how a mine was run, or never knew.

"The Santiago staff seems to feel we can handle the one shift up here. We'll give it a try." Reicher said.

"Well, I think it is a good idea." It was Juan Ortega. "Hidalgo and his locos need to know we can manage without them!"

"Thanks, Juan. Yes, exactly!" Reicher smiled and nodded his head. He and Barnett went into Barnett's office and shut the door.

Gerritt looked at Juan Ortega, now wondering which side he was on.

"You act like you are a long ways removed from the strikers, Ortega. Don't you feel any of your "nationalistico" spirit now?" he asked tauntingly, too tired to be nice anymore.

"Not when it comes to the mine, Wells. It's a matter of priorities." Juan's face was dark and sullen as he turned to leave.

"God, Gerritt, leave Ortega alone," Wes said, putting a hand on Gerritt's shoulder. "He's a good man and he's sitting on a fucking fence, can't you see that?"

"I know, but he's still a Chileno," he said getting up. "I'm tired of this whole shitty business. Going home to bed." Wes looked after him, thinking that Gerritt was probably going to enjoy working as an obrero in the mine.

While Gerritt lay in a crumpled sleep that afternoon, a truck went over a bench on the waste dumps east of the mine. It was a bad accident anyway, but being on the day before a threatened strike, a large crowd of men gathered quickly to see what the Jefes would do. Both empleados and obreros had been purposely slowing their work with the impending strike and this was a good excuse to stop completely.

Barnett and Reicher were out there as soon as they heard on the radio, but they had to shove their way through a crowd, which was there before them and smelled of sweat and garlic. The dump was eighty feet high and the huge yellow Dart lay on its side halfway down, crushed and stained, clinging to the side of the hill like a discarded toy.

"Must have rolled over at least once, the cab's all smashed." Barnett said. Dust rose up around it. "Wonder if it's going to slide anymore."

"No, it'll probably hold for now." It was Hugh Dillon, arriving with Ortega and Wes Bowen.

"Get those two dozers over here, altido, and cable." Reicher yelled at the oberos, who scattered, knowing what needed to be done. Even with the strike, this was still one of their own down there and they wanted to help.

"Is that oil on the hood?" Wes asked, then seeing the number 352 on the door, he knew who was driving. "Oh my God, it's Guillermo Arias! He must have gone to sleep!"

"Shit! Let's go down and see how he is," Barnett said. Barnett, Bowen, Dillon, and Ortega slid and skated down the hill, which was new dump and loose. Reicher stayed on top to direct the dozers that roared to life and were smoking their way over to the site. The crowd backed off to make way and men were pulling cable out, picking up dust that blew around them.

"God, it's fuel oil all right, the tank's busted!" Barnett said, reaching the wreck first. He looked in at the cab, then looked away and spit, throwing his cigar far down the hill. It was, indeed, Arias and he was unconscious. Barnett stuck his arm in the broken window, careful of the splintered glass and felt for a pulse in the man's neck as the others watched.

"Curt, you better get an ambulance quick," he hollered up to Reicher. "And get us some rope and a crow bar. We won't be able to use torches to get him out. I don't want a fire. And get that cable down here so this mother doesn't slide any further." Reicher disappeared into the watching crowd. They seemed like a weight hanging over the hill. Barnett turned to climb down. The truck was fairly stable, imbedded in the dirt.

"Any of you want to take a look?"

Wes climbed up with Juan, the truck swaying slightly. He'd never seen an accident like this in the States. The inside of the truck and the injured Arias were both covered with dirt.

"Jesus, is he going to die? He's got nine kids!" Wes asked Juan softly. The man was broken up, his legs pointing in weird directions and there was blood seeping through his trouser pants.

"Maybe not, Barnett called for an ambulance."

"Hey, you bastards get down! Here come the cables." Barnett ordered. They jumped down. The wind hit Wes in the face and he felt sick, leaned his hand on the truck and coughed.

"If you're going to throw up, do it down-wind, Bowen. Ortega, fasten these cables to the back axle." He handed Juan and two of the obreros the cables, being fed down from above, and a sack with wrenches and bolts.

"O.K., Hugh, let's see what we can do with this fucking door. Barnett tried the crowbar on the side. The door was dented in, the sides of it caught on the edges and it didn't budge. Barnett strained, his face turning red.

"How're we going to move him when we get it open?" Wes asked, thinking about the position of the man's legs and the night Arias ran over his pickup.

"He's not going to feel a thing. Here you get on this, too, Bowen. You've got some weight behind you." But they couldn't move the door. The crowbar only collapsed it further, bending and curling the edges inward. "Gees, what I'd give for a blowtorch."

"We don't have much time," Dillon said. "Let's see if we can take him out through the windshield."

"Alright," Barnett said after thinking a second. "Got those cables on, Ortega?" He hollered back at Juan.

"Yeah, just about. Yeah, there, the second one is secure. Winch it up a little, Curt," he yelled at Reicher, who motioned to a dozer out of sight. An engine started and the winch squeaked as the cable straightened out, feathering puffs of dust where it moved along the sloped ground. The yellow weight of the truck groaned in its crumpled sleep as the cable tightened. "O.K., slow it down some," Juan shouted from under the back of the wheels. "Easy. O.K. that should do it. I think it will hold."

"I'll go up top, I'm lighter than the rest of you," Hugh said, and he climbed up on the front wheel and onto the fender, slipping on the oil. Hugh's bony legs showed as the wind whipped his pants.

"Careful," Barnett cautioned. "Here's the crowbar."

"Watch out for your eyes," Hugh said. They looked away as Hugh started bashing at the windshield. He shut his own eyes in spite of his glasses, as the safety glass shattered and went everywhere, falling in on the injured man and into Hugh's pants cuffs. He mashed the remaining edges out with his boot, then handing the crowbar down to Bowen, stepped down onto the seat and grabbed Arias under his shoulders.

"Poor bastard," Hugh mumbled, as he struggled with the limp weight.

"My God," Wes gasped. "How did this happen?"

"A little slip, backing up just too far. With Arias, maybe slowed reaction. Fucker is always tired." Barnett said, disgusted. "Sure glad this fuel oil didn't catch fire, we'd have had a real barbecue."

Hugh's hand bled. He'd cut himself on the glass in the man's clothes.

"Can you take his shoulders now, Art? I'm going to have to straighten his legs a little or they'll never clear the window." The whine of an ambulance came and went in the wind.

Barnett climbed up on the tire to grab the man. His legs were mashed under the steering wheel. Dillon slid him carefully to the side and as he lifted the shoulders to Barnett he shoved on the legs to straighten them and felt bare bone in the bloody pants. Arias's legs bent in an unnatural way, flaccid as Hugh unfolded them and passed the broken body through the window where Wes and Art Barnett were waiting. The sound of the bones moving against each other made them all feel weak. Reicher passed down a sling and together they laid the unconscious man in it as gently as possible. He was dragged to the top on his back and swallowed by hands waiting to help him.

The four rescuers climbed wearily to the top. They were dirty and covered with blood, caked and dusted.

"Get a crane up here and pull this bastard up, Ortega. I know with the strike, it will probably sit here awhile, but get it up anyway," Barnett ordered. He took a new cigar out of his pocket as they all stood there looking down at the wreck, bit the end off and lit it. The crowd of men began to disperse after the ambulance left for the hospital, its siren fading.

"We better get back to the schedule, Art," Reicher said, sighing and climbing into Art's truck.

"Yeah," Barnett answered blankly, then looked back at the other three men. "Thanks."

Wes went about the rest of the day in a daze. He helped Juan set the crane and bring the yellow Dart, or what now vaguely resembled a truck, up the steep incline of the dump. They left it sitting on top, touched only by the wind. It reminded Wes of his own crushed pickup and he felt a chill, thinking of how fragile the human body is and how things, lots of things seemed to be coming apart. Arias now was a victim of his own smashed truck. The strike would pass, the truck would be fixed, Arias would probably live to go back to his nine children, and Gerritt, yes, maybe Gerritt would be fine. It was more like an unsettled feeling than anything, like a door with loose hinges that needed tightening.

CHAPTER 14

It was 7 PM before they had the schedule for operating the mine during the strike. The office filled again, the men waiting apprehensively for assignments, all hope of a settlement gone. Some came in directly from shift, covered with dust and there was a general unease. Wes straddled a chair, telling Gerritt about the accident.

"You should have seen Barnett," Wes said, the freckles disappearing in the lines around his eyes as he frowned. "He and Dillon have probably done this before, but Arias was all broken up. Made me sick."

"What did it do to the truck?" Gerritt looked up, imagining the effect of the fall on the metal of the cab. Wes was surprised at the question, the lack of concern for the Arias and his family. He pulled back in the chair and then answered Gerritt as coldly as he could manage.

"We pulled it up with a crane, O.K., but it probably won't be repaired soon, what with the strike." Gerritt didn't seem to notice Wes's reaction, as he was looking at Reicher and Barnett who just came in and the room grew quiet. No one was happy about running the machinery, save possibly Gerritt, but everyone had a common desire to help and for some sort of plan.

"Sheets for the week are going up on the board," Art explained, wearily. This was going to be a bitch and he knew it couldn't go well. He had tried to get Reicher to wait, but they both knew the pliego was far from being settled and that New York wanted the mine running. They had no choice. Juan thumbtacked two sheets on the board near the door.

"I don't want any bitching", Art said. "No one is going to be happy, so you won't be any better off trading with the next bastard. Curt doesn't think this will last long, but just get as good at what you're doing as fast as you can so we don't have any accidents. I've put the Chief Foremen as division heads and the rest of you under them. They'll organize you further." He seemed finished, pulled his papers together, then turned around to them again.

"Oh, and for those of you who were up on the waste dump today, Giuillermo Arias died at the hospital late this afternoon." Barnett hadn't wanted to tell them this and didn't look anyone in the eye. It was what it was.

Hugh Dillon and Wes looked at each other. Hugh took the live butt from his mouth and lit another cigarette. Neither knew Arias personally. The relationship was like the truck he drove, part of the mine operation that was OK as long as it functioned. But it was more personal now. Arias was alive when they last touched him, broken but warm, and it was a loss. Somehow driving the mine machinery seemed more dangerous than it did the day before.

"So you don't expect the strike to last too long, Curt?" It was Mike Marshall, the sandy-haired track foreman. He lay forward on a desk with his head leaning on his hand, wrinkling up tanned skin on his face. "What's your best guess?"

Reicher stood up to answer, putting his hand into his shirtfront, pensively.

"We really have no idea," he admitted, his shoulders sagging perceptibly. "The pliego is going badly, as I told you, and I haven't heard anything further. There are some tempers that will have to cool down. We're guessing two weeks, that's what we have the schedule set for." He waved toward the board.

"I'm going back down to Santiago tomorrow and will call Art daily to see how it's going." Curt continued, tight-lipped. "Just keep things running, if you can. Don't worry too much about production. They'll be on the same staffing as we are down at the plants and they have a full-shift, two-week stockpile now." He looked around for further questions, but the men were anxious to have a look at the schedule.

Gerritt didn't rush up to the board. There would be time for that, time to find what his specific job would be. It didn't matter in the least. He would feel good about running any part of the mine, getting his hands on a solid piece of machinery again, the oil, the smells and sounds. He only wished it was a permanence and not merely a gesture. Hidalgo, the economic impact of the strike on the company and the length of the pliego were far from Gerritt's immediate responsibility or concern. Right now he only wanted to feel the humming vibrations of an engine underneath him and forget about Eve.

"Aren't you going to check your job, Wells? You can't sit on your ass all day." Barnett had been watching him.

"Sure," he answered caustically. "I don't care to get trampled, that's all."

Barnett frowned, seemed about to say something else, then shrugged and went into his office. Immovable was the word that came to his mind. You couldn't reach Gerritt Wells. He needed a stick of dynamite put up his ass.

When Gerritt got up to look at the schedule, he smiled, finding he was to work a shovel. He was assigned to Hugh Dillon, which would be OK, too. Ortega and Wes Bowen had the trains, Alford the trucks, Marshall his regular job of track. Tully would try to get at least one shot loaded. There were only a dozen or so Chilean shifters to parcel out, the few men the Union allowed to work. Julio Romero was not one of them. It didn't matter, Gerritt wouldn't need him, but he thought briefly of Julio's loyalties and knew they would not lie with the Gringos in this situation.

Geology was in charge of the night watch. Everyone would take a watch once during the two weeks, with the following day off. Gerritt grunted, put his hard hat on and went home to sleep.

He reported early for work the next morning, a rarity that drew raised eyebrows from Barnett. By the time he had coffee, Dillon arrived and the two began to make a plan for operating the shovels. Gerritt insisted on using the #204 in the bottom of the pit and Hugh didn't argue. It was the largest shovel in the mine and would load more ore at 20 tons a bite. Hugh decided to load the #206 up on G-4. It was on a sulfide bench and the sulfide plant had lower stockpiles than the oxide plant. One of the Chilean obreros would load another sulfide shovel and the other Chileno they were assigned could run maintenance on the three machines.

"Looks pretty good," Hugh said, pushing back the papers. "You sure you can operate the #204? It's quite a bit different from the smaller shovels with that cabled boom."

"Sure, It can't be that difficult." He couldn't wait to get down there and inside it. Wes Bowen was less enthusiastic.

"Gerritt, be careful for God's sake! Driving a dozer is one thing, but that mother is four stories tall." Wes was remembering Gerritt on the dozer the afternoon shortly after their arrival in Cerro Verde, the look on his face of being somewhere else, disengaged from the act itself.

"Playing with the trains won't be a picnic either," Gerritt said testily, knowing exactly what Wes meant. He wouldn't have to work at distancing himself from the problems with Eve this time. She was in Santiago and the reality of the enormous shovel would be enough to make him forget everything else except the movement of that bucket. It was important to keep the mine running. Gerritt didn't want to jeopardize his position here; it was an unbelievable experience being a Shift Boss and now the small pleasure of running a shovel.

Wes leaned on the desk with both big hands. "I know. At least Ortega knows something about trains. He said he drove Machinista one summer here when he was in school. We'll be loading your shovel. Our Chilenos are going to load Dillon."

Gerritt drove down the winding roads to the bottom of the pit where he could see the #204 sitting idle. The wind wasn't up yet and the pit was still and gold in the early morning. He raced across the pit floor, bumped over track, looking all the while at the giant machine looming ahead, couldn't contain himself and felt a course guffaw rise up from an inner secret place where he kept unconscious desires. He gunned his truck and drove right under the #204, between the huge cat-tracks, then around and through it again, laughing.

When he stopped, the dust overtook him and he waited for it to clear, savoring the massive machine with his eyes, before stepping down from his truck. The shovel towered over him, an immense orange shape, the tracks it rested on as tall as the pick-up.

"Howdy, you big bastard!" Gerritt said to it, slapping his hand on its side, a sound, which echoed from the mine sides in the morning silence of the pit. "You and I are going to work together for awhile and am I ever glad to see you." He walked underneath where he could smell the oil. It dripped from the gearbox and from the swivel that turned the cab when it was loading. He wiped at a gear with his hand, smelled the grease, then rubbed it on his pants.

The inside of the cab was fairly clean, being glassed in and thus protected from the dust. Empty beer bottles and newspapers lay on the floor, attesting to the wait for trains to switch track above, and there was a stale smell of sweat and closure. Gerritt looked down to the ground far below and up the 100-foot boom to the bucket, empty now and swinging slightly on its cables. He settled into the seat and began to study the levers and gauges. It didn't take him long to understand, feeling over each of the dozen or so control levers that raised and lowered the bucket, turned the cab. When he started the engine a thrill went through his body, the vibration and the power satisfying him totally. It was a complete understanding and identification with the machine and he gave in to it willingly. Gerritt looked up to the top of the mine and could see Ortega and Bowen coming slowly down with the train. He had some time to practice and to be alone with the #204 after the giant machine was warm and then Wes and Juan were there and he began to load the cars one by one.

There were misses when Gerritt did not properly place the bucket before releasing the ore. At such times, the crushed rock spilled against the side of the ore car and they had to stop to clean off the track.

But on the whole the men got on well with the work that first day and Barnett was pleased, or perhaps relieved. However, it was slow going with the inexperience and there was a minor accident. One of the Chilean shifters, laying track with Marshall, jumped off a flatcar and broke his ankle.

On the third day, Ortega and Bowen were emptying a load of oxide into the crusher. Juan guided the train in as Wes directed him and would release the ore when it was in position.

"Yeah, a little further," he motioned, his hand on the trip for the dump as the car came into alignment. But Ortega gave the throttle too much and as Wes pulled the tripper, the side-dump car was partially past the crusher.

"Fuck!" Wes yelled, but it was too late. A whole carload of ore fell out, only partially on its mark. Half the load missed the gaping mouth of the crusher completely, fell three stories, tore out a flight of concrete steps and roared into the building below, collapsing a wall and part of the roof. Chet

Weir and the other metallurgists, who were having their own problems in the plant, nearly quit.

"Do you know how much time it's going to take to clean up this fucking mess?" Weir screamed at Barnett, his face round and red, puffed full in anger. Barnett couldn't say much. It took three days to get the oxide crusher operating again. The repair on the building waited, for lack of anyone to do the work and during the three days they hauled additional sulfide to the other plant's growing stockpile.

Barnett yelled at Ortega and Bowen, but only half-heartedly. He was beginning to realize the lunacy of trying to run the mine with the short and inexperienced crew. Reicher called every day from Santiago and was discouraged when Barnett told him about the crusher. There was no progress on the pliego and Hidalgo had been amused by the accident and said so publicly.

Gerritt was on nightwatch at the end of the first week. He had dinner after shift and then went to pick up Molly. Staying awake in the mine all night was difficult and boring. Molly was calling him lately, wanting to see him, so he had said yes for the company. By a mutual understanding from past arguments, they avoided discussion of Eve, who anyway was a thousand miles away in Santiago with her parents. Gerritt stopped at the mine office when he saw Barnett's truck still outside, but parked on the other side of the office and left Molly in the truck. Barnett wouldn't approve of her being in the mine.

"What's up?" he asked when Barnett heard the door slam and raised his head to see who was there.

"Been seeing some dust up around H-3, where Mike unloaded that track today, Wells. I don't know if it's just the wind, or if somebody's up there. You might take a look-see later." Barnett told him, putting on his coat and hardhat.

"Anything from Curt?"

"Naw, I'd have said so if there were. Fucking Union. They're killing us." And he was out the door. It was more than the man said to Gerritt in days, but he was sure it was not a confidence and only that Gerritt was there. He looked around the office. It seemed strange to see it quiet, unused. For the first time he saw it as a space instead of a meeting place and he thought briefly of Shem's barn and remembered that it was March and there would still be snow on the ground in Montana and the worry of how to buy hay if what you had didn't last. He shivered, glad to be where he was, and went on back to his truck. Molly turned on the radio. There was static, but no human voice.

"Not exactly the evening news," she said smiling.

Gerritt clicked it off and backed the truck out. They drove around the mine as the night fell, stopping occasionally to look it over. He explained what new work they'd done, before the strike. Molly hadn't been out to the mine for some time and she reminded him of that.

Fall was coming and the days were getting shorter. Gerritt liked the sunsets here. On the farm, the end of day was always green and pink, the colors of growing. Here the sun set in baths of gold. There were seldom clouds, the sky clear to keep the last light. Gold spread across the sky and reflected off the barren hills and benches of the mine, taking away the drabness for a moment as the last rays illuminated the dust.

Gerritt pulled the truck to a stop on an upper bench facing west and they sat there watching the colors fade, his arm around Molly and his hand resting on her breast.

He started. There was something on the south side of the mine, where Barnett said to keep an eye.

"Did you see that dust up over there?" he asked.

"Yes, but it could be the wind."

"Better check." He started the truck. Molly would have liked to stay there. She wanted to talk and his hand was warm and where she wanted it to be.

They drove up to the top of the mine, which took nearly five minutes and found no one. The track that Mike Marshall off-loaded that afternoon looked undisturbed. Gerritt got out and looked around but didn't see any fresh tire marks.

"Wind could have blown them away, I suppose. Barnett was so sure he saw some activity up here." They drove back down to the more distant, designated watch position.

After the light went, they sat eating candy bars in the truck. There would be no moon. In the darkness, both had their eyes on the upper bench. It wasn't long.

"There, see that?" Gerritt whispered, as though whomever it was a mile-and-a-half across the mine could hear him.

"I saw it too, but it's gone now."

"No, there it is again. There's not supposed to be any lights up there now. Let's go!" He dropped the rest of the candy on the seat and started the pickup, knowing that whoever it was would hear them coming. There was no other way; it was too far to walk.

When he was nearly there, the lights went out. Gerritt put the brake on the truck and turned the motor off, giving way to the darkness.

"Come on, be quiet," he told Molly. They both got out and ran toward where he could hear low voices on the night wind.

"I'm scared, Gerritt," Molly whispered.

"Go back to the truck, then," he said without looking back. It would be better if he went on alone.

"OK. Be careful." She disappeared behind him and he heard the truck door open, but not shut. Good, she tried not to make any noise.

He ran toward where he could hear movement and began to feel uneasy, knowing there was something wrong and that Barnett should be told. But he had already reached the top of the bench, the loose rock moving noisily under his boots. Ahead, he could make out shadows carrying the rail sections and bumping them onto trucks.

"Que hacen aqui, Señores?" he shouted at them. He cursed himself for leaving the flashlight in the truck. It didn't matter. Within seconds, lights from four pickups came on, the last sections were thrown in, doors slammed and they were gone, leaving Gerritt standing there surrounded with dark, choking dust.

He coughed and spit out dirt onto the ground.

"Shit," he said out loud, knowing he should have called Barnett when he saw the first light earlier. With two of them coming in from different sides, they might have caught the bastards.

He walked slowly back to the truck where he found Molly shivering.

"What happened? I saw all those lights and heard engines gunning. I should have stayed with you," Molly said.

"Wouldn't have made any difference. I forgot the damn flashlight. With that I might at least have made out a face or two. All I saw in the dark were the lights from the trucks and dust." He started the pickup and they drove over to assess the damage. There were two sections left on the ground. Gerritt kicked at a rock. Barnett was going to be pissed.

"Why in hell didn't you call me, Wells?" Barnett screamed at him the next morning. "That carload of track is on its way down south right now! Fuck! I should have stayed out here!"

"I know, I know. I was in a hurry," Gerritt said lamely. He knew he'd fucked up.

"You're always in a Goddamn hurry! For Christ sake, if you'd just stopped to call, we could have saved some of that track."

But they both knew that even with both of them there, the track would likely have been gone, and there wasn't any point in arguing with Barnett. Gerritt was furious with himself for not taking a flashlight, or at least driving up on them with his truck lights blazing.

The end of the two weeks came and there was no encouraging news from Santiago. Hidalgo had stopped coming to the meetings and was refusing to talk to the company representatives until a better offer was made. Reicher returned to Cerro Verde, there being nothing he could add to the negotiations.

The third week Gerritt nearly lost an arm. He was helping Ortega and Bowen get the train ready to load, climbed up the steep 80 foot bench above the shovel to two loaded cars sitting there from the day before. Ortega was slowly bringing down the rest of the train. Gerritt checked the brake coupling and finding it loose, was bent over it and didn't see the train running down on him. Wes Bowen was in the back car motioning to Ortega to come on forward. He saw Gerritt at the last minute, his head appearing, popping up between the two cars.

"Gerritt! Jump!" Wes yelled out, but not in time. And with the noise of the train, Gerritt didn't hear him. The locomotive and eight cars hit the stationary ones with Gerritt between. He happened to look up, saw Wes waving and brought his arm up just as the coupling jammed together, the rust and metal grinding and squeaking.

There was a pop in his head and everything went black. Gerritt's head bounced against the last car and he fell free onto the ground. Ortega and Bowen were there in seconds, standing over him as the light forced its way back into his brain. He looked up as into a bright light and, remembering the train coming at him, wondered if he was dead. Slowly the fuzz lifted and he saw Wes's red hair and the squatty Ortega. He put his hand up to his head where there was a throbbing pain.

"Goddamn, Wes," he said, sitting up with help. "Sure glad I saw you. My arm was in that coupling." Ortega was breathing deeply, his dark face so drained of color, he appeared grey. He lit a cigarette and handed it to Gerritt. The three of them sat on the ground next to the train, smoking. Without speaking, they knew they didn't want to do this anymore. Even for Gerritt, the fun was over.

Reicher blew up, telexed New York that it was impossible to continue with this sort of operation. It wasn't worth losing anybody and they had been lucky the accidents were not worse. After that, there was only the guard duty, four at a time to prevent any more looting.

Gerritt was left with a large knot on his head where he was thrown against the ore car. Jason Stoddard, Elaine Barnett's father, saw him at the hospital and assessed for a concussion. Stoddard, trained in Canada, was a slight, grizzled man with dark eyes, small and sharp set back in his head. There was none of the pale softness of his daughter about him, but Gerritt liked him immediately. He reminded Gerritt of Shem. They both held life back behind their eyes somewhere, knowing things he could not because he hadn't lived long enough.

"You people seem to be having some trouble playing with all the toys out in the mine," Stoddard said smiling after he examined Gerritt.

"Yes, well, it's not quite as easy as we'd thought." He was more embarrassed than hurt, disgusted with himself for not being able to get out of the way in time.

"So I see. You were lucky; there's no concussion, but you better take it easy for a few days," Jason said, raising bushy eyebrows thoughtfully. He had an idea. No, maybe it wouldn't help. Jason knew of the distance between Gerritt and Art Barnett, but only from Art's side. Though Stoddard liked his son-in-law, he also thought him a bit of a blowhard, knew he was often harder on the men than necessary. But Gerritt seemed easily as obstinate. Yes, perhaps it would be good for both of them.

"Why don't you go out to Piedra Negro with Art? He's going to take some supplies to the Clinica for me."

"Where?" Go someplace with Art. Right. Gerritt frowned, but Jason didn't seem to notice.

"Piedra Negro, out beyond Santa Bárbara de Atacama. Actually, I think he's also planning to take another look for Los Penitentes, some salt statues out in the salar. Nebulous things, people who say they have seen them can never tell you exactly where they are. The salar is a big haystack."

"Yeah, sounds interesting. There isn't much to do around here right now, what with the strike," and he thought briefly of Eve's hair, then of the impossibility of going anywhere with Barnett.

"I don't know if he would want me along, though. We don't get along so well."

"I know about that. Art is a goodhearted person, but a bit on the stern side. Do you want to talk about it?"

Gerritt stared at him. Yes, it might be good to talk to someone not so close to the mine. But there was Eve, and who was he kidding. Stoddard was Barnett's father-in-law. Talking about Art wouldn't be possible in a community this small. Confidentiality was almost incest.

"No," he said somewhat regretfully. "I'll work it out, but thank you, Dr. Stoddard."

"It's Jason."

"Thanks then, Jason. Glad you told me about the trip. Maybe Art would let me tag along. And Wes Bowen, yes, it might be better if Wes went too."

They stood. Gerritt looked at Stoddard and felt drawn to him, needing to talk to somebody. There was one thing he could tell him, something he had told no one. Not about Eve. Not about Barnett.

"I'm sorry we can't run the machinery anymore. I liked the way it felt. It's not complicated."

"No, it's not. But the shovels and trains are tools, Gerritt. Your education makes you the carpenter. I'd like to see you in a week or so, to be sure you aren't having any secondary effects from the injury."

"Yeah, sure." He put on his jacket, knowing that Jason didn't get it. Nobody did.

Jason Stoddard sat down in his old cracked leather chair and looked out the window at the pampa to which he had given his time. He was tired now and rubbed his grey eyebrows, pinching them together and deepening the furrow between dark eyes. Gerritt Wells would be back. Jason knew he was seeing Eve Driscoll, whom he had known since Driscoll first brought her, a lice-infested pitiful animal, from the cage in Antofagasta. Not many such babies were so rescued or so nurtured. But it was too late. Eve was an unreachable psyche, a tiny winged thing, incapable of meaningful exchange. Wells would want from her something she couldn't give. And Gerritt seemed to have his own stable of untamed horses, a desire for simplicity that didn't match his situation. Jason sighed, standing up. There was work to do. Out the window, he could see the parking lot where Gerritt was just getting into his truck.

Gerritt drove over to Wes Bowen's to ask him about going to Piedra Negra.

'Shit,' he thought. 'Barnett either knew everyone or was related to everyone in Cerro Verde.' Gerritt wanted badly to talk longer with Jason. Eve had been gone a month and he was still thinking about her, knew he was now Shift Foreman because of her. But she was so simple a human being, there was nothing to clutch onto. Not simple in the way that an engine was simple for him, certainly. She was, instead, unpredictable and illogical and did not respond to reason.

But then, neither did Molly. He hadn't seen Molly in more than a week. When he went to her now, she wanted to talk, talk about Eve, or what he wanted here in Cerro Verde, or what he wanted from her. Gerritt couldn't talk to her about these things. Molly would argue, try to tell him what he wanted was what she wanted. Things were getting all mixed up and he thought if he could get away, think about it all for awhile, it would get better and he would know how he felt and what mattered. He had to make a go of this, his first job after college. He had to make it here, there was no one else to help him.

When Gerritt asked him about the trip to Piedra Negra, Wes was interested but skeptical about Barnett letting them go along.

"Did you ask Barnett yet?" Wes said, "You know we aren't exactly his two favorite people!"

"No, I wanted to see if you could go first. That way we can take our own pickup and we won't have to ride with him."

Barnett was lukewarm, as he had expected.

"Jason told you, huh? Figures. Well, I suppose it's all right. Probably a good idea to take as many pickups as we can. This could be a rough trip. You'll need extra gas. Get some cans and extra tires from the Bosque. Blankets, sleeping bags, water, and food. There's a hosteria to stay in at Piedra Negro, but we may get stuck out on the salar and it's not the kindest of places. It's a big mother and there are no roads.

"So I've heard. Where'd you hear about the salt statues, from Jason?"

"Yeah, and from people at the Clinica in Piedra Negro. There's a kid out there named Roberto who claims he knows where they are. His father saw them once, supposedly. Salt formations crystallized around some rocks and supposed to be in the shape of praying monks, three of them. The pueblo named them Los Penitentes."

"When do you want to go?"

"Tomorrow, I guess, if we can get all the stuff together. Jason has the supplies for the Clinica packed. Ortega is going with me and Dillon and Alford are going, too." Barnett stopped, looking at Gerritt.

"Dillon actually wanted to ask you to go but he thought you might have a concussion and I think Bowen has guard duty, doesn't he? I don't care one way or the other." And he looked back to his papers.

"Wes didn't say. He thought you wouldn't want us along. If he does, maybe Marshall would sub."

"Marshall?" Barnett laughed. "If he's sober, he might. Mike's been spending most of his time down in Molino, getting himself fucked."

Wes did have guard duty, but found Mike and he reluctantly agreed to take Wes's shift the next night. It took them the rest of the day to gather up the necessary supplies. Alice packed their food. Gerritt thought there was enough for ten people and briefly that maybe being married, at least to someone like Alice, might be nice. Barnett sent them to the hospital to pick up the clinic supplies. Jason Stoddard smiled at Gerritt, pleased he was going.

They left early. Barnett was already chewing on a cigar, his breath steaming the cold air. Dawn hit them an hour out and its warmth melted Gerritt's bitterness, erasing the bad days. Jason was right, the pampa was cleansing.

New light outlined the rocks, slowly bringing in the day. He was driving his own pickup and being behind the wheel on such a morning gave him again a sense of control over his life. Taking supplies to Piedra Negro made them all feel useful, which was a good feeling in the meaningless days of the strike. And they were looking for the unknown salt statues, a safari feeling Gerritt imagined, knowing it was something Shem might have liked to do.

The sun was up and fully warming the earth when they reached Santa Bárbara. Wes slept most of the way, while Gerritt was deep in thought. He wanted to see Padre Simon in Santa Bárbara, or at least felt he ought to. No one objected, they all needed a stretch.

Simon was in his office in the museum, though it was barely 7AM. In spite of the warmth outside, the adobe building was cold and smelled like wet concrete. The big man stood up, wiping his hands on his dusty brown cassock.

"Sr. Gerritt. Que sorpresa!" He grasped Gerritt's hand in both of his big claws, looking around him for Eve. "Y La Chiquitita, Eva?"

"No. Esta in Santiago con su Padres."

"Ah, si, todavia," Simon said, disappointedly. The smile dropped from his face so rapidly that his beard seemed about to melt down into the cassock. It drew a response from Gerritt he hadn't intended.

"Le gusta Eva mucho, no cierto?" he said sadly.

The look of surprise at such a question from Gerritt brought a jerk up of Simon's head. He scrutinized Gerritt carefully, moving close to him, so close Gerritt could smell his stale, night breath.

"No, Señor Gerritt," he said slowly. "Yo amo Eva. Es como mi niñita, entiende? Eva es de la tierra mia, una niñita de la poblacion!" His eyes became blank as he spoke about her, his people, his earth. And he seemed very far away, in a way Gerritt understood. Gerritt reached out to him, put a hand on his shoulder. Simon was taller, a massive man, but Gerritt needed to touch him. The cloth of the cassock was heavy and felt rough, but he could feel the body warmth beneath.

"Yo entiendo." Gerritt said, looking straight at him.

"Si?" Simon answered hopefully, then shook his head sadly. "No, no puedes entender."

Wes appeared in the doorway. "Gerritt, we have to go, Barnett wants to get going. Holla, Padre."

"Yeah, I'll be right there," Gerritt said, his eyes on the folds of cassock around Simon's neck. Wes left and silence filled the space in the cold room. There was a crucifix on the wall, the only decoration and Gerritt looked at it, then back at the Padre who was studying him.

"Hasta luego, Señor Gerritt. Ten cuidad y guarda la Eva, por favor," he said slowly and seriously. Gerritt touched his arm again and went out from the darkness of the priest's cell to blinding sunlight, not aware at all of the men standing around the trucks watching him walk down the dirt street toward them.

Hugh Dillon and Felix Alford asked Wes about Gerritt while they were relaxing in the sun drinking beer, curious about Gerritt's need to see the Padre.

"What's he doing in there, Bowen?" Dillon asked. I didn't know he knew the Padre that well."

"He doesn't. We were only up here the one time. I suppose it's because of Eve," Wes explained.

"What is he going to do about her?" Felix wondered. "Seems to me he's a bloke looking for trouble with that one."

"I don't really know much about it," Wes said trying to be as vague as he could, then realizing that in truth he really didn't know much about Gerritt's feelings about Eve. And then Gerritt was there and Barnett and Ortega came back from the store with cheese and crackers and they were on their way again.

Gerritt was quiet, hoping Wes would go back to sleep and he could think. His short visit with Simon was unnerving, but he was glad he had seen him. Why was it that everyone appeared to be examining him all the time? Eve was his business. Why couldn't things happen as they fell, one following another? He couldn't explain his past actions, not to anyone, even himself. And he truly didn't know what he would do about Eve. He looked over to find Wes staring at him.

"Well?" Wes said, the freckles on his face wrinkled between his eyes as he frowned. Gerritt didn't say anything.

"I guess you don't want to talk about it." Wes hit his knee with a large fist in frustration at Gerritt's seeming lack of trust.

"No, that's OK," Gerritt said, looking over at him. He knew Wes was genuinely concerned. They shared a lot and Gerritt wanted badly to explain what little he understood himself, but was unable to come out with it.

"Shit," Gerritt said, shaking his head and pushing his hair back. "There's nothing to talk about. Simon asked about Eve. I told him she was still in Santiago. He was sorry she didn't come, that's all."

"OK," Wes answered, clearly unsatisfied.

Gerritt knew it wasn't enough. There were the things that weren't said in the cold room, the concern in Simon's eyes. There was the throbbing in his head when he thought about Eve and where they were going together, where they would end up. There was no sound basis for such a relationship, but he felt irrevocably tied to her now in some way, some way involving the land itself and the promotion. Strangely, he thought maybe Simon understood, and didn't like it. No, Simon didn't like him being in Eve's life. This wasn't something that could be easily explained to Wes, or to anyone. He tried to forget it all by looking out on the pampa and concentrating on the road ahead. They drove through the edge of the salar, disturbing the flamingos eating shrimp in the shallow brine. The graceful, pink birds flew up into the sky, scattering and settling back down in another place. No one seemed to know from where they had come to live and nest in this high valley so far from any tropical paradise.

"What's that volcano, Wes?" he said, to change the subject. The golden light of the morning had spread over the whole pampa now; the shadows were gone. It was still cold and the smoke from a cone-shaped mountain, set in the first rise of the Andes, curled straight up.

"I think it must be Linconquebur. It's a long ways away, about sixty miles, I'd say. It's new, Barnett said it hasn't reached its angle of repose." Wes opened the map of the pampa they brought with them.

'A new thing, another new thing,' Gerritt thought, looking at the volcano breathe into the morning. It was nearly a perfect cone, steep-sided and black, looking closer to them than the sixty miles because of its inconsistency with the surrounding and flat, older cordillera. Gerritt was tired of new things. He thought about the velvet grass by the creek at home in summer, watching a hawk look for supper.

The climb up to Piedra Negro was gradual, but the altitude was already over 12,000 feet. Barnett stopped the trucks several times to cool them down. The road was straight and of such a slight incline, that it seemed they always stopped in the same place and Gerritt felt surprise when he began to see the greenness flat up against the Andes that was the village of Piedra Negro. It clung to the base of the mountains, a spot of life on otherwise barren land, keeping the notion alive that life is somehow possible anywhere. Such villages disappeared frequently, with little remembrance, when the ground water that fed them stopped flowing. To the west, from where they had come, the land flattened and turned whitish, becoming the dry salt lakebed of the salar, running on into the horizon with no end.

Barking dogs and grimy children jumped around the trucks on the dirt street as they drove into the village. They could hear water somewhere, trickling through irrigation ditches and the air felt damp and fecund after the arid pampa. There were fig trees, heavy with green fruit and small pens holding scrawny livestock. The whitewashed adobe houses were dusted with dirt.

Art drove directly to the Clinica, which was further up the hill. By the time they reached it, there was a swarm of people behind the trucks, running and screaming in the dust, which roiled up twenty feet. The Clinica was a small building, whiter than most and clean inside. A short-wave radio sat on a table just inside the door, for communication with Jason Stoddard in Cerro Verde. The Clinica was staffed by local women, dressed neatly in white, who hugged each man in turn, thanking them profusely for the supplies, which they stacked in a storeroom. The women offered food and rest in the cool of the clinic, which was dark inside and smelled of antiseptic.

When they finished eating and emerged into the bright sunlight, a laughing boy, shoulder high, with a voice that cracked when he spoke as though his voice was changing, but too young for that, came running up to them.

"You want Los Penitentes, Señores? I know, I know," he croaked, jumping up and down. "Alla, Alla." And he pointed out toward the salar to some imprecise location in the distance.

The men stopped and Barnett went up to him.

"Are you Roberto?" he asked the boy, his hands in his pockets.

"Si, Señor. Los Penitentes, no cierto?"

"Ha visto, suyo?" Juan Ortega asked the boy suspiciously.

"No, but my father see. He tell me."

"Where is your father, Roberto?" Art asked hopefully.

"El cielo, up there," and he pointed toward the sky. "He with angels. We go find Penitentes now?" He jumped into the back of Art's pickup and stood there, legs apart, waiting.

"Hold on there, Roberto," Barnett said. "We aren't ready to go yet. Now tell us exactly where they are. You're sure you know?"

The boy's smile faded and he got reluctantly down from the truck and then stood looking defiantly at Art.

"I know, only I know. How much you pay me?" He was more serious now, worried lines creasing his dirty face.

Art turned to the others, seeing he wasn't going to get any precise directions from Roberto.

"What do you think, Juan?"

"I think he's full of shit," Ortega answered, spitting into the dust, not wetting the dry powder, just scattering it.

"No shit, no shit," Roberto said, shaking his head and feeling customers slipping from his grasp.

"Well, I rather think we should forge ahead, being we've come this far," Felix Alford said.

"We do have supplies for the night and who really cares whether we find them or not," Hugh said, "There's nothing doing back in town."

Gerritt shrugged when Art looked at him. Gerritt couldn't agree with the rest. What point was there in looking for something if you didn't know generally where it might be.

They asked around the village, but no one else had any clearer idea where to look for the obscure salt statues. That they were there seemed to be beyond dispute, but exactly where, no one knew. No one, except Roberto, who seemed so sure. The dry salt lake covered roughly 1500 square miles. It was a big hole, but they finally decided to jump in. It was the temptation of finding something and the search seemed as important as the discovery to most of them.

Water jugs were filled from the spring on the square. Gerritt saw with amusement that Roberto had already planted himself in Barnett's truck. Barnett would have to ride with the boy, who had on a bare minimum of clothing and threadbare socks covered by a worn pair of sandals the pampa people cut from old tires. There was dirt encrusted on the sides of his face, matting his dark hair in knots.

'Barnett at least had his cigars and wouldn't smell the kid,' Gerritt thought.

The road away from the village went across a dry wash covered with large rocks, but passable. The trucks rocked and tilted as they reconnoitered the gully and then they were on the salar again and it stretched out endless in front of them. Gerritt wanted only to press hard on the gas peddle and fly. There was no distinct road, the three pickups spread out abreast, driving flat out for an hour as Piedra Negro paled in the back distance.

"Well, Roberto, how are we doing?" Wes asked the boy when they stopped for a stretch. The wind had come up, blowing the salty dirt around them.

"I think OK. Maybe isquierda." And off he went to take a leak.

"Christ, Art," Hugh said when Roberto got out of reach. "Turn left. There is no left out here! Does he know where he's going?"

"Says he does." Barnett bit down on his cigar, blown dead long ago by the wind. "We're alright with the supplies."

"Yeah, provisions for the night," mumbled Alford. "But it's bloody cold out here already."

Gratefully, they climbed back into the trucks. The trucks were cold inside now, but at least broke the wind and had heaters. The low sun turned the pampa dust to gold again. The way began to get rougher, the smooth surface breaking up, cracks running like rivulets in dried mud, the edges all uneven and sharp.

Dillon and Alford broke a tire hitting a gully. They wasted 30 minutes fixing it and gassing the trucks. The jack sank into the surface when any weight was put on it and they had to set it on a board to raise the truck enough to change the tire.

By evening, everyone agreed they were making no progress. The salar was softening, nearing the center where there was still a suggestion that the whole expanse had once been a lake. There was no sign of the salt monks, or anything else in the endless salt plain. Gerritt was sure if there were ever any monks they had long since been blown away.

Finally, Barnett came slowly to a stop, as though there were some sort of joint realization of failure. Gerritt and Wes could see him talking to Roberto, then get out of his truck.

"We better make camp while there's still some daylight," he said to the other men.

Ortega was mumbling and cursing Roberto under his breath. Gerritt supposed as a Chileno he had a right to vent his feelings on the boy or at least to verbalize what they were all thinking. There wasn't a chance in hell of going back that night. Orientation was difficult at night and they wouldn't be able to follow their tracks on the hard pack.

They pulled the trucks into a circle in the driest place they could find, put up tarps and built a fire from some llareta they bought in Piedra Negro.

Once the sun set, the dark came quickly and with it the cold pampa wind. There was no moon, but the stars were brilliant, giving the sky an iridescent glow. With nothing around them to provide a landmark and the endless wind, they felt isolated. Gerritt felt he was on a pinnacle at the top of the world, exposed and vulnerable.

Hot coffee mixed with scotch warmed everyone up. Dillon had freeze-dried food from the States to cook and by the time they had eaten, everyone's spirits were much improved.

"Well, Roberto," Art asked, "So which way tomorrow?" Being warm again made things somehow right and possible.

"Si, Señor Art, only a little more far." The answer was confidant, a voice to trust.

They didn't stay warm for long. Rolled into sleeping bags, figuring on a dawn start, they huddled together behind a large tarpaulin. The wind roiled down the salar, blowing all the way from the Bolivian altiplano, seeking to beat everything flat in its path, an immense and equalizing force. Somehow the tarp got loose at one end, whipping out away from them. It walked its way, a sail without a boat, disappearing into the darkness before anyone could get out of his bag. The wind whistling under the trucks was then too much, with the sand and loose stones cutting into skin. They climbed in the truck cabs to spend the rest of the night.

Gerritt was dismayed to find Roberto in with him and Wes, sandwiched between them with his single, ratty blanket. The wind moved and bumped the trucks all night, coming through every crack and seam, seeking them out. It was eery and alive and Gerritt felt they had no right to be there.

Dawn came, pink and cold, watched by all. The wind seemed to have died down some, but the early morning was hazy and pink from the dust, as sunsets are during harvest.

Gerritt uncurled himself, pealing the sleeping bag off like a cocoon. He had slept in a cold sweat huddled against the bodies of Roberto and Wes. His body was stiff and his head ached; he shouldn't have come.

"God, what a night," growled Barnett, falling out of his truck. "I'm half frozen to death. Get a fire going."

The morning coffee was only a gesture; they were all too thoroughly chilled for it to warm them. And the trucks wouldn't start.

Gerritt sat in his pickup grinding away the battery when Roberto suddenly leaped from the door where he was huddled, not even having a jacket to warm him. He grabbed a piece of burning llareta from the fire, ran around to the front of the truck and shoved it up against the grill.

"I fix, I fix," he cried as if his burning bush would make it all OK again. Gerritt looked at him, thinking he was crazy.

"Turn, turn," Roberto shouted, waving one arm at Gerritt to crank the engine. To Gerritt's amazement, the truck caught, the fan pulling the warm air in and around the engine, warming the oil enough to start it.

"Goddamn it, grab some of that stuff!" Barnett shouted and everyone fell to helping. It was a hope that they could start moving again. Half an hour of heating the blocks and the trucks were all running. There wasn't much to pack up, most everything had blown away, and they were soon moving, but sliding now.

Barnett headed off toward the north on Roberto's advice. The surface got sloppier, a grey color in the morning sun, shiny and slick. Gerritt, following last, drove in ruts from the other trucks and was soon mired. Rocking the truck only dug him in deeper. He cursed as he got out, his boots sinking down three inches. This was worse than the spring mud on the farm.

"That's a rotter," Alford exclaimed looking at the mess, the wheels oozing down into the clammy muck.

"That's just what it smells like, something rotting," Gerritt said. He started rummaging in the back for a shovel.

After a lot of cursing, they got some boards under the wheels and managed to get out onto some firmer ground. Gerritt was covered with the grey slime.

"Which way now, mijito?" Gerritt said to Roberto, giving him as dirty a look as he could muster through the mud drying stiffly on his face. Roberto by now was in sheer misery, shivering and scared.

"I think, Señores, maybe we should have gone the other way from Piedra Negro," he said almost inaudibly.

Barnett bit his cold cigar in half, the outward part flying off into the muck.

"Goddamn it! So we should have gone the other way, eh? I'll tell you what, I'll tell you what!" He was turning red in the face and spit out the other half of the cigar.

"There are no Goddamn Penitentes on this salar or any other Goddamn salar! Any Goddamn sons of bitches stupid enough to kneel down and pray out here, salt or no, are going to get their asses froze off or blow away like we Goddamn near did last night!"

Roberto was quivering and ran behind the truck. Barnett was through with him, his feelings of the last fifteen hours finally vomited out of him. He leaned on the truck for what seemed an hour to Gerritt.

"OK, now, let's get these mothers turned around and get the fuck out of this deep freeze!" Barnett shouted to the others.

They had another hour of labor getting the three trucks turned around. Barnett got stuck; the boards didn't help. Flushed to the breaking point, he labored, jacking up both sides and putting spare tires on top of the boards. With help he was able to bounce the truck off onto drier ground. It was afternoon when they began the trip back over tracks sometimes covered now, but at least in a direction where they knew the salar would support them.

Roberto, afraid to ride anymore with Barnett, sat between Gerritt and Wes, quietly sobbing. He was a foolish boy, but proud and he had failed in his dream. His anguish infected Gerritt.

"It's OK," he said to him. "This is like a lot of things. You never really find what you are looking for, even when you know where it is. And it's a hell of a lot of trouble, just the looking."

It didn't seem to help. Roberto sobbed on, a fallen hero. Gerritt felt a rapport with this dirty kid. It was something that got him in the gut, the hunger for looking and then not finding anything, knowing it was still out there, sure of it, but not knowing how or where to look. It was an ache that couldn't be assuaged with food or warmth or kind words, that needing to know.

Distance closed the salar behind them. If Los Penitentes were to be found, it would not be that day. Gerritt shoved his foot down on the accelerator and they flew behind Barnett and the others back to what they knew as civilization.

Roberto, their uninformed leader, became a hero in Piedra Negro. He was given the presents they had brought for him, the new clothes, sugar, candy, and magazines. These things were to have been a reward for leading a successful expedition but, by the time they returned to his pueblo, Roberto was in such a depression over his failure to know, that Barnett opened up the boxes for him, with no objection from the others. His black mood quickly disappeared and he leaped and shouted about the arduous trip and his part in it that grew with the telling. No one in the pueblo asked if he'd seen the Penitentes. With the gifts, Roberto was suddenly a man of property and it was clear that, for him at least, that was enough.

For Gerritt the failure to find the salt monks dwelled. He was disappointed in Roberto, felt somewhat the fool for trying to comfort him in the truck on the way back. The kid was not crying for the lost Penitentes, but for the gifts he thought he would not now receive. To go back to his village empty-handed was for him the bigger shame. Even Wes blew it off as an experience in respect for the severe conditions of the pampa.

"Well this wasn't quite like camping in Montana, was it?" Wes asked Gerritt after they finally left Roberto and Piedra Negro.

"I don't know. The kid seemed so certain and Eve mentioned the salt figures once. Guess her maid, Hortensia, has family out here that have seen them. Eve comes out to Piedra Negro with Simon and Dr. Stoddard sometimes." Gerritt believed the statues were out there and to not know finally and objectively where they were was depressing.

"Eve has strong ties to the pampa, doesn't she?" Wes asked, looking over at Gerritt, wanting him to open up about her. Gerritt met his stare quickly, then turned back to look at the road.

"She was born here and is just more comfortable with people in the pueblos. Simon Gaerts protects that part of her like a tiger. I don't think he likes me much."

"Eve seems pretty fragile. I can see how he would be suspicious of a Gringo. You know, motives and such." Wes ventured. Gerritt turned to look at Wes again, this time more darkly.

"What motives? She is chasing me, buddy! I know it's probably not good to see her, but Eve has a softness about life I haven't ever seen."

"Yeah, Alice likes her, too. But she is spoiled and innocent. Just be careful, OK?" Wes was thinking about Eve using them and their house to see Gerritt.

"Sure." Gerritt answered, ending the discussion. But knowing Wes was concerned lightened his mood some. By the time they drove into Cerro Verde, they were talking about the endless strike and wondering if there would be news.

CHAPTER 16

Gerritt dreamed about the ephemeral Penitentes that night. Luminous and praying, they swayed in the wind and blowing salt and seemed to move forever away from him as he walked toward them. He woke up cold and found he had kicked off the blankets in his journeys and yet was sweating profusely. He lay there, incapable of even dreaming of finding them.

There was little discussion at the mine the next day of the failure to find Los Penitentes. Whatever talk came out about the trip was the kind of talk Gerritt remembered from Shem and his hunting buddies when they didn't get their elk. The elements became important, the exposure, the extreme cold, the tortuous wind were forces to be feared and spending a night out there was enough for any man. It didn't matter to Barnett or most of the others that they had been on a fruitless search. Los Penitentes were lost in the receding past. Having failed to see them, they no longer existed.

Gerritt sat the following evening, nursing a scotch, and thinking about the trip. Maybe he shouldn't have gone. At the very least, if you didn't try for something, you couldn't be disappointed. Maybe Roberto hadn't failed enough times; fiascoes accumulated in your bones.

And it was all tied to Eve. He feared failure in his job; he was bumped to a higher position before he was ready. But he knew it was what he wanted and must make it work. Eve was extra, the sweet bonus in all this. Maybe because it was all new, no one would get hurt. He thought about his talk with Wes. Whatever love was, this was not it. What he felt was fascination with Eve's innocence and the temptation in the power that she brought him. The mine workings, the machinery, control of all that was heady stuff. These things, these mechanical things, the earth itself, ruled him and would not disappoint.

The phone rang, bringing him back to the room, which was cold, and he decided to build a fire. It was Molly.

"Hi Gerritt," she began, but he only mumbled something, not wanting to see her then.

"Uh, I'm calling to say that I'm leaving Cerro Verde and didn't want to go without telling you." It was as though she had a speech prepared and needed to read it to the end. Gerritt shivered with the cold news, not believing at first that she meant it, then knowing it was true.

"It's just that things aren't working out as I'd hoped, Gerritt," she said seriously. "I didn't want you completely, you knew that. I thought for awhile we had worked out a sort of arrangement, that we understood each other in some basic way."

"I thought so, too," Gerritt said, realizing this was hurting him. "So what was wrong with it?"

"Oh, Gerritt, you really don't see, do you?" She was crying and he hated that. "You don't need me, and you won't need anyone ever. Eve is perfect for you. She will buy you a mine and you don't have to give her anything, at least any of the things that I would have wanted eventually."

He felt the warmth and stability of what Alice Bowen represented moving away from him like the salt monks in his dream, forever out of reach.

"Molly, don't go yet. I'm in control of all of this."

"Are you, Gerritt?" There was no answer. She waited a silent moment.

"Well, goodbye then. I'm going tomorrow morning and I don't want to see you. This is hard enough. I'll write at some point." She hung up. Gerritt sat there until the blankness on the end of the line clicked into a dial tone. Then he laid the phone down on the table, not hanging it up, as though it left some connection still open between them.

As a loss, this seemed to be major, the loss of some undetermined thing. Molly was as close to him as he had ever let a woman get. She understood his need for the mine. And she was leaving and he couldn't make her stay, was powerless to do so. She made up her mind. But in his incapacity to get in his truck and go over to her now, he knew, as Molly knew it, that he was on a new path and it was one way and you had to get to the end before you could turn around.

He shivered again, remembering the cold room. The overhead lights were uncovered and gave a harsh glare that reflected off the pale yellow walls. He built the fire, but didn't light it, sat there on the floor awhile and then got up and into his truck and headed for El Molino. He suddenly wanted a bar, noise, and people he didn't know who would leave him alone to get slowly drunk and forget the losses, whatever they were.

New Camp was crowded, mostly with women, which seemed strange to Gerritt for this time of night. The wind was blowing dust and whipping their long skirts around dark-stockinged legs. He thought about the strike, now in its fifth week, wondering how they had money left to spend. People stopped to watch his truck go by, people with dark, serious faces, cold looking and hungry.

He loved the road down to El Molino and quickly forgot the crowd in New Camp. The pavement was straight and dropped quickly in altitude and he felt he might be able to fly if he could somehow raise the truck wheels off the road. His foot pressed down on the accelerator in this escape from the crowd in the streets above, from Molly, from Roberto, from loss and confusion.

He stopped at Mi Corazon, a place Mike Marshall visited frequently, where there were decent pisco sours and young girls. It was shady inside, darker than the faded day, and Gerritt stood a moment in the door to consider going back to Cerro Verde. The air was fetid with smoke and sweat, hanging thickly around the dozen or so round, crudely built tables. There were a few people, but no one made note of his presence. The jefes from the mine were frequent visitors and their money welcome. A band of three old men played guitar, the Chilean music that to Gerritt seemed to go on and on with no end, but which now was what he wanted. That and drink. He took a table in the back, having pisco sours at first. They weren't as good as the Club's, but they went down. The floor underneath was dirt, worn in a slight depression where people before him sat. He ground his boot into it, glad of the opposing pressure of the hard earth.

When he ordered a bottle of pisco and a glass, a girl with long black hair hanging over one eye brought it, rather pretty, and who looked to be not more than fifteen. A red dress hung limply over her breasts, outlining the nipples clearly and ending above her knees. There was a weak smile as she placed the bottle on the table, then sat down beside him. She rubbed his arms and neck, pouring more pisco for him when he tossed off the glass, her breasts moving up and down as she touched him, talked to him. She put his hand under her dress so he knew she had nothing on underneath. It was soft and wet there. The band seemed to keep playing the same thing over and over again, the rhythmic music moving his head and blurring the girl. The last he remembered was thinking of Eve and starting to cry. The girl smelled strongly of garlic, leaning over him. He saw she was crying, too. Eve was walking away, taking the mine with her. It was sliding along somehow by her side, leaving the green hills at Shem's, the cool water, in the meadow. The hills were so green and soft. He could feel the breeze.

When Gerritt opened his eyes, he was laying on his side, a dirty pillow stuffed up under his head. He knew he was going to be sick, but as long as he didn't move it would wait and he wanted to figure out where he was first. The breeze was coming from an open window, open below a shade, old and crooked. Outside somewhere, he could hear children playing and closed his eyes, trying to think of the hills at the farm.

Someone close to him moaned in sleep. Gerritt turned over with a start to see black hair lying on the pillow next to him, the filthy sheet pulled up over a slight body. He remembered how he had gotten here, the pisco, the girl, the girl talking and touching him. The room was small, totally brown, furnished only with the bed and a broken chair over which was draped the red dress. Shoes, worn out shoes, lay thrown under the chair.

Gerritt reached down on the bed where his pants lay. His head was splitting and he knew he had to get outside. The girl moved. She was tiny, like Eve, and the long black hair fell all over the bed. Gerritt had an urge to touch it, was reaching out, when she sat up in bed, the sheet falling away from her breasts and looked at him. She wasn't anything like Eve and his nausea deepened.

"Dinero, por favor," she said, her voice as hard and empty as the morning and her breath sour with the death of teeth.

Gerritt stared at her. She was only a child. How had she come to this, what unhappiness and hardship had made her come with him? He got up, ignoring her, throwing on his clothes without buttoning them, stepping into boots cold from the night. He had to get out of here into the air.

"Dinero, Gringo!" the girl screamed at him, her teeth showing now, yellow, the gums inflamed with trenchmouth. She grabbed the sheet and started to come after him, but he reached in his pocket and threw some money at her, he had no idea how much. The last he saw of her, she was bending over, squatting naked to pick up the money, the sheet fallen on the floor around her in a pool of light from the exposed bulb.

There was no one on the street and he vomited the night up onto the dirt. It lay green on the brown earth, steaming in the cold morning. All of it did not help his remembering, nor made anything go away. The girl had maybe even brought the pain of yesterday back. He wondered down the street until he recognized where he was, saw his truck still parked in front of the bar. At the end of the callampas, the mud and metal calamina houses, Gerritt found a tank with a water tap. Two dead rats lay bloated at the bottom, but he turned the water on anyway and drank deeply. The cold liquid followed his esophagus down into his stomach, which was not ready to receive it, and then came back up again onto the dirt.

The trip back to New Camp seemed to take hours, his stomach grinding. He retched and spit out the window several times, not stopping because there was nothing now in his stomach to come up, just yellow bile from somewhere deep inside, throwing up the same things every time. Nothing had changed. Eve and the mine would still be there, his role in all of that unresolved. And Molly was gone and he knew that was a clear loss.

Gerritt saw the crowd in New Camp from a mile away and slowed as he came into it. There were people down the whole length of the up street, swarming, moving around like bees. A roar of angry voices greeted him, but opened to let his truck through. He had to roll up the truck windows, making the stench from the vomit on his clothes stronger. The crowd seemed to be mostly women and he remembered briefly the women on the street last night. As he progressed slowly through the mass, they crowded against his truck, their breasts pressing on the sides, their spit on the windows. Some had pans and banged on the truck, which echoed in his head like an empty hall, drumming on the hurt there. It was as though the whole of womankind was after him. Men stood near the doors of the stores, watching.

Finally, he was free, at the upper end of town, able to go faster, get away. It was part of a bad dream, what was going on in New Camp, and he wanted no part of it. By the time he reached his apartment, he wasn't sure those women had really been there. It was all mixed in his mind with Eve, Molly, the Mi Corazon girl and the farm.

The phone was still off the hook as he had left it the night before after Molly hung up. He looked at it and slowly replaced it on the cradle. If there was a time to make a call, to change what was happening, it had passed.

The sheets were clean and cool on his bed and he disappeared into a dreamless sleep.

CHAPTER 17

Felix Alford stood up with the steak plate, then set it carefully down next to the barbecue. His face went serious as he stood there staring out over the camp below them.

"What?" Wes started, looking up from his empty beer.

"Shut-up! Listen!" There was a tinkling noise in the distance that came and then blew away in the wind.

The mine had been silent for weeks, each day blending unremarkably into the next. The watch was boring. Since the night Gerritt saw the rail sections being lifted, there was no further incident, at least none that was seen. The unsuccessful trip out to find Los Penitentes was forgotten. An impatience was building like sweat that all felt but went unsaid because talking about it meant you had to explain it or take some action. The policy was still to wait.

"What is that, Felix? You've been through strikes up in Bolivia, I know?" Wes opened another Escudo and handed it to Alford, who was not paying attention. While Gerritt was sleeping off his hangover, Wes and Alice were having lunch with the Alfords. The men were barbecuing steaks, trying to keep the afternoon breeze from blowing ashes on the meat. It was chilly, the dry wind coming in off the northern pampa from the Andes carried not a trace of moisture.

"Frankly, I don't like the situation. It was like this in Bolivia, especially with the women. Perhaps here it will be more controlled." The steaks were smoking as he moved across the patio and put them on a plate.

"Controlled? What's there to control?" Wes asked. His red hair moved down onto his forehead when he frowned.

"Mmm, crowd emotion I should call it. A few people, usually the women, get together; begin talking about their problems. A few more join them. The next thing you knew a pueblo full of Cholas decided the gringo was the cause of all their problems. There it is again; did you hear it?"

"The strike doesn't seem to have hurt many people--I still see a lot of big new cars around. How do they do it? I bought a '38 Chevy!"

"Yes, but you see those cars represent a life savings, sometimes everything in the world a family may own. The empleados, and the obreros too, can't save their money in a bank because in five years it wouldn't be worth anything. Instead, they buy things, dollars, cars, jewelry, things that won't lose value here."

"So when it's time to go on vacation, they just sell something?" Wes said jokingly. It all seemed so impractical.

"Exactly. But about now I expect the buyers are getting a little sparse. Steaks are ready." The sound in the distance was getting louder.

"Sounds like somebody cleaning out their closet," Wes said, smiling. Then the crinkles disappeared from around his eyes when he saw that Felix was again staring seriously toward New Camp.

"What's that noise, Felix? I could hear it out the kitchen window?" Thea stuck her head out the door, her long nearly white hair blowing in front of her face.

Felix turned slowly and smiled at her. Thea was beautiful. The blond hair and pale skin glowed in the early afternoon sun.

"I suspect it's a protest of some sort. Not to worry. Wes and I better go down and have a look," he answered blandly and handed the steaks to her.

She looked at him a long moment, expecting more explanation.

"Well, all right then. But your steak won't be rare if I keep it in the oven. Don't be long."

"It will be fine. We'll just go have a look and be right back. And Thea," he paused. "I'm leaving my truck, key's are in it. We'll take Wes's."

She seemed to understand the import of leaving a means of transportation and disappeared into the house to tell Alice.

Wes and Felix hurried down the hill, the houses flying past in their peripheral vision as they intently looked ahead toward the main offices near the entrance to the Jefe Camp.

"My God, look!" Wes's eyes widened. From the main offices, the road went out of the gate and straight toward New Camp, descending slightly. It passed the brightly painted, new apartments, which were designated for the empleados. Near where these buildings started, a crowd of people was coming toward them, swaying and crashing together what looked like large pans. They filled the street, moving slowly upward in a wave a quarter mile long.

Wes and Felix climbed out of the truck to find most of the other Jefes near the office buildings lined up as if in a sort of stand. Reicher and Barnett were there already, as were Dillon, Ortega and Blain.

"I don't see Gerritt here, Felix. I think I'll run over to his apartment and see if I can find him," Wes said, swinging his large frame back into the truck.

"Well, OK then, but you better hurry back. They'll be up here in another 15 minutes and we may need you." Felix was worried, but Wells would be one more person. He wondered briefly where the Carabinieros were.

Wes thought about Alice, now at home with Thea Alford and whether Thea was telling her the stories she heard from Felix about giant, Bolivian Chola women peeing in dead Gringo's faces. This was insane. Things like that didn't happen anymore, did they? The banging was getting louder and he knew Alice would be frightened. Surely Gerritt must have heard it, too. Where was he?

Wes pounded on Gerritt's door several times, walking out to the street to listen each time to the growing clamor down by the offices. His truck was here; he must be inside. Wes was just about to give up when he happened to glance into Gerritt's bedroom and saw him sprawled on the bed, unmoving.

"Gerritt, wake up! Gerritt! Gerritt!" Wes screamed, banging on the large window, which shook with his blows.

Gerritt moved slowly, trying to ignore the noise from the window. It hurt his head and he unconsciously put a pillow up to cover his ears.

"God damn you, Gerritt! Open the door or I'm going to bust this window," Wes hollered in a lower voice, becoming really angry. When he pounded again, his fist went through the thin window. The glass flew away and onto the bed, cutting him only slightly. He looked at his hand, not knowing how he broke the window. It seemed like only a small effort.

Gerritt finally stirred seriously with the sound of the falling glass, turned over and blinked his eyes against the daylight shining around Wes, who was framed in the middle of his broken window.

"What the fuck are you doing, man?"

"Let me in!" Wes screamed at him. Gerritt nodded without saying anything else, staggered to the door, which he opened and then headed back for the bedroom.

"Put on your clothes. For Christ sake, what are you doing in bed at this hour of the day? Come on, where are your pants?"

Gerritt looked at him and then remembered, remembered his pants lying on the filthy bed. The girl, the child. He groaned and sat down heavily on the bed and leaned over on his hands.

Wes looked around the room, finding Gerritt's clothes on the floor, but when he picked them up they reeked of sour vomit and alcohol and he threw them down.

"You can't wear these. You must have really tied one on last night." Wes began rummaging in Gerritt's closet and came up with a pair of jeans and a shirt.

"Here, put these on", Wes said. Gerritt sat there, unmoving, thinking about how that girl looked like Eve from the back and then the shock of having her turn around to face him, the hard face, the rotten teeth.

"Gerritt, move it! We don't have much time." Wes was getting impatient and knew they needed to be there for whatever was about to happen.

"There's a crowd marching up from New Camp on the General Offices, banging pans. Everyone's down there. They need us. You've got to come!"

"Marching?" He looked up at Wes with red eyes and sallow skin, his black hair matted around his face. "What the fuck for?"

"Shit, I don't know. I think they're tired of the strike. Sorry about the window." Wes shook the spread and glass went onto the floor. He pulled the shade. He would have to call Duvillard to replace it.

"Yeah, maybe." Gerritt shrugged, he was slowly remembering the morning drive back from El Molino, the people in the streets, the spit on his truck window.

"Yeah, ...yeah. I saw them this morning, getting ready," he said with a mushy mouth. He stood up to dress, sat down, then got up again, feeling nauseous and weak. Somehow he brushed his teeth, splashed some water on his stale face, and was ready to go. With some effort he was able to concentrate on what Wes was telling him, putting the night away for a later time when he would be able to regurgitate it slowly, give it a meaning if he could find one.

When they arrived at the offices, the mass of people was only 200 yards away, still moving toward them. Wes parked the truck and they came around the building to where the other Jefes were standing. Reicher looked over at them acknowledging their presence, seemingly glad they were there. Blain had some binoculars and was peering through them, his tall lanky form like some rare bird species.

"My God," Blain exclaimed. "It's women. All women! Those are cooking pots they're banging!" He lowered his glasses and looked helplessly at the others.

"Rotter," said Alford under his breath, kicking at the dry earth. "Let's hope they only want to talk!"

Gerritt was now awake. He knew Alford's stories about the altiplano. Ned Tully used to work in Bolivia, too. Those were tough times. If you were a Gringo, you carried your papers with you. Life was temporary there and sometimes things happened after which you left quickly or not at all.

They watched the wave of women coming toward them and then the mass seemed to stop, arrest for a moment and turn inward. The women parted slightly in the middle and a large black and shiny limousine crept through the crowd noiselessly, inching slowly through the collection of humanity.

"That's Hidalgo, the bastard," Barnett growled around his cigar. "Might have known he'd be behind this."

The black Continental drove slowly up the hill in front of the women who resumed their march and pot banging. When the car reached the offices, it turned slowly around so it was facing the women. The windows were dark, it was difficult to see inside, but they were sure it was Hidalgo. And then the door opened and he got out, his greasy hair slicked back; dark glasses hid his eyes. Two bodyguards got out with him and they walked over toward the Jefes, but not close enough to talk. It was obvious they were observers of this reception, not participants.

Reicher watched the women come on, banging together the pots they cooked in, expressing their needs in the only way they knew how. Their pots were empty. There was no money left to feed their families.

As they approached the front of the offices, the tide slowed and spread horizontally, nearly surrounding the Gringos and the black car. Gerritt and Wes stepped back, letting Blain and Reicher move out in front. Reicher noticeably tried to stand taller, rocking back and forth on his heels. Putting his hand in the front of his shirt, he stood firm. The odor of the horde of women was strong and the wind blew it over them. Garlic from their breath, melded with sweat of many nights lovemaking. Womanly, fecund smells. These were the women of the mine, heavy with the weight of years and pasta and childbirth, with flat bottoms and protruding bellies and breasts. The bolos and hatpins from the old days in Bolivia were missing, but the blood of those earlier Bolivianas coursed in these veins. Slowly the din of the pans subsided, the swish of layered skirts grew quiet, waiting.

Curt Reicher stepped forward. Blain should have handled this. He was senior in camp when Driscoll wasn't there. But Blain's Spanish was minimal and he asked Reicher to speak.

The mass of women repulsed Reicher. He and his wife Nell lived the sheltered, clean, ordered existence of the Swiss. This presence, this conglobation of stinking humanity made him feel weak. The smells were suffocating, but this had to be finished now. Doing anything other than what he must do was unthinkable.

"Buenas dias, Señoras," he said with as much aplomb as possible in a circumstance that engendered only fear. A pan crashed to the ground and he started. The women moved restlessly and talked to each other.

"Comida, comida!" Shouts came from several places in the crowd.

"Silencia!" Reicher screamed back at them, and he got it. "Quiro hablar con una mujer no mas." Talking to this mass was clearly impossible and there had to be a spokeswoman, there had to be. They whispered and moved among themselves.

Gerritt squinted, examining them carefully and thought he recognized a few of the women he had seen in New Camp that morning. The day was bright and hurt his eyes, especially the reflections off the pans they carried. He looked over at the Union officials for a sign, but they stood blankly like spectators at a cockfight, with arms folded and faces vacant, unreadable eyes behind the glasses.

A woman separated herself from the mass and stepped forward. She was heavy and dressed in black. Her hair, twisted and matted up behind her round head, was greying. Dark stockings hung wrinkled in rings about her thick legs, and when she opened her mouth to talk with the women behind her, Gerritt saw she had very few teeth.

"That's Guillermo Arias's wife," Alford whispered to Wes and Gerritt.

"The driver killed in that truck accident?" Wes asked.

"Yes, she has 9 children."

Señora Arias narrowed her black eyes at Reicher, showing creases in her leathery skin, and letting the pan she was carrying clatter to the street as a last gesture of protest.

"What will you do, Señor Reicher?" she asked in broken English. "We are hungry, our children hungry. We fight nobody. We not ask for this huelga. We do only what Sindicato say to do. It is our way."

She looked for support from Hidalgo, waiting, expecting him to now come forward. Hidalgo did not move, but his mouth tensed up below the glasses and mustache. He appeared to make the Señora nervous. She wet her lips and wiped her hands on her black skirts.

"Señora Arias, we realize full well what this is costing you and costing El Condor. But the matter must be settled by the rules of the pliego." Reicher looked over at the expressionless Hidalgo, furious with him for being here. He was a presence, anymore, in everything that happened at the mine.

"And it must be settled in accordance with our company's policies and their ability to pay," he continued, directing this last remark to Hidalgo, spitting it out, this at least giving him some satisfaction.

"But Señor Reicher," the Senora pleaded, her hands raised helplessly. "We waited. Sindicato is your matter. Our worry is with los niños who grow thin and sick."

"Oh, brother," Barnett said around his cigar. "Shit! She's not starving, none of them are."

"But they are hurting, Art," Juan Ortega said quietly next to him. "The men don't give them much to run the house anyway and now with the strike things are worse. The huelga is not their fault."

Art nodded in disgust. Juan was right. The women had been told to come, another of Hidalgo's ideas to squeeze Gringo balls.

Gerritt felt his head throb at Ortega's words.

"What do you mean, Ortega? They trust that bastard, Hidalgo! Elected him again after he robbed them blind." Gerritt felt nauseous, wished he were back in bed.

"The women are here, Gerritt, that's real. Whether they support Hidalgo or not, we have to give them something." Juan's face was red.

Gerritt nodded; he couldn't protest. In this Ortega, too, was a Gringo. He would react as they all were to this whole thing. He looked over at Hidalgo, standing near the outrageous automobile paid for by Union funds, the bodyguards leaning on it, bitter and mean. The whole thing seemed suddenly ludicrous to him. The needs of the women were mixed up with the absurd true purpose of the act, this march on the company, this show of strength behind the heavy skirts and the clattering pans.

"I wonder if the women know they're being used?" Gerritt said aloud. Barnett looked over at him for a long moment, surprised at the insightful comment.

"Probably," Art answered to no one. "We'll give in a little and then Hidalgo can save face when he settles the strike in Santiago. Clever of him to think of this."

The women started moving again. They were restless and tired.

"What will you do for us?" Señora Arias pressed toward Reicher when he did not answer her last words. The force and weight of her pushed at him and though he did not move you could almost see him mentally take a step back from her. Reicher began with the prearranged conditions and Gerritt realized that management had anticipated a confrontation. Perhaps not in this form, but a confrontation in the Camp that would affect the outcome of the pliego in Santiago.

"I will open the Pulperillas," he started, but was soon interrupted by the commotion from the crowd. The murmuring and swishing began again and the pots clanged, but it was a different sound this time, coming because the women were crowding together to hear what Reicher was saying.

"Silencia, mujeres!" Señora Arias screamed and the women hushed.

"You will have to pay..." This was greeted by moaning. There was, after all, no money to pay. "But you may pay later and a discount will be in effect, but I caution you to buy only what you need until the huelga is finished. El Condor knows you have suffered and wants to help you now. Please return to your homes. The Pulperillas will open tomorrow morning. They will need today to prepare for you."

Señora Arias looked over at Hidalgo, her face filled with fear. Was this enough? If it wasn't, what should she do now? Her hand went up in front of her face and it seemed as though she might cry. Hidalgo gave her a quick, almost imperceptible nod and while they all watched in silence, he turned and got into the back of the black limousine. The motor was started. The car with its dark contents pushed its way quietly back through the accumulation of women, who touched it as it passed as though the act somehow lent them support. And then it was gone, swallowed by the mass that spawned it.

The Señora stood there looking intently at Reicher, the air still wired with tension.

"Well, Señora Arias," Reicher stepped toward her and began in his easy Spanish, taking her hand down away from her face and holding it in his. Her hand was rough and hard.

"You should be pleased. The pliego can be settled now. You and I have just negotiated some basis on which to live together another year. Take your friends and go back to your children where you are needed. I know your strength. Keep it," he said kindly, patting her hand.

She smiled, her dark skin crackling at the edges of her eyes, turning it warm. Reicher smiled back at her. In some elemental way, she knew he understood their need. But then, she withdrew her hand from his and backed away. Though she trusted his word, Reicher would always be the Gringo, the unreachable Jefe. Her daughters could work in his home, but they would never break bread with his family. It had been that way for too long to change.

"Gracias Señores," she said quietly and whatever else might have been said was left in the stagnant air between them. She turned and with the other women moved away down the hill leaving a hint of garlic and sourness.

Two days later, the office at the mine received word from Santiago that the pliego was settled and the mine was to restart operation immediately. It would cost El Condor, but the ore body was rich enough to cover it easily. Mining expenses remained cheaper than in the States and New York knew occasional settlements were part of the package. The fear engendered by the women's march was forgotten in the flurry of activity that ensued to ready the mine and equipment.

Gerritt was relieved to be working again. The slow passing of the days during the strike gave him too much time for reflection. He reconciled the night Molly told him she was leaving and then the girl in El Molino as a nightmare having nothing to do with his life. There was no other way. Otherwise it was too painful. With the settlement, Driscoll would soon be back in Camp with his family and Gerritt knew he would see Eve.

CHAPTER 18

The mine was running again. The familiar growl of trucks laboring up the steep mine roads sang to Gerritt. Shovels whined, moving on their axes, the sweetest sound he could imagine. Work, production, something for your effort. These were the things that were understandable, in which he could bury thinking. Drinking their noises and addressing their malfunctions was easy and it was busy enough that he could forget Eve completely at times. Although he suspected that she was the source of his discontent of recent weeks, her image was drowned in oil dripping from crankcases, and she disappeared in the dust of the recently resumed daily blasting. Gerritt could concentrate on his ore tonnages and nothing else, falling into bed each night too exhausted to dream. He was a Shift Foreman now, responsible for the eight hours allotted to him and he meant to haul more ore than any other shift and do it every day.

"Juan says you're hi-grading," Wes asked him one morning when they met for coffee after Gerritt's night shift. "Are you?"

"Nah," Gerritt answered blandly. "He's jealous because he can't beat my tonnages, that's all." He looked up at Wes, coldly, a muscle in his jaw moving involuntarily. Wes knew he was lying and he didn't do it well. They considered each other carefully. He wasn't ready to talk to Wes about it and Wes wasn't ready to believe in the deception. The matter was dropped, but did not go away.

There were times when Gerritt ignored a call from the Jefe Patio asking if the next train convoy should load waste. It gave him a devilish thrill to give the shovel operators loading waste the night off. By doing this, he freed trucks and was able to increase his ore tonnages to levels the other shifts couldn't possibly match. He knew it was wrong, but did it anyway and then covered the action in his mind as the right choice. It made his shift look good, but quickly created resentment among the other shifters. Hi-grading was not good engineering. The waste had to be removed, and always was integrated into the mine plan, balancing the amount for each shift. But not on Gerritt's; his shift hauled ore.

A week later, Barnett told Gerritt to stop by his office after shift, a friendly request, almost pleasant for Art. That afternoon, Gerritt sat down in the chair across from him, leaning back casually. Barnett no longer scared him.

Art looked at him for a long moment, trying to understand what Wells might be thinking and then smiling carefully and a bit snidely, began to read him out in a level monotone between his teeth which clenched the ever present cigar.

"You are hi-grading your shift, Wells. I've checked the tonnages of ore and waste carefully over the last two weeks." He threw a sheaf of papers across the desk to Gerritt, who ignored them, already knowing what they said.

"I won't tolerate it, as long as I'm Mine Foreman!" His face grew redder as he talked around the cigar.

"Not only is it bad engineering," he went on at a measured speed. "It's not fair to let the other shifts clean up your shit! Ortega follows you. He loaded one shift entirely of waste last week. That doesn't go here! Is that clear?"

Gerritt stared at him, his chair still tipped back, unmoving. He didn't care what Barnett thought. Art could pop a blood vessel and he wouldn't give a damn. It was still his shift, his own to do with as he liked. Gerritt knew that Driscoll and New York saw those tonnages and the name that went with them. Barnett was waiting for some sort of reaction from him, waiting for him to blow up, and Gerritt wouldn't give him that satisfaction. He knew as he sat there that Art couldn't touch him. The feeling was like one he had once as a twelve year old when he stayed hanging from the monkey bars after the recess bell was rung to resume classes; it was his first hard-on.

"Is that all?" he asked, still holding the other man with his icey stare. Gerritt couldn't have told Art why he was hi-grading, even if he had wanted to. It simply seemed the logical thing to do, an urge, an inclination rather than a plan. Perhaps he would back off a little. But he wouldn't tell Barnett that, not now.

"Yeah, that's it," Art bit down on the cigar. There wasn't anything else to say. He had his piece of Wells's ass. Maybe the bastard would listen, maybe not.

Gerritt let the front of the chair bump to the floor and slowly pealed himself into a standing position, looking at the furious Barnett sitting across the desk from him.

"OK," Gerritt said, pursing his lips. "Think I'll go get a beer."

Barnett sat there for a long time after Wells left, looking at the empty chair, wondering if he made a point, or was simply shooting with an empty gun.

That was also the week that Driscoll brought his family back from Santiago. Things were finished there, the pliego settled, the papers signed. The mine was safe from further threat of the huelga for another year.

Gerritt did not go to see Eve. She would call. He knew she would, but he wanted to give her this chance to let whatever was between them die its ridiculous death, or let her be the one to continue it. When the call came it wasn't Eve, it was her father.

"Hello, Wells. Joe Driscoll here," the gruff voice said, now so recognizable. There was silence.

"Uh, Wells?" Driscoll seemed nervous.

"Yes Sir, how are you?" Gerritt's surprise was total. So this was how it would be. Driscoll would tell him he would not see Eve again. Maybe she stayed in Santiago with her mother. He found he had a sudden ache, pulling at his chest like fright, that he didn't understand. Was it Eve? Or had Barnett gotten to Driscoll.

"Fine, fine. Yes, now that the pliego is settled, I'm fine. I expect you are glad to have the mine running again, too." But his voice was warmer. What did he want?

"I sure am!" Gerritt replied, relaxing some.

"Uh, how is Eve?"

"That's why I'm calling you. She would like to see you." He paused, the blank silence filled the receiver like water and Gerritt could feel himself slipping under. Driscoll continued.

"Anna and I want you to come to supper tomorrow. Nothing fancy, just family."

Family? What did that mean? Driscolls did not entertain except for the required yearly party at the Gerencia where he met Eve. He thought about Anna Driscoll, trying to remember her, and realized he couldn't recall her at all. He only saw her taking Eve away and was looking only at Eve. What did she think of him? What could he possibly say to her? Not knowing his own mother, Anna Driscoll was an alien being. A mother, especially of a girl he wanted to fuck, was completely foreign to him. He realized he hadn't answered.

"Uh, yeah. Yeah sure. I'm on day shift this week."

"Yes, I know, we'll expect you at 5. Goodbye then."

Gerritt sat holding the phone for a moment, as though there was something more to be said, and then put it carefully back on the hook. Driscoll would not have called him without reason. He would see Eve. The thought of her came back then. The softness of her hair and face, her smell, returned and stayed with him through the night. He wanted to tell someone. No, it would be better not to tell anyone, even Wes. Maybe especially not Wes.

Gerritt arrived at the Gerencia at 5 sharp; Driscoll seemed rather emphatic about the time, he thought. He showered after shift, deciding not to wear a tie but put on a clean white shirt, starched too much for his liking by the laundry in New Camp. The maid, Hortencia, answered the door and took his jacket, looking at him directly with the blackest of eyes. He wondered who she was currently sticking pins into, and hoped it wasn't him. Hortensia pointed to the library and he walked across the marble foyer, inhaling the fragrance from the growing vines and flowers, and onto the soft oriental rug in the library. Driscoll was sitting by the fire reading the Mercurio. When he saw Wells, he let the paper fall into his lap, but didn't get up.

"Hello Gerritt," he said easily. "What would you like to drink?" A mozo, dressed in a white jacket stood ready to receive his order. Gerritt glanced at him wondering how old he was; there was no beard on his smooth skin; the Atacameños didn't have facial hair unless they were of mixed blood.

"Escoces, por favor. Un poquito de agua," he told the mozo, who nodded and fixed the drink from a bar there in the library.

"Sit here," Driscoll indicated the chair across from him. Gerritt sank into comfort, the fire's warmth had entered the rich leather. The use of fireplaces was a luxury here as the wood had to be brought up from the south. The only thing to burn on the pampa was llareta, a slow growing fungus, and it was getting scarce.

"Thank you, Mr. Driscoll," he said stiffly.

"I think you ought to call me Joe, Gerritt. We have a lot to discuss." He took a long pull on his drink, which Gerritt assumed to be scotch straight, the way Alford drank it. But this was good scotch, a smoky single-malt, unlike the cheaper scotch Gerritt drank at the Club that came from the Argentine.

Gerritt looked at Joe Driscoll, the round, pocked face, the receding hair, and nodded as calmly as he could, not knowing why he was here.

Driscoll got up, laying the paper on the floor and walked over to the fire. He seemed to be pumping himself up.

"Mmmgh," he cleared his throat and looked down into the fire, resting his hand on the carved mantel.

"I, uh, we hoped that the time interval of the pliego would be sufficient for Eve to forget about you, Gerritt. She has done this before, becomes infatuated very easily. The doctors tell us it is part of her, uh, her condition. To be needed, I mean. And she also tires of people easily. I'm sure you can appreciate the problem we have here."

Gerritt nodded, chewing nervously on his lower lip. No, he did not appreciate the problem at all. He was feeling, instead, confined.

Joe smiled at him, then. "Well, our Eve definitely did not forget you." His voice was shakey. He looked away and took another pull on his scotch. Protection of your children is often difficult and not clearly defined. Joe

Driscoll wanted to be sure he was doing the right thing. But what was the right thing?

"So you see," he continued, "we are uncertain how to handle this situation. Eve is a willful child. She will see you even if she is forbidden it."

Gerritt smiled faintly, knowing this was true, remembering the circumstances of his first visit to the Gerencia.

"I've done a great deal of thinking about this," Joe said turning to him, "And I think that you, also, would come to see her if she asked. Am I right?"

All the past weeks piled up on him then. How could he answer when he didn't know, himself, how he would respond to such a request from Eve. But he knew Eve would call, was expecting her to call. It wasn't simple; she wasn't Molly. What if it didn't work? He would be screwed.

Driscoll seemed to see his confusion, but pressed for an answer.

"Would you see her, Gerritt?" he asked again, raising his voice slightly, and standing up straight.

"Yes, yes I would see her," he answered finally, knowing it to be true. She would call and he would come. But there was something else. Gerritt was drawn to Eve, as to the earth. She was of this place and he wanted to enter here, to stay. They looked at each other carefully, the only noise the crackling of the fire.

Driscoll sank into his chair, finished his drink in two swallows and set the glass down heavily on the table between them.

"Yes, well, I thought so," he said resignedly. "Anna and I think it is better that you see her, with our knowledge, here and with us present most of the time. We ask that you be indulgent of her. Eve is all we have," he said sternly. It was not a request; it would be expected.

There were footsteps across the marble entrance and Driscoll stood up; Gerritt followed his cue. Anna and Eve entered together as if summoned by a bell. Gerritt wondered if they were listening and decided it would have been impossible. Eve was dressed in a blue filmy thing that fell around her soft body and melted into the floor. He had forgotten how pale and beautiful she was. She ran to him, leaving her mother with an empty outstretched hand.

"Oh Gerritt, Gerritt, I missed you!" She pressed herself against him and he could feel the softness of her breasts through the thin fabric of her dress. He took her arms, knowing her parents were watching him, pushed her away a safe distance and kissed her lightly on the forehead.

"Dinner is ready," Anna announced. Gerritt had hardly noticed Anna, and now turned to smile at the worried face. He truly did not remember her. Was that how mothers looked?

"Fine, I'm hungry, aren't you, Gerritt?" Driscoll said, clapping Gerritt on the back and urging him toward the dining room.

Yes, Gerritt was ready to eat. The scotch was in his veins and he felt warm for the first time since he arrived in this place.

Dinner went well. Eve was so happy she infected the others, her laughter ringing against the crystal chandelier. They all relaxed. It wasn't as though anything was resolved or finished. But by discussing the relationship, talking about it openly, Eve's desire for Gerritt became tangible and, even if uncontrollable, it was now something that fell into the realm of organized thought and action.

"How's the shift going?" Joe Driscoll asked over coffee when Eve was finally subdued and sleepy with wine.

"Mmm, OK, I think," Gerritt answered thoughtfully. How much did Joe know? He must be careful. "I have a problem with Barnett now and then. I try to haul as much ore as possible and he sometimes doesn't agree with the way I do it."

He tried to sound forceful, in control of his shift. But Driscoll seemed unaware of the conflict between Gerritt and Art. Was there one? Gerritt was just now seeing that Barnett's reaction might be important. In Montana, he usually acted alone; indeed he made unilateral decisions all his life because he had to. Shem was there, but as an older uncle and never having been a parent he was not inclined to become one. He provided shelter and food, as was his responsibility for his dead sister's boy, but Gerritt was allowed to develop his thinking on his own, at times a lonely and confusing task.

But, Driscoll seemed not to know of any problem at the mine.

"Good, good," he nodded. "After all, that's what you're out there for isn't it?"

There was brandy by the fire and then Gerritt noticed the Driscolls both yawn and knew it was time to go. Eve walked him to the door, clinging to his arm. She didn't wear perfume, but she had a clean smell, like a baby. He put on his jacket, held by the mozo, then turned to her.

"Goodnight Eve. I'm glad you're home." He tilted her chin up with his hand and kissed her softly on the mouth. She didn't kiss him back, but her lips tasted sweet and were warm. He let his hand drop slowly, brushing lightly against the blue dress over her full breasts. She pushed toward him then, but he put his hands on her arms and kissing her lightly on the cheek, said goodnight again and left her standing in the doorway framed with the green and pink bougainvillea.

The wind was blowing outside as Gerritt got in his truck and he felt the warmth of the evening go out of him. The cold reality of all of this washed over. The Driscolls had just adopted him, but in some way he felt imprisoned in a cage the way Eve was found. What kind of cage was it and could he get out if he wanted to leave?

CHAPTER 19

Gerritt didn't see Barnett at all the following week. He was on afternoon shift and when he arrived at the office each day around three, Barnett was conspicuously missing. Felix Alford, whose shift preceded Gerritt's, gave him the briefing, not Art. At first Gerritt was glad not to see him. After their discussion of the previous week, he had no desire to talk further about how he ran his shift. When asked about Art's absence, Felix only shrugged and said he was away on leave. Away where? Felix didn't know. But did Felix know? Did anyone know? Gerritt didn't change his mine plan; he was running the shift in the same way. If his tonnages dropped suddenly, as they would if he began to load the normal amounts of waste, somebody, perhaps Driscoll might wonder what was going on, or what he did before to make his daily ore tonnage so high.

On Friday, Gerritt was beginning to get a little anxious. Barnett was still not around and the rest of the shifters seemed to avoid talking about Art. And Gerritt would be seeing Eve on Saturday. How long could he keep his hands off her when she was all over him? He was sitting at his desk after shift rolling a toy truck around he bought in New Camp because it reminded him of the mine trucks. He was sweating, though the room wasn't warm, and was just wiping his forehead on a sleeve when Wes and Juan Ortega came in for night shift briefing at 10PM.

"What's eating you, Wells?" Wes asked, noticing Gerritt's sweaty brow and obvious agitation. "The mine fall in?" Wes sat his large frame down on the chair opposite Gerritt.

"Shit, Wes. I haven't seen Barnett all week. What's going on around here? Has he said anything?" Gerritt's hair hung limp over his eyes, hiding the lines in his forehead, but Wes could tell something was eating at him. He looked sick.

"Don't know. He's out of here. I heard you had words last week over the hi-grading."

"Is that all? You're sure? It was nothing. Why did he leave, then?"

"Hi-grading isn't nothing, Gerritt! None of us like it. Maybe he was told to lay off you." Wes looked straight at Gerritt, waiting for him to raise his head, to respond to what they both knew was happening.

"By who?" His head jerked up and he stared at Wes, the muscles twitching in his jaw. He remembered he had lied to Wes about the waste tonnage and saw mistrust in Wes's eyes.

"Why don't you tell me, Gerritt. You're seeing Eve again, aren't you?" Wes wasn't mad at him, just disappointed. "What are you doing?" He shut the door to Gerritt's office. Everyone didn't need to hear this.

"God damn it, Wes," Gerritt said, standing up and throwing his hard hat at the wall. "I don't know what's going on. People go messing in your life. I can't stand it. I had such a clear idea of what I wanted and it's getting all fucked up. I don't give a good Goddamn for Barnett or what he thinks or what any of the rest of them think!" He paused and looked at Wes, who was staring at him uneasily.

"Maybe I don't even care what you think."

They stood there, some distance between them, the friendship smoking and about to burn up. Wes slid off the chair and put on his hard-hat. Something was wrong and he knew it. Gerritt was on some blessed wild horse and right now he just wanted to get out of the way.

"Wait. No, no, I do care what you think," Gerritt said quickly before Wes could leave. It bothers me because you are so straight about your job, I guess. We aren't at all alike."

Wes turned and looked back at Gerritt. He looked lost and Wes wanted to help him, but he had to figure out how and that would take some time.

"No, for sure we're not alike. I better get to work on my shift, Gerritt." When he went out the main door, it blew against the wall, banging loudly.

Barnett ordered the hydraulic cylinder removed after it shut on him; since then the door had been a free spirit. Wes reached back in the room without looking at Gerritt and carefully shut it.

Jason Stoddard was putting away some medical journals he was reading in his office when the phone rang Saturday morning. He wearily answered it, the hope of an early day fading. It was Gerritt Wells. Stoddard's ears had been burning all week. His son-in-law, Art Barnett complained constantly, before leaving for the States, about having the mine controlled by this man. And Hugh Dillon, always objective and fair, mentioned Gerritt's behavior to him at a dinner party the previous week. Jason wasn't sure he ought to see him, but Gerritt was insistent and he acquiesced.

Gerritt hadn't slept much. It took the entire night to decide to come to Jason at all. Why should Jason Stoddard help him when Art was his daughter's husband? Gerritt counted on Stoddard's integrity, and secondly on his curiosity.

"Well, Gerritt. It's been some time since I've seen you. How's the head?" he asked uneasily. Gerritt looked awful, unkempt and very tired.

"OK, thank you." He was quiet and didn't look at Jason, nor did he sit down. Maybe he shouldn't have come.

"How can I help you?" Stoddard said after a moment, when Gerritt continued to look at the floor in silence.

"It's about the mine," he began, looking up slowly at the doctor, whose concern showed in the grey furrow between his eyes. "About the mine and me and Barnett and Eve Driscoll. Somehow, I'm getting everything out of whack. At least other people say I am." He was thinking of Wes in particular.

"How do *you* feel about it?"

"God damn it, I don't know how the fuck I feel about it! Why do you think I'm here? Do you think I want to come to you! You're related to Barnett! I don't want sympathy, I just want to get everything straight." He was sweating profusely, beads of perspiration on his upper lip.

"All right, all right. Why don't you sit down, Gerritt." Jason sighed and turned his chair toward the window. How to begin? This was definitely a very anxious young man. He swung his chair back around to face Gerritt and leaned across the desk.

"Gerritt, I know about Eve. And Art was told early this week to let you run your shift as you wished." He was about to say more, but paused to see how Gerritt would react.

"Who, who told him to lay off me?" Gerritt screamed clenching his teeth.

"You know the answer to that one, Gerritt. Joe Driscoll is a protective father and wants Eve to be happy," Stoddard said quietly, watching for the reaction.

Gerritt shut his eyes and fell back into the chair. Of course! He had known, but he was realizing now that everyone knew, must know. He was empty inside and could feel his heart pumping blood as if into hollow spaces until he was dry as the summer dirt when there was no rain.

"Gerritt, I don't know what is making you see Eve Driscoll, what, if any, motives are behind it. I do think you should go away for a while; get some perspective on what is happening to you. You are nearly due for long leave to the States. I'm sure Blain would let you go home. Think about where you are going and what you want to do here in Cerro Verde. Art's doing that right now. I doubt seriously that he can live with your new influence. And that, of course, worries me."

"No, I couldn't leave now, not with the strike recently settled. We're too busy. It's not a good time." Gerritt heard the excuses echoing in his ears like echoes returning across a canyon and stopped with his mouth open.

"Of course you can. It will all be here when you get back and maybe you'll see things differently," Jason said softly.

"Maybe." Being away from the mine was frightening to him.

"Will you go to your parents?"

"They're dead," Gerritt said numbly to the floor, and then when there was no reply, he lifted his head and found Jason looking at him. It was the first time Jason saw real pain registered on Gerritt's face.

"A car accident when I was a kid. I lived with my Uncle afterwards. He farms in Montana." Gerritt could still remember the night, the confusion, the loneliness that had seeped into his veins like water into cold, leaky boots. He was taken to Shem's by neighbors, people who thought it kinder to tell him nothing. And Shem wouldn't tell him at first because of his own pain at having to identify his only sister with her head laying severed on the gurney in the morgue. No one would tell him why his parents weren't coming back. He lived in that uncertain space for weeks not knowing where he belonged. Now, Gerritt couldn't remember his parents' faces. The unpleasant memories of their departure had faded, dried and blown away.

"I would see Shem. He would like that," Gerritt said thinking ahead to the farm.

Stoddard sighed and sat back in his chair. He was tired, but glad there would be some temporary relief from the tension between Art and Gerritt. Maybe the time would allow them both to reconsider their situations, especially Gerritt. He seemed compulsively driven to maximize the output of the mine, at all costs. The men on which he trod and a sensible mine plan were not considerations, but rather hindrances to his own agenda. His anxiety seemed overwhelming. Something was driving him, but what? Jason felt the relationship with Eve was separate from the issues in the mine, but Joe Driscoll had compromised all that and Jason knew he needed to talk to Joe, and soon.

"Why don't you come back to see me when you return," Stoddard smiled at him. "And we'll talk about it again then."

Gerritt said he would call.

But going home was an indetermination, a lying in, expecting a live baby but catching a stillbirth in your hands. Gerritt went, hopefully returning to the green grass and fertile smells of the farm, looking for something that wasn't there. He called Wes to tell him he was going and Wes was pleased and genuinely wished him well, hoping Gerritt would come back as the person who had arrived in Cerro Verde with him a year ago.

Shem was plowing when Gerritt arrived and didn't come to the station to meet him. He hitched a ride from town with a neighbor who took the opportunity to share his previous winter's illnesses. The house was the same, maybe less clean and organized than when his Aunt was alive. But there was a chicken stew in the oven and the smells of a wood fire and food were welcoming.

His bed had fresh sheets and as he was hanging up the few things he packed, he heard Shem come in.

"Gerritt," Shem smiled at him and put out his hands. Shem was shorter than he was, stooped from bending over in the garden so many years, and he smelled of sweat and earth as Gerritt hugged him.

"Shem, so good to see you." He really meant it. There were so many things about Shem and the farm that were solid and dependable. He needed that strength right now.

"You look tired, Gerritt. They working you too hard down under?" Gerritt's face was lined and anxious. "I'm going to shower. Grab a beer. I'll be out in a minute. Supper is ready."

"Thanks. Smells like home." Shem smiled at him.

He found beer in the fridge and turned on the TV. The reception at the farm wasn't so good. He found a basketball game between two local junior colleges. The conversation with Shem was along the same lines, the neighbors, a barn that burned the previous winter. He didn't talk about the mine until they sat down to eat.

"Good stew." Gerritt raised his beer.

"So you seem to be doing well, Gerritt." Shem said and it was more a question. The few letters he had written his Uncle were non-specific.

"Yeah, I run my own shift now. Things move pretty fast. It's a huge pit. We are hauling upwards of 400,000 tons of ore a year, running around 2% copper. Just great experience, Shem."

"How long you planning on staying there? More potatoes?"

"Don't know," he said as he dished more potatoes out on his plate and got up to get more beer for them. "Right now things are good."

"Tomorrow you can help me with the barn. Want to get it cleaned out before winter."

"Sure," Gerritt replied. They cleared the table and sat down to the ball games. Shem dozed off. It wasn't that he didn't want to tell Shem about Cerro Verde, about Eve, but there was no basis from where to start with him. Gerritt wasn't even sure that Shem knew where Chile was. When Gerritt first told him he was going there, Shem asked what state it was in. It was simply someplace far away, impossible for his imagination to consider. Shem's world was the farm. When you had no hope of seeing or doing something, did it even exist? Gerritt thought briefly of Molly, tried to remember her face.

He stayed two weeks, mostly because his reservations for returning allotted that much time. He rested. They cleaned the barn and Gerritt helped Shem change the oil in the tractor and replaced a fan belt. They went into town for dinner one night. Town was the same. Small and crowded. There wasn't anyone he wanted to see there and was ready to go back to Cerro Verde after a week.

The farm and Shem failed to make him see anything about the mine differently. It was all the same. Eve was still there. Barnett was still there. Gerritt sat in the plane now, cursing Stoddard and Barnett. He felt as though he was coming from a dream, or was the farm the reality and Cerro Verde the dream. They couldn't both be real because the one did not know about the other. He existed in both places but was a part of neither.

Two young girls with long, dull brown hair, sat in front of him. They fidgeted constantly, making the seats in front rock and clack together. One of them got up on her knees and started going through the hair of the other, parting it carefully with her fingers and then feeling down in the seams and spaces looking for something. They paid no attention to Gerritt's stares, but went methodically on with their grooming and picking. The two girls changed places, rocking the seats, and their roles were reversed but the same, parting and looking, lifting the hair up and letting it fall. Gerritt felt a chill on his neck and realized he was sweating again. He wasn't comfortable observing their intimacy.

The girls sat down and he couldn't see them anymore and was grateful. Their attention to each other embarrassed him. The preening was an old habit, animal like, and full of primitive overtones. In some ways it was the way he felt about the mine and about Eve. The mine machinery was simple and Eve was simple. The complexities lay in the people who couldn't let them be. The mine was his beginning, something of his own. Shem would not, could not ever understand what went on there. Shem was squeezed out of a tube, a finished product, the farmer, and spread himself only on that world.

Gerritt was returning to his own life, or what would be his life, as he could make it. He needed a home. Even though a loose attachment, Cerro Verde was as much of a home as he had ever known. This time the ride up in the sterile white wagon was a known quantity. He was returning to the swelling hole in the ground to make it run and to Eve who kept the key to the door.

CHAPTER 20

No one met his plane in Antofagasta, except for Vera and the white company car. The wind had changed on the pampa and Gerritt arrived in Cerro Verde to find it covered with a foggy acid cloud, which burned equally the lungs and edges of the few growing things. Usually the prevailing winds prevented the sulfur fumes emanating from the sulfide plant from suffocating the town, taking the caustic smoke out into the uninhabited pampa. Rarely, the winds changed, and when they did folks stayed indoors and the lawns became tipped with yellow. Gerritt coughed as he took his suitcase out of the back of the station wagon; Vera stayed in the car.

The wind had blown dirt under the door of his soltero's apartment, again, and it was cold inside. He dropped his luggage and pack on the floor, found his truck keys in the kitchen and headed out to the mine. The truck started and hummed as though it had been waiting for him and he smiled to hear the engine break into life after the weeks away. Cerro Verde was his home now; there would be no other place. He thought of Barnett as he crossed the right-of-way change and a 100-ton Dart rolled by him, thought of the first day and how scared and pissed he was at Barnett for not telling them about it. Barnett would be back by now. He would go slower for a while on the ore tonnages, he decided. There would be other ways to make his way here.

Gerritt forgot the broken door when he went into the office. It banged loudly against the wall, and the men inside looked up to see who was there.

"God damn, hasn't that door been fixed yet?" Gerritt exclaimed to Marshall and Alford, the only ones there. Felix stopped stiffly, in the middle of sorting the day's report and stared at him. Gerritt wasn't expected until the next day, and the men seemed surprised to see him, almost alarmed, he thought.

"Hello Felix, Mike," Gerritt said smiling. "How goes it?"

"You tell us, Wells," Mike Marshall said sullenly. Tell them what.

Felix smiled, but unnaturally. "Rather well, I guess, Gerritt. How was your vacation?"

"So, so. I was anxious to get back."

"I imagine so," Felix answered, raising his eyebrows.

Gerritt was puzzled and, frowning, about to ask why, when Curt Reicher stuck his head out of his office door.

"Ah, Wells, you're back. Wasn't expecting you until tomorrow." Reicher looked down, considering something on the floor and pushing at it with his foot, decided it wouldn't help to delay.

"Why don't you come into my office," he looked up at Gerritt with serious gray eyes, a little sad. "We need to talk."

Gerritt followed him, looking around at Marshall and Alford who didn't move. Even the papers Alford held in the air were frozen. A chill of both fear and excitement passed through him.

Reicher's office was small and Gerritt always thought it stuffy. There was too much furniture, chairs and bookcases. A large plant sat on one bookcase, shading what little sun came through the narrow windows. Photographs of the Swiss Alps covered the walls, surrounding a large picture of Nell, his wife. Curt closed the door, making the room even closer and Gerritt felt himself back in the bullet of the plane earlier in the day and thought of the two girls and their grooming behavior.

"Sit down, Gerritt. I trust you had a restful leave?" Reicher sat down and leaned back in his chair, his hands behind his head, and regarded Gerritt carefully. The fluorescent lights buzzed.

Gerritt sat and reaching up to scratch his forehead found it wet. The room was definitely small.

"It was all right, I guess. The farm hasn't changed. I'm glad to be back." He didn't want to talk about the farm; there was absolutely nothing to tell Reicher about it, nothing at all.

"And well you might be, my boy," Reicher said thumping his chair down on the floor and leaning forward over the desk toward Gerritt. Curt Reicher liked to thump his chair down; it gave a sense of authority, he thought, and what he needed to tell Gerritt he definitely wanted to deliver with authority, such as he had. He wasn't happy with the news, but there it sat and he was the one to tell it.

"Gerritt," Reicher began, pursing his lips and hitting one hand into the other nervously. "Art Barnett turned in his resignation last week."

"What?" Gerritt rose up in his chair. He wasn't expecting this. Then he remembered the discussion with Jason Stoddard before he left. So it happened. In a way, Gerritt was relieved but there was something about it making him uncomfortable as well. Where did it leave him? Curt watched Gerritt's reaction carefully and saw the shock writing furrows in his face. He wondered what, exactly, worried Gerritt. For Reicher there was concern about Gerritt's policies as Shift Foreman, the hi-grading, the excessive fraternization with the workers in the mine, not acceptable for a Jefe.

"I know," Curt said quietly, seeing the disturbance in Gerritt. "I tried to get him to change his mind, but he is a strong person and he, uh, well, he felt he couldn't live with...", he stopped, stood up and looked out the window around the trailing plant.

"Live with what?" Gerritt asked, his face flushed and he felt hot.

"With certain influences from high up, Gerritt. I'm sure you know what I'm talking about." Reicher turned to the wall, to Nell's picture and wished they were in Switzerland, walking along the river near her mother's house, and not here where he was a manager with no power to manage.

"Yes, yes, maybe I know what you mean." Gerritt sighed, bent forward and looked at his boots, wringing his hands, wondering just what was said and done in his absence.

Reicher took a deep breath, turned reluctantly from his wife to Gerritt, put his hand in the front of his shirt and leaned back on his heels. It always helped him.

"Well then," he said smiling. "I think you ought to know that when Art leaves in two weeks, you, Gerritt Wells, are to be the new Mine Foreman."

Reicher made this statement like a pronouncement, a new law of the kingdom, over which he had total control. And he stood there waiting for Gerritt's response.

Gerritt didn't move. He sat there looking at the floor, Curt's words hanging in his ears, waiting to see if it was the thing to do to hear them. He wanted to fall through the floor, disappear forever, get away from this. Barnett leaving was a surprise but one he could deal with. Barnett's job, that was another matter entirely. He wasn't prepared for Christ's sake. What could Driscoll be thinking, doing something like this to him?

He thought of Marshall and Alford outside, the looks they gave him. Did they all know? Did Wes know? No Wes couldn't know, he was gone on long leave, too, Stateside. But what would he think? Gerritt hit the chair on the side with his fist and felt the sweat slide out from between his fingers.

Whatever the source, and Gerritt knew the source was Driscoll, the news was there, the power he longed for so totally, or thought he longed for. It was his, the mine was his to run. His! The realization made him shake and he could feel the beads of sweat run down the sides of his flushed temples and onto his neck. His mind raced, matching his heart and he looked up slowly into Reicher's gray eyes. Curt was smiling.

"Well, what do you think about this, Curt?" Gerritt asked him as slowly and steadily as he could manage.

The smile left Reicher's face and he grew serious. He hadn't expected to be asked what he thought about this; he wasn't usually asked what he thought about anything. And he had to consider the matter for a moment.

"It was a surprise, Gerritt, I can't tell you it wasn't. What is important is for the mine to run smoothly. Driscoll can make any decision he wants, but I have to see that things actually get done down here, which isn't always easy." His hand came out of his shirt and he sat down. This was his job.

"The shifters are good and I can help you."

Gerritt shrugged. He didn't know where to look for the kind of help he needed. How would Reicher know?

"Does anyone else know about this?" Gerritt asked, thinking of the men like Juan Ortega. What would he be thinking?

"Not officially. They all know Barnett is leaving; they surmise the other." No announcement had yet been made and Curt felt that Driscoll would wait until Barnett was no longer in Cerro Verde. Driscoll respected Barnett, as they all did. What a loss. It made no sense.

"There's one other change," Reicher continued, "Hugh Dillon is being transferred to a new project. New York wants to leach the tailings dump and he's going to design and head that project. It's a big one. We'll have to find a new Chief Engineer."

"A new Engineer? Oh," Gerritt said thinking and then knowing it was something he couldn't deal with at that moment. He blanked out. The news that he had Barnett's job was too big. It filled his brain to the point where nothing else could be considered at the moment.

"Well," Reicher said, realizing what was happening, "Well, that doesn't have to be decided right away of course. No, not at all. That can wait." He was talking to himself, because he knew Gerritt was no longer there. They shook hands and Reicher wiped Garritt's sweat on his pants as Wells opened the door and left without responding.

Gerritt had to get out of the office, think about this. He was visibly shaking now and ran out without saying anything to the men, letting the door slam against the wall and not shutting it this time. Ortega, who had just arrived with Dillon, pulled it shut. They all knew before Reicher came out to tell them.

Gerritt climbed into his truck and set out for the upper benches of the mine where he could be by himself. It was cold, July and winter. The brown dust roiled up on all sides of him in the acid wind. His hands on the steering wheel shook as he squeezed it. He stopped on the visitor's bench and leaned his head on the wheel in tearless sobbing.

Gerritt knew that in the States this wouldn't be happening to him, couldn't be. Organization in mining companies was strict and involved more men in the decisions; promotion was sequential. On foreign contract jobs, advancement was faster because there was a high turnover in personnel. Men came for a few years for the experience and then moved their families back home to the familiar suburbs and supermarkets. That was why he came here, that and his need for fewer people and a simpler life. And some of it had happened. There it was. He was Mine Foreman, things moving along, following each other, Eve, then her father, now this.

He looked up, hearing the mine, the sounds grinding up to him on the overlook. It was too good to be true, this place, all his. But it was true enough. He closed his eyes tightly and tears finally squeezed out. Yes, he would do it; he could do it. Reicher was right. There were good people, enough good people to carry him. There was Wes. There was Wes to rely on. Yes, Wes would help him.

Gerritt got out of the truck and walked over to the edge of the high bench where the chain went through posts, keeping visitors from the abyss below. It was cold all right, but he was no longer shaking. He smelled the dust, savoring the sounds of his life, thinking about Wes. It came to him then, Wes would be Chief Engineer, replacing Dillon. Yes, Wes Bowen would be the Engineer. They would work together, work this mine. He would talk to Driscoll then Reicher; it would be fine now. He knew it.

He began to walk back and forth thinking of the things to do, how to approach Driscoll, how to tell Wes. Ortega would be pissed as hell. He was always mentioned as next in line after Barnett. Maybe Ortega would leave, too. Yes, that would be OK. Gerritt looked at the posts along the edge of the bench. Several seemed to be leaning outward toward the pit again. He frowned, wondering how that could have happened, then shrugged and made a mental note to tell Marshall to get his ass up here and do something about it.

It was dark by the time he went home and his phone was ringing. It was Eve.

"Gerritt, where are you? Daddy is expecting you for dinner. Come. Come now!" The tinkling, slightly hoarse voice, the usual innocent demands of a cherished child.

Gerritt showered, washing the layers of sweat away, watched the shock and fear of the afternoon's news go down the drain. He felt refreshed, renewed. He was truly elated. It was crazy, but it was real. Good on that bastard, Barnett! Let him go have the easy life in California selling real estate if that was what he wanted. Gerritt wanted the mine, the mine! Wanted it with every breathing pore in his being. He put on a clean shirt and went to Eve.

The night of Barnett's despedida, Wes and Alice returned to camp. They went to Alford's for champagne before the party. Alice was pregnant and they wanted Felix and Thea to be the first in camp to know. The baby would come in the spring. Thea was vicariously thrilled. She wanted a baby, but Felix was 24 years older than she and thought that at 52, he was too old.

Felix filled Wes in on the happenings of the last few weeks.

"And I doubt Ortega will stay much longer. He's rather like Barnett in many ways," Felix said sadly. He felt the mine, as he knew it, was lost.

Wes was incredulous that Gerritt would be made Mine Foreman. This time it wasn't jealousy, it was fear, fear for the mine and what was happening to Gerritt. What would be his relationship with Gerritt now?

The party was at Dillon's. Hugh had the mine shop rig up a bar sink that ran beer and a bathtub faucet that dispensed wine. By the time Bowens and Alfords arrived, the despedida was far along.

Barnett saw Wes come in and, as though he had been waiting for the opportunity, staggered drunkenly over to him, spilling beer and belching loudly.

"There you are Wes Bowen, you bastard. Guess what you get? You get Wells!" he laughed, spilling more beer and singing raucously,

"Down in the deep dark Wells, down in the deep dark Wells! You know that song don't you Bowen? Hope you can stomach it because I can't!" He fell onto Wes, spilling beer on Alice. Elaine Barnett brought a towel for her, smiling helplessly. Barnett wondered off to get more beer.

"God," Wes said to Felix. "So this is how it's going to be." The party was crowded. Some people were dancing, but most were sitting around drinking and talking. Mike Marshall was with the schoolteacher who had replaced Molly, whose ample front was barely covered, and obviously the focus of Mike's attention.

Wes felt watched. Was he marked as Gerritt's friend? Was he Gerritt's friend? Certainly they had not left each other under agreeable terms and now all this happened. What a mess. The mine would hurt when Barnett left. He talked to Hugh some, and Hugh told him about his switch in jobs, which left Wes with even more questions. There were to be changes, was the bottom line. Maybe he should start looking for a job back home as well, especially now that he was going to be a father. Wes was glad when the party noise increased and he'd had a few drinks.

Henrí Duvillard, the Frenchman in charge of the Bodega, was coaxed into playing his violin. They all knew the act, having seen it many times before, but it was always fun to see and Henrí was so good at it. He wore a heavy black suit, too large for him. His violin was propped under his chin, his black hair slicked back and a Chaplinesque mustache glued under his pointy nose wiggled. The pantomime began with melodramatic, recorded violin music. His nose wiggled more vigorously and just as he seemed about to sneeze, he stopped moving and the third finger of his left hand emerged from the fly of the black suit, large and pink, to grasp the bow while the sneezing Henrí blew his nose with his other hand. Gales of laughter erupted as the pale pink penis held the bow when Henrí combed his hair or scratched his ear. Henrí, a straight and businesslike man at work, loved to act and this was when he was happiest, when he could make his friends laugh and this time forget they were here to say goodbye to a family they all loved. Even Barnett was holding his sides from laughter. Later, Barnett passed out on the floor, seemingly happy and content. It was a good way to say goodbye, Wes thought. At least being numb, Art could no longer be angry.

CHAPTER 21

B arnett's resignation was followed by a period of irritating limbo for Gerritt. The announcement of his promotion was delayed until Art left camp. Reicher tactfully managed to keep the two men from a confrontation by having Gerritt give his shift to Julio Romero, Gerritt's first Shift Boss at Cerro Verde, who ironically now found himself once again in that position. Julio was pleased; he liked Gerritt, remembered the intended kindness of taking him to the club for a drink.

As the days drew nearer to Art's departure, he was in the office less and Gerritt began hanging out there in the afternoons. He couldn't stand not being there, feeling like a small boy who is told he will get a new bicycle at the end of the week and it's only Monday. He took note daily of the progress Barnett made in cleaning out his desk, soon to be his desk. On the morning after the despedida, Gerritt hurried out to the mine. Art Barnett was essentially gone. He would be sleeping off the party and Gerritt didn't expect that he would see him again. According to Reicher, the Barnetts would leave for California the next day.

The Shifters would communicate now with Gerritt, adjusting to a change they knew to be out of their control. He sat in the Mine Foreman's office, now his office, going over the night shift reports from Alford. It all looked OK and he smiled putting it aside for Zuñiga to type.

The front door slammed against the wall and he turned still and cold inside, until he saw that it was only Ned Tully, stomping into the outer office and spitting tobacco juice loudly into a metal wastebasket. Ned moved his heavy body and dirty leather jacket past Gerritt's door, then stopped and stuck his head in.

"You're a piss-ant replacement, Wells," Tully snarled around the tobacco plug. Gerritt had no response and so made none, just looked at the man. He was right, but the fact could not be acknowledged. Failing to get a reaction, Tully sniffed and moved the wad around, then went on to his own office to plan the next day's shot.

So that was how it would be. Gerritt guessed that most of the men would feel that way, but few would have the guts to say it, as Tully just did. Tully was old and his time here almost done. He didn't care what Tully thought, but the others weighed, Dillon and Alford. And there was Wes. It would pass. The resentment would pass. He knew he needed to see Wes soon, but had purposefully come in after Wes left the office for his shift. Bowen would be hung over and Gerritt wanted to give him some time. What he had to tell him was special, a plan to work together and telling him that required a plan. Gerritt stared out the window, but the window was high and he couldn't see anything but blue sky and dust rising. It was enough, enough to know where he was and that the mine was now the node on his heart, regulating life itself. His fingers turned the cat tracks slowly on the model of the D-9 on his desk he brought back from the States. Gerritt longed to get back on a dozer as he did in those first days on shift at Cerro Verde.

'Now there isn't anyone who can tell me not to do that.' He thought. 'It's my mine.' He wouldn't do it often, but once in a while, yes, it would be OK. A chill went down his spine thinking about it.

He didn't hear the timid Zuñiga tiptoe in to bring the mail, but felt the warmth in the room, the breathing. He jerked around, his eyes going wide, waking up from wherever he was. Zuñiga jumped back, afraid of his look.

"Lo siento mucho, Señor Wells, lo siento," he said quickly. He remembered the many times Gerritt had yelled at him. Zuñiga's voice was fine and wiry and his shirt was half open in the front where buttons were missing, and it was ripe.

"For Christ's sake, Zuñiga, take a bath. You stink!

"Oh, lo siento, Señor. In mi casa, no hay mucho agua."

"Figures."

"El correo." Zuñiga carefully laid a few envelopes down on Gerritt's desk and backed out the door, then turned and ran in the direction of the engineering office.

The mail. 'What mail do I get, only advertisements for more equipment,' Gerritt thought to himself as he looked through the envelopes and discarded them? He stopped at the one on the bottom. It was a personal letter, small, square and he could see, from Molly Pritchard.

He turned it over and around, feeling it. He did not get so many letters in his life, letters to him specifically, that this wasn't unusual. The envelope was cream colored and thick, so there must be some pages inside. The return address said she was in Des Moines. He sat there looking at it for some minutes. It was from another time. So much had happened and he didn't think about Molly often anymore. Why did he have to now? Finally, he opened the envelope, tearing the address. She was fine. Had a job teaching third grade in Des Moines near her parents with whom she was living until she could get her own place. She was seeing a friend of her uncles, who was in law school. Her parents liked him. She was writing because there was something unfinished between them. They had shared some heavy times, she said, which were hard to forget. If he wrote, she said she would write. If not, she would leave it. Gerritt sat there remembering her, the feel of her in bed, how Molly loved the mine. He straightened the envelope with his fingers so the address could be read. If she stayed, would things be different? Probably not, he decided. The thing with Eve had so many parts to it, he couldn't even begin to compare the two relationships. Molly wouldn't get it. She didn't get it when she was in Cerro Verde and now, well, it had gone too far to turn back. He was into it big time. Gerritt folded the letter carefully, put it back into the cream envelope and dropped it ceremoniously into the trash.

He got up quickly before he could change his mind and went into the outer office. There was a radio there, crackling with messages from the Jefe Patio to the trains and shifters. It was time to call Wes. Gerritt sat down on the table next to the radio and picked up the mike, thought for a moment and then pushed the button.

"Hey, Wes Bowen, do you read me?" he asked loudly, and released the button. No answer. He waited, looking at the floor, which was streaked with dust. Zuñiga swept, but the wind and foot traffic made his efforts futile.

"Wes, escuchaste?" Maybe he was out of his truck and didn't hear. There were several messages from the Jefe Patio to the trains and then Wes's voice came over the static.

"Yeah, I'm here. How've you been Gerritt?" He sounded tired, probably from the party the night before.

"OK, yeah OK. In fact, really OK!" Gerritt replied enthusiastically. His heart was pounding, this was so important.

"So I heard." The smile left Gerritt's face. Of course he would have heard. He was at the fucking despedida last night.

"Say, Wes, why don't you come on back up to the office and have a cup of coffee with me. I want to talk to you."

"Can't," he answered too quickly. "Got a bad derail down here." There was silence and then Wes continued.

"You should come down here, it's a mess."

"Fuck the derail. The palanqueros can fix it and Mike's there isn't he? I need you here." There was a long pause and Gerritt felt his face grow hot. He was counting on this.

"Yeah, well, OK. I'll check out that shovel on D bench on the way up. It's down for some reason." Wes didn't want to argue with Gerritt on the radio, the whole mine was listening. The derail was major and he shouldn't leave, but he knew Gerritt would have his way. And so it was beginning. Wes was tired and hung over from the party, but he sensed a change in Gerritt's voice. He was in charge and knew it.

Gerritt hung the mike on the hook, realized he was shaking again and went quickly back into his office, burying his head in his arms on the desk, where no one could see him. He had to do something with his hands while he waited for Wes, to get ready to talk to him. He pulled a box out of the drawer. It was another model he brought back from the States, a tractor like the one Shem had on the farm, the one he used for plowing. Gerritt opened the box, took out the directions and started reading them while he fingered the pieces inside the small plastic sacks.

It was over an hour before Wes Bowen opened the door and came in the office. Gerritt was so absorbed in the model that he didn't hear Wes walk across the wood floor and stand in his doorway. The earnestness and concentration with which Gerritt was piecing together the model astonished Wes. Wasn't he worried about the mine, about what was happening to them all?

"Gerritt?" Wes said carefully, not wanting to interrupt his concentration. Gerritt looked up then, not taking his hands off the model.

"Wes! Good to see you. Sit down, sit down." Gerritt had forgotten how large a man Wes was. He nearly filled the doorway, his arms hanging loosely down by his sides and slightly forward as a primate carries himself. The hard hat covered his red hair and his face was dusty from the mine. He looked worried.

Zuñiga stuck his head out of engineering to see who came in and Gerritt hollered at him to bring coffee.

"What are you doing?" Wes said, indicating the plastic debris on the desk. He sat down in the chair and took his hat off, but held it in his hands, not leaning back, as though he meant only to stay a few minutes. They regarded each other warily as Zuñiga brought the coffee, sat the cups on the desk, steaming into the air between them, and tiptoed out as quietly as he could.

"Oh, nothing really. It's a model I brought back from the States, something to do." He pushed the pieces back and leaned on the desk nervously, realizing Wes disapproved. Wes looked straight at him.

"You should be out in the mine. We had a bitch of a derail this morning, four cars off. Didn't you hear on the radio? It'll take all day to right them. And that shovel on D bench has electrical problems; I just sent a crew down there." He considered Gerritt carefully. He seemed not to be listening, as though he were thinking of something entirely different.

Gerritt shrugged. He'd get out there soon enough when Barnett was gone. And then, the tonnages would go up and it would all be OK. For now he needed to tell Wes something and he didn't want the derail or the electrical problem to distract their attention.

"How was the party?" he asked, to change the subject. Wes moved, uncomfortably on the edge of the chair. He had no idea where Gerritt was headed.

"It was OK. Barnett passed out. We all drank too much." That about summed up the party, which was really more like a wake. Barnett was buried and Gerritt, Gerritt was here in front of him, already sitting at Barnett's desk.

"Congratulations on your, uh, your promotion. Is this what you wanted?" Wes was saddened by all this and at the moment felt very tired. But Gerritt was not finished, not nearly finished.

"Yes, yes it is," he said positively but Wes responded only by staring at him.

"Look Wes, I know how I got here." The words floated in the steam from the untouched coffee. "This wouldn't happen at home, but this isn't home. The fact is that I'm now Mine Foreman. And we got rid of Barnett, the bastard." Gerritt chuckled, then stopped when he saw that Wes didn't find the remark humorous.

The insult to Barnett was uncalled for. He was a decent man and one hell of a Foreman. Wes didn't want to listen to this anymore and he stood up.

"Well, I'm happy for you, Gerritt," he said with as little enthusiasm as he could manage and still get the words out. His tall frame leaned over the desk as he looked at Gerritt and then he turned to go.

"Wes, wait, I'm not done," Gerritt said, standing up so he could more nearly look him in the eye. "Wes, we can work together, now, don't you see?"

"Work together? What do you mean, Gerritt?

"Work together, Wes," he repeated. "You and me, building this mine, running this mine." Wes stared at him; he wasn't getting through. Gerritt stiffened.

"We are offering you the position of Chief Engineer, Wes Bowen! Dillon is going to work on a tailings project. So what do you think?" Gerritt was glowing now, at least on the outside. He tossed the shock of black hair off his face and sat decisively down in the chair, putting his feet up on the desk, waiting for Wes to reply. He watched Bowen's face flush from the bottom up, as if the blood were slow to rise in his tall frame.

"Gerritt, you can't do this! Neither of us is ready for this!" Wes felt a heavy pressure in his chest and the lightness of air and dead quiet you know before severe weather comes. He sat down, again on the edge of the chair.

Gerritt's feet thumped onto the floor and he leaned forward to Wes.

"We can learn. And besides, this place has the best bunch of shifters and maintenance people around. It'll run itself!" Gerritt's blue eyes wrinkled up at the corners with enthusiasm.

"I don't know. What does Reicher think?" Wes shook his head slowly in disbelief that he was sitting here listening to this.

"I discussed it with Driscoll and then the two of us talked to Reicher. He thought it was a fine idea." Gerritt pulled out a handkerchief, unconsciously, to wipe his forehead where the sweat was itching. That wasn't exactly how it happened. Driscoll, indeed, told him that Dillon would be transferred to the tailings project and Gerritt mentioned Wes Bowen as his replacement. Driscoll was thinking of Juan Ortega. Gerritt told him he couldn't work with Ortega, and although Joe Driscoll was obviously distressed, Gerritt assumed the matter was closed. It was. Reicher was not pleased that he was the one to tell Ortega, but he did it. Reicher carried out orders from Driscoll no matter the consequences. Ortega quit, as Curt knew he would. Juan was a good engineer and no, no this was not "fine". But the decision stood.

Wes looked at Gerritt carefully, trying to make this all make sense, turning his hard hat over and over in his hands.

"I really don't know what to say to you Gerritt. This is a big step, would be for both of us. What if we couldn't pull it off? Felix said Ortega's quitting."

"Let him! We'll get a new shifter down from the States, and we have Julio. We don't need Ortega. What do you say, Wes? Are you in?"

"In?" He looked up at Gerritt, who held him with the gaze of a fascinated child. In for what? What would this turn into? Gerritt was waiting for his answer and all he could do was sit there, thinking that this couldn't be happening. He needed time to sort it out, reorder things. It was all so illogical.

"I want to think about it. This is happening pretty fast." Wes wanted only to get out of there.

"Sure, sure, take your time." He had to exude confidence. He couldn't let Wes know how much he was needed. If Wes wouldn't help him, no one would.

Bowen got up then and left without saying anything else. Gerritt heard the door slam and a truck start. He sat there, nervously, drinking the cold coffee and then went back to his model because his hands were shaking again.

The rest of the day existed for Wes Bowen only in the time it took to get through it. The shovel was somehow repaired, but the derail would go on into the afternoon shift and Wes wouldn't see all the cars back on the track that day. Thankfully, Gerritt was gone when he filed his shift report.

Chief Engineer. The offer dangled as though it was on a spring in front of his eyes. His mind searched inside for some reserve or resource to meet it squarely and, finding nothing there, he felt his hands forming fists in frustration as he drove home. That Gerritt was now incorrigible was beyond question. Logic and fairness were alien; he was firmly fixed on what he wanted and what it required to get it, no matter how insane the consequences. Sanity. Was that actually the issue, could it be? Driscoll and Reicher accepted it. Did that make it all right? Wes didn't know. He was sure, as he pulled into his driveway, that if he turned this promotion down he would be forced to leave Cerro Verde. There was Gerritt holding the piece of candy, offered before dinner. He could see the white teeth and laughing eyes.

"God-damn you, Gerritt!" he swore out loud, getting out of the truck and slamming the door.

Alice was baking something; the heavy smell of fermented dough filled the house. It was a good and easy, restful smell and seeing her there and needing her, he fell into a chair in the kitchen. Pregnancy made him see her in a different way. She was full now, her heart, her body was full of him and Wes loved her with a warmth that helped the wretched day.

"What's the matter, Wes?" she asked, wiping flour from her hands. "You look awful, sweetheart." She smiled at him, reaching out and he pulled her down into his lap and kissed her hard, so hard she leaned away.

"What is it?" She got up and poured coffee for them, covering the dough she had been kneading with a damp cloth. And then the whole thing came out for her onto the table between them. Wes tried to explain what Gerritt said, how he looked, though there was no understanding it.

Alice considered, nodding her head, her soft eyes caressing his pain.

"What is happening to Gerritt, Wes? He just seems to get in deeper and I'm frightened for him and for you. Maybe we should get out of this place, too."

"I think he's always been what he is now. He's alone, Alice. And I think scared as shit. Eve got him more than he dreamed of. In some ways he probably does care for her. I know I don't have the experience to be Engineer and Gerritt knows it too. And he hasn't got what it takes to be Mine Foreman." They sat there together for a minute considering in silence.

"Hell," Wes said, "Gerritt is Mine Foreman, it's not what if anymore. That is real, he's there behind the desk, Art's desk. The mine is running itself. He's certainly not doing anything to help it along."

Alice shook her head, sat up in the chair and pushed the dishtowel away from her.

"What I think, Wes, is you have to decide based on what you can do, not what Gerritt is doing, or what he is or will be next week. It's a job. If you can do it, do it. If not we can leave."

Wes was just beginning to think about this when they heard a truck driving up to the back door. They looked at each other and Alice got up to look out the window.

"It's Gerritt," she said, a worried look on her face.

"Shit, I don't want to see him now."

A door slammed and then the crunch of work boots in the gravel and the door buzzer before he walked into the kitchen.

"Hi Wes, Alice." He gave them a warm smile, just like any other day. It was all going to be OK, Gerritt was sure now.

"Say, something sure smells good in here." He walked over to Alice who was taking rolls out of the oven and gave her a quick hug around the waist and took one of the hot rolls off the sheet, juggling it in his hand over to the table.

"Always said these rolls are better than sex, eh, Wes." Gerritt let the roll cool as Wes looked at him, in awe of his incredible audacity.

"Got any beer?" he asked Wes.

"Sure, help yourself," Wes answered, but didn't get up.

Gerritt opened the frig, seemed to think a moment, looking. Their refrigerator had different things in it than his, family food, he thought, and then he found the Escudo, took one out for himself and one for Wes.

"Know that derail you were bitching about this morning?" he said to Wes and he sat down at the table. Alice was cleaning off the counter where she was kneading the bread.

"Yeah, is the afternoon shift cleaning it up?"

"Well not exactly," Gerritt said, biting his lip. "They were having some problems when I went down there this afternoon, so I told them to leave it until tomorrow."

"You what! Where was Mike?" Wes was astounded. Gerritt made no sense. The derail was on main-line track. Nothing could go in or out of the mine until it was repaired and the trains running again.

Gerritt sighed and slumped back in the chair.

"Mike was sort of the problem. He came down about the time the guys were packing up and God, was he pissed! He wanted them to unload and finish the damn thing right there. I wouldn't let them. I'd said they could leave. Mike got in his truck and drove off."

"Why, why didn't you let them finish, Gerritt? That's main-line track?" Wes said as calmly as he could manage, the words coming from between grinding teeth. Alice was wiping the counter in front of her faster and getting very nervous, listening to this conversation.

"I don't know. They'd have been on over-time and I didn't see the rush on it as long as Barnett is still here. Maybe night shift can finish it."

"So what do you want from me?" Wes was livid. It was a stupid thing to do. Overtime was a hell of a lot cheaper than a hold up for ore carrying trains the next day. There wasn't any way to help now.

"Talk to Mike, would you? I need him on my side and he's been getting damn hard to get along with lately. He's also still bitching about those posts up on the visitors' bench. Why doesn't he just fix them like I told him to do!" Gerritt was nearly screaming, like an angry child having a tantrum.

"On your side, Gerritt?" Wes's voice was louder too. Alice turned to him in alarm.

"And just what is your side? I thought running the mine was a common interest to all of us. Have I missed something here?"

"Just talk to Mike, Wes. I need you to talk to Mike." Gerritt tried to say this as calmly as possible.

"No, I won't talk to Mike," Wes said firmly. "There isn't anything I could say to Mike that would help you! Gerritt you need to let him do his job! You have got to let us all do our jobs! It's not going to work otherwise." Wes realized he was leaning over the table screaming at Gerritt.

Gerritt sat there in awe of Wes's anger.

"But that's not what I mean. If I tell him to do something, he damn well better do it!" Gerritt's white eyes widened.

"Oh, for Christ's sake, Gerritt, come on. I can't believe you see it that way. You better let it slide. If Mike goes to Curt, well Mike is right. Let him get that track cleared first thing in the morning, OK?" Wes was quieter now, imploring him to see the situation clearly. Confrontation with Curt Reicher would not be good right now. Curt would still feel like he was sitting on a fence, with Barnett just leaving and an unknown taking his place. It was not a good time for choices.

"Well, I don't like it, Wes!" He slammed his beer bottle down on the table making Alice jump. Gerritt looked over at her and his expression suddenly softened as though the whole thing had disappeared instantly from his thoughts.

"Hey, Alice," Gerritt smiled at her. "What do you think about old Wes here being the next Chief Engineer?"

Alice paled as she dropped the the rag into the sink and began to wash her hands. She didn't want to look at him.

"I don't think he's quite decided what to do yet, Gerritt," she said evenly, as the flour left on her hands dissolved under the warm water.

"What?" Gerritt looked at Wes, incredulous that he should need to consider the matter any longer. What was the conversation they just had about, if it wasn't about running the mine together. That's why he came to Wes with this problem; Wes would know what to do.

Wes looked down at his beer, which he held in his hand but hadn't touched. The sweat from it was running down over his hand.

"I want a day or so to think it over, Gerritt. Alice and I have a lot to think about right now." He looked over at her and then at Gerritt.

"We haven't had a chance to tell you. We're having a baby, Gerritt, and it makes me think in a different way."

Garrrett stood up and turned first to Alice and then to Wes. He didn't know what to say. Alice was going to be a mother. Was that what it was, keeping the house, baking bread, stocking the refrigerator, having a baby. Would she have the same sad look on her face someday that Eve's mother had. Did it all hurt so much? Gerritt wished he could understand it, feel it. Was it something you learned when you, yourself, were a child. Whatever it was, he didn't have it. He felt himself, suddenly sad. Alice saw it in him and went to put her arms around him.

"Say that's great, the little mother," Gerritt said to her, holding her out and looking at her stomach. "Where is it?"

Alice laughed then, embarrassed.

"Silly, I'm only four months and you can't see yet, but soon." She was pleased. The morning sickness was gone and she could feel the baby move inside her. She wanted everyone to share this happiness and Gerritt certainly seemed to need it.

"Congratulations, Wes." Gerritt extended his hand and Wes took it in his. They shook hands for longer than it took for the congratulations. Neither wanted the happy moment to end, to return to the decision that had to be made. Gerritt went for another beer.

"It's not that I don't want the job, Gerritt. I have to decide if I think I can do it, that's all." Wes sighed. It was all so sudden, he felt dizzy and wanted time for the whole thing to be swallowed and digested.

"I guess you didn't think much about that when you took Mine Foreman, did you?" It was a question Wes had to ask, to know.

Gerritt sat back down and turned the beer slowly around in his hands.

"Sure, you need to know that. I owe you that." Gerritt tried to answer a question he did not understand.

"I'm scared as shit, Wes," he said, and this was true. "I figure I'll grow into the boots, you know what I mean." But he wasn't sure this was true.

"Well, we don't always think alike. So I'd still like a few days, OK?" There was silence.

"Sure, Wes, take your time." Gerritt's voice was almost too calm then. They finished the beers, talking to Alice about the baby. Gerritt got up, finally, and gave Alice another hug on his way out and was gone. He seemed already somewhere else and Wes wondered if he was thinking who else might take this job. Wes felt a catch in his stomach at that thought and knew, then, how badly he wanted to be Chief Engineer.

CHAPTER 22

Wes was distracted all the next day, thinking about Gerritt, the job, Alice. He would leave it, then break out in a sweat and it would all come back. The right thing would be to decline a position for which he was not yet ready. But was the right thing the best for his future, for Alice, their child? It was afternoon before he thought of talking to Hugh Dillon and found him after work in the Club bar having a beer. Hugh became Chief Engineer when he was a little green, too. His father was a past Mine Manager and Hugh's rise in the company was quick, some thought too quick. But Hugh was capable and did well. He was also sensible and right now that was what Wes needed more than anything, a second and rational opinion. What was happening with Gerritt, not only was moving too fast, but also was not logical.

Hugh obviously had a hard day. There were lines of dirt and sweat down the side of his face. He was sitting alone, rubbing his hand across his jaw, when Wes sat down beside him.

"Hi Hugh, how's it going?" Wes said, motioning to the mozo for a beer.

"Lowsy tooth giving me fits again. Think one of these days I'm gonna have the whole lot pulled." Hugh had bad teeth. That and his heavy smoking gave him an unhealthy look. He couldn't be too unhealthy, Wes thought. Hugh and Rene had five children and Rene was pregnant again. He was recently conscious of observing pregnancy in other families since he and Alice were now expecting their own.

"Been to the dentist yet?" he asked as his beer was set in front of him and he grasped its coldness.

"No, the butcher will want to pull it and several more probably and I've got a report to get out by the end of the week on the leaching beds for the new tailings project."

Hugh turned to look at the other man.

"What's up, Wes?" he said, knowing exactly what was up.

"As a matter of fact, it's not going well. I came down here to talk to you, Hugh."

"Sure." Hugh was expecting this visit, what one person knew here, all new. He slid off the barstool and walked over to one of the booths; Wes followed him. The bar smelled old. Men were playing pool in the next room and a jukebox played scratchy records. Wes looked at the wood steps coming down into the bar from the first floor, wondering how many people it took walking down those stairs to make the depressions in the wood that were clearly visible. They sat down.

"You going to take the job?"

"I don't know yet. I want it, I just didn't want it this way. It's too soon for me, for Gerritt."

"I know what you're going through." Hugh raised his eyebrows, looking seriously at Wes.

"I thought you might," he nodded.

"But I don't think I'll be much help to you. You know what's inside you. If you want it bad enough, you'll do the job."

Wes looked down at the wood table covered with carved names and initials of people that were no longer there, gone or dead. They were sad names because they weren't drawn after a climb up an apple tree in summer. Cerro Verde was a longer journey than that. Some of the marks were incised with indignation, others cut in boredom. But most important, they were a permanent mark saying that the table had been touched, someone was there. Not being there was a completely different form of dying, Wes thought, and more than anything he wanted to leave a mark. The baby was part of that and this job in the mine was another.

"Yes," Wes replied firmly. "Yes, I think I want the job enough."

They talked then about the mine and the engineering department. The mine was getting deeper and Management wanted a tunnel to the sulfide plant built through the bottom of the mine and then to the plant. Hugh had things well organized, and Wes was grateful for his help.

"One more thing, Wes," Hugh remarked as they said goodbye at the trucks outside, where it was now cold. "You won't be able to do anything about Gerritt, nobody can. He's got management sewed up. Just run the department as best you can. The sulfide tunnel is important. I left the preliminary designs for you. Zuñiga knows where they are. The mine is getting too big to haul bottom ore up and over, but you're going to have trouble about this with Gerritt."

"Yeah, I know." Wes sighed at the prospect. Gerritt was into high-grading and wouldn't want any effort put into such a tunnel."

It was surprising to him how there is a progression that you grow into and accept without shock. The sudden holes that open, requiring you to jump across and you have to decide how much you want to be on the other side and weigh carefully the risk of falling in if you can't jump far enough.

Wes ran into Rita Blain, when he stopped to get milk at the Pulparilla on the way home. She was with one of her maids who held the market basket patiently. Rita was perfectly groomed as always, her red hair in tight curls. You never knew whom you would run into.

"So, Wes, will you take the Chief Engineer position?" she asked after congratulating him on the baby. It surprised him that Rita would know about both, but as Wes knew, in Cerro Verde the whole camp knew where you pissed.

"Yes, I think so, Rita," he answered carefully.

"Everyone has a price," Rita laughed. "Even me."

Wes went back out to the mine that night after supper. He spent some hours going over maps and the tunnel designs, thinking about his relationship with Gerritt and what it would be like working with him. The Engineer was to make the mine plan and the Foreman was to carry it out. There was sure to be conflict, not only in opinion, but in practice. Wes hoped his practicality would balance Gerritt's impulsiveness.

The next morning, Wes had to look for Gerritt; he wasn't in the office. A call to him on the radio was answered around the static.

"Up on the south rim fixing a dozer. Come on up." When Wes drove up he saw Gerritt and an obrero, covered in grease with parts of the engine everywhere.

" Good God, Gerritt! What are you doing?" The obrero shrugged at Wes, knowing his Jefe was not supposed to be doing this work.

"Shit, Wes! This feels so good to get my hands dirty. I love it! I heard the dozer was down on the radio and drove up here early this morning. Raul is going to get a part."

The obrero got quickly in a truck and drove off leaving Wes and Gerritt alone. They stood in the morning sun, the wind already blowing, staring at each other, each knowing what the other was thinking. Wes decided not to say anything about the grease on Gerritt. Maybe it was not now his place.

"I came up to tell you I want the job, the Chief Engineer job. I'll talk to Reicher when I get back to the office." He thought Gerritt looked relieved.

Gerritt wiped his hand on his pants and offered it to Wes, who took it.

"Thanks, Wes. I need you." They looked at each other a long moment.

"I know," Wes answered, worried about what that might mean. And was he now so different from Gerritt. They were both stomping over better judgment in boots that didn't fit, knowing they couldn't do something and doing it anyway.

There was one other man Wes had to see. Juan Ortega. Juan's resignation made Wes realize how much the events of the last few weeks were going to cost. Wes avoided him in the first days after acceding to Gerritt, knowing how the two promotions would affect him. It was easy not to think about it, as he was busy rearranging Hugh's office, pouring over engineering books and reviewing surveying skills. And Juan did not return to the mine after his resignation.

Wes saw him coming out of the Club one afternoon and haled him.

"Juan?" Bowen called. Ortega ignored him, walking quickly to his truck. "Juan Ortega!" Juan stopped with the keys in his hand, digging at the dirt with his boot and not looking up as Wes approached him.

"Juan," Wes said frowning. "I'm sorry about all this." Wes liked him. This hurt, and Wes thought briefly that there must be some other way.

"Are you?" He spit out the words, his black eyes burning through Wes. "Or are you just another bloody Gringo bastard." Juan looked sad, as though he wanted to believe in their friendship, but there were two many differences between their positions at Cerro Verde to allow it now.

"I guess I'm a Gringo bastard, if that's the way you want to put it," Wes answered, knowing that accepting the job made this true.

"I didn't think you'd quit. It's going to be damn tough out there and we need you," he said sincerely. It was desperately true.

"Yeah, I know. You need the Chilean to do the work, while the Gringo gets the credit," Juan spit out.

What was there to answer? He was right. Ortega had worked hard, done his job well and deserved and was qualified for one of these promotions. Had he gotten one, everyone would have said yes, good show, Juan, yes you deserved it. And then Wes and Gerritt reached out and took all that away, again.

"You know I don't think that way, Juan. You're one of the best engineers this place has seen. Please reconsider." If he did, would it make all this right?

"I couldn't. You don't expect me to anyway. I can't stand to work with Gerritt, much less for him! You go ahead and give in to him if you want, but I can't. He represents every Goddamn thing your country has done to mine and he makes me sick in the gut! I've been shafted ever since I came here by El Condor, and I've had it!" His voice rose steadily as he spoke and his face reddened.

It was an American company and though on Chilean soil, the copper income benefited the American employees first when anything was passed out, anything at all. The Gringos got the big houses, the help with their taxes, the foreign contracts with paid transportation to the States. It was unfair, but as long as you were a Gringo, the inequities were somehow overlooked. The fact that the company and American employees paid enormous taxes and the whole thing provided employment and revenue for thousands of people seemed to miss the point of whose ground was being mined. The copper belonged to the Chilenos. Wes felt depressed to be a part of something he could not now control and to have let himself slide into it so easily.

"What will you do?" he finally managed to ask quietly.

"One of my brothers has a marble quarry on the way to Antofagasta. I'll go down there," he replied flatly and looked away, anxious to leave. Someday they might meet again in a better time.

"Good luck then." Wes offered his hand. It was a long moment before Juan took it in his, just briefly touching. The wind seemed to separate them and Wes stood there as Juan got in his truck and drove away without looking back.

CHAPTER 23

For Gerritt, Ortega's resignation was a gift. The mine would do without him. Ortega carried a huge chip on his shoulder, a burnt-in bitterness no Gringo could ever assuage. Gerritt needed loyalty and constructive help; Juan Ortega would give neither. And now there was Wes, Wes was Chief Engineer. Wes was his friend and would help. He was right about letting Mike Marshall repair the track. The argument over the derail was resolved as Wes said by waiting. Gerritt simply came in late to work the next day. By the time he arrived, the cars were back on track and nothing more was said. It warmed him, thinking how easy it was. Gerritt continued to get his hands on the equipment when he could. It gave him a feeling of power, being in charge, from the equipment to the men who ran it.

Coming in late solved other problems, or avoided them. The night shift did morning report, briefing the day shift on what had been done, what was left to do. It wasn't hard for Gerritt to arrive late for work. He spent most evenings with Eve and sometimes ate breakfast with her at the Gerencia. He liked watching her play with her stuffed animals and decided to get her a puppy when he could. Her simplicity touched him, as nothing had since he left the farm.

Gerritt wasn't entirely sure what his job as Foreman entailed, other than as supervisor of the shift bosses and seeing as much ore was loaded as possible. There was no debriefing from Barnett, who left Cerro Verde without returning to the mine after the despedida, and wouldn't have given him any help anyway. Gerritt was counting on Wes.

But there were problems. Wes took the balance of waste and ore removal seriously, as was good mining practice. Gerritt only cared about the ore tonnages. He moved trucks and shovels around and Wes moved them back, but not until more ore was loaded than waste. Curt Reicher shook his head, watching the polite sparring going on between them. It couldn't last.

The plans proceeded for a crusher in the bottom of the pit where sulfide ore would be processed, then transported on a conveyor system through a tunnel to the smelter. It was an enormous undertaking, entailing the blasting of a hole through the mountain from the bottom of the pit to the smelter on the other side, the tunnel that Hugh Dillon designed before leaving the engineering work to Wes.

"Bowen has the plans finished for the tunnel," Curt Reicher said to Gerritt a month later. "Sounds good."

"I know, I know, Curt," Gerritt had replied disgustedly. He was not pleased with the plan; it took too much time from the business of loading ore.

"He wants to move the bloody access road and I can't spare the equipment."

"I think Wes feels the rock isn't stable enough for a tunnel at the end of the existing road. It needs to be moved back," Reicher explained, carefully.

"And I said we can't afford the God-damned time to build a new road right now!" Gerritt was adamant. He hadn't looked at the rock stability studies Wes had done, but it wouldn't have made any difference. He wasn't going to move the road.

Gerritt didn't discuss the tunnel location with Wes. Both of them were avoiding disagreements when possible, fearing a confrontation. The weekly meetings became increasingly difficult. These were planning meetings where Wes presented the engineering plans for the following month, where blasting was to be done, ore and waste loaded, and track laid. And, of course, plans for the tunnel. This one, as always, was held in Curt Reicher's office. The closeness bothered Gerritt, the smells of the other men, the plans in which he took no interest. Ned Tully was always there and Leif Erickson, the geologist. Ned was a contrast to Leif who always wore a white shirt.

No matter what was decided, Gerritt planned to run the mine as he saw fit. Out the high window the dust was roiling up from the mine and he longed to leave the crowded room and go outside. As Wes read his report, Ned Tully complained about moving a drill down to the next bench.

"We need it up top so why does it have to go down?" he asked spitting into Curt's wastebasket. Curt cringed.

"There's still part of that lower bench that has to come out if the mainline track is going to go through there." Ned shrugged accepting Curt's explanation apathetically.

"This looks good, Wes. If we take out that lower bench, we can begin putting the track in there while the next shot is being drilled." Curt seemed pleased. Gerritt put his feet up on Curt's desk, drawing a quick look.

"Right," Wes replied. "The track has to be moved to make room for the tunnel entrance." He said this directly to Gerritt. It was time to move on this.

Gerritt's feet thumped to the floor. He didn't want that bench moved, didn't want the new track laid and damn it he didn't like this tunnel placement.

"That bench is a big nothing, Wes. It's all waste. How do you think that's going to look on the monthly? Fucking lower the ore tonnage one hell of a lot, that's what!

"Sure it is, but we'll get the track in with no wasted time and the area will be cleared for the tunnel. The plants have enough stock-pile anyway to keep the copper production the same."

"Shit on the stock-pile!" Gerritt stood up over Wes. There was silence in the room. "I want the ore grade and tonnage to stay high. That's what they look at in New York!" His shouting surprised himself, as well as the others.

Didn't anyone see what was important here? It was all so clear to him. But no one said anything. He was flushed and hot, continuing to glare down at Wes who looked plaintively to Curt.

"Sit down, Gerritt," Curt said calmly. And Gerritt lowered himself into the chair, his breath coming in great gulps as he looked at his feet, feeling the discordance.

"Well, I guess that about does it for today," Reicher said, quickly standing up before anything else could be said. Wes had confirmed the tunnel placement in the meeting. It would be better now to let things slide along. Surely Gerritt would realize the bench had to go. He would be reasonable eventually. He would have to be.

Curt turned to Leif Erickson, who said little.

"You have those new cores ready, Leif?"

"Sure," he replied quickly. "Want to see them now?"

"Yes," Curt said relieved. "Come on, Wes, let's have a look." They stood and Wes looked hopefully at Gerritt as they left the room.

After the meeting, Tully moved the drill back down to the lower bench, as Wes had requested, and the bench was shot. But the next day, the trucks were elsewhere, on Gerritt's orders, loading ore, not waste. He was the Mine Foreman, director of mine operations who gave instructions to the shifters, told them where and what to load. When another day went by with none of the waste trucked out, Wes had to do something.

He found Gerritt sitting in his office working on the dozer model. The mine was humming outside the window and he looked surprisingly detached, not noticing Wes at the door. Wes took his hard hat off and dropped it on the desk. Gerritt jumped.

"Hey, Wes, watch where you slam your hat, you might break my model." Couldn't he be careful? Wes looked mad, there were furrows sliced between his sandy eyebrows.

"Fuck your model, Gerritt! I've got something to say."

"For Christ's sake then, sit down."

"No thanks," Wes leaned across the desk at him. "Not one rock of that shot has been taken out. You're hi-grading the pit!" The words fell bluntly on Gerritt's ears. Of course he was.

"I don't know why, Gerritt, and I don't think I want to know why. But you can't run a mine this way!" He banged his fist on the desk.

"The hell I can't!" Gerritt stood up then to face Wes, his white eyes wide. "Use your head, Wes. We'll slow down soon, when the tunnel construction begins. Now, I want it to look to New York like this place wasn't managed at all until I...until we took over." He smiled, sure that would make a startling impression, the suddenly increased production under his new management. But Wes was shaking his head, looking at him in bewilderment.

"Gerritt, are you crazy? You'll have this hole so fucked up in a month, we'll never get it straightened out. You can't do it. I won't let you!"

They stared at each other. Gerritt felt the blood rising in his head, ready to explode from his ears and Wes disappeared from view momentarily. Why couldn't Wes see his plan? No, Wes thought he was nuts. Did everyone? Did Driscoll know about it? Well, maybe he should slow down with the hi-grading a little. His head started to cool, returning to the room, to Wes glaring at him, his face flushed.

"OK, Wes, calm down, calm down. We'll go more slowly. Can't guarantee I won't do this again, but go ahead, take some of the trucks tomorrow." He talked slowly, careful to be a little patronizing. He couldn't afford to lose Wes.

They both sank down into chairs, Gerritt nearly collapsing. He felt weak and shaky, like a poker player who has lost his pot and lacks resources for another hand.

"You've got to let us clean up that mess from the shot in the bottom of the pit and get the new track laid." Wes said slowly and firmly.

Gerritt squirmed in the chair and wished Wes would leave. He was getting his way now, wasn't that enough?

"Yeah," he said, not looking at Wes. "OK".

When Wes was gone, he sat there for a long time, looking at the model. It made sense, the pieces fitting together in order, with no argument. He wished Wes was like that, where he could take him out of the drawer and then put him back when he didn't need him. Yeah, he would have to go slower, he thought, make it all look like it was his idea. Gerritt was sweating. He took out his handkerchief and wiped his forehead.

That evening he decided to walk up to the Gerencia instead of driving, to clear his head. It was cold, the wind blowing at him as he went up the hill. He could hear the mine working and the stars were out like light fixtures, so bright you could see the snow on San Pedro and San Pablo.

Gerritt tried to think Wes was right. At any rate, he must be more careful. He would continue to hi-grade when he could, but not when it screwed up the blasting or laying track. Maybe it was a lucky thing Wes blew up, yes, probably a good thing. It cleared the air and it would be better now.

He arrived at the Gerencia sweaty. The wind had taken away his heat, but now inside, beads of perspiration broke out on his lips and forehead and he realized his handkerchief was damp.

Eve took him in and washed his face with a warm rag and kissed him.

"Poor, poor Gerritt. You work so hard for Daddy." There were tears in her dark eyes to see him so tired and sad. He watched her face as she was intent on her task of cleaning, comforting. Eve was so soft, her heavy hair a contrast to her frail body. She couldn't possibly know or understand the reason for his despair, her silent virginal nourishment cooling him from somewhere outside. In her earthy goodness lay the basic truths of why things happen. A slow fate was taking them all, like a train on the track in the mine, already being made to turn by the direction of the rails, and Gerritt was no longer sure who was driving.

CHAPTER 24

In August the wind blew incessantly, the local people saying there hadn't been such ferocity in its force in years. It raised the earth into the air and threw rocks and gravel at windows and faces alike, pitting and cutting all it touched.

The mine offices were little protection, the pre-fab walls moving where the wind sought places to enter. Mike Marshall sat in the engineering office complaining to Wes Bowen again about the posts on the visitors' bench.

"Wells gave me holy shit about those last month! Wait until he goes up to check them now! The bastards are leaning out again and I don't know the fuck why. I recemented the fuckers in myself last time."

"Maybe someone's running into them," Wes offered, half listening as he cupped his hands around a cup of steaming coffee to warm them. "How can you even see whether they're straight or crooked in this rock blizzard?"

"Oh, you can see all right. The whole lot of the bloody things are pulling at their chains like champing horses ready to leap over the edge." He thought a minute. "And this is the third time, the third time! Something the fuck is going on up there, something weird! You gotta go see this!"

Wes was about to say he would go have a look, when the building shook violently, the walls waving, the chairs they sat in moving. By the time they were on their feet the sound shock hit like a crack of thunder directly overhead, frightening because whatever it was could not be the wind. Windows crashed in around them, jingling and tinkling as the glass fell to the floor.

"Shit!" Wes screamed as hot coffee poured down his front.

And then the wind did come, blowing through the jagged, open cuts in the windows, at last able to enter the building freely. It lifted maps and papers, floating them around the office like sailplanes. Bottles and pencils rolled from the desks, crashing to the floor and Wes and Mike grabbed at anything within reach. Zuñiga came running in from the bathroom, his pants around his hips.

"Que pasa, que pasa? Madre de Dios, que pasa?" he screamed, his prickly, unshaven face wild with terror.

Leaving the mess in the office to the hysterical Zuñiga, they ran outside, finding Reicher standing there looking toward the south end of the mine where an enormous cloud of dust obliterated the view.

"This is bad, I know it's bad," Reicher was saying in a daze.

"Christ, it's not time for the shot. They don't ever blast before the shift change at 3," Mike said, shaking his head.

Wes looked at his watch. It was 11:30AM. There must be something wrong, something really wrong inside that brown curtain at the other end of the mine.

"Let's go," Reicher said to Wes. "Radio the Jefe Patio to send everybody down there."

Two benches above where the explosives trucks were loading for the afternoon shot, Ned Tully and Gerritt Wells were moving some cable around for a drill crawling slowly up the incline on cat tracks.

"Wish that sucker would hurry. I've got other things to do," Gerritt was saying impatiently.

"Ah, Gerritt, my boy, you need to learn not to hurry things. Life moves fast enough." Ned smiled at Gerritt, and that's the way they were when the shock wave hit them. Neither heard the blast itself; they were too close. The force of the air front threw them both against the rock boulders where they were working and knocked them out.

Gerritt came back into the day on his side tasting blood and the grit of dirt in his mouth. He raised his head, which seemed heavy, and wiped at his mouth with his hand. It came away red. He was on his elbow when he saw the boot not two feet from him. It was a plain, workman's boot, laced and worn, sitting there unmoving in front of him. Inside it was part of what had been a leg, grotesquely sticking up now with jagged edges of broken bone and blood vessels, brown with dust. No, he couldn't be seeing that thing, he was sure of it! He looked away, rolling over, his shoulder hurting.

Ned lay nearby. He wasn't moving and Gerritt crawled over to him. There was a deep gash in Tully's head where it hit the rock, but he was breathing.

"Ned, Ned, you OK?" Gerritt pulled at the khaki jacket sagging limply over a big stomach. Tully moaned, but didn't move. Gerritt walked over to the edge of the bench, trying not to look at the boot. The wind was blowing at his back, trying to push him over the edge. There were still smells of exploded powder coming up at him and other smells he couldn't identify, sweet and bitter. He knew there were three trucks down on that bench, the truck carrying the nitro pellets and the other two trucks with the equipment and men. Where Gerritt remembered the explosives truck, there was something that looked like a big hole and the other trucks were twisted and bent into shapeless metal sculptures. And there weren't any men. Where were they, Gerritt thought, incoherently? They were there before. He remembered the shouting and cursing as they loaded the shot. Where were they? There wasn't anyone there, only an enormous hole.

"Gerritt?" Tully called feebly. "Help me up." Gerritt turned and ran over to the old man.

"Is it gone?" Tully rasped.

"Yeah, gone," Gerritt whispered, choking. "Gone I don't know where."

"Can you get me up."

"I don't know." Gerritt tried to raise the heavy body, but his left shoulder kept going down, giving way under the weight. It didn't hurt; it just didn't function.

"Your shoulder's hurt," Tully said to him. They both looked at it. His arm hung in a funny way. Tully somehow managed to stand, leaning on a rock. He saw the boot then, and Gerritt remembered. They walked over to it, and Tully began to cry, silently, the tears cutting white scars down his cheeks.

And then Wes Bowen was there, glad he found them safe, if injured. Gerritt's arm was out of joint. Wes shoved him down, put a foot on his chest and pulled. The arm popped in, Gerritt screamed, and then got up slowly.

"It won't hurt much now, you're in shock," Wes said. "But it'll hurt later."

Tully mumbled something about the boot, better bring the boot. Wes picked up the thing and threw it into the back of the pickup. The drill that was moving too slowly for Gerritt now lay over on its side, the driver crushed and dead against the ground. A piece of metal from the drill pushed through his chest, pinning him to the earth.

They drove down to the bench below in Wes's truck. There was smoke and dust everywhere making it hard to see. Gerritt fell out of the truck with Ned and Wes.

"Got to find the men," Ned said over and over. At first it seemed they had vanished, vanished with the truck that was now only air in a hole, a deep hole in the earth. And then they began to see them, the pieces of lives, laying on rocks, blown yards from where they stood, loading the shot. Gerritt knew then why he hadn't seen any men from above; he looked for whole people. What was, what really was, were parts of men, laying everywhere, broken and smoldering on the dry brown rocks or smashed sourly up against the side of the bench. Acrid smoke from the explosion, yellowish and bitter, blew with the wind, which whipped gravel and cut faces.

More trucks arrived and the rescuers began to cough and vomit from the smells. There was murmuring, a looking around the fringes and then they began to find a few men left whole, blown far enough away or like Ned and Gerritt protected by rocks from the shock waves of the air blast. But some had been too close and their screams filled the air, rising and falling with the wind, almost a part of the wind of death that seemed to share in the agony. They were sought out, their broken bodies laid on stretchers from the ambulances that began to arrive.

Gerritt stumbled over a hard hat, picked it up and handed to Ned.

"Muñoz," Ted read on the hat. "Oh, dear God! He was the foreman. Where is he? He would have been right here. Where is he?" Tully began to walk in circles around the hole, the twisted wreckage of trucks. He couldn't find Muñoz anywhere.

A stretcher passed them filled with an unconscious man, his clothes, skin, even his mustache burned away. Body fluids oozed down his side, not bloody, more as though his body was weeping.

"Mañuel, Mañuel," Ned called after the stretcher, and then buried his face in his hands and fell to the ground, his shoulders shaking uncontrollably. "That was Mañuel Ortega, Juan's nephew. He's 23!" Ned cried up at Gerritt, who stood there not knowing how to help. It couldn't be true, it was too awful. His eyes began to spill out on his cheeks.

The stretchers kept passing him and Gerritt heard vaguely the sound of ambulance sirens. The dead, the silent ones, and the pieces of men were lined up in a row near the back of the bench. The man from the drill on the bench above had been brought down, a hole gaping in his chest. Gerritt didn't know him, but he had an overwhelming need to know who he was, recite his name, say that only a few minutes ago he was on the drill, alive.

Reicher walked over and asked something about a list of who was on the shot today, but Tully only shook his head, tears streaming from clenched eyes.

Three priests arrived, dusty cassocks swirling about them in the wind. Gerritt watched as their helpless words blew over the bodies. "Cordero de Dios, ten piedad de nosotros, danos la paz."

"Danos la paz, danos la paz!" Gerritt screamed into the wind as he walked away from their ministrations. "Give us peace, peace, peace!" Why couldn't they have the power to sweep the whole thing away and begin the day again, begin everything again! That would mean something. What good were their words now, only words. As though dying was something you did, an everyday thing like taking off your clothes or resting after you made love. No, this was anguish, wrenching of flesh from bone, so hurtful it was beyond fixing, beyond peace. There could be no peace.

Gerritt began to feel a running off of the mind where his thoughts made no sense, went round and round like the cherries in a slot machine. Nobody knew, nobody knew anything, there was no way to know. And then he was on the ground retching up onto the dirt, throwing up the whole horrible violation of life. And he was alone.

There wasn't time for Gerritt until later and by then he was back on his feet, blankly helping the others assemble bodies. Things slowed. Trucks began to arrive from New Camp with coarse wood coffins. The dead men that were whole were carefully placed inside, labeled and went off down the hill. But no one seemed to know what to do about the pieces of men, the grisly puzzle pieces that didn't quite fit together. The three priests talked quietly. Burying parts of men wasn't something they did every day, it was a thing to be weighed, handled in a proper and dignified manner. But how could you dignify this?

A limousine drove up, a black one with Hidalgo and a white station wag-on with Joe Driscoll. Gerritt shrank away. He somehow didn't want to see Joe now, to be associated with such waste.

Hidalgo and Driscoll walked around the wreckage, paying little attention to the human debris lying askew on the ground, the wind trying to bury it all where it lay. There was discussion about the lie of the various trucks, the hole where the munitions truck had stood, some loud words from Hidalgo and then he climbed into his black tank and was driven away. Reicher and Driscoll walked over to where the others stood staring at the remains.

"There were supposed to be 35 men up here today," Reicher said to no one in particular. "They took 8 to the hospital and 19 down in coffins. That means 8 are still missing." They all looked down at the arms and feet and clothing on the ground.

"There's not enough of anything here for eight men, Curt," Driscoll said. The fading afternoon and strain made his pitted face older.

"I know," Reicher looked away, pale. There was a long silence. "Bring in eight more coffins. There are eight more missing and there will be eight more coffins."

They're gone, Gerritt thought. Some of them gone, blown away, disintegrated, pieces now of air and sand. Muñoz, the foreman and seven others. He watched them put pieces of bodies into the eight boxes, then saw a boot. Mike picked it up. It was only a boot, but matched the one he had seen on the bench above when he first came to that morning. Without thinking, he ran to Wes's pickup and grabbed at the other boot where Wes had thrown it and ran toward Mike. Gerritt hugged the boot hard in spite of the ache in his shoulder. It was firm and brown, and inside was what was left of the leg, a man's leg like his. The bone fragments pressed into his shirt, he could feel them on his chest.

Mike reached out for it, but Gerritt held fast, staring at Mike and then began to laugh. The laughter shook him, racked his entire body, his white teeth blooming through the sooty mouth. But Mike had no patience, he was sick of the whole mess and he hit Gerritt across the face. Tears flew into the air and down to the ground and then Mike realized that Gerritt was crying and laughing at the same time. He grabbed the bloody boot and threw it into a coffin just in time to catch Gerritt as he fell.

"Don't take his shoulder," Wes screamed at Mike. "It was out of joint." Wes ran over. "Is he out?"

"Looks like it," Mike said, "I didn't think I hit him that hard." Gerritt moaned briefly and then was silent.

"OK, let's get him in the truck and take him home. There's not that much left to do here. What about Tully?"

"Felix took him to the hospital to get his head sewed up but I guess he'll have to wait in line with the mess coming from here."

The priests had begun to light candles in makeshift shrines as they drove off. There wasn't much to say in the truck. Gerritt leaned limply on Mike. He and Wes managed to get him home and laid him on the bed, partially undressing him and covering him with a blanket.

Wes dropped Mike off and then drove home, finally thinking of Alice. She would know by now and be worried. There wasn't any way to tell her about this. Only that there were a lot of men who wouldn't be going home that night or ever. She would understand that, Wes thought. Yes, she could understand that. Alice was up waiting for him. Rita Blain called her earlier to tell her what happened and that Wes was not hurt, a kind thing, Alice thought. Rita needed to talk about it, too. As much as she didn't like this place, it was her home and Ian's mine. The explosion hit everyone here.

When Wes finally came home, Alice could only hold him in silence.

CHAPTER 25

Sometime in the night, Gerritt woke up shaking. In front of his eyes were the dead men, their limbs flaccid and dripping blood. Helplessly, they waved, calling him to come back, come back. They came closer, weaving in and out, not dressed in anything, their bodies having no form. Then he was seeing their faces, beginning to see their faces. God, it was Shem, a thousand Shems, waving in front of him attached to the mutilated bodies, the ghosts dancing in his room.

Gerritt was awake, leaning on his hands and he shook his head to clear it. The forms, the faces melted into the white curtain pulled in front of a slightly open window, moving back and forth, toward him, then away.

"Christ," Gerritt said out loud. "What in hell is wrong with me?" Taking a deep breath he remembered the day, the explosion. There was still grit in his mouth from the blowing dirt and his arm hurt when he leaned on it. He sat up in bed, reaching over to close the window, stopping the curtains from moving. It was cold, cold to be living, colder to be dead. He felt bare, peeled back like an orange with no covering or resource left, the juices draining out of him.

He stood up and went for some Tylenol for his arm and a drink to clean the grit from his mouth. He didn't turn on a light. The light from the refrigerator was enough to knock an ice tray out into the sink and pour a heavy scotch. The wind outside was moving the walls, making them creak. Gerritt shivered.

Back in bed, he sat leaning against his pillow emptying the drink into his stomach, feeling the burning, warm sensation radiate into his body, and thought about why the dream ghosts looked like Shem. Gerritt did not know many of the men killed, like Tully did, but it was sickening anyway. Maybe that's why their faces became Shem's. He certainly could not wish Shem dead. His Uncle was all he had in the world and he loved him though they now had no common meeting place. Maybe it was only that he had seen Shem recently, and it meant a leave taking rather than a death, a leaving of what Gerritt had been on the farm. And here were all these men gone now, blown to bits. Lots of goodbyes. Maybe he was saying goodbye to himself, and what he was before Cerro Verde.

He drank the scotch quickly and setting the glass on the floor, fell asleep again. The next time he woke, he could see light coming through the white curtains. He was wet with sweat and dreaming about the nameless forms again, they moved in front of his eyes almost as if they wanted to be counted, recognized, given a meaning. And this time there was not only Shem, but Eve and Wes and the dead men from the explosion. The faces of the man under the drill, Mañuel Ortega, faces he hadn't seen, the ones that had vanished, ran through his mind. They were all mixed up together and all the same person, they all looked alike, all passing away from him. He was losing something he couldn't identify.

Gerritt sat up and wiped his forehead, breathing heavily. What was it? There was no sense in the floating forms. He was suddenly frightened, wanted to see Eve, wanted to be sure she was all right. He looked at his watch. It was seven; he would phone and go up for breakfast.

A shower took away the white forms. Gerritt pulled the curtains back and let in the day. He felt better. He was alive; Eve was alive. His shoulder hurt, but that would pass. Thinking of the explosion sickened him again, so he tried to think only about Eve, seeing her, smelling her. After breakfast, he would go out to the mine.

What he saw first when he arrived at the Gerencia, was Driscoll hunched over a table in the breakfast room, morning light flooding the place through skylights, illuminating the flowers and plants. Driscoll sat with his head in his hands leaning over a piece of untouched melon and swaying slightly back and forth.

Gerritt sat down by him, and the maid poured coffee.

"Joe?" Gerritt asked softly.

The older man looked up. His face was pale, withdrawn as though he were reaching into this room from another plane. His eyes were puffy. Driscoll probably had the same sort of night.

"Are you going up there?" Joe asked him finally. They looked at each other, sharing for a moment the suffering.

"Yes, I have to go." He didn't want to look at it all again, but supposed everyone would be having the same feelings this morning.

Driscoll stared ahead at nothing and drank his hot coffee "Well I can't," he said, setting the cup down noisily on the saucer, "Tell Reicher if he wants me, I'll be here until the funeral this afternoon."

"Sure," Gerritt answered and watched Driscoll leave the room.

He sat there, staring at the bougainvillea in the hall and finished a second cup of coffee before Eve came in, smelling of soap. Her hair was damp and hung limply over her shoulders and onto a pink dressing gown. She kissed him on the head and sat down.

"I'm so glad you called, Gerritt. I've just got this most wonderful thing to show you. Mum brought me a tea set from Lima. We'll have to use it this very afternoon. Alfredo loves it." She sparkled with her news. Her world was so lighted by small things. Gerritt looked at her sadly.

She probably didn't know about the explosion and if she did there would be no understanding. Was that good? Was it good to miss such gut-wrenching pain, to be free of loss, any loss? He stared into her dark eyes, looking for an answer. They moved back and forth reading his face. Her lips were trembling and she reached out for his hand.

"Gerritt, are you going to cry? I know about the big smoke in the mine. It shook my chair and Hortencia told me." She looked at him desperately. "Oh Gerritt, please don't cry. Dead is being happy. When you die there are blue skies and you fly into forever and birds are singing. Padre Simon says so."

Gerritt raised his head up to look at her. There was an ache in his throat and he couldn't swallow.

"Don't cry, Gerritt, please don't cry. I hate it. It's true. When you die, it's beautiful. Simon promised, he promised!"

"OK, Eve. I'm fine now." How could he not be fine? She knew so perfectly. The only one who could know. For her there were no complications, no intricacies, no disappointments. All of life was simple and good, even the end of it.

He pushed her dark hair behind a small white ear and held her very close.

"I love you, Eve." He said quite honestly. If ever he could love anyone, it must be Eve. She gave everything and asked for nothing.

"I love you, too, silly." She pulled back to smile at him, a radiant, happy smile. "Well then, let's have tea. Hortencia?"

"No, Eve. I can't. Not now. Maybe, maybe this afternoon, or tonight."

Hortencia came in and Gerritt looked at her. She was not a pretty woman but had always been neat, her brown uniform starched and ironed, almost to the point of severity. This morning she was totally disheveled. Her hair, which she wore braided around her head, had not been combed and pieces pulling out of the braids straggled down or stuck out at odd angles. Her face was puffy and red like a drunk's and her uniform looked wrinkled and slept in.

"Hortensia!" Gerritt exclaimed when he saw her.

She looked at him. The coffee pot in her hand started shaking. Gerritt caught the pot before she dropped it. He set it on the table and made her sit down by Eve

"Los siento, Señor. Mi hermano, mi hermano..." Her face dissolved in sobbing.

"Your brother, oh God. Lo siento." Gerritt felt helpless. Eve began to cry, too.

"I have to go to the mine. I have to go. Eve, talk to Hortensia. Make her rest. I must go." Gerritt felt if he stayed another minute, he would be crying with them. As his heels clicked in escape across the marble foyer he could hear Eve telling about the blue skies and singing birds. How he wished he could believe all that. Oh, how he wished.

He drove by the mine offices and seeing no trucks in front, went on up to the explosion site. The mine was silenced today, desolate without the sounds of machinery, and a deep melancholy was already descending on him before he arrived at the scene.

Wes and the engineering crew were taking pictures of the twisted truck wreckage, which was blown over three benches. There was the hole, nearly five feet deep where the explosives truck had been. The other trucks looked almost as if they were melted and then frozen in a dripping, contorted state.

"For Christ's sake, Wes, who wants pictures?" Gerritt asked.

"New York. And Curt said we better have some for legal reasons before anything is moved."

"Yeah, I suppose. What a fucking mess."

Ned Tully walked over to them. Gerritt could see a heavy bandage around his head under the hard hat and his eye was swollen below where the stitches would be. He was crying, wiping occasionally at his eyes.

"You alright Ned?" Wes asked.

"God in heaven, no I'm not! These were all my boys. I've worked with some of these men for thirty years. And you ask me if I'm all right! I'll never be all right again, I can tell you!" He hung his head and shook it sadly.

"Do you know what happened, Ned, do you have any idea?" Gerritt asked. His head was swimming. He was seeing Ned exactly as he looked in the dream, hazy and floating.

"Can't find anything here to tell me, that's for damn sure!" Ned said. "We were using some old explosive, trying to use it up, but it wasn't that sensitive. It couldn't have gone off by itself."

"What do you mean, old?" Wes said, suddenly turning to him.

"Oh just some stuff, we'd ordered a long time ago. It's been sitting in the polverine about a year, I think."

"Would it have been dangerous?" Gerritt said softly. He didn't want to upset Ned.

"Christ no, Wells!" You trying to tell me I don't know explosives?" He shoved his puffy face into Gerritt's.

"No, no, not at all Ned. I, of all people, know that." He was remembering the time Ned had told him to move the shovel. Tully nodded, dropped his head and wandered off.

Wes had to continue with his photography and Gerritt was left standing alone there, the wind already blowing dirt in swirls. He put the collar up on his jacket and began to walk around. Reicher didn't seem surprised at Driscoll's absence. He only nodded at Gerritt's message, intent on the paper in his hand where he was trying to draw a rough map of the truck locations, or where they had been.

Near the hole where the explosives truck used to be, Gerritt stood over a twisted piece of wreckage. The chunk of metal was or must have been, he decided, about three feet long and a cylinder of some sort before it was blown apart. There were traces of blue paint on it.

'A brake cylinder,' he thought to himself. 'What is a brake cylinder doing over here? If it were from the explosives truck it would have been blown far away or disintegrated?' Gerritt stood there for a long while trying to decide where it was before the explosion. Absently, his mind way ahead of his body, oblivious to the men working around him, he walked over to one of the surviving trucks, the one facing the hole. It was burned out, blackened and bent by the blast and fire following, as a relic of war might be. Gerritt walked around to the right side and there were the remains of a brake cylinder, now opened and bent, the compressed air expanding in the fire's heat. But when he walked around to the other side there was a hole where a cylinder should be, and half the truck was gone.

Gerritt looked at the wreck, then at the hole left from the explosives truck and the piece of a brake cylinder sitting in front of it, then back at the truck. They weren't more than 10 yards apart and were in a direct line.

Why hadn't anyone noticed this, Gerritt wondered. How did you explain the brake cylinder from this truck being so close to the hole? He couldn't. His head ached from the effort.

"You done with the pictures?" He asked Wes a little later.

"Yeah, why?"

"Well, I think I'm going to take that piece over there down to the Bosque and have a closer look at it." He stomped off before Wes could ask why and Gerritt couldn't have answered. It bothered him, that was all, and he needed to think about it.

He lifted the heavy metal chunk into the back of his pickup. It wasn't level and when he drove it over the rough road, it clanked and rattled as if trying to tell him something. The Bosque stood outside the main entrance to the mine, three large metal calamina buildings where the machinery was repaired. It was empty today, the only sounds those of the wind shaking and rattling the siding and roof. The men usually employed here were otherwise occupied today, or not likely to return at all.

It was difficult to get the brake cylinder wreckage into the building. It's torn edges caught on the truck bed and then on the door, but he finally wrestled it onto a workbench and turned on the light. Even with the light, the building was dim inside and he went for the flashlight in his truck.

He chipped at the blue paint on the edges and looked all around inside, not knowing what he was looking for. Was the explosives truck blue? There were charred marks all over it, but they could have been from any form of fire, perhaps the explosion itself. Without a chemical analysis of the ash residue, it told him nothing. Still, Gerritt was sure it meant something. He sat for a long time on a bench across from the twisted metal, staring at it and listening to the wind.

The funeral began at 2PM. Gerritt was late, didn't want to go at all, and couldn't get inside the Church. A cold wind was blowing the sand on the street, which pelleted the sides of his pickup as he parked several streets over. There wasn't any need for him to go inside. He didn't believe what the Priests were doing or saying would make a difference for the men in the coffins. For them it was over, done with; they were dead. Words wouldn't bring them back nor ease them into whatever came next, if there was anything. For some reason, he thought about Padre Simon, wondering if he knew and how he would view this loss.

The service seemed to be ending, as coffins started coming out of the Church, followed by several Priests. Gerritt stood watching the boxes come. Inside each was a man or what was left of a man. Then he saw Simon, walking heavily, his head bowed, his hands tucked inside the dirty brown cassock. Of course he would be here. What a business, Gerritt thought, to have this sorrow on your shoulders. Why would a man choose such a life of his own free will? Padre Simon walked very near him, stopped momentarily and put his hand on Gerritt's shoulder. It was heavy and Gerritt could hear him wheezing through his beard. They looked at each other, darkly, and then Simon went off behind the coffins.

After the Priests came Hidalgo and all his officials, then Driscoll, Reicher and the others. Gerritt fell into step with Wes.

"Where were you?" Wes asked, irritated that Gerritt skipped the sad affair.

"Checking out that brake cylinder."

"What brake cylinder?"

"That piece of wreckage I took off in my truck. I think it's a brake cylinder and it's got some blue paint and powder burns on it, but I'm not sure from what."

Wes turned to look at him thoughtfully. The square filled with people from the Church and others who also were not able to get in, as the thirty-five coffins were loaded onto pickups. The crowd cut the wind, but stirred up dust like cattle milling around. A band struck up a dirge and started out, followed slowly by the trucks, the clergy and then the people. The sobbing of women could be heard over the lament of the instruments, a sound like sheep bleating, coming in waves on the wind.

The sorry train of weeping, wailing humanity wound its way across the square, then crossed the Up Street, the Down Street and past the identical houses and apartments of the obreros. The cemetery rested a quarter-mile outside of town, walled in by whitewashed adobe. Once clear of buildings, the dust roiled up in earnest, enveloping the band of mourners. The taste of sulfury grit in his mouth brought back the day before and why they were here, the remains of that day carried in the boxes.

It took some time for the procession to pass through the narrow gate of the cemetery and, as at the Church, there wasn't room for everyone. The ceremony there lasted only a few minutes. The bodies were placed in a beehive mausoleum to wait for what they were promised in the Mass. Gerritt felt uncomfortable. He remembered his parents, but couldn't see their faces anymore. It was noticeably colder to him inside the white walls and smelled of stale flowers. People stood for a long moment as though anticipating something. The funeral they saw in Antofagasta the day they arrived came back to him; it was so long ago. Was this all there was? The elaborate church service, the wailing cortege and all of it to end on a silent shelf. There was no need to wait. Whatever came next, they couldn't follow any further. As if in agreement people began to leave, streaming out in straggling lines back to town.

Wes and Gerritt walked beside each other not talking. Their trucks were back by the Church and they headed in that direction.

"Bowen! Wells!"

They turned to see who was calling. It was Curt Reicher, running to catch up with them. He was frowning.

"Glad I caught you," he said breathing hard. "You need to be in the office early tomorrow. Hidalgo is coming around 8AM. I want to have a meeting before he arrives."

"What's the problem, Curt?" Wes asked. His large form was hunched over against the wind and grief, his hands stuffed in his pockets.

"The Union thinks maybe the accident was caused by faulty explosives. They want an investigation."

"Christ, Curt," Gerritt stormed. "There's nothing left up there. They saw it."

"I know, I know. But Hidalgo's heard something about the explosive being old. I'm having Tully check the records. We'll talk about it in the morning." Reicher walked back to where Hidalgo was still talking to Blain and Driscoll.

"Shit, that bastard! Every place he walks he leaves dirty footprints." Gerritt's hair was blowing wildly in the wind as he spoke. All he could think about was losses. How much was now gone that could never be recovered.

"There can't be anything to this. Tully's not stupid. He's not going to use anything dangerous." Wes looked at Gerritt, but their minds were working backwards to all they knew of Tully, trying to read his character.

"No, no I'm sure he wouldn't." But Wes was thinking. "But, what if…" he stopped, kicking at the dirt with his foot, sending clouds of dust up around his leg.

"What if what?" Gerritt said turning to look at him.

"Well, Curt called this morning. Seems Mike Marshall was down in Molino last night and overheard someone say something about suicide."

"What?" Gerritt was incredulous. "Mike's probably hearing things. He was juiced, I'm sure."

"Maybe." Wes said and started walking slowly toward the trucks.

Suicide, Gerritt thought. That was never a consideration. His mind went back to the wreckage of the brake cylinder, trying to make some connection. The two seemed unrelated, and yet Gerritt still had a gut feeling about the twisted metal that lay on the Bosque bench. He'd find out, yes, some way he would find out, know why he'd picked up that thing.

CHAPTER 26

The mine was shut down for a week. The order came from New York, which surprised everyone. It was a measure of the shock of this accident; rarely was anything more important than production. Even New York needed to mourn the loss. The hole that was the mine was desolate when Wes went out after the funeral, a cold wind blew gravel against his truck as he parked at the office. There was only the wind and the rock, the way it was before anyone ever started digging there. Curt wanted more pictures of the explosion site before anything was cleared away. Zuñiga was waiting for him, sadly sitting next to the camera equipment he had readied. They spent the rest of the afternoon photographing the scene from every angle. The photographs showed just the barren rocks and the twisted pieces of machinery. He did notice that one of the trucks was missing a brake cylinder and took detailed pictures of what was left, though he wasn't sure they would be much help.

The phone in the office rang. It was Mike Marshall. His voice was slurred and Wes was sure he was drinking.

"What's that, Mike, I can't understand you. Slow down, slow down." There was noise in the background and Wes was sure he was calling from a bar.

"Suicide! He left a suicide note." Mike screamed to make himself heard and it made him cough. Wes heard him vomit and the line went dead. Great, Wes thought, remembering Curt mentioning this at the funeral.

He left Zuñiga to process the film and went to find Gerritt. He didn't answer Wes's knocks, but it was open so Wes went in and found him lying on the bed. Gerritt rolled over and sat up. His face was red and swollen as though

217

he had been crying, but maybe he was lying there for a long time, frozen in one position.

"Want me to pick you up early tomorrow for the meeting?" Wes asked, slumping down on the other bed. Gerritt stared at him a minute.

"No, naw, I don't think I'll go. It's just a lot of shit with Hidalgo and I don't want to get involved. You go ahead. It's better if I don't think about it right now. See you in the afternoon maybe.

"There was a strange call from Mike at the office this afternoon," Wes said tentatively. Maybe it wasn't a good thing for Gerritt to have more specters right now, but he didn't want to keep this to himself.

"Said there was a suicide note and then hung up. Drunk and sick someplace down in Molino, I think. Do you know anything about a note?"

Gerritt looked up at him, his mouth open.

"No, just what Reicher said yesterday." He was still staring but elsewhere. Wes got up and left him there. Gerritt wasn't responsive. If he was going to react to this, it wasn't now.

Gerritt sat there for a long time. His mind went to the brake cylinder out in the Bosque, but it didn't make any sense. The phone rang. It was Eve and he went to her, not wanting to think about anything at all for a few hours.

Wes didn't sleep and kept Alice up. Alice was now heavy with their child and he worried that the shock of the last few days would affect the baby. She wanted to go to the doctor, but Jason Stoddard was far too busy with the wounded that had been left from the explosion and wouldn't have time for her. They were up early and Wes left for the office, wanting to have a look at the blasting orders from the day before, as if that would help the understanding of what happened. The daylight was just breaking orange and clear, with no dust from the mine to dull it. Wes saw that Curt Reicher's light was on as he went in. Curt must be thinking the same thing. Ned Tully would know the shot plans, but he wasn't there yet and was in bad shape at the funeral.

"Morning, Wes, thanks for coming early." He looked up, strain clear on his face. "Is Gerritt coming in?" Wes shook his head. Curt's eyebrows went up and then he bent back to the papers on his desk.

"I think I found what we want. Ted said last night he was pretty sure this lot was ordered more than a year ago. It sat around in the polverine, and might not be good."

"Why wasn't it OK? Oxidation?" Wes thought back to his classes at Mines. You just learned about explosives, their function, and use, not about how you actually dealt with them in a situation like this.

"Yeah, probably. Ned thought it might have been too sensitive and is blaming himself for using it." The cold fact stood there between them. Ned Tully had forty years experience. It shouldn't have happened.

"Well, Hidalgo's going to love that!" Wes said. The door slammed, it was Ned. He seemed to have aged in a withering sort of way. He wasn't chewing his usual plug and his eyes reflected no sleep and a deep sadness. Ned loved the men he worked with, worked next to them lifting the sacks and loading the shot, swearing and spitting, and enjoying the work. Ned had no children of his own and this was as close to being a parent as he would get. It was a parent's loss and he wasn't sure he could survive it. He felt old and tired and slumped down in the other chair in Curt's office.

"Did you find it?" Ned's voice was flat and hoarse.

"Yeah, it's here. About 20 tons were purchased 18 months ago. It's been in Polverines 21 and 22." The Polverines were the underground storage cellars for the explosives. They were some distance apart and nowhere near populated areas. You could see them from the gravel golf course outside of Molino. Bare brown pimples, they scarred a landscape already pocked with digging.

"That sounds about right," Ned said, clicking his teeth together nervously. He was missing his cheek full of tobacco.

They all nodded, looking down in thought. There it was, the purchase of death, there written in stark black and white in front of them. Curt waited for Ned to begin. There had to be a beginning somewhere, an explanation for all this. In an hour they had to have it. The rest of the mine staff would be there and the jury of Hidalgo and his men would want answers.

"I don't know what could have happened," Ted said finally. He looked about to cry again, but his own voice kept him from it.

"I don't, I don't. I've been out to that fucking site a dozen times and there is nothing there to tell me. It just went up! It shouldn't have, but it did."

"Are you sure it shouldn't have, Ned?" Curt wanted to be sure for Hidalgo, not for them. One telling from Ned was enough.

"Goddamn it, yes! I've worked with that stuff for years and you can throw it and jump on it. Without a fuse it's as safe as a bag of cow shit! I know it!"

"OK, OK," Curt said, calming Ned. It wasn't going to do to tear up the earth in front of the Union. The whole thing would have to be presented in an organized way, and they didn't have much time.

"Ned," Wes began, remembering now Mike Marshall's call. "What if the stuff was fused in some way? What would it take to set something like that truck off?"

"What do you mean, fused?" Ned turned to Wes, incredulous. It had not occurred to him. Explosives were something fragile and glasslike to him and to the men who worked with him. Their power engendered respect. They moved the earth where man could not.

"Who would do that?"

"Well, I suppose Hidalgo is going to ask that question so we may as well," Curt said looking at both of them for something, anything.

"What about the suicide note? Mike Marshall called me this morning, drunk and incoherent, said there was a suicide note and hung up. I didn't think much about it, but you heard something, too, Curt." His words fell on thick, dull, air.

"Julio heard about it and told me," Reicher acknowledged, not knowing what it meant.

"Christ," Wes screamed, jumping up. "I better get Mike up here altido". He called Mike at home, no answer, then reached him on his radio. He sounded sober and was on his way in.

"Yeah, I guess there was a note of some kind left." His radio crackled and Wes told him to get his ass directly to Curt's office. He was there in a few minutes.

Mike leaned against the door, there being no more chairs in Curt's office, looking at the expectant faces. He didn't know much and looked like hell.

"Lucho Figueroa's wife found a note. You remember him, the one who was always asking for you to bring back stuff from the States for him. He must have been close to the truck because we never found him, not even a piece of him." Mike belched loudly.

"What about the note, Mike, what about the note?" Curt was so calm. Wes found himself sweating. It was nearing 7AM and Hidalgo would be there at 8AM.

"Well, what about it? I don't know what it said exactly. Videla told me. The note said he was going to end it. That's all Videla knew."

"Why did he have to take so many people with him? How did he do it?" Ned gasped.

"Now look, everybody," Curt looked at us all. "No one knows for sure this was the cause. Let's not go hanging labels on people just yet."

"Well, something set that Goddamn ammogel off, I can tell you," Ted declared. "It didn't just fuck itself!"

There was the grinding noise of trucks coming up the short hill to the side of the offices. The rest of the staff was arriving for the meeting. Leif Swenson hurried in, nervous and afraid he had missed something. Felix Alford and Hugh Dillon arrived together dressed in starched khakis ready for the confrontation. Ian Blain, soon after and then Joe Driscoll. Only Gerritt was missing. Curt briefed them on what they knew, which wasn't much. Ned repeated insistently that the truck couldn't have gone up by itself. Mike talked about the "note", and there were raised eyebrows and wonder.

Wes retreated to his office, having a thought about the brake cylinder, and tried to reach Gerritt. He found him at the Gerencia.

"Yeah, I'm not coming down there," Gerritt said emphatically.

"Well, there really was a suicide note and Ned thinks someone may have set the explosion. What do you think about that brake cylinder you found?" There was silence on the other end of the phone.

"Shit," Gerritt said between his teeth. "Not sure how. I'll see you later." And he hung up. Wes sat there looking at the phone for a minute. Gerritt was just out there someplace.

Zuñiga was doing his morning tasks, making coffee and cleaning the office. Although today he was having a little more trouble than usual, since there was still broken glass everywhere and the papers and maps were in complete disorder. He had nailed cardboard over the windows and gave Wes a helpless look.

"Señor Jefe," he said. "Don't worry. I get the place ordered up and the windows fixed. No worry." Zuñiga looked at his skinny feet moving nervously inside his shoes.

"Señor Jefe, there is talk. Figueroa, no cierto?" Yes it was true.

"He would not do this thing. Muy malo. He was a good man."

'Yes,' Wes thought. We are all good men. And yet some of us do bad things every day. He wasn't sure Figueroa couldn't have done it, no matter how good a man he was. But Wes nodded to Zuñiga. It was better Zuñiga think that being a 'good man' settled it all.

Wes poured coffee and went back out to the main office, where the meeting was gathering. Chairs and tables were moved around to accommodate everyone. At 8:15AM, a car pulled up outside, the black limo. Hidalgo brought two lawyers, abogados, with him. They came in first and held the door for the man. An electric tension filled the room. The abogados looked like Hidalgo. All Chilean officials looked the same to Wes, a rubber stamp. Dark hair, long, and greased back. The dark glasses so you couldn't tell whom they were watching. Black suits, appropriate for mourning. Driscoll gestured to chairs at the center of the main table and everyone sat down. Lucius Alvarado, one of the company lawyers from Santiago had flown in. Ian Blain and the entire mine staff sat tense and ready for the confrontation.

It did not go well. The morning sun broke through the windows heating the room and soon it was stuffy. Wes sat next to Ned, who had finally taken a plug in his cheek and spat into the wastebasket every few minutes. The panging sound was somehow comforting as a sound is when you are used to hearing it. Wes sat thinking about the cylinder, trying hard to make some connection, and wondering what Gerritt thought. He was glad Curt and Ned knew about the note as it was one of the first things brought up.

Hidalgo suggested that perhaps Figueroa was paid to do this, which was ridiculous. Even Hidalgo would know that. Curt remained calm, but every time Ned would pang his brown spit into the basket, Curt would frown. He knew Ned thought the proceedings were shit and that they had to figure out what had actually happened.

Joe Driscoll finally asked Hidalgo what he thought the company ought to do, explaining that the future support of the widows and family would be handled without question.

Hidalgo considered, totally without expression, fingering his black, greasy mustache. Ned grew restless and Wes could sense the anger rising in him. Ned seemed sure that something or somebody had set off that truck and that was good enough.

"Quizás," Hidalgo began, his voice syrupy and slow, as though he wasn't sure what he was going to say next.

"Perhaps, we will run some tests with the explosives to see how safe it is. You say it is safe, but how do we know? You test it. Then we will talk again."

It was over. No more talk. A short silence and Hidalgo got up and swept out the door and was gone, followed by his henchmen. The room seemed empty and quiet. Hidalgo hadn't said what he meant by 'testing the explosive'. No one seemed to know. Then a loud pang into the wastebasket and Ned spoke. Wes watched as the brown glop slid slowly down the side of the basket and onto the paper and other waste.

"What the fuck does that bastard want us to do, shoot it at ten paces?" Ned broke the shell of silence. People began moving around, getting more coffee, and murmuring suggestions. Ian thought it might be good to drop-test it from an airplane at different altitudes. That seemed as good a plan as any.

"Juan Ortega's brother, Jorge, is a pilot and flies a small plane out of the airport in Molino. He's a dentist, I think. I'm sure he would help."

Wes wasn't so sure. Juan Ortega probably didn't want to hear from anyone at the mine ever again after Gerritt took his job. And a cousin of Juan's was killed in the explosion. It seemed like he wouldn't take to his brother helping out.

"OK, who's going to do it then?" Curt asked, assuming they could get Jorge to fly. "We'll need volunteers to go up with some sacks of explosive." No one readily spoke up. Most had families and were thinking about them.

"Hell, I'll go," Ned said finally. "It's my end anyway. Seems like I'm the only one that thinks this stuff isn't going to blow up when you touch it." Ned looked over at Wes.

A thousand things were going through his head. Alice, the baby, Gerritt, the brake cylinder, all the dead men. To Wes, dying was something you did when you were ready. It was all the people you left that generated the hurt. Volunteering to die himself and now made him hesitate, losing the today, not seeing the baby. There was a time for it, but the thought of it coming now made him angry. Then he thought about the widow Figueroa, and wondered if she was angry, too, and would want to know what happened.

"I'll help you, Ned," he heard himself saying. Curt agreed readily. It was settled. Somehow doing something, having a plan, was a good thing. Even though they were all unsure of how it might come out, the action eased the tension.

"Let's get on with it. You know Jorge Ortega, Ian?"

"Yes, his office is in the Union building in Molino."

"Fine. You and Tully try to see him today to set something up." The meeting was over. Felix came over to talk to Wes.

"Are you sure you want to do this thing, Wes. You have a baby on the way."

"It's OK. I think Tully knows what he's doing." He wasn't sure that he would tell Alice exactly what he was going to do. But, underneath, he believed Ned; the age of the explosive had nothing to do with the accident.

CHAPTER 27

Blain and Tully weren't gone long. Jorge Ortega readily agreed to fly for the tests. It was almost as though he knew they were coming, was expecting them. Mañuel was his cousin, too, and Jorge had been giving him flying lessons. Now he was dead. Tully grumpily told Wes to meet him at seven the next morning. The tests were scheduled at 8AM, too early for anyone but the Union and the company to know about them. It wasn't clear what dropping the bags of explosive from an airplane would prove. Certainly the same bags sitting on a truck would not be expected to go up. Hidalgo would know that and Wes wondered if he, too, felt this was only a gesture, and because they didn't know what else to do. Wes called around for Gerritt after the meeting and found him at the Gerencia.

"It's not a good place up here," Gerritt said. "Joe is inconsolable and is just drinking scotch."

"Yeah, well, nobody knows what to do. We're going to drop some of the amogel from a plane, Jorge Ortega's plane, to see if it explodes."

"What? That's crazy! It's not going to go off!"

"Right, but we're doing it anyway. I'm meeting Ned at 7AM tomorrow. You need to be there, Gerritt." Wes had been thinking. Gerritt was in charge of operations now and should assume that role instead of playing at it. Silence on the other end of the phone.

"I'll pick you up," Wes said finally.

"OK, but this is ridiculous. I still think this has something to do with that brake cylinder."

Gerritt was ready when Wes pulled up the next morning. He hadn't slept much after going home to his own place. The supports on a brake cylinder in one of the other trucks must have blown up somehow. He supposed someone could have done it and wondered about Figueroa.

"Maybe Figueroa blew the supports out, Wes. Or he could have just set the explosives truck off to blow himself up."

"Why would he take all his friends out, too? That seems a bit much."

Tully was late, arriving at the office strained and nervous. Ignoring his own tardiness, he ordered Wes and Gerritt to follow him. They stopped at the explosives bodega to pick up two other men who would help with the loading. One had a bandage over his eye and the soft sad look about him of one who survived when others did not. Both had known the dead men well and got into their truck with serious looks, innocently honest, as though they were all engaged in an earnest mutual pursuit. Gerritt ached for their illusions.

The pampa was bathed in the gold light of early morning as they drove down to Molino. The road seemed like a long pointed stick ending in the spread of town a thousand feet below them. The newness of each day on the pampa never failed to amaze.

But Molino was the same as the day before at the funeral; dimly dirty in the daylight. The callampas of town glistened at the water faucets where constant dripping made mud under the feet of grimy children. Gerritt felt nauseous, remembering his recent night at the bar and the dead rat in the trough. They passed the Guarderia, the day home for children run by a thin Salvation Army couple. Its whitewashed walls stood out against the darkness of the early morning.

Molino, like New Camp, had an Up Street and a Down Street although the town was nearly level. Near its center, there were nicer houses and stores. The streets off the main street here were paved and there was less dirt and more hope. Then, they were through, winding past more callampas, a nitrate plant, and turning onto a narrow, dusty road.

The polverines rose ahead of them as they turned again, each with its own road. The separate mounds reminded Gerritt of gravesites. There were markers for each one, wood steles to tell what lay inside. Tully stopped in front of number 22. The dust of the two trucks caught up with them and they waited until it blew away to get out.

The door to the polverine opened to Ned's key, squeaking as it rubbed against the sandy earth. It was cold inside and there was a musty smell mixed with ammoniacal gases from the explosive.

"Think six sacks will be enough?" Ned asked, spitting brown tobacco juice on the floor.

"I guess so." Wes said. The sacks were stacked neatly in rows. They were so ordered and dealt such disorder.

Gerritt walked over and touched one. It felt like lawn fertilizer, the round white pellets that make grass green. It was hard to think these innocent pale beads could blow a mountain away, could make something into nothing. The others were having the same thoughts. They were standing, staring, too, as though they had been searching for something and found it, only it was disappointing.

"Let's go!" Ned growled.

The sacks weren't heavy; they weighed maybe twenty pounds each. The men put three in each truck and covered them with tarps against the sun.

The ride to the airport was in silence. Ned drove more slowly and carefully, as if he had a truckload of babies in the back.

"That stuff wouldn't go if we crashed, would it?" Gerritt asked uneasily.

"Ned said it needs dynamite to blow."

"How come he's driving so slow then?"

The airport wasn't far and they could see at some distance the crowd of trucks and Hidalgo's black car. A small Cessna stood on the edge of the runway, a man was checking the oil.

"That's probably Ortega out by the plane," Wes mumbled. "Hope he knows how to fly that thing." Ortega was a small man with a head of wooly hair. He finished his task and disappeared into the small concrete structure that was the only building on the strip.

The men crowded around the trucks when they stopped.

"Is this the explosive?" Hidalgo said in English, lifting the tarps in one of the truck beds. It was more a pronouncement than a question. Everyone was there, Driscoll, Blain, Reicher, Dillon, even the Chilean shifters.

"I'm going up, not you," Gerritt said to Wes. Wes looked at him and nodded, gratefully, glad he hadn't worried Alice.

Hidalgo was accompanied by his lawyers and toughs. They discussed the test once more, no one wanting to get on with it.

"Where's Ortega?" Reicher finally asked. No one seemed to know.

"I think he went into that building, whatever it is," Gerritt said.

"They're building a terminal. Go get him, Wells."

Gerritt walked over to the unfinished structure, still feeling queasy from the day before.

When the terminal was planned, the government was to pay half the cost and the company half. It would have been a large structure with a lighted strip, but the government had reneged or run out of money. Now there was only a half-finished cement skeleton, left to face the ravages of wind and pampa gravel. The tower had no windows and no radio and a family who took care of small private planes and gassed the daily DC-3 that came in from Santiago inhabited the base. The caretaker was a shriveled little man with too many children, who hung up tarps against the wind and made some few pieces of furniture. Washed clothes blew from a rope line on the side.

Ortega was in the kitchen eating an avocado sandwich and gulping down orange Fanta mixed with beer. The meal made Gerritt feel as though he could vomit again.

"Siente se, siente se," he said. "Would you like something to eat?" Under the brush of black hair a narrow mustache moved in a circular motion when he chewed.

"No thanks," Gerritt said, swallowing down the lump in his throat. "Somos listo."

"Bueno," he smiled and the mustache relaxed and bent upwards. "Are you ready to blow up the pampa?" He said laughing and stood up. When he laughed you could see the gold teeth in his mouth, appropriate for a dentist.

He threw a few coins to the sagging wife, wiped his face and strode out the door, taking large steps for so small a man.

Curt Reicher was crossing the concrete expanse to the tower when they came out. He seemed anxious.

"Can we load up now?" He asked Ortega.

"Claro, Señor Reicher!"

Three of the sacks were carefully loaded into the front seat next to Jorge. Ned got in behind Ortega and Gerritt followed. As he climbed in, Gerritt put his hand on the bags. He wanted to squeeze them in his hand like he had done with sacks of beans and rice on the farm at home. The plane was smaller inside than Gerritt had imagined, the whole atmosphere cramped. He felt confined, walled in with Ned Tully, a large man who smelled of stale tobacco, and a wailing monster in the bags of white death. Ortega was whistling and Tully chewing on his plug. Neither seemed nervous.

Gerritt was relieved when at last the engine roared to life and they began to roll down the runway, though the sacks jiggled and moved ominously. They lifted from the ground and for a few minutes he was absorbed in the sight of people and houses receding from his eyes. Ortega circled around to gain altitude and yet still be over the eager audience below, their heads straining upward like a bunch of flowers waving in the wind.

"We're a thousand feet above the strip. Is that high enough?" Ortega shouted, the sound of the motor grinding loud in their ears.

"Yeah," Ned hollered. "Let's get out into that open space east of the runway. Then we'll drop the sacks."

The door was hard to open because of the wind. Gerritt leaned over the seat, pushing out on the handle while Ned shoved the sacks out one at a time. It was cold at that altitude and air filled the plane, quickly chilling them. Ned hurried. The sacks fell out one after another, each with a grunt from Ned.

They watched them grow smaller, sailing away below as Ortega circled back. The flower faces on the runway followed them down. When each sack hit the earth, small puffs of dust rose, no more than there would have been from the impact of a rock.

Ned said, "Humph," and Ortega sighed and smiled, banking the plane for a landing. Gerritt felt his whole body relax, part by part, feeling the bones under his skin. When they landed, he could read the relief in the welcoming faces. Only Hidalgo frowned. Was he disappointed?

What Hidalgo wanted, they found was to have the other three sacks dropped, just to be sure. This time Gerritt climbed into the plane with no trepidation at all. Tully was right, there was nothing to fear from the sacks of explosive alone.

And when the second sack exploded, he felt only a sort of disappointment, a letting down, as though someone he trusted failed him.

Tully was furious.

"Son-of-a-bitch, that can't happen! Son-of-a-bitch!" He kept saying over and over. But it had happened and they all saw it, the large cloud of white smoke and the pop like a gun going off a few seconds later.

Jorge Ortega watched the white puff going up, his eyes widening to a crescendo and his head hitting the top of the plane inches above him when the sound of the explosion reached his ears.

"Dios mio!" he cried and turning to Tully he completely forgot the plane for a few seconds and it began to weave crazily across the sky, him looking and correcting and then turning back to Tully with a wild look in his eyes. Gerritt grabbed the safety strap, frightened, and Tully kept saying "Son-of-a-bitch, Son-of-a-bitch."

"What's wrong? What happened? You said there would be no explosion!" Jorge screamed. He was panicked, the sweat beginning to run down from the dark mound of hair. Then he remembered the third sack of explosive sitting inauspiciously beside him there on the front seat, its sides squished in where hands had pressed into it during the loading. Jorge seemed to erupt from his seat and the plane went into a steep climb. Gerritt's stomach dropped down to his feet and back up again.

"Get it out of here! Out! Out!" He screamed at them, the plane bobbing around.

"Hold the Goddamn plane steady," Gerritt screamed. He could barely manage to bend over the seat to the door, the plane was lurching so badly.

"OK, Ned, shove it out!" The sack plummeted toward the earth and Gerritt slammed the door shut. It was silent in the plane after all the shouting. Ortega was maintaining the plane in a proper position now and with no further words, circled for a landing. Gerritt felt sorry for him. As a dentist, he would be completely unfamiliar with explosives. Tully should have explained the test to him in more detail. At the very least Jorge needed to be prepared for the sound of the stuff going off.

The last sack did not explode. It wafted its way down and bumped onto the pampa harmlessly. Ortega sighed, relieved, but Gerritt was sure he would not go up again for any further testing.

It wasn't necessary. Though everyone was upset about the one explosion, it was still clear that it wouldn't go off by itself; something would have to deal it a blow. It was almost like a human reaction; something must hit it for it to hit back.

There were great arguments there on the airfield and afterwards in the offices about what the tests meant. Hidalgo finally stood up, followed by his henchmen, said the tests didn't mean anything, and walked out the door to his limo.

"So where does this leave us?" Curt Reicher asked the group after the door slammed on Hidalgo.

Gerritt stopped by the Bosque on the way back from the airport. With set lips, he loaded the twisted metal wreckage into the truck bed and drove back to the offices. After Hidalgo left, he went out to get it and banged on the door several times with the heavy thing before Mike Marshall opened it.

"For Christ's sake, Wells, what are you doing with that piece of junk," Marshall said grinning.

"Just hold the goddamn door open, will you." Gerritt struggled to get the thing through the door and dumped it on the floor. Everyone heard the commotion and turned to see the object of Marshall's derision.

"What's that, Wells?" Reicher asked disgustedly. "I want to discuss next steps now." Curt was annoyed.

"It's a piece of brake cylinder I found up near the accident, and I think it's important."

"Oh yeah?" Reicher said. "There's hardly enough left to see what it was."

Tully stood up, bit off a new plug and leaned on the door looking at the wrecked cylinder.

Thoughts had been growing in Gerritt's mind. Some fuse or concussion was needed to set the explosive off.

"Suppose Figuoroa had taken a stick of dynamite with him that day and set it off next to the brake cylinder after carefully parking his truck so it was aimed at the explosives vehicle. Then pshew, it would be like a torpedo!" Gerritt gesticulated with his hands. He was excited by his idea and looked at Wes for approval. It was all making sense at last.

Wes examined the twisted metal.

"That's crazy, but maybe just crazy enough. What do you think Ned?" Wes said finally.

"Could this have been blown up with dynamite by Figuoroa and then torpedoed the explosives truck? Could it, Ned?"

Ned switched the tobacco plug in his mouth from side to side, thinking.

"Maybe." And that's all he would say. Gerritt stood there looking at him helplessly. Tully should know, if anybody knew, whether it was possible.

"That's just a wild idea, Wells," Reicher said impatiently. "There's no way to prove it."

"Well, I know that's the way it happened, I'm sure of it." Gerritt was surprised when this came from his mouth. Was he sure? He had certainly given it a lot of thought and in his mind, it was necessary to resolve the cause. When you died there should be a reason. Gerritt never understood why his parents died. Death should finish something. If it didn't, a death meant nothing.

"Oh fine," Curt said, hitting his head with the palm of his hand. "I can see trying to explain this to Hidalgo. He'd laugh."

"I know who would know if it was true. The widow Figuoroa! Maybe I'll just go down and have a little talk with her, then." Gerritt was incensed when Reicher shrugged his shoulders and disappeared into his office. The group broke up then with nothing logical or final to consider.

"Gerritt, come on in the office and talk awhile." It was Wes, pulling his arm. Wes's hand felt cold on his flesh, but he followed.

"What are you planning to ask her?" Wes said. In the background, Zuñiga was nervously cleaning up the office and watching them.

Gerritt sagged down into a chair.

"Reicher's given up." Gerritt felt Zuñiga's cold stare on him. He knew the man understood English, though he pretended not to.

"I don't think it's so much that he's given up as that it really doesn't matter what caused it. The men are dead, nothing is going to bring them back. This will put the widow through a trauma, an unnecessary trauma. Don't you care about her? What about her feelings?"

It seemed to Gerritt that the widow would want to find out the truth, too; know what happened. Knowing was so God awful important. He looked over at Zuñiga. Some terror seemed to be overtaking him. He was shaking and burst over to Gerritt.

"You no go, Señor Wells, no go! You get hurt! Not friendly there. Malo! Por favor, no sale!" Gerritt's eyes widened. A fury grew up from in his chest, fury at ignorance, the fear of truth. Why didn't people want to know? He stood up, almost throwing the chair back against the desk and stalked out slamming doors to the office and truck, started the motor and drove to New Camp.

He had some difficulty finding the address and cooled considerably by the time he turned down Señora Figueroa's street. When he saw the crowd of men in front of her door, he knew it was hopeless, he would never see her. But he drove up close to them anyway, leaving the engine running. They were a cruel looking bunch of men, scowling, and leaning against the sides of the house and fence, trampling the flowers in the small yard.

Gerritt saw a shadow of a heavy woman pass the window inside the house. Wanting desperately to reach out to her, ask her, know, he rolled down the window of his truck and turned his eyes away from the men. He didn't see the rock coming. It hit him on the forehead above his eye, not hurting really, but he knew it was cut, like when you slice your finger with a knife.

"Vayase, vayase Gringo!" the men shouted angrily, picking up more rocks. He automatically shoved his foot down on the accelerator and shot down the street, a hail of rocks hitting his pick-up, and didn't slow down until he was well on the way home. Only then did he reach up, the trickle of blood seeping down into his heavy eyebrow itched strangely.

He knew then what Tully's "maybe" meant. It meant mind your own business. Gerritt felt quashed, his enthusiasm extinguished, put out like a bucket of water spilled on coals. The steaming desire to know was still there, gnawing at his insides.

'The bastards,' he thought. 'Keeping me from her.' It was a concrete and logical request for him, this wanting to know. But Gerritt would never find answers from Señora Figuoroa, not today, not ever. What he couldn't understand was the unbridled anger at the Gringo for everything bad that happened here.

The cut over his eye required only a band-aid and a scotch, though it attracted much attention the next day at the office. He told them little. There was nothing to tell; so little evidence to go on, he could prove nothing. The wreckage of the brake cylinder disappeared from the office and in time from conversation.

Reicher doubted the Señora would tell Hidalgo about any dynamite, even if she knew. And Hidalgo only continued his pursuance and harassment a few days, then let the matter fade. It was impossible to tell what really happened and reason seemed to sink into the sand of the mine, where it lay buried.

According to Zuñiga this wasn't the first time something of the sort had happened.

"Happen cada dies años in Cerro Verde. Muy malo and same Augusto. No why." This was the third such accident to happen in the mine, one every ten years, always in August, and without explanation. But Gerritt couldn't accept a superstition. Unlike a machine; there was something frightening and unsettling about how weak men were, how they reacted to emotion. There was no answer. Gerritt finally let it slip into the recesses of his mind where he hid things he didn't want to remember.

CHAPTER 28

The mine went back to work. The offending explosives in Polverine 22 were quietly disposed of, burned far out on the pampa where the winds would take the smell and memories of the explosion away to the cordillera.

Gerritt's recurrent nightmares remained, specters that hovered above, waking him in the night. Sometimes there were other faces, sometimes Shem, sometimes Eve. She floated above him with the window curtains, blowing in the cold breeze through his open window. He was able to imagine her there with him, but not truly there, more a symbol of her, of the earth, the mine, the explosion, everything he was. He began to feel as though Eve were some irrevocable part of him, intertwining with his insides, attaching herself like a web. Relieved each morning to have the night over, Gerritt eagerly went out to the mine, to reality. The dripping oil and groaning of machines were where he felt at home. As long as the mine was running, he would be all right.

The tunnel for the conveyor system was begun on the outside of the mine near the sulfide plant. It would be located where Gerritt wanted it; he'd won that point. When the day came to start the drilling and blasting, as Mine Foreman, he simply sent the crews to the site he wanted and little more was said. The access road to the bottom of the mine was saved and the time it would cost to build a new road would be applied to hauling ore. It wasn't ideal, and Wes objected.

"I see you sent the drills outside the mine, Gerritt. I thought we agreed that we needed to move the access road inside and start there!" Wes leaned on the door to Gerritt's office that afternoon. Wes was not pleased. Gerritt looked up from a model of a dozer he was working on.

"We can't have the tonnages decreasing, Wes. You know that. New York wouldn't like it!"

"New York understands we have a tunnel to construct and it should go in at the best site! They understand it may hold up hauling ore for a week or so."

"Well, I didn't like it! We're starting outside the mine and it will come in under the existing access road." He went back to his model. That was it.

Lowering the tonnage was something Gerritt would not do right now. After the meeting where it was decided to move the road and start the tunnel inside the mine, Gerritt went down himself to look at both sites again. He carefully examined the sight where the tunnel would come through into the bottom of the pit from outside, drilled at a slight incline. He refused to lower production by building a new road. The rock looked solid enough, but the benches were much steeper in this part of the mine.

The first blasting for the tunnel was done with great ceremony. Government officials came up from Santiago, but not President Frei. As a socialist, Eduardo Frei Montalva would not attend a triumph of an American company. Gerritt did not understand his reticence. Frei's government received enormous sums of money from Cerro Verde. The conveyor would increase production by 10%, cutting down on haulage times. It seemed an event to mark, for all involved. Instead, the Minister of Mines was there, a dark, serious man who contributed a proper dignity to such an auspicious occasion. A square cement collar was built around the edge of the tunnel entrance outside the mine; it looked very much like the entrance to an ancient tomb.

The night after the ceremony, Joe Driscoll gave a party at the Gerencia to celebrate a record production year. Gerritt was on a high. He knew Driscoll credited him with the production increase and the party seemed, because of that, to be for Gerritt. Lobster was flown in from the coast and tables were heavy with roast pig and sides of beef. Everyone on dollar row from the mine and mills was invited. There were cocktail parties beforehand, but Gerritt went up to the Gerencia early and had a drink alone with Driscoll. Their conversation was mostly about the tunnel and the successful putting to bed of the explosion and aftermath. His place there and in Eve's life seemed to have been accepted.

The tables were set up in the atrium of the Gerencia where blooming bougainvillea near the glass ceiling floated over the guests. The crowd soon arrived, waited on by mozos in white coats who served drinks. Alice and Wes were among the first to arrive. Alice was very pregnant.

"Hi Gerritt. We aren't staying long. My legs are bothering me," Alice said. One of her hands supported her back.

"Yeah, I think we will probably go home early." Wes was nervous about her. Jason Stoddard told them it was normal at the end of pregnancies, but it was their first baby and they worried about everything.

Rita Blain was drunk when she arrived and weaved around laughing loud-ly and spilling red wine down the front of her green dress. She hit Rene Dillon accidently in the eye with her purse and hung on everyone, even Gerritt.

"I hope you know what you're doing, you bastard." She whispered in his ear hoarsely. He squirmed out of her grasp, trying to ignore her. She smiled insolently at him, then went weaving off to bother others.

The band was from Santiago and beat out the "tah..ta-tah," of the Latin music on a steel drum and tire rim until Gerritt felt the music moving through him, coming out the tips of his fingers and toes with the scotch. Eve was dressed in black with white pearls that shimmered against her dark skin. She loved to dance, hugging him closely; she was soft and her thin dress excited him. Her black hair hung full and loose down her back and Gerritt ran his fingers through it as they danced, and down her back to where the small buttocks curved out. He left his hand there, thinking about the soft wetness that was below. He wanted her, but how? Gerritt buried his face in the fragrant mane at the side of her head, a thought occurring to him. And why not? Yes, why not. It was time.

He pulled back from her to look at her face, a round moon smiling up at him, pale and happy. He kissed her lightly on the lips.

"Eve," he whispered. "I want to marry you! Marry you tonight." Why hadn't this occurred to him before? It was a perfect idea. It would seal every-thing, make it sure, permanent.

"What? Marry? You and me? She said softly. "Like Momma and Daddy/"

"Yes," Gerritt said into her ear, holding her close now, feeling her body rub against him. She was silent. Gerritt knew it would be an overwhelming idea, one she would need time to grasp. But, he couldn't let her talk to her parents, not yet, not until it was done.

"Eve?" He asked, waiting. "Eve, I love you."

She drew away from him, to look at him seriously.

"Is that what people do then?" She said questioningly. She was totally dependant on his judgment, he knew that.

"Yes, we'll do it tonight, OK?"

"Oh yes! Let's tell Momma," And she started away from him toward the table where Driscolls were sitting. Gerritt grabbed her to him.

"No. Let's make it a surprise." They danced together in silence then for awhile, Eve giggling softly. They were close and she was so warm, he felt flooded with light. It was right, he knew it. The others would see that in time. It was meant to be. There was a reason for him being here. Yes, it was the right thing, the only thing. Then the necessity of a license occurred to him, but he passed it over being sure that Padre Simon could fix it. Yes, they would go to Santa Bárbara.

Late that night after the party, Gerritt drove up to the Gerencia, coming from the backside and cutting his motor to coast down to the large building. He didn't want to wake the maids. He explained everything carefully to Eve. He would knock on her window and she was to pack things only for the night without telling Hortensia and come to the side door. It was farthest from the sleeping people in the house.

Eve appeared in the window when he knocked softly, but she wasn't dressed. He motioned for her to open the window.

"Aren't you ready?" he asked in a whisper.

"No. Is it time? I was packing Alfredo's things."

"Screw Alfredo."

"What?"

"Never mind," he rasped. "Hurry and get dressed." Gerritt sighed, leaning against the outside wall. He didn't want to think what would happen if they were heard. It was a clear night with no moon. The wind was stilled, but at this altitude there were no crickets, or noises of any kind. He turned back to the window and saw Eve scurrying around, the nightgown came off, the clothes were thrown on. She picked up two armloads of something and came to the window.

"I'm ready. Oh Gerritt, I'm so excited!" She had a small bag in one hand and Alfredo in the other.

"Come on, come out the window since I'm here." She climbed up clumsily, her pale spidery arms gleaming in the black night. When he grabbed her, his hand slid up under her dress to her crotch and as he felt the warmth there briefly, there was a surge of blood in his body. Eve giggled and he put his hand over her mouth briefly to quiet her.

In the truck, he coasted down the hill, not starting the engine until they were beyond where Driscolls would hear. He headed out on the road to Santa Bárbara, deciding what he would say to Padre Simon when they woke him.

The truck flew. Gerritt hardly noticed the passage of time. Eve drew over very close to him, her hands like waves of oil on his body. She wanted to touch every part of him and he had to push her away to keep driving, keep from stopping. She kissed him on the mouth and her tongue, which had always kept its place, was suddenly searching, rubbing on his teeth, tickling his lips. He grew hotter, his breathing faster. Eve giggled, tried to sit on his lap, feeling the hardness of his body. Gerritt didn't think he could make it, then he saw the silent groups of adobe houses, the pueblo that was Santa Bárbara and he started laughing to himself. They looked at each other. Yes, he would have it all.

They knocked on Padre Simon's door together, holding hands. The night cooled Gerritt. He wiped the sweat from his forehead. They knocked again, then heard stirrings inside, a shuffling of feet and the saguaro cactus door opened. Simon was used to being awakened in the night for birth and death, but was unprepared for these visitors who wanted something in between. The Priest was in a huge night shift, his giant feet stuck out the bottom and splayed on the bare floor.

"Eva, Eva," his voice shook. "Que pasa? Que haces aqui?"

"Nothing's the matter, Padre," she laughed. "Gerritt and I want to marry now. You come to the Church, OK?"

Padre Simon looked incredulously from one to the other, then his gaze settled on Gerritt, eating into his countenance, searching for a reason to this insane request. Gerritt stood firm.

"That's what we want, Simon, what I want. It's the best thing under the circumstances."

Simon's eyes opened wide, realizing the significance of Gerritt's words. He seemed to breathe heavier, as though he were trying to control something inside. Perhaps he was expecting this. Sometimes things arrive that you don't wish for. He knew it was no use to argue.

"Eva", he said deliberately still looking at Gerritt. "Eva, you know where my robes are. Go and get them for me." She smiled, squeezed his hand and ran into the next room.

The two men stood there regarding each other.

"What have you done to her," Simon said finally through clenched teeth. "If you hurt her, I will kill you. I will kill you, do you understand me?" He was forward now, glaring and talking into Gerritt's face, his night breath, old and stale.

"You couldn't do that. You are a Priest." Gerritt said to him, calmly, knowing he had done nothing to her.

"I am a man also, Señor, and Eva is like my daughter. Is she with child?"

"Yes." Gerritt lied quickly, cutting him off. It was the only way. Simon would have wanted to wait otherwise.

Simon wheeled around, the grey nightshirt flying after him. He hit his head with his hand, then hit his fists together, then in pure exasperation, he hit the wall.

"Why!" he screamed. "Why do you do this thing? Why don't you go back to where you come from? Eva is not of your people, not for you."

"I love her, Simon." He did love her, loved her body and what having her would mean for him.

Simon spit on the floor in front of him.

"What do you know of love for someone like Eva? She is a bird, a butterfly, a rare thing that cannot be caught. She will fly from you, Señor! There is nothing to hold onto!"

The anger, the empty night rained down between them. There was no meeting of opinion here, could never be. They heard Eve's steps returning across the stone floor, tapping, echoing on the walls. She stopped in the doorway with the heavy robes, feeling the tension.

"Oh, I love you both so," she dropped the robes loosely on the chair, cried and ran from one to the other drawing them nearer together.

"Alright," Simon choked back tears. "Wait for me in the church."

The air outside seemed fresh after the fetid atmosphere of Simon's sleeping rooms. They crossed in the dark to the Church, pushed open the squeaking door and went inside. Eve knew where the candles were, took one, lit it and handed it to Gerritt, then lit one for herself.

"Come." She said, taking his hand.

The candlelight reflected in dancing bird patterns off the white walls of the little adobe and cactus Church. Eve went into a pew near the front, genuflecting and kneeling. Gerritt sat down beside her. After a short time, she turned to him.

"Don't you pray?"

"No. I don't need to," he whispered. What was this, praying? Asking for impossible things from something that didn't exist. All he wanted was here, right here next to him. Eve was the answer to supplication for anything, woman or job. She would be an entirety for him. Wax ran hotly down the side of the candle and onto his hand. He barely felt it.

"I'm cold. I wish Padre would hurry." She sat back next to him and he put his arm around her.

"En el nombre del Padre, Hijo y Espíritu Santo," Padre Simon said ceremonially from the back of the Church. They stood. He had washed and dressed in his white robes for Eve. They followed him to the alter. He set a bench for kneeling in front of them. Eve knelt, then reached up for Gerritt and pulled him down beside her. Simon read the words in Spanish quickly and formally, hardly looking at them. Eve didn't notice how stern he was; she looked only at Gerritt and he at her.

Gerritt had never thought much about getting married. Now it seemed he was only swimming in Eve's black eyes, the candlelight reflecting in them as little white dots. He watched her chest raise and lower. What was she feeling? It was over quickly; there was no Mass. Simon stalked out of the Church and over to his house. Eve and Gerritt followed slowly, wrapped in each other's arms, Gerritt's hand resting softly on her breast.

Simon waited for them outside his own door.

"You sleep here, it is late." He motioned them to another entrance on the side of his office, then disappeared into his bedroom. There wasn't anything else left to say.

"Alfredo?" Eve asked of Gerritt.

"I'll get him and your things."

It seemed cold outside now by himself and he hurried back to Eve, shutting the door tightly. She was already in bed, her clothes thrown carelessly on the floor. She lay smiling at him, her hair all over the pillow.

He began to breathe heavily as he undressed down to his shorts, and got in beside her. She was warm, a light in the freezing bed, which smelled dank and coarse. Her breasts rose in his hands, firm and full. She started to giggle softly, wiggling away from him.

He kissed her open mouth, drinking in the sweetness and stifling the giggle, feeling himself grow hard and ready. She was a mound of softness, flowing to him, giving. He rolled over on her, rubbing her stomach, the soft hairs, pushing her legs apart, feeling where to put himself.

Then he was inside her. She was wide, open and large, really too large, as though she were not the virgin he knew her to be. It was wet and warm inside, but loose, flaccid, as if he was pushing his penis into warm butter.

Eve began to giggle when he entered her, moving all around and he had a difficult time staying inside her as he began to pant, feeling himself coming. Her giggling grew worse. She was twisting from side to side, her breasts jiggling against him. Just as he began to climax, she jerked down and he emptied himself on her stomach, gasping to catch his breath. And she was still coming at him, giggling. He wiped the semen from her body with his shorts, then played with her easily, tickling her and sucking softly on her breasts until she shuddered in his arms and was quiet.

Gerritt lay there for what seemed hours, the ends of his nerves vibrating with the excitement of what he had done. Eve rolled away from him and began to snore, but he only became more sensitized. It was as though he were mentally floating above the bed, feeling every hair on his body rubbing the rough sheets, the hairs triggering little sharp spasms. Eve's breathing rocked the bed, aggravating his passion. He got up, he had to get out of the room, into the night, think.

Clumsily, he found his clothes, stubbing his toe on the bed, and sending pain showers through his brain. The night was still black and cold as he climbed in his pickup and headed out, not conscious of where he was going, or what he would do.

Gerritt simply pressed his foot down on the accelerator, following the road ribbon into the mountains, not seeing, not thinking, his nerves standing on the edge of the seat. The stars were dim and far away, and it was as though the whole of the pampa had withdrawn into a dark hole and he was driving into its center, disappearing. Something ran out in front of the truck and he skidded to avoid it, waking slightly from his focus on escaping.

"Probably a fucking viscache," he said to himself, the small wild rodents that lived out there. It was damnably cold; he could feel it seeping into the truck in spite of the truck heater.

Shapes began to pass along the sides of the truck. He was in the Cordillera de la Sal, the wind-worried rock configurations on the road back to El Molino.

The grotesque formations began to close on him. At first they would seem directly in front and then fly past the side when it appeared collision was imminent. Gerritt was soon ducking and dodging as if he were the truck itself trying to avoid the rocks. His vision grew myopic, he couldn't focus, the night and the rocks all running together, swimming inside his eyelids. He stopped the truck, killed the engine and listened to the silence and the wind, leaning his head on the steering wheel.

Nausea overtook him, waves of it, coming from every hair ending. Climbing down from the truck, he found he could barely stand, braced himself against the back of the vehicle and threw up onto a silent road, the wind passing through his shirt.

He managed to stagger around to the front of the truck, trying to see the surrounding land, squinting his eyes at the dark. Then, he felt faint. Everything seeming to blend in with the night, and he fell backwards onto the dusty road in the darkness below the headlight beams.

When Gerritt returned to consciousness, he was shivering, coiled up within himself like a baby against the cold. The wind had stopped blowing and he could see the dim outline of morning in the Andes to the east. He sat up, thinking about his body, where he was, the rock formations now more visible beside him and not quite so frightening. What happened to him? Then he remembered where he was, what he had done, where Eve was, and quickly picked himself up and got back in the truck.

It wasn't easy turning the truck around on the narrow road. His stomach ached, but from emptiness, he thought. His mind was clear now, lucid, formed.

There was no doubt in his mind where he was going or why. As he began to drive back to Santa Bárbara and to Eve, he saw in passing a wet spot on the road and remembered vomiting. He was glad he was alone.

The sky, lightened and bluish, chased the night away, the last stars faintly giving up to the day. The pueblo was quiet except for a dog smelling around the edge of a house. He parked and went to Eve. She was still soundly asleep, turned away from him, her black hair loose, falling freely on the sheets. Gerritt had a flash in his mind of the girl in the Molino brothel. His stomach tightened and he tiptoed over to the bed, turning her over gently.

But it was Eve, for sure it was Eve, her open, pale face smiled at him in sleep. He sat on the bed looking at her for a long time. There was not a mark on her face. It was as pure as a child's, a piece of china. Her long lashes feathered out, lying softly on flawless cheeks. She was so perfect.

There was a gentle knock on the door and Padre Simon pushed it open with an elbow. He was dressed in his heavy brown day cassock and carried two cups of steaming coffee in his big hands. Simon towered over Gerritt, looking at him a long moment and then at the sleeping Eve. He laid the license on the table by the bed. It seemed there was a smile, ever so slight, barely visible through the thick beard as he handed Gerritt the cup and motioned for him follow. He hadn't expected to find Gerritt awake and dressed.

Simon's office was dirty and smelled of stale food and age. Gerritt suspected that he worked and ate in the same place. Simon was so many different men. He was an amateur archeologist, a priest, and commanded respect from everyone, particularly Eve. Gerritt needed him to be supportive. They sat down and each man regarded the other carefully.

"I called the Gerencia," Padre Simon said seriously, then took a long drink of the steaming coffee.

Gerritt shivered and looked at his watch; it was seven. He was cold from lack of sleep and he needed any energy, sapped by vomiting in the pampa, to go to his brain. There was much to think about. How to tell Driscoll? What would Wes think? Did he care what Wes thought? Did he care what any of them thought? Was Simon talking to him? The office was dark, the only light came from the door. Simon's face was shadowed with worry.

"Hortensia woke Driscoll. She would have anyway, once she looked in Eve's room." Still there was no reaction from Gerritt. He sat, a man asleep, lost in his own thoughts and deep concentration.

"Señor Gerritt!" Simon said more loudly. "I said, I called the Gerencia!" He bent his head to see Gerritt's face, but could read nothing in the cold eyes. Gerritt jerked up as if awakening and stared at the Priest.

"You did? When?" He almost spilled his coffee. Holy shit, he thought. Driscoll already knows.

"Before I came for you—I called." Simon took a gulp from his cup and swallowed loudly.

"Oh," Gerritt said sadly, the realization of the profundity of his actions clear. "So they know." He was afraid to ask their reaction, but knew it would be forthcoming.

"Yes, they know. I love Eve too much to worry them. They take it badly; they want you to return at once." Simon got up to pour more coffee from a pot sitting on a hotplate. There were electrical cords strung along the walls and ceiling connecting it to the one outlet near the door. Gerritt traced them mindlessly.

"What about the baby, Señor?" He ran his fingers through his thick hair. He had made things worse by lying, but Simon would never have married them otherwise, he was sure of that.

The priest poured more coffee for them both, clanked the pot back on the hotplate and sat down heavily.

"I didn't say that to Señor Driscoll, because it is not true. Is it?" Simon looked up over the coffee cup straight into Gerritt's eyes. There was a keen perception behind the black gaze that took Gerritt by surprise.

The man must have lost the night thinking about this, weighing values, working the various possibilities. And now to come up with such a statement, Gerritt knew the Priest understood his motives perfectly.

"No," he answered as directly as he could.

Simon continued to examine Gerritt carefully, looking at him askance.

"I came very close to coming in your room last night and pulling you from that bed. But too late. I gave you the sacrament of marriage, I cannot take back."

Gerritt's eyes widened. The thought of the giant Simon coming into the room filled him with apprehension. But what was he talking about rights, what about his own right to privacy. Gerritt seethed. What Simon thought or did in public was one thing, but when he talked of coming into his bedroom, that became a breach, a chasm of fault not even a Priest could leap. He stood up and the Priest did, too. Gerritt's anger paled in the man's stature. Yes, Gerritt realized, Simon could have bodily thrown him out.

"Surely no silly sacrament would have kept you from such a desire." He said through clenched teeth.

"It's something you wouldn't understand. That and my love for Eva. But if you hurt her you will be sorry, that I promise you, Señor!" Simon shook his huge fist at Gerritt.

They stood there, the air hot between them, neither moving, and then Gerritt broke away, longing for space.

"I'm going to wake Eve. We're going back. Stay away from us. I don't need your God, your pretentious caring. Eve belongs to me now."

The Priest was silent, looking after Gerritt sadly as he went for Eve.

She was still sleeping when Gerritt woke her, waking lazily to the day. He sat watching her dress slowly, the buttons and snaps taking her some time.

"Can I help you?" He offered, anxious to get under way and away from Simon.

"No, silly. Hortensia makes me do it all myself. She says it makes my fingers strong. Do you think it makes my fingers strong?"

"I'm sure," he said smiling. She was so beautiful.

Padre Simon was not to be found when they were ready to leave. Eve fussed, she was hungry and wanted to say goodbye, but Gerritt told her they needed to get back to Cerro Verde, her parents were worried. She was silent going back, but sat very close to him, as though she were now frightened and needed his warmth and security.

Cerro Verde was quiet, a Sunday morning; people would be sleeping off the production party. But the Gerencia was not quiet. The minute Gerritt and Eve entered the door, the servants hurried quickly out of sight, save Hortensia who rushed to a surprised Eve hugging her fast, her tears falling on Eve's cheeks.

And then Joe and Anna Driscoll were in the doorway of the library, standing stiffly in a sad receiving line. They were dressed formally. The four of them faced each other as at some sort of match, deciding which partner to parry first. Joe Driscoll seemed about to speak. His feet were placed widely apart, his arms extended forward like he might be about to begin walking. And his face, his face, Gerritt had never seen such a face. It was bloated, distended, red and throbbing. Rays of anger, of feeling, radiated from him like a sun. He was filled to capacity with controversies he didn't know how to deal with, a force of hate and indecision combined with love and helplessness.

Anna Driscoll simply stood and rung her hands, wrapping them around each other as if she were drying them.

"Oh Eve," Anna finally said. Eve rushed to her Mother's arms and Joe spit his breath out, leaning forward and walking toward Gerritt. When he reached him, Joe took Gerritt's arm, squeezing it too tightly. Gerritt painfully withstood the temptation to pull away, sensing the older man on the brink of telling him to leave.

"Congratulations," Joe finally said through clenched teeth, then released Gerritt's arm.

"I need a drink," Driscoll said and led Gerritt into the library. Eve and her Mother disappeared, their arms around each other.

It was 11 AM and Gerritt did not need alcohol. He still felt slightly sick from the previous night. But he accepted the double scotch, sipping carefully, feeling it burn its way down into his empty stomach. He looked up at Joe Driscoll, and felt somehow sorry to be causing this confusion and pain. Forever came in many forms. Eve was lost to her Father now in a way over which he had no control.

"Eve is happy," Gerritt said smiling sincerely. She was happy. She was always happy.

"Yes, I suppose she is." Driscoll took a long pull on his drink. "Are you happy, Gerritt?" His mouth turned slightly down in derision.

"Of course. Eve is like a new morning for me." But was he really happy? Gerritt looked into the amber drink. He never stopped to think in a situation whether or not he was happy. It seemed to have nothing to do with getting through a day. Happy? What was happiness? Gerritt didn't think he understood the concept.

Driscoll nodded. They sat together in silence. There wasn't much to say. It was done, the thing Gerritt didn't know he intended and the thing Driscoll feared.

"You will live here for the time being. Anna will want to have a house fixed for Eve."

Gerritt nodded. It didn't seem to matter. They sat there together a long while, saying little. They were meeting on a different level now and they both seemed to want a quiet time to absorb the new relationship.

Gerritt moved into the Gerencia that afternoon. They had Eve's suite of rooms, a bedroom, bath and the blue sitting room where they spent so many hours. They took their meals with Joe and Anna and after dinner Joe and Gerritt talked about the mine over brandy and cigars. They settled into a routine of acceptance.

Cerro Verde was acquiescent. It was as though the marriage, the Union of these two, was something that had been awaited, planned on. Gerritt was pleased there was so little reaction. Even Wes was unaffected.

"This place eats absurdities," Wes told him once. Perhaps that's what it was, yes, the absorption of the absurd. There was not a thing Cerro Verde would not accept. They were too far, too far from the organized world to have its habitual inclination for propriety.

The mine ran smoothly for Gerritt those first weeks and he began to wonder if perhaps he truly did have everything he ever wanted. Driscoll insisted that he and Eve take a few days away together and they went to Rio.

CHAPTER 29

Wes was glad Gerritt was gone. It meant he could get some things done without interference. He prepared his mine plans and engineering for the tunnel carefully, and as always Gerritt only partially followed them, changing things as he saw fit to keep the men hauling ore. It was almost as though he had to have the final say, needed that advantage to make him content. Wes saw him several times standing at the top of the mine, a lonely figure estimating the limits of his control, remote and uncommunicative. Whatever was contributing to the unbalance, Gerritt's priorities were shifting. Why else would he have eloped with Eve; it was irrational. Or had he always been that way, needing to make decisions alone? Wes wasn't sure. And then most everyone was neurotic at one time or the other and had some obsession. Wes's was keeping everything. He couldn't throw things away and had the original boxes and wrappers of everything he purchased, unless Alice was able to discard them without him noticing. Gerritt had a drive of some sort, pushing at him, drowning him. Wes hoped the marriage to Eve would bring about stability, but doubted that would be the case. And he was worried about Alice. The baby was overdue; Jason told them he would induce at the weekend if nothing happened before then. Alice was uncomfortable and anxious about having a first baby in a foreign country without any family nearby.

With his mind wandering and so much to do, Wes wasn't prepared when Mike Marshall burst into the engineering room and threw his hard hat on the floor. Zuñiga nearly fell into the map basket again. Wes looked up from the light table, rubbing his eyes. Working over the fluorescent lights with superimposed plans was a strain.

"You bastards have got to listen to me!" Mike screamed. Curt Reicher raised his eyebrows as he walked into the office and handed Wes some papers.

"What's the matter, Mike?" Curt said smiling. Mike's face was flushed and sweaty.

"Those Goddamn posts are leaning out again! This makes the third time I've dug up those fucking things and re-cemented them. I'm not going to do it anymore! Even if they fall down into the pit, I'm not touching them."

"Calm down, Mike," Curt said slowly, frowning. "They aren't going to fall into the pit or anywhere else."

"Oh, yeah," Mike said disgustedly. "You just wait. There's something funny going on up there and you just better get on up there and see what it is because I've had it!"

Wes looked at Curt. Things went through his mind. What makes rock move? Earthquakes. Blasting. Rock failure. He shook his head. The rock in Cerro Verde was exceptionally stable and had stood for years. Curt seemed thoughtful, staring out the window toward the visitors bench.

"OK, OK, Mike," Curt said with deference. "There must be a reason for your posts moving. Let's go take a look." He clapped Mike on the shoulder and went for his hard hat.

"At last," Mike shrugged his shoulders, relieved to be taken seriously. "Let's go, Wes." The three of them climbed into Curt's truck.

"When did you last reset the posts?" Curt asked as they drove up to the top of the mine. The road went out to the mine entrance and back up to the southeast side.

"Oh, about a month ago, just after we broke ground for the tunnel. I even had them set slightly inward, and you should see them now."

The pickup groaned going up the last rise and they came out on the Visitor's Bench. Curt drove over near the edge and cut the motor.

"My god," Wes said incredulously, as he unfolded his tall body from the truck. "You're right."

The wind was blowing fiercely, whipping the pampa gravel against the truck. Their pants wrapped around their legs as they walked over to the edge to look at the now leaning posts of the guardrail. They were three feet high with a chain joining them together like a safety rope holding mountain climbers from the void below. The posts were indeed chueco, crooked, out of line. They all leaned slightly outward and over the edge, as though the open pit were calling to them and they were answering. Some three or four were twisted, the cement bases raised up from the earth. Either Mike had done a damn sloppy job of putting them in, or something else was moving them. Wes didn't want to think about the latter possibility.

Curt stood with his hand in his shirtfront, thinking.

"Let's have a look around. It can't be anything too serious. This bench may be sliding a little, but it's been here 30 years, it's not going anywhere." Curt seemed confidant and Wes sighed. He wanted to have that look. Something didn't feel right.

The bench was at the top of the mountain and the area they had to search was fairly flat, the wind throwing clouds of dust at them. They spread out across the bench and walked slowly away from the edge, their eyes down, looking for something they didn't want to find, cracks in the brown earth.

For a long time there was nothing to mar the barrenness of the ground in front of him. Wes grew mesmerized with the brown flatness, rough and pebbly. Then he saw something and bent down, pushing the dirt aside with his fingers. Yes, it was there, a narrow, jagged crack running away from his hand in both directions. He looked down toward Curt who was 50 yards away and also bending over something.

"Do you see it?" Wes yelled at him.

"How wide do you make it to be down there?" Curt's voice sounded far away, the wind swallowing it.

"About a millimeter here," Wes answered.

"Same here. Mike, you see anything?"

"No, nothing. Yeah, wait a minute. Come here!"

Wes and Curt walked quickly over to where Mike was brushing at the loose rocks another 50 yards back from the edge. Another crack in the earth wound its way to the north out of sight, seemingly not connected to the other two. Curt stood up and wiped his forehead like a sweating runner.

"I'm not sure what this means," Curt said seriously, looking at the leaning posts. "It could mean the rock is failing on this bench. Maybe it was cut at too steep an angle. We don't cut benches this steeply anymore. It must be close to vertical.

A chill went down Wes's spine. He felt as though he was standing on floating soil, coming away from a riverbank. What about the benches below this one? Were they all collapsing? Would the whole side of the mine weep its way into the bottom of the pit? It was an incomprehensible thought. Wes remembered Gerritt and was again glad he was in Rio.

They continued to search for more cracks, criss-crossing the area, but found no further breaks in the earth. They mapped two parallel cracks, about 20 feet apart, the first one some 40 feet back from the edge of the bench and visible for more than 100 yards. As they drove in silence back to the offices, Wes tried to figure in his head how much rock there was in that section of bench, probably more than five million tons, he decided.

"I'm going to call Ian Blain and Ned. Tully's been here longer than those cracks." Curt said confidently. "Do you think you could find the records on those benches, Wes?"

"If there are any records," Wes said glumly. "Maybe Zuñiga knows."

"Fine, only don't tell him why you want them. In fact," he said, leaning over the steering wheel so he could see both of them. "Don't tell anyone else yet, not until we know what we have. I'm not going to Telex New York just yet. They'd think we were crazy.

"You want those posts put right again?" Mike asked Curt.

"No," he answered clicking his tongue." I think we better close the area for a while. Put up a rope barrier on the road up there." Mike nodded agreement.

Zuñiga looked at Wes with questions swimming in his watery eyes when Wes asked for records on those early benches. But Wes offered no explanation and went back to the tunnel plans on the light table. The office was again neat and ordered after the explosion, and Wes was sure if records on that top bench existed, Zuñiga would find them.

Presently a few maps and the mine journal were laid carefully on Wes's desk as though they were made of dry papyrus and would crumble with a heavy touch. There was another searching look and then Zuñiga left him alone.

Wes found little in the records to help them, though the journals were an interesting history. There were entries concerning a new hitching post in front of the mine offices. Somebody's horse had kicked over the old one in the days before trucks were brought to Cerro Verde. There were dates on where the blasting was done and how much earth was removed, but nothing about the angles of the benches. Wes walked into Curt's office with the information and found Ian and Ned sitting there, anxiously.

"What did you find, Wes?" Curt asked quickly. "I was just about to take them up there."

"Not much. Mostly blasting and tonnage records and some superfluous info like fixing a hitching post."

Ned smiled. "Yeah, I remember those days. A stable boy used to deliver a horse to your house before seven every morning."

They discussed the cracks and the implications. Ian plainly wasn't worried.

"The ground probably has stopped moving or will stop soon. We don't know how long those cracks have been up there and there's too much earth involved, millions of tons. Entire benches can't go sliding down into the pit." Ian said, his chair tipped back. The alternative was too destructive to contemplate.

Ned looked thoughtful and Wes wondered what he thought.

"I hope you're right," Ned said as he spat into the wastebasket. "But something is moving Mike's fucking posts."

"What do you suggest then?" Curt asked Ian, tapping his teeth with a pencil.

"Let's watch it for awhile. Wes, can you get some stakes and wire up there and marked without too much commotion? I don't want the Union hearing about this yet."

"Yes." Wes answered. "I can take another Jefe instead of my surveying crew."

Wes asked Felix Alford to help him set the survey stakes. Felix was visibly nervous after he heard about the cracks.

"I'll meet you up there, Wes," Felix said. "I want to go have a look right away." Wes and Mike gathered the equipment themselves and when they arrived on the bench they found Felix and Ned Tully tracing the cracks.

"These Goddamn things go on forever." Ned exclaimed. "I don't like this at all."

"Ian didn't seem too worried." Wes answered as they unloaded the stakes and transit. They set the stakes at three different points along the cracks and ran wire between them, then determined their position with the transit. If the cracks widened, the stakes would move further apart, the difference showing in the next survey.

"What do you think, Ned?" Felix asked Tully as they stood together looking at the blackness down inside the tiny separation of dirt and rock.

Ned considered a long moment. He looked tired and older since the explosion.

"I think it's going to slide, that's what I think. Look at those posts at the guardrail. Mike's replaced them three times now. This baby's moving!" He spit brown tobacco juice on the ground in front of him, the dust flying away from the warm liquid.

"Christ," Felix cursed. It was enough to say. The whole side of the mine sliding into the pit seemed impossible. But that's what it looked like was happening.

It took them two hours to run the wire and stakes and take the initial measurements. It was crude, but would give them some idea of the rate of movement. Wes could feel the fear coursing between them, running from one to the other. There was more power under their feet than he could imagine, and the thought of it leaping down into the abyss of the pit made him shudder. Ted was old and honest, open about his gut feelings. Wes wondered what Curt and Ian really thought. Maybe when you got to be in their position you weren't allowed to acknowledge fear. If they were afraid he certainly hadn't read it in their words or manner. Wes knew he was not ready for that kind of responsibility. He wanted only to get off the bench and home.

It was nearly dark when he pulled up to the house, Rosa the maid ran out to his truck.

"Señor, Señor, the baby comes!" she screamed.

He found Alice in bed. Her water had broken and soaked the bed and she was moaning.

"Alice, are you OK?" Wes asked her. Of course she wasn't, he could see that. She was clammy and weak.

"Why didn't you call me?" he yelled at the maid.

"Te llamo', Señor, pero no esta"! It was too late to investigate why he hadn't gotten the message. They had been up on the bench for a long time. He wrapped Alice in a blanket and put her in the truck. She had a contraction just as he started down the hill and he stepped on the accelerator. They were 10 minutes from the hospital. He called the tower and had them call Jason Stoddard. He was waiting for them when Wes drove up to the emergency entrance. Jason took her pulse and felt her abdomen. Alice opened her eyes to look at Wes. He felt so helpless.

"Baby has turned and is breach. I probably will have to do a section, but she should be OK. Let's go." He motioned for the gurney and then they were upstairs and Alice disappeared into the OR with Jason. Wes stood there staring after them before a nurse led him into the waiting room. The cracks, Gerritt, the mine, all disappeared into a well of concern for Alice and the baby. How had he let her be alone when this happened?

After what seemed an interminable amount of time, another nurse motioned for him to come. Alice had been cleaned up and was in bed in the maternity ward. She was awake and warm now with an IV in her arm. The baby hadn't yet arrived.

"Alice, Alice, I am so sorry I wasn't there. Are you OK?"

"I think so. Jason said the baby turned; the head is not down. It hurts so much and I don't think I am getting anywhere. Hand me that pan, I think I'm going to throw up." She vomited into the pan, leaving Wes feeling ill himself. Stoddard came in with a nurse.

"We are going to do a section, Alice, but everything will be fine," he explained as the nurse put something into Alice's IV. Jason motioned for him to follow.

"She's lost some blood. Couldn't you get her here earlier?" Jason asked him.

"We were up on the visitors bench and out of the trucks placing some wires! The fucking mine is collapsing," he screamed to Jason.

"OK, OK. Relax. Things will be fine. The baby is a little stressed. I should have the baby out in a few minutes and will find you." He didn't say anymore as Alice was on a gurney heading to the OR and Jason followed.

Wes thought the next hour was the slowest of his life. His mind wondered from the day he met Alice to the day she told him she was pregnant, to the mine, the cracks, Gerritt, the blood on the bed at home. He looked out the window at the always cloudless, dark blue sky and could hear the mine in the distance. The guilt hung on him like a wet rag, chilling him to the bone. How could this be happening? Alice was so perfect and he had let her down. If something happened to her, he couldn't live with it. She was his rock and without her he was nothing.

"Wes, Wes?" Jason was shaking him. "You have a little girl. She and Alice are fine. Alice is weak but she should be OK by tomorrow. The baby is perfect- -nearly 8 lbs. Alice is in the recovery room. You can go see her for a few minutes, but then she needs to sleep."

"Oh God, oh God, thank you!" Jason clapped him on the back and Wes followed him. Alice's head was propped up and she smiled weakly as he came in and held her, sitting on the edge of the bed to reach her.

"Oh Wes, have you seen her? She's beautiful."

"Not yet, I wanted to see you first. Are you OK?"

"I think so. The pain is gone. I'm just tired. Jason said the baby wouldn't have delivered on her own. I'm not sure why she turned. I was cleaning shelves yesterday and maybe the reaching....I don't know." She was drifting off.

"Alice, stop thinking about it. You are both fine and we are blessed." He waited until she was asleep and then went to see his daughter. The nurse motioned for him to come in to the nursery where he washed and put on a gown before she handed him the baby. Feelings of instant love for this new life overtook him. How could you love something this much, he wondered, as he touched the baby's face. Then he remembered that they hadn't decided for sure on a name. Here he was talking to his baby and he didn't know what to call her. Then it came, Georgia. It was one of the names they both liked, his grandmother's. As he kissed his baby's tiny hand he whispered her name. It was a miracle, so special, so amazing, he couldn't comprehend the depth of his feelings, but just stood there for a long time looking at the child until the nurse tapped him on the shoulder and laid Georgia back in her bassinette. Even then, Wes was loath to leave her.

He drove back to the house to tell Rosa and to call their parents. He also called Felix and Curt; their wives would pass the word on. Alice's room would be filled with people in the morning and he was glad she could sleep now. Rosa fixed his supper and he went back to the hospital. Alice was awake and he asked her about the name and she wanted Georgia as well. They brought her in and the three of them lay on Alice's bed until Alice and the baby went to sleep again. Wes lay there thinking about the day and how nothing would ever be the same again.

CHAPTER 30

Gerritt stood looking in the bathroom mirror. It was going to be impossible to shave. He had gotten severely sunburned in Rio and it was blistering, leaving patches of sore, reddened skin. He reluctantly took his electric shaver from the medicine cabinet and a plastic bottle of hand lotion fell into the sink making a loud thud.

"Shit," Gerritt said under his breath. The bathroom they shared at the Gerencia was small and Eve seemed to think she didn't have to move her things over. Driscoll was having a house fixed for them and it was nearly ready. Gerritt couldn't wait. Living and eating with Driscolls was fine for a few days, but the pretense of sociability was wearing on him. He longed to be alone. Only that wasn't going to happen, not ever again. There was a lot of baggage that went along with Eve, not only the parents but also her maids and nurses. She had a whole "staff".

The shaver buzz echoed off the walls and Gerritt watched the pieces of dead skin fall from his face and float into the sink as he ran the machine carefully over his patched cheeks.

The whole trip had been a disaster. Eve was silly and trite. Her excitement turned her giggly and Gerritt spent the flight to Rio calming her, finally forcing champagne down her. By the time they arrived, she could barely stand on her own. He put her to bed and spent the evening in the bar and walking on the beach.

They made love the next morning, the cool sea air blowing in on them. It could have been so good. Eve was soft, pure, and smelled clean. But she became a writhing, wrongly responsive mass when she was excited, totally uncontrollable. Making love to her was exhausting. He tried several different approaches, warming slowly to her, and another time mounting her immediately, a chase on the bed. But it was all the same. It was all he could do to stay inside her until he came. She wanted him constantly, her hands were all over him, but it wasn't in her power to receive him. Gerritt usually emptied himself onto the sheets or onto Eve.

And then he got sunburned. Floating out on an air mattress to be alone, he had felt at one with the rocking waves, getting out beyond the point where they would push him onto the beach. He looked at Eve for a while, sitting under the umbrella shading her eyes and looking out across the water to him. It was good to be alone, the water warm, the sun soaking into his skin. He was drowsy and dozed. By evening he looked boiled and raw and felt feverish. Gerritt ordered dinner sent up and took a cold shower. He began vomiting about midnight, his face and body burning hot. Eve held his head and washed him off with cold rags.

Gerritt couldn't see her and began to get worried. He would open his eyes and see Shem or Molly and once Barnett was hanging over him throwing his hard hat. The room seemed to turn and he had to turn with it, his pillow forcing his face around when he felt himself falling.

Finally he slept, losing a whole day. It spoiled his enthusiasm for the trip and scared Eve. She wanted to go home and Gerritt missed the mine; they returned three days early.

He put some cream on his chapped face. There wasn't any helping how he looked, and knew he would get razzed, but the mine was where he wanted to be and he felt happy driving out to the office.

The office door shut correctly now and Gerritt smiled thinking of the day it shut on Barnett. He saw Wes leaning against the door of Curt's office. Wes smiled, but went on talking to Reicher.

"I repeated the survey three times to be sure. I couldn't believe what I was seeing. It's moved two millimeters in six days."

Curt was reading a paper on his desk, his fingers worrying his temples. He looked up. Gerritt had never seen him so serious.

"All right. Thanks Wes. I'll Telex New York this afternoon. I don't know what they'll say, but they need to be advised."

"Good. I reset the stakes. We'll resurvey in two days."

Gerritt looked from one to the other, not understanding the conversation.

"What's this about cracks and surveys?" he asked tossing his shock of black hair away from his face.

"Good God, what happened to you," Wes exclaimed, finally really noticing him. "You look like a burn case."

Gerritt shrugged. He didn't like to feel different. Handicapped people made him uneasy and he felt handicapped right now.

"Oh, a little too much sun," he said, trying to be nonchalant, his white teeth a sharp contrast to the red, bubbled face.

"No kidding," Wes laughed. "Hey, Gerritt, come on, I've got something to show you. We may have a problem." Wes had forgotten the sunburn and turned serious.

They walked over to Gerritt's office. It was the same. The clock above the door still said nine o'clock and the dozer model he was working on the week before lay spread out on his desk as he had left it. He sat down and Wes sat down in the chair across from him. A stack of mail lay in front of Gerritt and he quietly wished Wes would go about his work so he could attend to it and check the daily tonnage records.

But Wes wasn't going to budge.

"Remember those posts up on the visitor's bench that Mike was complaining about?"

"Yeah the ones he said were leaning out?"

"Mmmhumm. Well, Curt and I went up there right after you took off. We found cracks, two of them, extending about 200 meters down that upper bench and a third crack a ways back. The survey we did shows there's a mass moving up there! It moved two millimeters in six days, Wes waited for this to sink in. Gerritt was fingering his model. He frowned. What was Wes talking about? Cracks? There were cracks all over the mine. He raised his head and looked at Wes.

"OK," he said smiling condescendingly. "Let's go have a look. If you say there's cracks, there must be cracks." Why was Wes always making so much out of nothing? Wes was a meticulous person, but Gerritt felt he was a little anal about things at times.

Gerritt rode up in Wes's truck. The window was open and he had his arm out the window. The day was warm and not much wind, but the air moving into the truck felt cool on the sunburn. It was good to be back, the grind of the machinery in the background almost a song for him.

"How was the vacation?" Wes asked, looking over at him.

"OK." It hadn't been much of a vacation. Gerritt felt more tired than when he left.

"Well, I got kind of sick with the sunburn. Didn't feel like doing much, I guess."

"Oh yeah? Did Eve get sunburned, too?"

"No, I was out floating around on a goddamned air mattress."

Wes laughed.

"You really got one for sure. Hey Gerritt, guess what? I'm a father!" Wes beamed. "Alice had a little girl! We named her Georgia. She's amazing! You have to come over to see her."

"Congratulations," Gerritt said, looking at Wes, but not understanding. He wouldn't ever have this with Eve, whatever this feeling was. It seemed special and he felt an ache and thought about his parents. As they were nearing the top of the mine, Wes grew serious. He maneuvered the truck around by the edge of the bench where he and Curt had stopped the week before.

"Jesus Christ, look at those posts." Gerritt exclaimed and walked toward them. They were leaning out even more than when Wes had first seen them. Gerritt felt the chain, drawn taught between the posts. It was stiff and didn't give when he pushed on it.

"Where are the cracks," he asked nervously. What was this? What was the ground doing? Gerritt felt unsteady on his feet.

Wes began to pace back from the bench edge in giant steps, his lanky form bending forward at the waist, his head tilted toward the ground. Gerritt watched him; he looked like a stork or a child playing a game, stepping off some territory. He stopped and Gerritt walked over to him.

"Here, look at this."

Gerritt's eyes followed Wes's down to the ground and there were the cracks. Gerritt squatted down to brush away the gravel blown into them. The cracks ran crookedly away from his sight in both directions.

"There's another one forty feet back and parallel," Wes said.

Gerritt considered them, felt them, looked at their length. No, he would not let them be what he feared. He couldn't let them be what he feared. That was a total impossibility, he would not allow it!

"This is what you're so excited about?" He tried to force a laugh. Wes looked at him strangely. Gerritt kicked at the crack with his boot. "Looks to me like it could be ground desiccation. You know how cracks craze the ground." He tried to sound confident.

Wes looked at him in disbelief.

But, Gerritt, these are getting wider! That's what the survey said, that's what I was telling Curt. Do you see what that means?" Gerritt didn't answer. He looked across the mine to where a shovel was grinding in regular rhythm. It was the only noise.

"This area is above the main road into the mine, Wes." Gerritt said not looking at the other man.

"I know that."

"Well, the road just can't be in danger, can it? We won't let that happen. Maybe it's only settling. Yes, that's probably it." Gerritt said, kicking at the crack again, as though he could cover it up and forget about it.

"I don't think so." Wes said slowly in a lower voice. Gerritt looked up at him then. Wes was deathly serious, his face pale and drawn. What if it was moving? Where would it go, into the pit? No that was unthinkable. No he wouldn't even think about that possibility, couldn't conceive of such repercussions. What would happen if it all fell? How much was there to fall? No it was better not to think about it.

"I see," Gerritt said slowly and carefully. He could feel the sweat on his upper lip and wondered if Wes noticed. "Well, I hope you're wrong."

The chatter and commotion at the Gerencia that evening went right over Gerritt's head. All he could think about was the mine. How could it be collapsing? He wouldn't let it fail. It couldn't be happening, not when his career was on the move. The explosion and the pieces of men laying all around came back to him in the night and he saw them all and the hole and the truck remains being covered by the mine falling in on them, burying them with Gerritt's plans and hopes. He pushed Eve away when she tried to come on to him. She started crying, but he didn't care. He didn't have a family like Wes's and would not likely ever have that. But he had the mine and now the mine was failing. Eve finally went to sleep, but Gerritt lay there with white and red visions of unidentified loss running through his mind.

CHAPTER 31

The house Garrett and Eve would have remodeled was the house Barnett and his family lived in before he resigned and left Cerro Verde. It was up the hill near the Gerencia, which pleased Anna as she wanted to look after her daughter. The Driscolls seemed to be there in Cerro Verde most of the time since Gerritt and Eve married. The four of them went up to look at the place and determine what changes should be made.

"Oh, it's so cold!" Eve said as they walked in.

"No one is living here now, Dear, so the furnace is not on. Here, put on your sweater." Anna said solicitously.

There were three bedrooms, in a plan similar to Wes's house, but the living and dining rooms were larger. Gerritt looked at the dining room, thinking about Blain's house and the garden.

"Joe, what would you think about putting a garden room off the dining room here. It opens into the front yard so there is room?" He asked, thinking aloud. Then realizing what he was asking, he looked over at Joe. But Driscoll only pondered the question.

"Good idea. What do you think, Anna? It would be nice for Eve."

"I think it is a fine idea," Anna answered. Gerritt smiled. This was going to be so easy. Joe and Anna liked him and could see Eve was happy.

"We need to do some things in the bedroom. Eve will need shelves for all her stuffed animals. And they need to add another maid's room." Gerritt's heart sunk. He was hoping the animals would stay at the Gerencia. And Eve was also bringing Hortensia and another maid who would cook and help with the cleaning.

"It's going to take a month or so to do this," Joe explained. "But we will make it nice for you, baby." He hugged his daughter. Gerritt resigned himself to it all, but was nervous about the mine. The cracks worried him. He would be fine as long as the mine was working and hoped the slide would not happen or be minimal.

March found the conveyor tunnel fifty feet into the mountain. It was the main concern after the business of running the mine and Wes was pretty much left alone with the weekly surveying of the stakes and wire. Discussion of a possible slide was dropped at the mine meetings, the men taking a lead from Gerritt who said there was nothing to worry about. Wes reported the weekly movement, which stayed about the same, the crack widening approximately 2 millimeters every time they surveyed. Wes sounded like a stuck phonograph needle producing a repetitive noise that was heard but ignored. They went up to look at the cracks several times, but the change wasn't noticeable to the eye and Curt was unimpressed with any urgency. The tunnel to the smelter was the main focus.

About the middle of March, Wes and Felix were up doing the weekly surveys, tending the stakes and wire like a newly planted lawn. The survey was getting to be so routine that he did it while thinking about Georgia and whether she would soon sleep through the night. Fortunately, Rosa got up with her, but Alice usually got up, too, and he longed for a full nights sleep. But he would not be able to remember what he had been thinking about when the results of the survey that day finally hit him. Wes and Felix looked at each other in disbelief.

"OK, mate," Felix said quickly. "Let's repeat the survey. We must have done something wrong." Soberly they repeated their work, step by step, measuring each angle, calculating carefully, hoping they made a mistake.

The bench top looked the same, flat and windswept, the noises from the mine diminished by the distance and depth below them. But the ground they were standing on was not the same. It had moved four millimeters from where it was last week. Six millimeters, an increase of four over the past week! Not much movement for this enormous part of the mine, but enough to scare the shit out of them. Wes sat down right where he was; he had to think it out. If they ran back to tell everyone now, would the rest of the staff be as worried as he was? No, he decided. Gerritt had them wrapped; no, they wouldn't be. It was easier not to think about this. They were all fighting it. Curt had contacted New York and they replied to monitor but were not alarmed either.

"New York ought to be down here measuring this slide. They ought to be making these surveys, Goddamn the lot of them", Wes said to Felix, realizing this was the first time he had used the word, slide.

"Then maybe when they got an increase and knew they were surveying the same way day after day – maybe then they'd believe it." He now understood how Mike Marshall had felt when he kept observing the "moving posts" on the visitor's bench, and no one believed him. Wes and Felix agreed they would wait for the weekly meeting, survey one more time and try to convince everyone that something was happening. Ned would be there and would be supportive.

The planning meeting went routinely. The tunnel work was proceeding; the total tonnage was up.

"And Wes, what's new with the cracks? Still two millimeters?" Curt asked smiling and expecting, needing the same answer.

Then Wes was able to spit the whole thing out there on the table in front of them all. It was like throwing up all the unrest inside him. Curt and Ted and Gerritt and the rest sat and looked at him, all of them expressionless.

The six-day movement was six millimeters! Twenty million tons of rock and dirt were moving down into the mine, collapsing into the air, only the bottom of the mine to stop it. He tried to convey his strong feelings about the two millimeters, now the six; what it all might mean. Curt picked up the phone before Wes finished and Gerritt could say anything. Wes heaved a sigh of relief. Curt was calling Joe Driscoll.

"Joe?" He said when he got him on the line. "You better come on over, there's some surveying results I want you to see." Curt's voice was tired and weighed down with worry. He liked things to run smoothly and avoided conflict at almost any cost. This time there was no possibility of ignoring what was happening; the bench was failing.

"Maybe it's just slipping and will stop when it begins to push against the bottom," Gerritt said hopefully.

"I've seen a few of these buggers in the coal mines in Australia," Mike Marshall said. "But they were shallow strip mines and the slide could be cleared out in a few days. When you start talking about a half-mile chunk of earth... well, that's a fucking lot of rock."

"How's it moving, Wes, can you tell anything?" Curt asked. Wes must have frowned because he said, "I mean, is it moving out or shearing down?"

"Don't know. You can't tell with movement as slow as this." They discussed the thing over and over and it didn't get any better. Joe arrived and a meeting was called for the afternoon with some of the Engineers from the plant to be included. Joe had seen a slide in New Mexico once and it wasn't pleasant.

Wes felt better about the whole thing now. At least everybody understood the problem. Joe Driscoll did indeed know a little about slides.

"From what I saw at Silver City," he told them that afternoon, "They never seem to be complete. This one we had there wasn't very big, but it made a hell of a mess. It just slid down into the bottom of the mine and then when we started clearing it, it slid again."

They all agreed on drilling down into the area from the top and attaching some wires down inside the drill holes to see how much vertical movement there was. Joe Driscoll would try to get a geologist down from New York with some seismographic equipment. The main mine staff stayed after the meeting to discuss the next days planning. Wes tentatively proposed that they ought to start thinking about building a new main road into the mine, down the other side in case the existing one needed to be closed. The road they used now ran directly under the slide area and everyone working the mine went in and out that way. Gerritt exploded at this suggestion. He sat slumped down in a chair during the whole meeting offering nothing, not wanting to hear any of it.

"For Christ sakes, Wes, the thing isn't going to come down tomorrow and I doubt it will ever come down! I think we've just scared ourselves. God – that thing has stood there how many years now? A hundred or more! If we start building a new road its going to tie up a lot of men and that's going to affect production, and that, ole buddy, is all I care about." Gerritt was standing up, over Wes, who had to admit he had a point about building the road early when it really wasn't needed, so Wes let it go.

New York was notified by Driscoll and this time they received a reply. One of the Vice Presidents, Bill Dixon, would be down on the next flight to take a look. He started in the compay as a shifer, like Wes and Gerritt and moved up rapidly.

Dixon wasn't at all what Wes expected when he arrived later that week. A waspish little man with hawk-like jet eyes darting here and there, he didn't miss a thing and Wes understood quickly how he got where he was. Gerritt sensed the same thing and hardly let Wes get a word in. Wes wondered if Bill Dixon saw through Gerritt, but was too concerned with the problems to think about it long.

"I realize you are all worried," Dixon told them in the general meeting just after he arrived. "I am, too! The conveyor tunnel would open right under this Mother. But the important thing is not to panic. You can imagine what would happen if the stockholders should get wind of this information. It would be magnified beyond reason. It really must be kept quiet until we know just what we have here." His voice was silvery and soothing and seeing him recognize the need for patience and consideration was encouraging.

"The first thing I want to do is to see the cracks." He directed when the meeting shrunk to the mine staff. "I did a lot of engineering on those benches underneath it, you know."

Curt drove Bill up to the site and Gerritt and Wes followed.

"Impressive, isn't he?" Gerritt said on the way up, almost to himself. Gerritt could see himself in the same position, giving studied advice.

"Yes," Wes answered. "But probably not impressionable." Gerritt and Wes looked at each other, each knowing the other too well. There was no need for Wes to explain what he meant by the remark.

Dixon walked up and down along the cracks, scuffing at the stones with an expensive black kid shoe. He was dressed in a business suit and his tie blew away from his shirtfront as though someone were holding onto it and tugging him here and there. He looked at the simple surveying Wes set up and at a drill that was moved in. Wes was suddenly ashamed they hadn't done more. Dixon walked the full length of the finds and then back to where they stood. Gerritt was chattering and showing him where the holes were to be drilled and where the stakes were.

But Bill turned to Wes. "So what do you think, Wes? Your reports don't mince words." Wes was surprised. He didn't think anyone in New York read the dry engineering reports he sent up weekly.

"I think we better know when it's coming down." Wes chose his words carefully. There wasn't any better way he could think of to express the concern inside him for this failing rock.

"OK then." He nodded his head. "What do you need?"

They needed a seismograph, an instrument to measure the movement in the earth and Dixon said they would take care of it, plus send someone to set it up. Wes could see that this would occupy their thought and energy for some time to come. Gerritt was just agitated. It meant changes, changes for the ore production, which was his focus.

But Wes was calmed and for the first night since the baby arrived, slept through the night. Nobody would ever know when the mountain began to slide, but they would know when it was finished.

Dixon made good on what he said. It wasn't three weeks before the seismometer arrived. A sensitive, expensive box of wires and tubes, the instrument was fairly straightforward and Wes felt they could have installed it themselves. However, it was brought down by a representative from the firm. A short, fat little man named Harold Hudgins, arrived one morning in Antofagasta with his boxes of instruments and wire. The baggage was treated with serious suspicion by the Aduana and impounded.

"God-a-Mighty," Harold Hudgins exclaimed when he arrived in Cerro Verde after having to leave the reason he came behind with customs. "What kind a country you folks got down here." It was hard to explain to someone who didn't live this problem daily.

And to make matters worse, it rained. There hadn't been rain in Cerro Verde for years and the day after Hudgins arrived, it rained. And that set him off again.

"God-a-Mighty, you fellers tell me you got the driest desert in the world down here and the day I come it rains!" He liked cigars, so he and Ted hit it off fine, the one puffing, the other chewing. That afternoon, the equipment came up from Antofagasta in a big white company station wagon. Wes wondered what the customs agents in Anto were paid, but was sure Hudgins's instruments cost the company more than a few cases of scotch. But it really was no help to have the equipment at last in their grasp because the mine was powerless. Since it never rained, or hardly ever, 5000 Volt cables as thick as your arm were run snaking over the ground to the shovels and buildings in the mine. They were supposed to be propped up on rocks, so if the unlikely ever did happen and it did rain, the cables wouldn't lie in puddles. However, this was pretty tough to enforce when the "in case" chances of it raining hard enough are about every three or four years. Yet there they were, with it raining and needing the power in the mine like needing a beer on a hot day.

"Now look here," Hudgins told them. "Ah've come an awful long way down here and Ah have to be in Tennessee on Friday, so how are we gonna get this little shit put together if you don't have any power?" There wasn't even any power in the mine offices. Everything had blown. It would be several days, before the mine would dry out enough for current to flow freely again. Bernie's office where they were had windows and was light enough to talk by, but was hardly equipped to work in, and then the machines, themselves required juice.

"How much room do you need?" Curt asked.

"Oh, not much. Ah'll just get this thing put together and that'll be all you need. You can do the rest."

"OK," Curt said. "There's generator power to the houses. Let's take it on up to my house and we can work on it there."

Wes and Gerritt went with him. Nell Reicher was mildly surprised when they barged in with all the boxes, tracking mud on her carpet. But she graciously accepted them as though they were her bridge club. The dining room was large and after the table was spread with newspaper the unpacking began. Wes began to see why they sent a technician down with the equipment. It was unbelievably complicated, and very few sensors were assembled. They worked until dinnertime and were to come back after dinner.

"I have to be at the Gerensia for dinner tonight," Gerritt said weakly. "There's some diplomat from Santiago, Joe wants me to meet." He looked dimly displeased. The construction of the instruments was interesting and challenging and Wes didn't envy him at all. Hudgins squinted at him wondering what the likes of Gerritt was doing meeting diplomats, but everyone else understood why and showed no emotion, just acceptance, and Hudgins didn't ask about it. They were at work again by 8 PM, soldering and cutting under Hudgins' watchful eyes. Gerritt didn't return.

"No, that one, that one!" he'd say when they picked up the wrong piece. Wes burned his finger on the soldering iron, but Nell was there with a band-aid and he kept working. Four hours and as many scotches later, they were finished. Hudgins turned the thing on to warm up and they all sat down to rest.

"You all ought to be able to record somebody pissing on the other side of the mine," Hudgins laughed. Nell had, thankfully, gone to bed. His language had gotten worse with the scotch. He had a right, though. Hudgins's knowledge of seismology was phenomenal. He drew out where they were to place the thing and where wires should be attached for optimum response.

Hudgins left the next day. The rain stopped, but they weren't able to install the seismometer before he left and it stayed there on Reicher's dining table for two more days.

Wes had a cement pad poured back about 100 feet from the cracks to set the instrument on and a wood house built around it. The preparation took longer than he thought to set the thing up, stringing the wires and getting the power into it. Gerritt never said why he didn't return the night they were putting the instrument together, but he came up with the idea of drilling into the face of the slide area. Wes thought it a little dangerous, but the value of the information finally won over and Gerritt took two men and went over the edge of the bench about halfway down. There were plenty of footholds and in a few hours, holes were drilled and the wires attached with no mishap. They settled in to watch.

The first movements they detected were earth tremors, tiny earthquakes you can't feel yourself. Signs that deep down below there was a rising restlessness. The Andes were still on the move and at times vicious earthquakes discouraged habitation. The movements of the slide itself looked different on the paper. The movement magnitude of their little piece of rock didn't change much, but the frequency and distance did. At first movement was noted only several times a day, but the movement increased and by the end of April, they were detecting a change of 2 millimeters a day. No one was getting very excited about it. Now that the monitor was installed, it seemed to ward off worry.

And there were other problems. About a week after the seismograph was in and recording, Wes was finally back to work on some maps he had been putting off doing for weeks. His vacation was coming up and there was so much work to be done he wasn't looking forward to it, even though they were taking the baby to meet the grandparents. The phone rang and it was Gerritt put through from the radio out near the tunnel.

"Wes, can you get down here altido?" His voice sounded scratchy from the transmission, but urgent. "I got a big mess here."

Wes hustled on down expecting to find some minor problem to which Gerritt had over-reacted. He drove up to the concrete entrance of the tunnel and found all the men standing around outside, worried looks on their faces as well as Gerritt's. Gerritt ran up to the pick-up door and opened it when Wes stopped.

"Tunnel collapsed!" he screamed breathlessly.

"Anybody inside?"

"No, thank God, but it's a real mess. C'mon." And they headed toward the entrance. Rafia, the Jefe Empleado, passed them some lanterns, but didn't offer to go inside with them. Wes figured he was glad to have some goofy Gringos take that responsibility.

The tunnel was cool and dark after the glare of the sun on the light brown of the ground outside. It looked good, the walls seemed firm and solid. Wes was surprised there could have been a collapse. They had done some studies on the rock drill cores before the tunnel was ever started and determined that the integrity of the rock was such that it wouldn't even have to be shored up inside. It could support itself. But there it was.

A hundred feet into the tunnel the air began to smell dusty and the light beams lost their directness in the mealy air. Wes coughed.

"Happened about an hour ago. Dust just cleared enough for me to go in before I called you. Look at this."

He shot his light ahead and through the thick air Wes could see the tunnel ahead of them filled with earth and rock, gravelly and loose from the ceiling to the floor beneath. A wall of debris closed it off.

"We're lucky with this one," Gerritt breathed gratefully. "It's going to have to be shored up."

"This wasn't predicted from the core studies. There should be no instability whatsoever here."

"Well, there it is – fucked up right at your feet!"

He was right. The rock that came down looked fine and powdery like it was ground up and spit out. The tunnel would have to be shored up and cleared before any more work could be done.

Rafia and the others were sullen and silent when they were told they were going to have to go back in there. Wes wondered what they thought he and Gerritt would do about it, just close it up? In a way Wes didn't blame them. If it came down once...well, thinking about it wasn't going to help.

Curt was worried they would have trouble with the Union. Joe Driscoll met with Hidalgo after the seismograph was installed to tell him about the slide area, but Hidalgo already knew. Knowing how he operated, Gerritt wondered if he wouldn't figure out some way to make an issue. And now this collapse of the rock in the conveyor tunnel would threaten further relations.

The mess in the tunnel was cleaned out and Gerritt had steel girders put in to support the ceiling and work began again. Wes talked to Curt about his vacation and Curt told him to go. He was hesitant; there was too much happening. But he knew Alice would be disappointed, so the first of May they left for the States.

CHAPTER 32

Wes going away was a loss, not saying exactly what it was, but a part of Gerritt seemed to be missing. He did enjoy the sudden freedom from accountability; Wes was becoming the only one who would cross him. Freedom from Wes's opinions was what Gerritt needed right now. The move into the new house was a joke. Eve moved in with all her things from the Gerencia, furniture, gifts from her parents, even Hortensia and another woman to cook and clean for them. It wasn't that the house wasn't nice. Gerritt had never lived in such an amazing place, which included the indoor garden. The first night after Eve went to bed, he went out and lay down on the cool grass and imagined that he was somehow back at Shem's where things were simpler. He tried to smell the soil and plants, but they were different and try as hard as he could, he was unable to transport his mind back to Montana. It had slipped away. It wasn't that he needed to find the exact place because it wasn't the same as he remembered when he went home to visit. It was his tie to the farm, soil, smells, creek that he wanted to recapture. And it was gone. He wasn't sure where, it was just gone.

The rest of the house looked a little like the Gerencia.

"I'm just bringing a few of Eve's things down so she feels at home," Anna Driscoll said, as furniture, dishes, curtains and colors for the paint were duplicated. Eve was pretty useless for all of that and Gerritt had no time to think about it with the mess in the mine and really didn't care. The bedroom, though, he did care about, and it was this part of the house that particularly upset him and made him want to escape to the green grass of the garden room.

Eve's room at the Gerencia had been transplanted to this new house. The pink and blue colors, all the stuffed animals, and her tea set. This wasn't a bedroom conducive to conjugal pleasures, but was rather like an adult nursery. Eve loved it.

"Isn't this bedroom just too perfect," Eve cooed as she snuggled up to him in bed.

Their connubial pursuits were like the room, childlike. Eve continued to be all over him until he made love to her, but it wasn't satisfying for him. Her flaccidity and silliness was a turn-off. He was often unable to perform, sometimes had to stimulate himself in order to do so and he wondered how long it would be before he couldn't even do that. He thought about going down the hill again, but figured if Driscoll found out he would have his head.

And the mine was falling apart. All the things that he loved about it, the smooth operation of the machinery, the productivity, were in some ways better than sex for him. Nothing gave him more pleasure than physically feeling the rock, hearing the shovels, watching the trains. It was a high like no other. And it all started a downward turn after the explosion. And now the slide. Sometimes, he would pretend the problems in the mine were not happening, that they would go away, that the mountain would somehow put itself back together. He often worked late in his office alone, putting together models of trucks and dozers that were sent down from the States. He could lose himself in that and make the slide go away, and avoid going to Eve.

During the mine meetings when he had to face it all, he actually came up with some good suggestions and was never sure where they came from. Part of his mind still ran with the daily work, attempting to solve problems, but the rest of him was in denial. The girders had been installed in the tunnel at enormous cost, but would they hold?

"These will definitely support the tunnel," Gerritt said in meetings, confidently, and everyone believed him, wanted to believe him. Inside he wasn't sure, and he chose to avoid going into the tunnel to check on them.

It wasn't much of a vacation for Wes. His mind was back at Cerro Verde. Alice spent money like her purse was a plugged sink drain that has suddenly been unclogged. Shoes for Georgia were $300. She wasn't even walking and Alice was buying shoes for the next year.

"Well, the shoe salesman said her foot was fat and that it might slim down in which case she might take a narrower size when she learns to walk, so I had to buy two sizes of everything." Alice explained. Wes's eyeballs rolled. So what could you say, the kid had to have shoes that fit.

They saw friends and visited with their parents to whom Georgia was the ultimate gift and the center of focus. Friends asked what had happened in the last year.

"Well, the upper benches are not supporting themselves and we are worried about a slide," Wes explained. Everyone seemed amused and when he talked about the explosives accident they would say, "Is that right?" so he eventually quit talking about it. There was no way to explain what was going on in Cerro Verde. It was something shared only by those who were there. Alice and Wes realized they were having something they could not possibly share with anyone at home and it was a lonely feeling in a way, as you feel when you move into your own life and away from your family. They were going back 8000 miles away from "home", and yet home now seemed to be wherever they were. Wes was so anxious to get back to the mine that he began having nightmares about the slide. Alice would wake him up and he would be sweating and shaky. The trip back seemed interminable, the plane changes in the congested O'Hare airport, and in stuffy Miami. And then the long trip via Panama and Lima to Antofagasta. The baby was tired and cranky, as were they, with the hours of travel and luggage to manage. At last on the way up from the coast Wes was breathing easier and when the smoke from the concentrator came into view he knew he was back and felt joy and relief. It was short lived.

The morning after their arrival Wes was a little hung over. They went to Dillon's house for dinner after leaving Georgia with Rosa, the maid. Alfords were there, too and they had a few scotches. The slide movement had increased.

"Gerritt doesn't talk much, Wes," Felix Alford said to him. "He seems withdrawn, and is always busy entertaining visitors to camp."

Wes wasn't surprised, a social obligation would now be expected of him by the Driscolls and Gerritt lacked these skills.

Curt looked at Wes with relief when he sank into a chair across from him.

"So glad you are back, Wes. The slide is moving eight millimeters a day and New York is concerned," Curt explained. "The wires on the face broke and were replaced. Gerritt did the replacement and fell and sprained his ankle." An hour and a half later Wes emerged from Curt's office wondering why he had been so anxious to get back.

The face of the slide had begun to spall, its steepness shoving pebbles down the face to fall far below. And there was trouble in the tunnel again. When Wes asked what kind of trouble, Curt just replied, "See if you can get Gerritt to take you out there. You won't believe it if I just tell you."

When Wes emerged from Curt's office, Gerritt was finally in for the day. He looked awful. Grey and sallow, like a man who spends too much time indoors.

"How are things?" Wes asked.

"OK," he said with no enthusiasm.

"How's Eve??"

"She's in Santiago with her folks. They're going out to Viña for a few days." The Driscolls had a place in Viña del Mar and spent a good deal of time there. There were casinos and Joe Driscoll liked to gamble.

"Well, thought you would be down there, too." Wes chided. Gerritt didn't seem to hear him.

"Did Curt tell you about the tunnel?"

"Only that you'd show me the problem."

"I haven't seen it and don't want to." He looked away.

"Come on, Gerritt, let's go", Wes said, picking up his hard hat and heading out the door. Gerritt followed but would have liked to be elsewhere, only he wasn't sure anymore where elsewhere was or how to escape to that place.

Wes watched him. The only word that came to mind was sadness. He knew that Gerritt was not pining away for Eve, nor worried about his position in the mine. It was something else, a disappointment, some unredeemable loss. He decided to try taking Gerritt's mind off the mine.

"Remember that school teacher you met here? Molly? We had a letter from her when we got back." Wes said tentatively, looking straight out ahead of him at the gravel road rising upward.

"Oh," Gerritt said with disinterest. "Yeah, she OK?" He asked this last after a small silence as if reminding himself who she was and that she had sent him a letter some time ago.

"Yes. She's teaching in New York someplace, don't remember where she said. I could bring you the letter." Wes waited for him to ask for it, but he cut off the conversation as though they had been talking about the gas mileage of the truck. And Wes let the matter drop.

"The girders I put in the tunnel failed." Gerritt said looking at Wes as though steel girders were life itself. "Haven't seen them, but Curt said they went. What the fuck is going on in that mountain? They should have held, they should have held." His head hung and swayed as if detached.

"Well, I don't know, Gerritt. Maybe the slide. Let's have a look." They pulled up at the site.

No one was around. Curt had pulled the men out of the tunnel, considering it unsafe. There wasn't too much change in the tunnel itself since Wes had seen it a month earlier. Not much additional work had been done. It took a week to clear out the original mess and then to install the steel inside. They walked into the coolness with lamps, the light walking ahead of them. Gerritt's voice echoed off the walls.

"Now down here is where the shoring started," he was showing Wes, pointing with his lantern. They walked on further, about 50 feet. Then Gerritt turned his lamp on the ceiling and Wes did the same. Above their heads were three steel girders, about 3 inches by 4 inches of solid steel resting on steel posts cemented into the ground below. These firm, stiff, solid representatives of the strength man can manufacture were twisted like so many pieces of taffy on a hot summer day.

Each girder was fit around the rock above it like it had been cast in that grotesque and agonized form, the rock pushing and shoving against the steel as a tumor might into healthy flesh. It was a sickening sight. Gerritt looked at them and wiped his eyes. He remembered how seeing Wes's pickup after Arias ran over it made him feel. Somehow seeing solid things hurt was painful. Was everything he knew and believed this vulnerable?

"How long has it been this way?" Wes asked him.

"We got the girders in a week after you left, I guess. At least I'm sure these were up then – this was the worst of it. Julio started telling me they were moving about two weeks later and I laughed at him. I laughed!" Gerritt's voice broke and Wes looked over and saw how this was affecting him.

"And the men are jumpy as hell, now." He went on. "They are talking about just forgetting the whole thing. The Union is giving some trouble over it, too."

"Yeah, I know." Curt had told him.

There was a crunching behind them in the darkness and a light swinging in illuminating only some khaki pants with thin legs that pushed bonily at the knees from inside. The man took shape as he approached the range of their light beams. It was Hugh Dillon. The angles of his face made sharper in the indirect lighting, he looked older and he wasn't smiling.

"You see where you guys screwed up again?" he said half seriously, then "When you going to clean this shit up?"

"Soon as I figure out how to get some of those men back in here," Gerritt said, regaining his composure.

"First, half of this side of the mine is falling down and now your tunnel starts falling in. What's going on?"

Falling down. Mine benches, tunnel, failing rock. They were all standing there, the three of them looking at each other. It would be hard to say just who it occurred to first, or if it came into their minds from the earth above them. Whatever, whoever, they all knew at once that the rock failure, the slide in the mine had to be related to the caving in the tunnel. The tunnel was far away, maybe 500 feet from the last cracks they knew about, but it had to be.

"Jesus Christ," Gerritt muttered, "How can I support a whole mountain coming down on top of me?"

"You can't." Hugh said to no one.

"But the tunnel is already so far in with no problem. There ought to be something we can do." Wes said. They all knew how much money had already been spent. New York would give up the tunnel reluctantly now if at all. "Let's go up directly above the tunnel and have a look."

They were awhile getting up to the top of the mine above the tunnel, the mine roads being interconnected, but indirect. Hugh called the Jefe Patio to ask Curt to meet them. The radio crackled with the day shift going about the business of running the mine, the dispatching of trains to the sulfide plant and trucks to the waste dumps. It all sounded so normal, so good, belying what was going on underneath.

The edge of the mine directly above the tunnel was somewhat higher than the slide area and the wind whipped around it trying to blow them off. What they were looking for came fast. There were cracks here, too, but different in a weird way from the cracks back of the slide area. These were short, wider, and looked like they had been formed from a settling action. It was as though an old man had sighed and his brow wrinkled up in creases showing the age and weakness of his skin. They were a disheartening sight.

"Do you think this could be from the first collapse?" Curt asked.

"Maybe we ought to have the geologists look at it," Hugh offered.

"Christ, they wouldn't know a crack in the ground from an ass-hole." Gerritt growled. He had no respect for geologists. He considered them theoreticians that couldn't fix anything.

"Well, it wouldn't hurt," Wes said. He discounted this judgment as he did most of Gerritt's opinions. "At least another eye or two wouldn't hurt, since none of us seems to know what to do."

He looked at Gerritt. Beads of sweat seeped across the top of his forehead, clotting a few hairs together. It wasn't a hot day and the wind was drying even the saliva inside Wes's mouth. He glanced at Curt and Hugh, their brows were smooth and dry and unconsciously he rubbed his own and his hand came away with no sweat on it. It was as though Gerritt was standing in another climate, hotter than theirs and windless, insulated from the things that touched them.

"I'll think of something," Gerritt said too quickly. "Something." And saying that "something" he moved off in the direction of his pick-up.

"Gerritt OK, Wes?" Curt asked.

"I don't know." And he didn't know. Gerritt was anxious, that much was obvious, but seeing these cracks opening and wrinkling the surface in front of them and knowing they reached down into and through the earth beneath their feet to the tunnel they were building scared the shit out of them all.

That night Wes felt he had to see Gerritt, or maybe just wanted to mull over with somebody the things that were going on in his mind about the cracks and the slide and the whole thing. Wes called him after dinner and asked if he and Alice could come over for a few minutes. It had been obvious after a few months that Eve was not going to entertain. She wasn't up to doing it, although she had maids and mozos at her service. Alice heard Eve was back from Viña and they both wanted to see her, too, and the house.

"Sure, come on over for a drink," Gerritt said, enthusiastically. After they got Georgia down and Rosa was sitting in her room with her, Wes and Alice headed over.

Eve answered the door in an expensive silk robe of some kind, but she welcomed them. At least she seemed all right.

"I'm happy you came. Nobody comes to see us." Eve's lower lip came out in a pout. She grabbed Alice by the arm and pulled her into the living room faster than Alice was prepared to go and the two of them seemed to weave and waltz, and just as Wes was ready to lend help they regained their balance and somehow were in the main part of the house. The living room was large. A hundred people could have mingled easily now. Gerritt was slumped down in a large brown leather chair across the room, a drink in one hand and a TIME magazine, their standby of communication, in the other. The sweat had disappeared from his brow and he had on a loose blue shirt and some old jeans. Wes sighed, feeling better about him.

"Get you a drink?" He stood up.

"Sure."

"How about you, Alice?"

"OK, but just a glass of wine, Gerritt. I'm still nursing."

"I'll help you." Wes said and followed him out to the kitchen. They went through the dining room and through doors at the end he suddenly caught sight of green grass and flowers.

"What's in there?" Wes stopped dead still. Gerritt stopped, too, was silent a moment, his forehead frowning and his lips tipped up on one side in a slight smirk.

"That's the rose garden. Eve wanted flowers inside like up at the Gerencia, so Joe had that built. It's quite a deal. Let's get a drink and I'll show it to you."

They went on into the kitchen, a huge room inhabited, Wes was sure, only by the cooks and maids. It was all new and spotless and he wondered if they ever ate anything in this house. Wes was almost tempted to open the cupboards to see if there were boxes and bottles and packages behind the sterile doors. He thought to himself that when Alice saw this place she would want him to go down and fight with Duvillard again about having work done on their kitchen. Getting remodeling done in this place was always a mañana sort of thing. If they didn't do it today, they might the next, or the next. Unless of course you were Joe Driscoll--or Gerritt Wells.

The drinks were handed around. Gerritt gave Eve a glass of Fanta. She licked around the rim of the cool frosty goblet as though it were an ice-cream cone.

"Did you see the rose garden?" Alice asked him, her eyes dazzling.

"Not yet."

They passed through the dining room and double doors and stepped out onto squashy soft and silent grass. The room was large, glassed in above and the sound of ventilator fans hummed securely somewhere. At the opposite end from where they stood was a raised brick terrace with a lawn swing and tables. There were flower borders all around and the place smelled earthy and wet and warm like a greenhouse. Eve had her roses, mostly yellow and there was a huge poinsettia blooming in one corner. It really was a most extraordinary place. It would have been surprising anywhere, but most especially so there in the middle of the desert. Gerritt was babbling on about his tomato vines, which grew up the side of the wall on a white trellis, and Wes found his mind wandering.

"...and Joe let me do the ventilation system. It's all on timers and the humidity is automatically controlled." Wes felt that this was something Gerritt could really relate to – a mini-farm right here in his own house, something for him to do with his hands, for his hands to feel and operate. You could see the pleasure in his voice when he talked about it.

"...but I can't ask just anybody to come up here and see it. They wouldn't understand."

No they wouldn't, Wes thought. It was escapist in a way, but obviously was something Gerritt needed. They went back into the living room and sank into the plush furniture and Gerritt and Wes began to talk about the mine. Eve was still showing Alice the rest of the house.

"I have an idea about what to do with the cracks." Wes offered.

"Well, I'll think of something." Gerritt answered, as though the entire thing was his responsibility. He threw his leg casually up on the side of the chair giving the impression that some brilliant solution would occur to him at any moment. Wes waited and there was nothing, and he began to explain his idea.

"So, I thought maybe we could drill down over the tunnel through the cracks and pour cement in there until it comes out the bottom." This came to him driving home that evening when he was thinking about gluing a plate of Alice's, she had broken. It was pretty far fetched, but the more he thought about it, the more it seemed possible.

"What?" Gerritt sat up and turned around to face Wes. "Christ, Wes! Do you know how many yards of concrete that would take? God, that's out of the question! You just go on with watching your slide over there and I'll figure out something. Cement!" And his eyebrows went upward followed by his eyes and his whole face.

It really wasn't that ridiculous of an idea. Cement was used in many mines for shoring purposes. And it had worked before. Granted this was a larger project than those reported. Gerritt's surprise and dismay made Wes uncomfortable, but before he could say anything Gerritt jumped up.

"I got some brochures in the mail the other day about a new support system for tunnel ceilings, I'd like to try. Come on in the bedroom, I think I left them in there somewhere."

Wes followed him and decided against making any comment at the time, shelving his idea for a later session with Curt, but wondering if maybe it really was impractical.

The bedroom Gerritt went into was right off the living room and when Wes went in, he must have backed out, because Gerritt noticed his reaction. The room was filled with dolls and stuffed animals. They sat everywhere – on the dressers, on the beds, in the chairs. The place looked like a toyshop. On top of that the entire room was an over-powering color of pink, the same pink as the nightdress Eve had on. Wes wanted to leave it, but Gerritt was rummaging around on the dresser knocking teddy bears and dolls off on the floor.

"Goddamn crap of hers," he muttered. Wes didn't say anything; couldn't think of anything to say.

"Here it is." He raised some wrinkled brochures out of a drawer. His eyes met Wes's and they just stood there for a few minutes looking at each other. Gerritt knew Wes had taken in the room and was breathing in the sweet, stale smell of old toys that hung there like yesterday's dinner. Wes waited for him to say something to break the air between them, but he didn't. Gerritt just looked at him, and Wes could feel him reaching out and it was too much.

"How are things between you and Eve, Gerritt?" He had to ask it. The question was already there.

He broke. His shoulders caved inward and the stare fell to the floor.

"Rotten! That's how they are…rotten! There's nothing at all between us. Can't you see from this junk in here? She's a nothing. She's like a beautiful, breakable vase my Aunt had that I tipped over once and almost broke. A big nothing!"

The little beads of perspiration were coming out again and Wes noticed them below his short sideburns, dampening his lower face and making him look older.

"I'm sorry." And Wes was. Sorry for what was happening to Gerritt, caught now in a position he had seemed to want so badly. Gerritt didn't look at Wes; he looked at himself in the mirror, then threw his head back and laughed.

"I want another drink." He said finally and seriously and went out of the bedroom and into the kitchen.

In the living room the women were talking calmly and quietly and it was a relief to be with them.

"Eve's just telling me about going to the Virgin Islands with her parents next week." Alice said gaily.

There was a crash from the kitchen, tinkling and falling sounds that stopped and then Gerritt swearing. Wes went in and found him nursing a cut finger.

"Goddamn bottle slipped. Looks like I finally broke the vase," he said. "Not bad, though." He squeezed at his hand trying to stop the bleeding with pressure. "Guess I don't need another drink, do I." There was sweat all over his face now.

"Guess not." Wes said worriedly. "We should go, it's getting late. You OK?"

"Sure, sure, this is nothing. See you in the morning." He paused for a moment examining his finger closely as though he might find some answer there to what he needed. "Wes," Gerritt looked up at him. "Thanks for coming."

Alice had gone into the bedroom to get her coat and when she came out her eyes were open so wide Wes thought someone had stuck a pin in her behind. And he quickly shuffled her out the door before she said anything to Gerritt.

"Did you see that room?" She said in wonder when they were in the pickup and on the way home. "It looks like a museum in there. How do they sleep in there?"

"I gather they don't. At least Gerritt doesn't."

"Oh." She looked out the front windshield as they went down the hill, over the bridge that spanned a small quebrada and back up the hill to their house. "I'm sorry."

"Yeah, that's what I said. Look...I don't think you better tell any of your friends what you saw tonight, at least not about the bedroom, OK?"

"All right" she said seriously as though they were partners in a conspiracy. Maybe they were, but only because Gerritt's life was now so intertwined with theirs and Gerritt had no one else to help him. Wes didn't like it, but that's the way it was.

CHAPTER 33

The following morning Gerritt went out to the pit early and alone. There was too much to think about and he wanted to get back to the basic rock and air and start from there as if there could be a new beginning. Inside he knew it was no use looking here. The rock itself had let him down. Instead of a hard and stable support, there really wasn't anything he could count on for sure. His relationship with Eve was fantasy. Eve wanted to be close, but Gerritt wasn't sure what close meant. He barely remembered his own mother, and his Aunt also left him at an early age. Although Shem loved Gerritt as his own, no woman had nurtured him. He had become an inside person, attached to the external world of machinery. Women could be with him, but not ever reach his center. They touched him, smelled him, loved him, but couldn't take anything away.

It was the same with other men. Wes was his friend, he knew that, but Gerritt was incapable of letting him inside to help.

The oval hole loomed up out of the ground, blossoming into the morning light as he drove up over the crest and then took the main road down into the mine, the road that went directly under the slide and continued to the end of the pit, some 2 miles away. Gerritt stopped under the slide area, as if to dare it to fall. The air was still cold from the night at this hour, but the wind was lost in the upper reaches of the pit and it was silent where he stood, or nearly so. He looked upward at the giant steps that reached back and up to the top. From this point, the bench faces looked so steep that he found himself tipping backwards on his heels as if the mountain itself was pushing him. They seemed to rise forever above where he stood, steep and somber. Men had cut the faces that gazed down on him and he wondered who they were, those men, and had they ever wondered if they were cutting too steeply, scraping that last bit of ore, squeezing the sides until now they could not support themselves?

It was then he heard it, at first not thinking about it, accepting it as a morning sound. A tiny, cracking, searing sound coming from the rock face, like a crick in the knee when your joints don't work well anymore. It wasn't much, but it was there, saying that it was still moving, the particles within the rock rubbing against each other, relieving the stress, adjusting to a more comfortable position. Pick-ups with men for the morning shift roared past him and he waited for the silence to overtake him again to be sure what he had heard and, yes, it was there.

Pebbles from the face twanged on the roof of his pick-up. The inside of the mountain was moving and soon the outside would follow. He wondered how much more it could take. He must have stood there a long time because finally the noises of the day shift starting up the shovels after shift change drowned out the cracking of the slide and there was no point staying any longer.

Gerritt looked down the length of the pit. The 704 had begun loading waste there in the bottom. Turning, eating the rock with its huge eight-yard bucket, turning, spitting the mouthful into the waiting truck. Eating, spitting, it was carving more benches like the ones he was standing under. Because of what they knew now, the new benches wouldn't be as steep as the ones above him. Gerritt thought they were probably making other, new, mistakes and vaguely wondered what they were.

He turned his pick-up around and headed back out of the mine around its outside to the road that went up on top and past the ancient graveyard protected from any industrial encroachment by the superstitions of the workers. The wind had come up here and he knew if there were noises they would be blown away.

He saw Wes's truck and stopped.

"Morning, Wes." Gerritt felt apologetic about the previous evening, but couldn't frame any comment.

"Just checking and resetting the seismometer." Wes was bent over intent on this task. The slide was still moving at a fairly regular eight millimeters a day, at least that hadn't changed. They went over to the edge and looked down at the sensing wires stretched down over the face. One had broken again and would have to be replaced. The sounds of the machinery in the bottom of the pit a half-mile below them drifted up faintly and they both had the same thoughts of the whole section of this side of the mine sliding slowly down to meet those noises. Wes shivered.

Shaking his head, hoping to clear away those thoughts, he turned and crunched his way along the crack line 100 feet back from the edge down toward the area above the conveyor tunnel. Gerritt followed, his head down.

The wrinkling and collapsing of the earth there seemed worse than Wes had remembered. Maybe the light was different this morning. The more he looked at the cracks there, the better the idea of pouring concrete into them looked, and he determined to present the idea firmly to Curt, but didn't mention it again to Gerritt. Gerritt just cursed and went back to his truck.

There wasn't time to talk to Curt until later, as when Wes returned to the mine office, everyone was visiting with a new geologist, Bob Fulton, sent by the New York office. Wes was glad to see he had arrived with more wire and monitors for the seismograph.

"Oh, Wes, finally," Curt's raised eyebrows and his hand in his shirtfront mirrored his anxiety. "This is Bob Fulton."

It was his hand, his right hand that Wes noticed first as it wrapped its long fingers around his. His index finger seemed to extend on around somehow and when Wes looked at it he looked quickly up to Fulton's face, embarrassed. There was an extra joint on that finger and it protruded beyond the others. The thin face that greeted him was long and sad as if someone had pulled the skin on his jaws down making his whole face sag. Even the smile he extended did not make the colorless eyes turn up at all near the corners.

"Pleased to meet you," and a bass voice welled up from somewhere out of his tall form, nearly as tall as Wes. Bob Fulton was on the verge of being grotesque and Wes turned from him to Curt as quickly as he could.

"Bob's got all your stuff," Curt offered. "As soon as it gets out of the Aduana anyway."

"Good," Wes said, looking at Fulton again, but he was still the same. "I'll take you out to show you around. Oh, by the way, I want to see you later, Curt."

"OK. And ask Zuñiga to get a desk for Bob in Engineering."

The praying mantis followed him into the engineering office and looked around while Wes talked to Zuñiga, who wasn't too happy about having to reorganize around another person.

"Si, Señor Jefe, como no." he said with no enthusiasm and pursed lips.

It wasn't long before Wes realized that Fulton was a gift. He was an expert on rock movement, and had spent some time with the U.S.G.A. studying earthquake monitoring in Alaska. It was quickly clear as he took him out to the site that Bob was going to be a real help. And his strangeness wore off.

"You seem to have made a good start here," he said of the set-up. "But the seismometer has to be put further back. See here. You're getting interference from the mine machinery." The long finger pointed to the unsteady base line, tracing a jagged line across the paper. It wasn't of great magnitude, but made slight movement of the slide undetectable.

"We'll have to drill, which makes me a little nervous, but no other choice." Wes took him over to the cracks above the conveyor tunnel, but did not tell him what he wanted to do about the cement, not knowing him well enough to trust him with an idea that was at best far-fetched. Bob never said a word about the wind or the bleakness of the pampa surrounding them. His strange body, his speech, he fit in here somehow. It was as though he was always meant to come to this place and only now arrived.

When they came back to the offices, Gerritt was there. Wes could see into his office as they came in. Gerritt was staring out the window and didn't turn around to acknowledge them, although Wes was sure he must have heard their work boots clomping on the floor.

"Gerritt?" Nothing.

"Gerritt!" Wes said louder. He turned around slowly and stared vaguely through him as though he wasn't there and Wes was sure he didn't see Bob at all. And then with a great effort boiling up inside of him, the little dampness on his forehead that maybe only Wes noticed, the quickening of breath, he was getting ready to be in the same room with them and to be who they expected him to be.

Bob glanced at Wes; he could feel Bob's eyes asking him what was going on. He would have to be told something, but what? And Wes determined to tell him as little as possible and then the thought went through his mind. Why did he not want to tell him? Maybe it was because there had to be an explanation, a reason for all this, and there wasn't any. And then Gerritt was back with them.

"Morning," he said looking from one to the other. They sagged down into the chairs in his office.

"This is Bob Fulton, Gerritt."

"Yeah, Curt said you were here." He offered his hand, which Bob took and Wes waited for Gerritt to notice the extra-long finger, but there was nothing, and Wes felt a twinge of guilt.

"I've shown him around." Wes offered and Bob laughed, the sound rattling like empty cans down an alley.

"It'll take me a year to find my way around this place. The mine roads are like a maze." They all smiled and it loosened things up some. Wes imagined how he must feel and looked at Gerritt remembering their first days with Art Barnett.

"There are some suggestions I can offer for the use of the new equipment," he began to tell Gerritt what he had told Wes earlier out in the pit. "I told Wes the seismometer has to be moved away from the mine. We'll have plenty of wire now. Is there any place you might suggest?"

"How about the powder magazine?" Gerritt suggested, cogently. There was an old underground storage for explosives way back of the slide. It wasn't being used and had a cement floor; it would be an ideal place.

Wes looked at him carefully. Sometimes Gerritt was so lucid, and other times, just a few minutes earlier, he was somewhere else entirely.

Gerritt and Bob went on out to look at the powder magazine and Gerritt was going to show him the tunnel. Wes wanted the time to see Curt.

Ned was in Curt's office, his feet propped up on the desk and the two of them were smoking the sour cigars Ned loved. The office stank, and Wes didn't want to talk to Curt about his idea for the cracks above the mine tunnel in front of anybody, especially Ned who he was sure would find it ludicrous. But, apparently Ned had already been there too long, or had work to do, or sensed his need for privacy, because he vacated the chair with a thump of his big feet on the plywood floor and in a cloud of smelly cigar smoke he was gone.

Wes dropped into the still warm chair, silent for just a moment too long.

"Something wrong, Wes?" Curt asked. Of late, with the change in Gerritt, that was usually the subject of talks with Curt.

"Well, no. Not exactly. It's just that…well, I have an idea about the cracks above the tunnel. You know… how we might shore it up so the drilling can continue."

Curt smiled, easing back into his chair and biting on the cigar so that it bent at an angle up from his mouth. It had been months since anyone had a decent suggestion about how to proceed with the tunnel.

"Good!" He grunted from teeth clenched onto the cigar. "Let's hear it."

"I'd like to open up the cracks from the top with a drill rig. We'll have to close the tunnel for a while, of course. Gerritt can't get anyone to go in anyway. Then it occurred to me that if we pour cement in from the top until it comes out the bottom the ground could move around it and not bend the girders. If the slide does collapse into the pit, we'd have to clean out the tunnel entrance, but the main part of the tunnel should hold. The rock isn't likely to crack further on because by then you would be beyond the parallel of the slide area." It all spilled out at once. Wes was so worked up over having held this in that he didn't look to see what Curt's reaction to this would be.

"…Ever been done before?" Curt asked and grimaced. Was Wes losing it, too?

"It's been used for underground shoring of cracks between levels. That seems good enough."

"Well, there's a considerable distance variable here…much more than one level!"

"I know, I know." Wes sensed his hesitancy. "But something has got to be done or we forget the tunnel."

Curt looked thoughtful. 'Ah,' Wes thought. 'He's at least giving the matter serious consideration.' But the enthusiasm was short-lived.

"Let's wait awhile, Wes." Curt's eyes burned pleadingly and yet firmly into him. "Gerritt thinks he can handle it for now. He's got some new kind of steel girder being trucked up from Santiago. That's a lot cheaper than the cement would be and…well, more sophisticated, don't you agree?"

"It may be more sophisticated, Curt," Wes was angry, knowing that Driscoll would support Gerritt's choice. "It won't work! You've seen those twisted girders down there. They bent like paper clips. There's no steel that can hold back that fucking mountain and you know it! We're just wasting time!"

By the time Wes finished his piece, Curt had swiveled in his chair and was looking out the window at the day blowing brown and dusty past his window. His fingers felt the cigar Ned had given him, turning it round and round. Then the short body wheeled abruptly around, the booted feet bumped heavily on the floor and the teeth bit the tip of the cigar off and spat it in the wastebasket.

"Wes…" It was an ultimatum. Curt's eyebrows raised and lowered, studying him carefully. "Wes, you know and I know that no Goddamn girders will hold, but Gerritt doesn't know that, or says he doesn't know." His teeth bared as he said "Gerritt" very carefully.

"…and you see," he continued slowly and deliberately. "Gerritt has cleared the girders with Driscoll and New York both! They've been ordered and are on the way up here right now…airfreight no less. So discussion about whether they are going to hold or not has absolutely nothing to do with whether or not we use them. That's it. Now, I don't want to hear anymore about it!" And with an air of finality and firmness, as though the whole thing had been entirely his decision and a good one, Curt pretended he really was the boss and began to relight his cigar.

Wes was so furious he could feel the bile rise up inside of him and stick in his throat making him want to throw the whole thing up and get rid of it once and for all. His ears throbbed and he only wanted to get out of that room. End of discussion. There was certainly no point in saying any more to Curt at that point.

Wes nearly ran into the engineering office and as he came through the door, he caught Zuñiga off balance carrying some maps, which he nearly dropped on the floor. Bob Fulton was already there working, looked up at him and smiled. Wes was a little surprised to see him. He and Gerritt certainly hadn't spent much time in the tunnel.

"Back already?" Wes said too loudly and threw his hard hat on the desk. It rolled off onto the cement floor with a clatter. Zuñiga jumped about to spill his maps again, but seeing it was only Wes's hat, laid his armload carefully on the drafting table and nervously rushed over to pick it up.

Bob considered Wes for a moment, biting the tip of an eraser.

"Yes," he nodded slowly. "Gerritt seemed in a hurry and really, I didn't want to spend any more time inside that tunnel than I had to. It's a God-awful mess in there!"

"Yeah, I know." Wes sat on the edge of his desk, the anger from his conversation with Curt leaking out slowly from every pore. There was a small silence between them with Bob regarding him tentatively. Wes could see the questions in his eyes."

"Look, Bob...uh...about those girders in the tunnel..."

"Yes." He said quickly hoping they could talk.

"Well, they're going to be replaced with some new kind of steel girder Gerritt is having sent down from the States."

"What?" Gerritt didn't mention that in the tunnel.

"That's right. I just talked to Curt and it's all settled. Must have happened after you left New York. I don't like it either. The waiting, I mean. You know, with the slide movement increasing all the time, more and more pressure is going to be put on that tunnel." Wes didn't want to explain any more about it, because he couldn't justify the decision. It was going to be done that was all. Wes slumped, feeling as Curt must have when he turned away from him a few moments before, closing the matter off because there was really no more to say, no sound explanation to give.

Bob tapped the pencil eraser on his desk several times, took a long drink of his coffee and sat back with his arms folded, his long index finger poking out weirdly over his sleeve.

"Wes, what's going on? What's with Gerritt? I see he's your friend, but I will have to work with the man and I sense he is difficult."

"Friend, yes...and difficult...yes, too." Wes stood up and walked over to the window, stuffing his hands into his pockets. He looked out at the cold crappy day and tried to figure out what to say.

"Christ, Bob, I wish I knew what was wrong with him. He's got some kind of bitchy fight going on inside of him about what's important and what's not. A lot of it isn't logical, but I guess when he gets it straightened out, we'll all be better off."

"And what do we do in the meantime?" He sensed in Bob's long sad face a feeling of threat from Gerritt.

'Oh God,' Wes thought, 'Just one more thing to worry about.'

"We get along OK." He tried to sound defensive of the relationship with Gerritt. After all, Bob was the outsider. "You will, too." But it didn't come out as sincere as he had intended. And Bob looked at him a long time, about to say something else, and then let the matter drop.

That weekend Wes and Alice went to a party at Tully's. Ned's wife, Claire, was a knick-knack enthusiast and when Wes walked around in her house, he always felt like he was going to crash into the little tables that sat around loaded with glass animals and dishes. It seemed like a horrible place to have a party considering the number of people who drank heavily in Cerro Verde. Bob Fulton was there with his wife, Dierdre. She was loud and brassy. Her red hair was cut short like a man's and it made her look even more forceful. But she was sexy, too, in an earthy sort of way with enormous breasts and wide hips. She and Bob didn't seem matched. Bob was quiet and serious and said little when he was near her, which wasn't very long. Gerritt and Dierdre spent the evening together. Eve didn't come. Wes figured she was probably out of town with her parents, but after seeing the house, he wondered if she would have come at all. And anyway, Gerritt didn't belong to Eve, he never had, and it looked like Dierdre didn't belong to anyone either.

Alice was pissed. She liked Eve and protected her simplicity.

"Did you see the way Gerritt put his hand down on Dierdre's bottom when they were dancing?" She asked him on the way home. Wes really hadn't noticed, because he was thinking that the whole thing was starting again and Dierdre was only another diversion for Gerritt. Only this time the woman was married and this saddened Wes because he liked her husband.

CHAPTER 34

The next morning was a Monday. Wes woke up wishing he could get into his truck and take off by himself, the pampa gravel flying behind him. Maybe out to the Rio Salado to fish. He thought about walking up and down that small salty stream with the wind blowing at him and being able to sit down in the matted grasses and think this whole thing out.

Instead, he played with Georgia for a while, bent down to kiss Alice and went in to work. Gerritt and Zuñiga were the only ones in the office. Gerritt was working on something at his desk that looked like another model. Plastic pieces were everywhere and he was concentrating as though it were a mine plan and did not look up when Wes paused at his door. Maybe now was a good time to talk, as they were alone. Wes filled coffee mugs and walked back to Gerritt's office, handed him a cup of coffee and sat down, not even able to say good morning. The room smelled like the airplane glue that was open and oozing on the desk. Gerritt kept on at his work, concentrating on gluing a tiny piece onto another tiny piece, and when he finally got it in place, he looked up at Wes.

"What's bellyachin' you?" he asked smiling. There was still something between them that made a friendship possible, but it took work.

"I hear you've ordered new girders from the States."

"Yeah, should be here next week." And he picked up the tube of glue and another piece of plastic. No explanation, just that they were coming.

"We need to start work on a new road into the mine, Gerritt." This got his attention. Gerritt remembered the sound of the spalling rock and the creaking of the slide he had heard in the early morning the week before. He stopped what he was doing, but didn't look up.

"Not yet. Don't want to move crews off production right now. We'll wait for the girders."

Wes picked up his coffee, as he stood up. It was lukewarm and bitter, but he drank it anyway. There wasn't any point in continuing the conversation.

"What do you think of my model?" Gerritt asked, the discussion erased from his mind.

"What?" Wes's eyes were looking out the window at the dust blowing off the rim of the mine like snow drifting and going nowhere.

"This model, here," he said again. "That crane salesman down last week from Denver brought it for me. I asked him the last time he was here. Model of the 704 shovel…it'll be 10 inches high.

Wes looked at the parts all over this desk and then at him. Gerritt had escaped and wasn't there anymore.

"Nice, Gerritt," he said and went back to his own office where Zuñiga's rustling of papers and maps brought him back to reality.

Drills were moved to prepare an area for the seismograph in the powder magazine back from the slide. Wes, Bob and Curt also agreed that some blasting might be done to remove rock from the top of the slide. Somehow it all seemed futile, but they went on day after day watching and waiting.

August came with no decision about the concrete or the new road. Wes finally talked to Bob Fulton about it, venting his frustration.

"What the fuck are they waiting for, someone to get killed? Gerritt sits in his office working on plastic shovels." The spalling was getting so bad that gravel the size of quarters was now falling on the truck cabs and Wes couldn't blame the drivers for complaining. They feared something larger coming down on top of them.

The drilling, 50 feet back from the edge, didn't seem to affect the slide movement at all. After they blasted the first time they waited a day before moving a shovel and trucks in to remove the debris. But nothing happened.

By September, they drilled and blasted three times with no perceivable change in the movement of the slide. Then one night after Dies y Ocho, Wes awoke to a noise that sounded like thunder. Alice sat up in bed; it awakened her, too. The sound rumbled from far away and kept getting louder, like an approaching train. There was a scream. It was Rosa, their maid. The scream was muffled at first and then wide open as she burst through their door, all modesty forgotten.

"Terremoto, terremoto!" she screamed. "Afuera, afuera altido!" The earthquake was alive and there with them. They jumped out of bed and the three of them ran for Georgia. Wes grabbed her, still asleep in her blankets and they started down the hall, stopping under the door lintel of her room. The walls were moving back and forth and they could hear glass crashing in the kitchen. He thought maybe they would be safer where they were, rather than risk something falling on them outside. The look of terror on Rosa's face sent chills up and down his spine.

"Afuera, ahora!" She screamed, her face red and sweaty.

"Let's go, Wes. Rosa knows." Alice begged. Rosa's look frightened her. And they followed her out through the living room where the drapes on the windows were rippling as though someone was tugging on them from below.

There was an eerie light outside, the first light of morning all grey and gold coming from behind the hills in back of them to the East. There were screams everywhere and others running from their houses. The road that went down the hill was waving like a long loose black ribbon.

When they got out, Wes felt foolish for hesitating. There was nothing to fall down on them outside, no trees or tall buildings. There was only a vastness into which fear could disappear, but which also lent a sense of lacking support as you might feel hanging on a rope over a dark and empty space.

Rosa calmed a little then. At least she stopped screaming, but she had waked Georgia who was crying. Alice sobbed in short wet breaths and there were marks on Wes's arms from her grip.

"You're OK little girl, you're OK." He wrapped the blanket tightly around the baby, kissed the top of her head, and hugged her to his chest. Her cries quieted to a whimper.

Wes looked out toward the mine to the South, trying to imagine what this madness was doing to the slide and the night crew who would be nearly finishing their shift. The view that way was hidden by dust from the ground movement. For the first time he felt really frightened.

It seemed to last forever, but finally the growling quieted and the ground beneath them stopped shaking. The black ribbon of a road ceased to wave and the earthquake was over. Suddenly, they realized that they were all standing there with very little on and embarrassed, like sleep-walkers waking in a strange place, they hurried back inside. It was cold, which Wes hadn't noticed, and he shivered.

Alice put Georgia back to bed with a bottle. There was no sleeping for the rest of them. Wes knew he would have to get out to the mine as soon as he could. They surveyed the damage to the house, but it wasn't serious. The houses in Cerro Verde were built on reinforced concrete slabs, of concrete blocks and rebar. They were cold in the winter and shook in an earthquake, but they didn't come down. And for that he was grateful. The bodega however was a disaster. They had their liquor stored on the top shelf and the bottles had marched like so many soldiers right off the edge and onto the floor. A few were still poised there and these Wes carefully moved to a lower shelf. The scotch and bourbon were sloshed everywhere, mixed with broken glass and cans and boxes of things. The flour bin, which was open, was a mess of glass and liquor.

Rosa fixed some coffee and sat at the kitchen table with them, which she didn't usually do. It seemed all right to her then, they were somehow all the same and needed to talk to each other about what had just happened. She was quite upset about her parents in El Molino and Alice told her to go down later to check on them.

"La Grande Pachamama monte en colera," she said, explaining the earthquake! Wes tried to convince her that it was a matter of rocks moving and underground pressures, but she would have none of it. The earth Mother was angry, it was as simple as that.

Leaving Rosa and Alice to clean up the bodega, Wes hurried out to the mine. The day was just coming on through the settling dust. You couldn't see the sky yet and everything looked brown and hazy in the artificial lights of the trucks and shovels. To Wes's surprise there wasn't all that much damage

302

down in the mine either. He could tell from the bottom of the pit where the road turned steeply upward to the mine offices, that the slide was still intact. If it had gone, there would have been no road to drive on. The offices too were standing, having been constructed in the same manner as the houses of concrete and rebar. But the tower of the Jefe Patio was down and would need considerable repair to fix it. There were, fortunately, no injuries. As soon as Curt and Bob arrived, they went up to the top of the slide. They expected the wires of the seismograph to be broken, but were not prepared for what they found.

Driving up the road where the edge only slowly becomes visible, it was minutes before they could take in what they were seeing. The drill they had placed up there a few weeks before was leaning out at an angle toward the edge. There was a semi-circle of rock and earth, extending to the original cracks some 100 feet back that had relaxed. It looked like a giant jaw with receding gums, an old man succumbing to the aging process.

"My God, look at that drill!" Curt exclaimed. "How are we going to get that off there?" No one had a ready answer. The drill was away from them, floating out there on a new island of earth as though it were an ice-flow. A giant crack in the earth opened where the section was dropping away. Its blackness continued on down into the rock and out of sight.

"Let's get some wires on this thing and the monitors going and then maybe we can see if it's moving and if it will be safe to move the drill." Bob was gesturing with his extra-long finger. He was the only calm one. Wes was sweating.

"That sounds good," Curt agreed. 'Nobody touch that damn thing until we find out where we are." Wes knew he was talking to Gerritt, who wasn't there to hear him.

By afternoon, Bob Fulton had a crew assembled to replace the wires and they went up there again with the men in the back of the trucks. Wes had a sinking feeling when he saw Gerritt's pick-up, stepped on the gas and then screeched to a stop. He ran over to the edge where the earth was slipping, but it was too late. Gerritt was already out on the earth island, on that drill and starting up the motor. Rafia, on safe ground, appeared to be attaching a cable to Gerritt's pick-up.

"Gerritt!" Wes screamed. "Get the hell off that thing!" What are you trying to prove!" But Gerritt couldn't hear him. And even if he could have heard, it wouldn't have made any difference. There wasn't anything to do but add their own hands and truck. They helped Rafia anchor the cable and stood there watching Gerritt as he slowly climbed up and started the engine on the small caterpillar tractor attached to the drill. Smoke belched from the Cat sitting about 30 feet from the solid ground where they were standing and down four feet where the dirt island had pulled away from the face. If the face slid any more, the weight of the drill going down would have snapped the cable, or worse, pulled Rafia and the pickup down with it. Gerritt put it into gear and inched forward. The drill crawled to the edge of the slipped earth where Wes and Bob could hook their truck to it as well. With the two trucks and the Cat, they managed to get the thing up onto safe ground.

"There," Gerritt said, pleased with himself. "That's done."

"Yeah, done," Wes said between his teeth. "What are we supposed to tell Curt? He said nobody was supposed to touch that thing."

"I don't give a damn what you tell him! The drill had to be moved and it's done. Done!" And with that he marched off to his truck. Rafia shrugged his shoulders and followed him. Bob and Wes spent the afternoon resetting the wires and didn't see Curt until the next morning. The slide had moved 10 millimeters, and they told him the drill was "safely" moved. They didn't say how or by whom and Curt didn't ask.

Wes wondered whether Gerritt gave any thought to what was involved in going after that drill and decided that no he probably hadn't. He seemed to have no regard for his safety or anyone else's. Didn't he understand he could have been killed? It was as though dying was something you did, like changing clothes or resting after you made love.

CHAPTER 35

Most of the houses in camp suffered minimal damage from the earthquake. The epicenter was in Tocopilla on the coast and the adobe slums there were mostly destroyed. The mine shut down for a few days because the men had to check on relatives or friends. The road to Tocopilla was closed; the two small ribbons of asphalt heaved up in spots making the way completely impassable and people had to go to Antofagasta and then up the coast to Tocopilla. The mine sent equipment and men to clear and repair the roads.

They were without electricity for a day but that was a small discomfort. In Cerro Verde, the earthquake was only an inconvenience, other than the dangerous moving of the drill that faded into the list of Gerritt's irrational actions that Wes passively tolerated and protected. It was the inhabitants of the callampas there in the small towns around that suffered. These hovels, rudely constructed of mud bricks and corrugated tin or cardboard roofs, fell down like children's blocks, crushing whatever was inside. Some 200 people died in the earthquake. Rosa's family in El Molino, to her great relief, was all right and having determined that the "Pachamama" had not been angry with her, personally, she came back to work at Wes's house. Alice sent her down with food for her family every few days.

Gerritt's "super girders" were flown down from the States and duly installed, replacing the twisted ones. Rafia and his gang did the work under protest and Wes didn't blame them at all since the roof of the tunnel was spalling rock all the time and the creaking and grinding of the massive weight above was enough to send the most hardened underground miner toward the daylight. It wasn't easy, getting the old metal out where it twisted around the caved in rock and bent in every direction. Welders from the plant had to come up to cut the steel before it could be removed. The girders were in at the end of September, the beginning of spring.

Gerritt was coming in very late in the morning and once when Wes ran an errand for Alice in the middle of the day, he saw Gerritt's pick-up in back of Fulton's house. He had just seen Bob Fulton in the office and wondered if Bob knew Gerritt was screwing his wife. Gerritt seemed to be moving into a place where he didn't care what happened to himself or anyone else.

The weekly meetings became more routine with Wes's reports on the slide movement, which stabilized after the terremoto, not stopping, but moving at a rather constant 10 mm a day.

Then Gerritt's reports on the tunnel progress after the special girders were installed dropped off and Wes was concerned.

"Tunnels doing fine." That was all Gerritt would say.

"Let's do a check tomorrow morning," Wes said after three weeks.

"8AM here," Curt nodded and Gerritt mumbled something and went back his office.

Gerritt didn't show up for the morning meeting. Curt, Wes and Bob went on ahead without him. When they got down to the site there were no workmen and Rafia the Chilean shift-boss was absent.

"Christ," Curt cussed against his cigar. "What in the hell is going on?" Wes hadn't been in the tunnel for a week, trusting Gerritt's reports.

The dozers and shovels sat silently on the flat area in front of the entrance and it was the wind they heard when they got out of the pick-up. Nobody said anything as they went into the tunnel. There was debris everywhere. They kicked rocks and the sound echoed hollowly along the walls. In about 100 feet where the first collapse had been were the new girders. They were red and the paint on them was cracked where they were twisted, bent and broken. Bob ran his long finger along the uneven surface. The power of the moving earth above them was immense.

"God, I can't believe it! It's just weird, spooky even! I wish we could get the manufacturer down here, they would never believe it." Bob was incredulous as he took pictures of the carnage. They all were.

That is, all except Curt. He was furious.

"Why the hell didn't Gerritt say something about this? And where is Rafia?"

Wes couldn't answer him. For all he knew Gerritt had not been in the tunnel for a week either.

"Come on, I want to find him." Curt was in a hurry.

"Can we stop up top, I want to check those wires going down over the side?" Bob asked.

"Oh all right," Curt growled.

He drove the truck into the ground. They dipped and skidded around corners and roared up in a cloud of dust in back of another pick-up above the slide area. It was Gerritt's truck. Curt bit down on his cigar and spit out the piece, grunting at the same time, and exploding from the pick-up in his haste to find Gerritt. Bob and Wes looked at each other, not sure they wanted to be around.

But Curt couldn't find him.

"Where is that bastard?" he yelled at us. They were walking over to the edge where Bob was going to check the wires. The top fell away at about a 30 per cent angle, but it seemed steeper looking from the top. The dust was blowing at them and Wes had to squint, but halfway down the embankment, hanging on with fingers and his mine boots, was Gerritt, trying to replace one of the wires which had indeed broken as Bob had feared. The face was moving too much now. Little pebbles constantly fell away and bounced their way noisily to the bottom. They were pinging on Gerritt's hardhat, but he didn't seem to notice. He was too intent on the wire he was twisting and didn't see them. Curt finally gave up looking for Gerritt near his pickup and came over to the edge. When he saw Gerritt, he was about to holler at him. His face was bloated and red with anger, but Wes grabbed him by the arm to keep him from calling out. Wes was afraid if Gerritt looked up at them he might lose his balance and there was nothing underneath him. Instead, they just stood there watching this crazy man crawling on the collapsing ledge and knowing they were unable to help him. Gerritt finished replacing the wire and began climbing back up. Wes didn't know how long they stood there watching him. It was painful and he continually dislodged rocks from the unsteady and loose face that went tumbling down underneath him. They were all relieved when he reached them. Gerritt was dripping with sweat, his hair matted.

"There," he gasped, "Your fuckin' wire's back in place." He said to Bob.

"There's not going to be anymore of this, ever!" Curt screamed. "What are you trying to do, kill yourself? That's the goddamndest stupidist thing I've ever seen anybody do! The next time you do anything like that, your fired!" It was an empty threat. There was no way Curt could fire Gerritt; it just couldn't be done. Gerritt looked at him blankly and let Curt go on.

"And another thing," Curt screamed. "What the hell is going on down in the tunnel? Where is everybody? Why didn't you tell me those girders weren't holding?" He was puffing smoke in Gerritt's face, but Gerritt just stood there waiting for Curt to calm down.

"Well, Curt," Gerritt began, rubbing the sweat from his forehead. "I was going to tell you about it this morning. Rafia said yesterday they weren't coming back to work today because of all the crap sloughing off the walls."

"And what about your miraculous girders?" Curt rocked back and forth on his heels, making him look like a little general.

"Well, there's one more thing I'd like to try."

"One more thing, one more thing, one more thing!" Curt could hardly contain himself. "No, Gerritt, there's no more things to try! We've run out of time. We're going to drill in from the top and start pumping concrete into that Mother and if that doesn't work the tunnel is going to be closed!" And with that he stalked away, having had the final word. Curt climbed into his truck and roared away, completely forgetting about Bob and Wes.

They rode back to the mine office with a seemingly subdued Gerritt, although he muttered, "You bastard!" to Curt's retreating back and told Wes he thought the cement idea was a good one and that he sent a telegram to New York that morning suggesting it. Wes shook his head in disbelief.

308

CHAPTER 36

New York telexed approval for use of cement; they didn't know what else to do. It took a week to move in more drills and get the holes drilled. The Union jefes started hanging around the mine after hearing reports from the empleados and obreros about what was happening. Gerritt was helpful and actually happy to have something to do. The wires popped again on the face of the slide, but Curt gave the order that they were not to be replaced...by anyone. Gerritt seemed to get the message.

When the cement began to disappear down the drill hole, Wes breathed easier. The mountain sucked up the cement like a thirsty calf. Yards and yards of concrete just vanished into the dark drill holes, and when they went inside the tunnel, it still looked the same, spalling from the ceiling. Curt became worried and they all were puzzled. Where was it all going?

"There's a limit, there's a limit, now!" Curt would declare, but he never said what that limit was and they just kept pouring cement down. After 10,000 square feet of concrete, Curt, Wes and Gerritt were down in the tunnel looking disgustedly at the mess there when something plopped onto Gerritt's hardhat. He put his hand up and then brought it down to examine in his headlamp.

"Cement," Gerritt hollered. "Sweet God damn son of a bitch, it's cement!" They all screamed and jumped around like little kids on Christmas morning. It was beautiful! The concrete oozed out and they caught it in their hands and threw it at each other, their voices echoing down through the tunnel and against the walls.

They were embarrassed when they returned to daylight and found the crew. Rafia and the others looked at them in silence for a moment and then all burst out laughing at their jefes covered with cement, but laughing mostly, when Wes thought about it later, because they knew what the cement meant.

There was a mess to clean up in the tunnel. The concrete continued to pour through and they waited to see what would happen when it hardened. It held. There was some spalling near the entrance and a little beyond the cracks, but limited blasting was begun again in the tunnel and if the cracks in the slide were causing movement, the rock was at least moving around the cement wall they had built down through the mountain. And so the tunnel was saved temporarily. But the earthquake had done its damage.

The rate of movement in the slide increased daily. There were no more big "terremotos" then, only the little temblores they never noticed by feel, but knew were there because the seismograph said they were. The slide was a living, moving thing to them, but in time they came to accept it as a growing canker whose pain becomes a daily burden. They measured, they monitored; it was always there. It was discussed in the mine meetings.

"The movement is slowly increasing, so no sign of stabilization, yet, Wes reported. The slippage was going as they thought it might. No one wanted to discuss the end result, when the angle of breakage reached a point where the whole thing would come down the rest of the way. There were various opinions.

"Maybe it will just stop soon," Gerritt was hopeful. He couldn't face a stoppage in the mine operation that would result from a slide into he pit. Some thought it would just continue to move until it reached an angle of repose, as the sides of the volcano Linconquebur on the pampa were doing.

"Couldn't it just slide until the weight of the debris stopped the fall?" Wes was trying to see an end to it. Bob Fulton knew differently. These millions of tons of rock were slipping away from each other, being too steep for mutual support and there would come a point he was sure where friction, the force holding it together, would be overcome by the vertical rock movement.

"I don't think so, Wes. Yes, the weight of the debris will eventually stop it from further movement, but how extensive does it have to be before that happens. We just don't know."

In December, one of the 80 ton Darts was crawling slowly back up the main haulage road under the slide. It was loaded with waste and headed for the waste dumps outside the mine on the west side. With the motor groaning and the driver intent on the road in front, he didn't hear the rocks coming. Let loose by the mountain relaxing, pushing out, releasing anything loose on it's face to tumble downward, two boulders about 3 feet in diameter and several lesser ones fell at precisely the moment the Dart was passing underneath. The driver thought at first that his truck had exploded and, in shock, wet his pants. The larger rocks pierced the roof of the cab, but did not go through, just making cavities and tears in the surface. Everyone was radioed and out there in a matter of minutes.

Julio Garcia, the driver, was just being helped from the truck. Gerritt recognized him from the explosion. Garcia had helped removed bodies, tears running down his face. He was grimy from the dust and looked shaken up. A short, sweaty little man, he wiped his forehead with the back of his sleeve and then noticing the wet patch on the front of his pants, he tried to hide it with his hat.

"Que pasa?" Gerritt asked him.

"No se, no se," Garcia looked up at the slide area and then at his truck. By now the full impact of the shock had reached him and he forgot the wet pants, his eyes wide in horror. "Señor Gerrittt, la montaña se calle!"

"Something like that." Curt said nodding his head. The truck looked like it had been opened by a giant can-opener. They climbed up on the cab to get a good look at the damage and from there could see a black car barreling toward them in a huge dust cloud. It was Hidalgo.

"Fuck," Curt said in disgust and spit into the dirt a long ways down from where they were standing.

"Christ, haven't we got enough shit around here without him coming to stick his nose in it?" Gerritt bent down to run his fingers over the angular edges of metal where the rocks had cut the cab. They were sharp and mean and he thought how like Hidalgo and capable of cutting they were.

"Careful what you say," Curt warned, looking at Gerritt. "I don't know how much he knows." The car drew closer and the dust cloud bigger. Wes wondered how he got here so quickly. Hidalgo had his own pipelines in the mine, but Gerritt was surprised at their efficiency. Maybe he was watching from one of the upper benches or maybe the Jefe Patio called him.

They climbed down off the truck and stood there as Hidalgo drove up with the rest of his greasers. The car stopped and the door opened, but it was a moment before he got out of the car. He took a good look at the truck, said something to those inside the car and only then got out.

Hidalgo lit a cigarette, his henchmen crowding around him to protect the match from the wind tearing at them. Then he pulled on some black leather gloves carefully like a woman does, adjusting each finger, fitting the glove to his hand, and only then did he venture up on the truck to see what happened.

It didn't take more than a few minutes. Gerritt didn't think Hidalgo cared what it looked like. He was making a point.

"Tiene suerte, Amigos," he said through a mouth closed down tightly on the cigarette, the ashes now long and smoldering and ready to fall. His eyes were squinting and he seemed vaguely amused by the whole thing. Perhaps he was disappointed that nobody was hurt.

Garcia was squirming now and sweaty from shock, the cold wind making him grimly aware of his wet pants.

"Get your truck out of here and to the Bosque, Garcia," Curt ordered. And Garcia shrunk into his machine and gratefully roared away.

They all stood there for a moment looking up the wall. Ian Blain arrived, having heard that Hidalgo was there and the incident might involve the Union. He looked nervous and anxious to get out from under this potential waterfall of rock. Ian seldom came down into the pit. Finally Hidalgo broke the silence.

"Que pasa con el otro camino?" he asked.

Curt looked at Wes. The other road. Oh yes, the other road, a new road on the other side of the mine. Curt wouldn't be able to say anything for sure, because the order for it would have to come from New York. Gerritt turned away from them and kicked at a rock, sending it bouncing and bumping off the last bench and into the bottom of the pit.

"Vamos a ver," Curt answered Hidalgo in Spanish. We'll see, he said, but Wes was sure the order for the new road would not be long in coming. It was apparently enough for Hidalgo and he got back in his limo and left. When they were gone, Gerritt turned around and Wes could see the desperation in his face.

"We aren't going to stop using this one right now are we?" He seemed frantic, his icy pupils swimming in the whites of his wide-open eyes. Curt thought a minute before answering. Wes found himself leaning forward to hear Curt's answer. Wes didn't want to stop using it either, but a real accident could mean injuries, death, at the very least trouble with the Union.

"No." Curt answered slowly. "No, I think we can continue to use it for a while. I don't like it, but we can't just shut down the mine until a new road is built."

Gerritt breathed, relieved that production would not be halted. He felt personally responsible for it; the daily tonnage was all that concerned him. And now men would have to be moved onto the project for a new road. A chill went down his spine; there was no other choice but to start on the road. He knew that.

"What about Garcia?" Ian had to think of the Union and possible strike threats. "And the other drivers?" You think they will be willing to drive under this Mother? I sure as hell wouldn't! I don't know about you!"

"Oh Christ, Ian," Curt's face wrinkled up in disgust. "These palanqueros, most of them have been driving these monsters for years! They aren't going to let a little thing like this rattle them." Wes could see Curt wasn't really sure of that because the beads of sweat were coming out above his upper lip and he was rocking back and forth on his heels again.

"Let's just wait a day or so." Curt said trying to calm everybody. "We won't know what they'll do until we ask them. Hidalgo at least didn't say anything about closing the road right now." That was encouraging.

It went better than they thought. The use of the road was cut for that day, but by evening, they had the go ahead from New York on the new road and Mainline Track and Gerritt and Wes had projected a two to three month ready time for the road. Mike Marshall seemed to think the track would be ready even before then. The next morning the trucks resumed their regular route under the slide and the drivers seemed content with the promise of the new road.

Bob and Wes started to work on some graphs of slide movement and direction hoping they could come up with a date of some accuracy. A date for collapse. It wouldn't be complete, they were fairly sure of that, but there had to be a time when the majority of that weight would be released into the bottom of the pit and they needed to know when.

It was a complicated study with both vertical and horizontal vectors to consider, but they finally came up with a date of some time in late January or early February. It was like setting a date for a death, the death of a mountain. And it spelled a failure of the early engineering in the mine, which made Wes reflect on how the science of mining engineering had changed over the years. You could only operate with the information in your own present. He thought again about what he was missing and didn't or couldn't know. And now the mountain was falling down in front of them because the early miners didn't understand rock mechanics. Wes went around with uncertainty and hope on his shoulders; the uncertainty of maybe not knowing enough and the hope that no one would be hurt. The due date didn't seem to trouble Curt or Gerritt or Joe Driscoll ...maybe because they were in operations and didn't have to worry about the engineering, or maybe because they just didn't want to think about it.

CHAPTER 37

It spoiled Christmas that year. Wes always had a hard time getting in the mood for Christmas in Chile when it was the middle of summer. Alice tried hard to make things nice and she succeeded for herself and Georgia and that was all he cared about. His little girl was pulling herself up now and would soon be walking. He treasured the time holding her, smelling her clean baby scent. Georgia was all the Christmas present he needed.

Wes took Gerritt out fishing when the work on the road was underway. He wanted to get Gerritt's mind off the decreased production in the mine, which had suffered severely. They decided to stop by Chieu-Chieu. It had been several years since they went out to the pre-Incan graveyard north of that little pueblo and they thought they might still find some beads and arrowheads among the mummies. Wes wanted to get Gerritt away, not only from the mine, but from Dierdre Fulton. Eve was in Santiago with her parents most of the time. Joe Driscoll seemed to distance himself from the troubles in the mine and Gerritt wondered how much of their absence was due to his failing relationship with Eve. He was becoming increasingly morose.

Alice wouldn't go with them to Chieu-Chieu, she hated the place...said it was creepy. It was in some ways, but Wes always was amazed at the survival of those mummies for a thousand years out there under the sand and wondered where he would be in a thousand years.

They stopped in Chieu-Chieu for water at the public cistern that stood in a square covered with unkempt brush and flowers and then drove out the mile or so and turned off to the graveyard.

"Wonder if the guy with the hole in his head is still out here?" Gerritt said remembering the bodies they saw on the last visit.

"Yeah, and remember all the heads lined up in a row."

But when they parked the trucks on the little bluff above where the cemetery was, there was nothing. Wes climbed out of the truck and stood there looking out at what had been masses of mummies as far as you could see and now there was just sand blowing at them from everywhere. He was sure this was the right place.

"C'mon," Gerritt cried. "Let's go have a look. There has to be something left somewhere." But they walked all over the ancient burial ground. Even the holes beside bodies were filled in, though whether by hand or by the wind was hard to tell. Gerritt was running all around, stopping sometimes to dig with his hands. When Wes caught up with him Gerritt looked at him wildly.

"They're all gone. Where did they go? Somebody must have taken them. There's just nothing here. Padre Simon! That's who did it. He's taken them up into the hills, damn him."

"I think we'd better go, Gerritt." Wes took his arm and shook him gently, but he shrugged off his hand and ran all the way back to the pick-up.

It was cold and desolate, a really dismal day there even for the pampa. Wes wanted to hurry, to say something to Gerritt who was leaning on the fender of the pick-up, his head in his arms. Then without acknowledging Wes's presence he pulled out the rag from the back of the truck and unwrapped the femur he had taken from the site.

"Here's your bone old man. I don't want it anymore." And Gerritt flung the bone as far as he could, grunting with the effort. It sailed up into the air like a propeller and landed some distance away, raising a small cloud of dust. The brown of the pampa engulfed them; there was nothing to be seen anywhere. Wes had never felt so alone.

He knew, that Gerritt felt it, too. He looked up at Wes sadly, the wind blowing at a rivulet of sweat on his forehead.

"Nothing I ever look for is there when I get there." Gerritt said to him. "It's never what I expect." Forgetting fishing, the reason for the trip, they climbed into the pickup and drove as fast as they could back to town.

Wes's thoughts on the way back drifted to a different conclusion. Maybe Padre Simon didn't like his ancestors being picked over by Gringos. That made sense. But, the missing mummies meant something else to him. Besides the shock of seeing something once and then having it not be there when you go back, it reminded him of the mine slide. Nothing was static, not dead people, and not even rock.

Rita Blain came back for Christmas that year, bringing her girls from boarding schools in the States. She didn't spend much time in Cerro Verde after Ian bought her the condominium in Miami six months ago. Wes wondered if she was happier now and perhaps drank less. At least she had the sense to leave.

Wes came home from work one day close to Christmas and found her visiting Alice. Rita was sallower, maybe from the air-conditioned life in Miami and seemed more staid and serious. But she was still having her afternoon gin.

"Well, Wes, you old son-of-a-bitch! Alice says you've had some troubles since I was down."

"Yeah?" Wes looked at Alice wondering what she had told Rita.

"You know how these things are. We're all one happy family here, now aren't we?" Her voice growled in the usual coaxing way. She wanted some information, Wes decided, and he determined to make her work for it. There was a silence after her inquiry about all being a happy family and finally she broke it, jumping to her feet and leaning on the fireplace as though the height over them gave her the advantage.

"Joe Driscoll was through Miami last month." She blurted out as though that explained it all.

So that's it, Wes thought. He must have said something about Gerritt. He still said nothing, but could sense Alice looking from him to Rita wondering what was going on. Finally, Rita turned to Wes, her face reddening, angry that an explanation was not forthcoming.

"For God's sake, Wes, what is wrong with Gerritt?" She slammed the glass down on the mantel, gin sloshing out and with her hands on her ample hips stood over Wes.

"He got everything he wanted, didn't he? He married that empty-headed kid just to get where he is…and don't tell me he didn't know what he was doing! He knew…oh brother did he know what he was doing! And now he's going to louse the whole thing up if he's not careful and ruin Eve's life while he's at it!" She was really going now, shaking her arm and fist at Wes, a diamond bracelet on her wrist sparkling when she moved it.

"We were going to have a nice quiet Christmas in Miami," she kept on. "Ian was coming up for the holidays…the girls were coming from school. And then when Ian was planning his trip, Joe told him he thought he better stay to keep an eye on Gerritt. You must know why he's acting this way…you of all people. Wes!"

Wes didn't know what it was about the whole thing, whether it was the look on her sagging, flaccid face, or the pressures of the slide or what. Later Wes would think about this time, deciding and admitting to himself that Gerritt was torn from him. No longer could he be his friend, at least in the way he saw friendship. Gerritt didn't want or need him. Had he ever?

"Will you please stop asking me about Gerritt?" Wes was screaming back at her, but not really at her, he didn't even see her. "Will everybody stop asking me about Gerritt? How should I know what's the matter with him? Is anything the matter? Maybe it's everyone else. Maybe something is the matter with all of us. Maybe he's the only sane one around here." He felt a touch on his arm and Alice was there.

"I'll get you a drink." Her voice was soft and she went on out to the kitchen.

"If you think a drink will help, it won't." Rita looked at him through the gin glazed green eyes. Wes's head was between his legs and he raised up to look at her, surprised at such honesty. But then she hadn't compromised herself. She left Cerro Verde because she hated it. Her glass still sat on the mantel where she had slammed it down and she didn't reach for it. Wes wondered if maybe she had to work hard at being a drunk, maybe it wasn't really her.

"I'm sorry, Rita." He hadn't meant to scream at her. "It's just that I'm fed up with everybody asking me about Gerritt. Sure I know there's something wrong. I thought when he married Eve that would be it, there wouldn't be anymore hurt, that he had what he wanted."

"Well, didn't he?" Rita asked, sitting down at last. Alice handed him a scotch that looked as though Rita had poured it.

"Gerritt's not happy." Alice said sadly. "You've seen the house, haven't you?"

"Yes, I've seen it. Its God-awful!" Alice handed Rita her glass, but she didn't drink from it.

"Maybe he doesn't know how to be happy." Wes said to them. "He's bellyaching everybody out at the mine and for what I don't know. He's a competent engineer and operator, really more than competent."

"Well, I know one thing," Rita said slowly and carefully, "He better treat Eve carefully or he's going to be out on his can. I talked to Anna Driscoll yesterday. She's trying to keep Eve in Santiago as much as possible. Anna and Joe both know something's wrong. And Joe's seen Gerritt's pickup around... down in Molino and over at Fultons. What's between Gerritt and Dierdre Fulton?"

"Yeah, well, something, I guess. It's pretty hard to switch beds in this place without everybody knowing about it. But I can't tell you why because I just don't know."

"You're about as helpful as an empty gin bottle, love," Rita tried to joke, but her remark was also empty.

"How long are you staying, Rita?" Alice asked.

"Have no idea. May stay until Ian can go back with me. We are going to Santiago tomorrow to see Anna and Joe and then on down to Viña for a few days. I'll bring you some books tomorrow. Better be getting along. Ian likes to know where I am, you know. Thank you for the drink, dear. You have a darling baby. Don't bother showing me out."

Then she was gone, the sweet smell of gin following after her.

CHAPTER 38

On an early morning in the first week of January, as a sleepy palanquero was driving his Dart back for the last load on night shift, a brownish gray boulder of about 100 tons made ready to meet with that Dart as it passed underneath on the road. Deep in the mountain the slide was creeping outward, downward, rocking the floor underneath that boulder. And finally, sticking out just a little too far into the mine, leaning toward nothing, it let go. Taking some seconds to fall the thousand feet, bumping along the sides of the pit on its way and dislodging other debris that tumbled along, it boomed and broke its way down the mountain to a meeting with the truck. At the very last second, the driver, perhaps thinking about the warm woman waiting at home for him in bed, or waking from the rhythmic humming of the motor, stepped on the gas and lucky for him. The gigantic rock fell into the bed of the truck instead of on the cab. He didn't even see it coming; the sound of his engine covering the crashing from above. The truck stopped dead.

It was quite a sight. The rock went through the truck bed, smashing it down, squashing the tires out into a squat position, and picking the cab up in the air. It looked like some paper toy that a little boy had overloaded. The driver came out of it with only a concussion, but it looked worse when they first found him unconscious with head cuts and blood running down onto the seat. His head hit the roof of the truck in a springboard action when the boulder hit the bed. This rock was five times the size of the ones that hit the cab of the truck a few months earlier. The driver was Victor Arenas, Rafia's brother-in-law. Jason Stoddard arrived with the ambulance. They removed him carefully onto a body board. Arenas regained consciousness briefly, looked up at the enormous rock in his truck bed, started shaking and then passed out again as they loaded him into the ambulance.

They were lucky again. At least no one was killed. Arenas's neck and back were fine and the concussion was minor. Hidalgo shook his head in disbelief. Ian and Curt came down to look at the truck and immediately closed the road and mainline track. The new road wasn't finished yet, but it didn't make any difference to anybody, anybody except Gerritt. He bitched and stomped around but no one listened. At that point after the two accidents, enough was enough.

There was explaining to do. The Union wanted to know what was going on. Hidalgo with his brash, blustery manner had been more than patient, Wes thought. At least more patient than he gave him credit for. The time of waiting for something to be said definitively and officially about the slide had come. Perhaps an admission at least that it was there, that in fact the mountain was falling. It was a time for reckoning with the problem, for facing up to what they already knew.

At the first mine meeting in January, Wes was surprised to walk in and find Ian Blain and Joe Driscoll present as well as Hidalgo. First thing, before they got down to the urgent mine business, Driscoll stood up. His hair was graying around the edges, but he still had most of it and combed it all straight back with some sort of gel, making it look shiny and solid at the same time. His pocked face had aged some since Wes came to Cerro Verde and he wondered how much of his concern and worry was due to Gerritt and Eve.

"The Union wants us to formally explain about the slide to the Union Board in Santiago." He began. It sounded like he was apologizing to them for it all.

"I know you are all busy, but we are going to have to send someone down there right away or they are going to be up here on our backs."

That would be all they needed, a bunch of nosey Union officials getting in everybody's way. Hidalgo was bad enough.

"One person should be enough, but it will have to be someone who knows what is going on with the slide. So that leaves management out." Driscoll was asking for one of the engineers to go. Wes was trying to think who could possibly do it when Curt spoke.

"Well," Curt put his hand inside his shirt and leaned back in his chair. "I suppose it will have to be you, Wes." He looked at Wes as though he was the last resort, and Wes felt like he probably was. Curt didn't want to send anybody. Gerritt would have been impossible. Bob Fulton didn't know the mine that well. There wasn't anyone else.

"Me!" Wes heard himself saying. "My Spanish isn't good enough to explain all this, Curt! Besides, how could I leave the slide…there's too much to do?"

"Well, I can't go, and Gerritt is too busy with the new road and track. Fulton can handle the seismographic work. And… there really isn't anybody else. It's only for a few days."

"Y no hay problema con la lengua. Tenemos una persona que habla Ingles, tambien." Hidalgo said.

Wes didn't like the thought of having to explain things through an interpreter, but neither did he like the idea of trying to put into Spanish what was happening there at the mine. He couldn't even explain it in English and the whole idea of having to discuss the slide with strangers and people who had never even seen the mine filled him with apprehension. But he knew that was it. He would have to go. Alice was not surprised.

"Of course you have to go. You are the most logical one out there, Wes," she said. "And you are good." She had to stand on her tiptoes to kiss him and fondly ruffle his red hair.

"I just hope it goes well. We don't need more Union jefes up here." Wes frowned. The mine meeting was a Monday and on Thursday, Wes was supposed to see the Union Gerente in Santiago. That gave him only two days at the mine, two days to get things organized. Bob Fulton and he planned to set up a movie camera across the mine from the slide to get the whole thing on film when and if the slide went. It had taken them two weeks to get the right camera equipment down from the States and it needed to be set up in a stable place protected from dust. Across the mine from the slide was an area they were preparing for another Patio and it was that place they decided on for the photographic equipment. They were able to get it set up and he showed Zuñiga how to operate it. If the slide went at night, there would be no pictures, but if they were able to photograph this thing, it would be of interest for years.

Wes talked to Gerritt in his office just before I left. Gerritt was nervous and pale, and kept pulling on his ear.

"The road should be ready before you get back." Gerritt said quickly. It was morning and the sun was coming fast through the window behind him, its light framing him, making his hair frosty and his movements without weight. A fly, rare for Cerro Verde's altitude buzzed fitfully on its back on the desk. Gerritt reached over for a paperweight made of a piece of chrysacola, green and shiny, and as Wes watched, he squashed the fly onto the desk, looked at the stone, then wiped it on his khaki pants and set it down again. Wes wanted to say something, to bring Gerritt back to where they had been months, a year ago.

"You OK, Gerritt?" He finally heard himself ask.

"Not sleeping much. Can't in that bedroom of hers."

Wes nodded. That was easy to understand. Maybe his house, built for Eve, was driving him into the bedroom of Fulton's wife, just the need to rest on a bed in a room furnished with the usual pieces…a bed, a dresser, a lamp, maybe a picture of the ocean.

"Why don't you try to get away for a few days when I get back, go down to the coast or something?"

"Can't," he said, his eyes despairing. He wouldn't say why but Wes knew it was himself keeping him here. The firm ground of the mine, the machinery, the track, the trucks, was all he had anymore. There was nowhere for him to go and he could not leave it, especially when the rock itself seemed to be leaving him.

Wes didn't want to leave either, but for different reasons. After moving with that slide all these months, watching it accelerate, peel, fall little by little, it was inconceivable to him that he wouldn't be there for the big bang, the time when the larger part of the rock involved fell in front of them. He told Bob Fulton to call him in Santiago the minute he thought it might go. Union or no Union, Wes would come back up there to see it. It meant too much to him.

Garritt lay on the cool grass in the garden room of his house, a large scotch nearly spilling over onto the ground beside him. Sprinklers were on earlier and the grass was still wet. The liquor was the only thing that took him away now. The scotch and the wet grass were his biggest hope of reminding him where he came from. A farm in Montana. And where he was headed, he didn't know. It was all going, all of it. Now that the mine had stopped working, there was nothing for him to care about. No planning for the next day's shifts, no comparison of tonnages, track laid. Nothing to report to New York. Eve was in Santiago now with Joe and Anna. She mostly cried for the last few months and Gerritt couldn't reach her and didn't want to try anymore. Eve was incapable of responding to him and he gave up touching her. She didn't understand, couldn't understand and that always led to the tears. In a way he was relieved that Joe and Anna took her away. Eve belonged with them. What would he do now? The slide was coming. He supposed that when it was over, he would just clean it up and start again. But the waiting was unbearable. He got up to pour another scotch and laid down again, fell asleep on the grass and woke in the early hours cold and alone.

CHAPTER 39

The Union officials came to the company offices down the street from the Hotel Carrera, a dismal, art deco imitation of an American hotel on a square across from the cold grey government offices in the Palacio de la Moneda. At least it was summer and the square was alive with flowers and the air clear allowing them a view of the snow crown of the Andes to the east. Wes wanted to be outside, not in a stuffy room pressured by the five-member board from the Union, trying to explain, only to have his words translated into colloquialisms and clichés he couldn't understand. He used Spanish where he could and sometimes, when he thought he had explained something fully, found the interpreter saying it over and adding comments he was sure were not included in his explanation.

Driscoll and Blain were with him, however, and their Spanish was fluent. Wes watched their expression and occasionally they interrupted to clarify something. It was a sweat-rolling interrogation. Wes was put on the spot to explain the whole thing. Across from them were Hidalgo and four other Union Jefes. Wes remembered two of them who came to the mine after the explosion. The five of them were in black suits as though for a funeral, greasy hair, plastered back flat and shiny. Four of the faces, dark faces, some with mustaches, including Hidalgo's were round and well fed. The man on the end was old and sat next to Hidalgo. Although he was dressed the same, his countenance was sadder and he even seemed to drift off at times. Wes would think he wasn't listening and then he would lean over to whisper something to Hidalgo. Wes was dressed in his mine khakis. He had brought maps of the mine and the seismographic information to show the increasing movement of the slide. The questions were endless.

"Have there been any serious accidents, Señor Bowen?"

"No, we have not had any serious accidents."

"But what about the large boulder falling on the truck last week? Do you not consider that serious?"

"Yes, of course we do, but no one was hurt seriously".

Then the murmurs and discussion beyond reach of his ears.

"And what is being done about new access?"

"Yes, the new road should be complete in two weeks."

"But, what if there is another accident?"

"The old road under the slide is closed," Blain interjected. "We have taken every precaution to clear the area under the slide, since it is imminent." Blain could be authoritative and Wes was grateful for his presence.

"Imminent? What do you mean, Señor?" And on and on. Wes showed the graphs he and Fulton carefully prepared showing the collapse projected for late January. They seemed impressed with the work, but still the questions kept coming. The next day, Hidalgo wasn't there. He had gone back to Cerro Verde to watch and report back to the Union. The slide needed to be watched. Wes cursed under his breath that he was not there, too.

"The spalling is increasing, Wes! When are you coming back?" Gerritt didn't want to be there alone.

"I don't know. They don't seem to finish and ask the same questions over and over!" He was growing anxious and impatient.

Finally, on the third day it seemed they had covered every inch of the operation, the monitoring, the safety plan. But the committee still didn't seem satisfied, they hadn't established fault with the company or found a cause for this disaster. They seemed disappointed. Then Bob Fulton called. They were interrupted in the meeting by a small boy in a white shirt and scrubbed face.

"Teléfono, Señor Bowen!" He said urgently. "Emergencia in la mina!"

The inquisitors broke into excited jabbering and made much of escorting Wes, Blain and Driscoll into the next office to receive the call.

"It's going, Wes!" Bob said desperately. "You better get your ass back up here if you want to see it! The movement and spalling are increasing rapidly!"

"You God damn well better hold it until I get there!" Wes felt like a small child, forced to stand in the corner away from the game.

"Can you get up here today?" said the froggy voice crackling with phone static.

"I'll get up there some way. You just hold that slide!"

"Sure, sure," he laughed. "Any other miracles you'd like us to work on?"

The committee understood the urgency. Everything had been covered and in some ways, Wes thought the finality of the slide actually occurring ended the discussion. The only one who seemed recalcitrant and made any protest was the shriveled, older man who seemed not be listening during the hearing.

Blain and Driscoll left with Bowen, but getting to Cerro Verde that afternoon was more difficult than they anticipated. The one Ladeko flight to El Molino had already spread its wings for the day leaving no public transportation home available. Blain checked in the Condor Copper offices and found that Henri Duvillard, the Bodega Manager, was down from Cerro Verde, apparently in town to do some buying. He had a freight flight going back in an hour. Blain ordered him to hold it for them and Hidalgo actually offered his limousine, which took them out to the airport. Ordinarily this fruit and vegetable wagon did not carry passengers, but after much persuading, Ladeko agreed to let them ride up with the cabbages and tomatoes. Wes was grateful that Blain knew about this possibility. Otherwise he would be sitting in Santiago on his duff while the mountain fell without him.

The trip up was bad. Though the vegetables and fruit were fresh when they were loaded, the heat in the plane and the hours since their delivery wilted even the sturdiest head of lettuce and the whole mess stank, rankly around them. Blain and Driscoll were markedly uncomfortable. Their positions had accustomed them to a certain standard of travel; this was not first class. That and the rough afternoon air over the pampa was too much and after the five hours in that plane and the two stops they made in Copiapó and Tal-tal, Wes couldn't stand it any longer and threw up into a paper sack he found on the dirty floor only minutes before they landed.

He called Alice from Santiago to pick him up in his truck, and she was there waiting. Rita and her driver took Ian and Joe. They all headed to the mine.

"You look green," she said as he climbed into the truck.

"I feel like I've been made into vegetable soup," he said. "What time is it? It seemed like it took days to get up here."

"A little after three."

Alice had a good foot for the accelerator in Wes's truck and they flew up the long, straight road to Cerro Verde. Wes saw the Carabiniero eye them suspiciously as they roared through New Camp. They went straight to the Patio where the camera equipment was set up and he found Bob Fulton, Gerritt, and the rest of the Jefes. There was quite a crowd, the tension in the air was palpable.

"I'll be damned, you made it!" Gerritt said, the strain in his face showing. Wes looked into his eyes for a long moment. They were empty and helpless.

"Private jet no less, the vegetable express," he said with mock smugness.

"Well, you're barely in time," Bob was serious.

Across the mine from them, nearly half a mile away, Wes could hear the slide. Without looking he knew it was there, waiting, dropping its excrement into the pit below them. Crumbling, weeping the brown rock that could stand no longer and just had to sit down. Its surface bubbled with the action like a boiling pot, but it was still just the surface, the face only that was moving. The great bulk of the thing had yet to come. Curt scurried over, anxious and busy. Ian and Joe were out of place in their business suits. Rita stayed in the car and Alice joined her. It was windy and cold.

"Hello, Wes. Glad you made it back. We stopped the rest of the work in the mine yesterday, the dust was getting so bad." Curt brought out a handkerchief and blew his nose loudly into it.

Ian stood there with his hands behind his back looking out at the thing as though his concentrating could hold it back.

"We'll resume...uhm resume work immediately after it goes won't we, Curt?" Gerritt asked nervously. They all turned to look at him. "I mean there won't be any reason why we couldn't will there?" There was a silence except for the cracking of the rock from the slide face.

"Goddammit, Gerritt!" Curt screamed at him. "How the hell do you think we can run a mine with the whole bottom of the pit full of rock?"

"Well," Gerritt said calmly, "If we get right on it Curt. Don't waste any time getting the fucking mess cleared up…"

"I don't know, Gerritt," Fulton shook his head. "Seems like we ought to let it settle first. It might be moving some more. We'd have to at least be sure of that."

"Shit! Nobody cares around here whether we dig another ton of ore!" Gerritt stalked off to his pick-up and gunning the motor until it screamed, he roared off making more dust and Curt sneezed into his brown streaked handkerchief.

They got back into the trucks to get away from the wind and waited. Alice and Rita went home, and came back with a bottle of scotch and glasses. The liquor felt good going down.

Gerritt couldn't stand to watch with the others. Everything he worked for was falling into the pit, disappearing from sight, fading into some obscure past and uncertain future. Sure he could clean up, but how had this happened? The rock disappointed him. It was supposed to stand, resolute and unshakable. He drove up to the Jefe Patio at the south end of the mine, parked his truck and pulled out the scotch bottle from the glove compartment.

An hour later the Jefe Patio, Lopez, radioed Wes.

"Señor Jefe," Lopez said excitedly, "Vengo no más! Se va!"

Wes gulped down the scotch, grabbed his hard hat and got out of the pick-up. He looked at his watch; it was 7PM. The sinking sun reflected on each dust particle made the air gold around them and gave everything a halo. They all sensed something special was about to occur. Wes thought about Gerritt and where he was, guessing he was headed closer to the slide.

Wes checked with Fulton about the cameras and he had everything set, and Zuñiga was wiping the lenses every few minutes when dust would settle on them. He brought binoculars for Wes.

And then with a shuddering roar the mountain began to move downward. There was a sudden silence among the watchers where there had been excited jabbering, an awe for what they were seeing. Or perhaps it was fear, fear of the earth's power. Across from them, not more than a mile away was what looked like a waterfall, cascading dirtily over the lip of the mine and churning its way the thousand feet down to the river below. Only it wasn't green water and cooling, it was dry dust and sucked the breath and moisture from them all as it fell. The air, pushed ahead of the slide rushed dust up at them from the pit and they could barely see. The roar was like water, the roar of a river in flood caving its banks and wiping everything from its path. The ground shook underneath them, lasting for what seemed an interminable time and finally the dust was so bad where they stood that it hid the vicious movement of the rock. Some of the spectators climbed into their vehicles to get away from it. Wes couldn't leave, but put his handkerchief up to his face. He stood hypnotized by the power of the falling rock. He could feel himself coughing and gagging from the dirty air, but it was part of him, part of everything that had happened there and he took it in.

When at last the growling began to subside and he could look elsewhere, Wes saw all the men who worked on this thing. Curt Reicher and Bob Fulton, Lief Swenson, Ned Tully, Ian Blain and Joe Driscoll, their faces fuzzy with the dust clinging to their hair and eyebrows. Only Gerritt Wells was missing.

Curt was still sneezing and blowing his nose and there was a muddy smear across his face. Joe wiped the dirt from his glasses. Rita and Alice sat in the white station wagon, with Vera. It was caked brown now with fine dust, but Vera had cleared the windshield with the wipers. Ian started to get in the car and Wes saw Rita say something to him and wave her hand. He knocked his shoes on the side of the car and brushed himself off before getting in.

Bob and Wes looked at each other. There wasn't much to say. That was it. What they waited for. What passed between them all was relief, resignation that it had at last happened. With the equipment and expertise they had managed to predict the mountains fall, could prevent it happening again. And most important, there had been no serious accidents.

The sun was setting and the wind finally blew the dust away from the slide enough to see the bottom of the pit. It was orange in the evening light and very shadowed, but where there had been road and track in the bottom of the pit was now a pile of rubble 500 feet long and slanted up toward the top for hundreds of feet. Rock was still falling, but the roaring had stopped.

Wes scanned the mine with his binoculars, looking for Gerritt and saw his pickup up near the Jefe Patio.

Just as well, he thought, maybe he couldn't watch the destruction of everything important to him. Yes, it was good he wasn't there with everyone else. The mess down below in the pit would only increase his anxiety. It would take months to clean up.

"It's been a long day." Bob Fulton said. He was out there with Lopez at 6AM. Zuñiga was folding up the camera equipment. "At least we have something to work on now. See you in the morning, Wes." And Bob left him there; Alice was waiting in the pickup. The others drove off, too, waving and happy that it was over. The waiting was over.

Wes stood there a few more minutes watching the light get flatter until the slide looked smooth in the coming dark. Maybe Bob was right. At least it was down on the bottom now instead of hanging there over them. The mountain was no longer a threat. Maybe they could clean it up now and start over. But it didn't seem like it would be that easy.

Up at the Jefe Patio, tears fell in streams from Gerritt's face. Something important and dear to him just died, irreparable and permanently gone. He pounded on the steering wheel as his body shook with sobs. It was over. The tunnel, Eve, and now the mine, falling away from him as though he carelessly dropped them. Gerritt always had losses and disappointments, but they involved people and he had learned not to count on anyone and to escape when he was pressured. Innocent Eve was not a solid thing, the mummies at Chieu-Chieu were gone, flesh was transcient and not to be understood. A mine, however, was a solid thing and machinery ran or could be fixed. But he knew now even the rock wasn't static. As he watched the benches cascade down, drowning in the dust, he felt himself falling, losing his balance and becoming one with the slide. Before the dust settled, Gerritt pealed out and went home. He sat in the garden room in his make-believe house and drank scotch from the bottle, thinking about the farm, anything to forget what just happened.

As light came through the glass roof, Gerritt opened his eyes. Remembering the day, the tears came again and he wiped at his face with his jacket sleeve, which he still had on. His mouth was dry and sour from the scotch. Shivering, moving slowly, he picked himself up off the grass. He knew where he had to be.

CHAPTER 40

Wes slept fitfully. He knew he should have looked for Gerritt, but he was dead tired and all he wanted was to be with Alice and Georgia. It would be several days before any clearing could be started. The angry earth had to settle. The next morning, the air was clean and when he went out to the mine, he could see what they had. It was still coming down, pebbles drifting over the loose surface that now sloped smoothly down from the top where the thing had broken away. There was an indentation at the top, a half-moon shape, but a ragged one, jutting into the upper bench, the jaw supporting a tooth that had now fallen out. The wind whipped around dislodging more stones from the unsteady surface and sending them tumbling into the bottom of the pit. Wes stood there outside the mine offices looking at the thing for a long time. There was a silence now, as the mine machinery was shut down and it made him feel alone with that caved-in mountain, used, but at last free of tension.

It was then he heard it, the sound of a dozer motor. Wes turned his head to look for it, but the machine itself was not to be seen. There was only the grind of the engine, but it woke him up and he went inside the offices. Curt was there, rummaging on his desk for something he probably would never find.

"What's the dozer doing out there?" Wes asked, flopping down in one of the chairs. "I thought the mine was completely shut down until further notice."

"It is." Curt answered not looking up from his search and finally he found what it was he was looking for, matches to light his cigar. He struck a match and was holding it out for his cigar to grasp the fire when he moved it aside and looked at Wes.

"What dozer? You heard a dozer?"

"Yeah, couldn't see it, though, it must have been..."

"Shut-up!" And they both listened because the sound was getting louder and Curt waved out the match which by now was about to burn his fingers, threw down the cigar and flew out the door, knocking over a chair and screaming.

"Goddamn Gerritt. I told him...I told him!"

Wes followed wondering what was going on, but when he got outside he knew. And then he could see it. On a bench, the second one down, crawling along the ledge toward the slide in front of him was a man on a dozer, its steady whine and growl advancing on the fallen mountain. Curt was running futily toward it waving his arms.

"Goddamn you Gerritt, I don't care who you are! You come back here you fucking bastard...you're fired!" Curt stopped running, but the angry words kept erupting from him. And when Wes caught up to him his face was red and he was crying.

"Look at him, Wes. That crazy bastard is going to work that slide! I told him last night to stay away from it. He called me at home about it all breathy and sounded insane! Said he'd have to start on it today. I didn't think he meant to do this!"

"Come on Curt, let's see if we can get a truck up there and stop him." There wasn't now a road onto that bench and they had no idea how Gerritt got a dozer out there. They took Curt's pick-up and drove it back down the main road and around to where they thought Gerritt might have gone down and sure enough there were dozer tracks leading up to the edge of a little ridge and down about thirty feet where he must have slid the dozer down because it was too steep to get it down any other way.

"What's he doing on this bench?" Wes asked.

"Christ, I don't know. What's he even doing out on this slide. Come on, we'll never get the pick-up down here, lets just run over."

They slid down the incline where Gerritt had taken his machine and ran across the bench. The sound of the Cat was out of earshot because they were around a corner from it. They ran about a quarter of a mile until they could see Gerritt again and hear the motor. Wes would always remember that time of running the intervening space between them, his lungs pounding with the effort of reaching him and at the same time not knowing what they would do when they got there. Curt was left behind, his smoke-crusted lungs giving way to the speed and distance.

But there was no need to say anything to Gerritt. When Wes rounded the corner and he was in sight maybe two or three hundred feet away, his front-end loader was already pulling out onto the slide. Wes saw him halt the machine and with a puff of smoke and a roar, lower the bucket to begin moving that mountain out of the way so he could mine copper again. In his apparent determination he didn't see how close he was to the edge and with the first effort of the bucket to raise its load and the machine to turn and deliver it over the side, the entire circus twirled in front of Wes's eyes, balancing in its effort to stay erect. And then it was lost.

The yellow thing with Gerritt on it rolled down the slide, tumbling and turning like one of Georgia's Christmas toys, taking part of the mountain with it, so the whole thing fell in unison and Wes stood there crying and crying…"Gerritt! Jump! Jump!"…and raising his hand up in a helpless gesture. When Curt reached Wes he was on his knees and Curt lifted him up. They helped each other back the half-mile to the pick-up, both of them crying and voiceless.

The Cat was hours coming off him. The acrid smell of broken flesh and spilled engine oil whined in Wes's nose and the twisted wreckage burned into his eyes like a crude metal sculpture. When at last they reached what had been Gerritt, he was still stubbornly breathing and Jason Stoddard gingerly picked him up and rushed him to the hospital.

Jason didn't bother to clean him up; he was too broken to move. Wes looked at Jason with a question, and Jason shook his head. Someone had washed at the face, smearing blood and dust back into his hair. Gerritt bled slowly onto the clean white hospital sheet as Wes stood over him and watched his breathing slow and then stop. He could feel the warmth drain from Gerritt as though he were taking off a sweaty jacket. Jason listened with his stethoscope and nodded when it was over and then left them alone. The sense of loss sickened Wes.

How had the time passed when he could have helped him? It was gone, fallen away like the day does when you wish you had one more hour of light. He knew Gerritt was heading toward that ride and not every man going over a waterfall in a bucket wants to be saved. Gerritt walked down his hallway and was now in another room, gone, like rain disappearing into the sands of the Atacama.

When Wes called Shem to tell him Gerritt was dead, the connection was poor and Shem sounded very far away. Wes told him there was a mine accident. Sadly, there was no way to explain it all. Maybe Shem understood. The old man accepted his nephew's death with resignation, as he had accepted that of his parents. Shem felt Gerritt needed to stay on the pampa.

There was no service for him; just a sadness that crept into the minds of all who knew Gerritt. Several months later, Wes drove out onto the pampa where he could no longer see the mine, only the empty space where the brown ran on out to somewhere open and free. He stopped the truck. This would be the place. The wind was blowing toward the east and the Andes. Wes picked up the box with Gerritt's ashes and got out. When he opened it the wind reached inside, took Gerritt slowly in its arms and carried him away. The Atacama keeps its secrets. They are there still, whispering across the dry land.

Made in the USA
San Bernardino, CA
24 June 2019